Enter a world of samurai and geishas,
ninjas and Zen masters—
a world of violence and beauty that will
take you on an extraordinary
journey through nineteenth-century Japan.
Enter the world of...

CLOUD OF SPARROWS

"The adventure-chasing spirit of.
James Clavell lives in this triumphant debut
novel....This is a riveting read, alternately
playful and suspenseful....Terrific."
—*People*

"[An] ambitious first novel...
boasts plenty of Edo-era pomp and pageantry."
—*Publishers Weekly* (Starred Review)

Praise for

Cloud of Sparrows

"The adventure-chasing spirit of James Clavell lives in this triumphant debut novel. . . . This is a riveting read, alternately playful and suspenseful. . . . Terrific."
—*People*

"Exotic, entertaining . . . [an] exceptional first novel . . . with an ambitious, unexpected ending that cuts deeper than a samurai sword."
—*San Francisco Chronicle*

"The book seizes you from start to finish. Much of it is laugh-out-loud funny . . . it is also, at key moments, wipe-your-eyes sad."
—*The Washington Post*

"[An] ambitious first novel . . . boasts plenty of Edo-era pomp and pageantry."
—*Publishers Weekly* (starred review)

"Nimble [and] adventure-filled . . . a likably straight-up samurai epic."
—*Entertainment Weekly*

"A rousing tale of Shogun Japan."
—*New York Post*

Cloud
of
Sparrows

**TAKASHI
MATSUOKA**

A DELL BOOK

CLOUD OF SPARROWS
A Dell Book

PUBLISHING HISTORY
Delacorte hardcover edition published October 2002
Dell mass market edition / September 2003

Published by
Bantam Dell
A Division of Random House, Inc.
New York, New York

All rights reserved
Copyright © 2002 by Takashi Matsuoka
Cover image of sword © The British Museum
Cover image of temple © Index Stock Photography © 2002/Orion Press
Endpaper map illustration by Michael Gellatly

Library of Congress Catalog Card Number: 2002022255

ISBN 0-440-24085-9

Manufactured in the United States of America
Published simultaneously in Canada

OPM   10 9 8 7 6 5 4 3 2 1

For HARUKO, WEIXIN, *and* JENNA
May they always guide me with their
courage, wisdom, and grace.

Contents

I.

NEW YEAR'S DAY,
January 1, 1861

1. The *Star of Bethlehem* 3
2. Outsiders 32
3. Quiet Crane 62

II.

BEAUTIFUL DREAMERS

4. Ten Dead Men 91
5. Visionaries 138
6. Lord Genji's Death 169

III.

DAIMYO

7. Satori 195
8. Makkyo 225
9. Bitoku 278

10. Iaido 308
11. Yuki to Chi 345
12. Suzume-no-kumo 361

IV.
THE BRIDGE OF
LIFE AND DEATH

13. Apple Valley 385
14. Sekigahara 425
15. El Paso 499

V.
NEW YEAR'S DAY,
The First New Moon
After the Winter Solstice,
In the 16th Year
of the Emperor Komei

16. Quiet Crane 523
17. Outsiders 532
18. The *Star of Bethlehem* 550

VI.
CLOUD OF SPARROWS

List of Chararacters

GENJI: *Great Lord of Akaoka; leader of the Okumichi clan*

SHIGERU: *Lord Genji's uncle*

KUDO: *Lord Genji's security chief*

SAIKI: *Lord Genji's chamberlain*

HIDÉ
SHIMODA } *Samurai of the Okumichi clan*
TARO

HEIKO: *A geisha; Genji's lover*

HANAKO: *A housemaid of the Okumichi clan*

LORD KIYORI: *Genji's late grandfather*

SOHAKU: *Abbot of Mushindo Monastery (and the Okumichi clan's cavalry commander)*

JIMBO: *A Zen Buddhist monk (and former Christian missionary)*

ZEPHANIAH CROMWELL
EMILY GIBSON } *Christian missionaries*
MATTHEW STARK

KAWAKAMI: *Head of the Shogun's secret police*

MUKAI: *Kawakami's lieutenant*

KUMA: *Ninja assassin in Kawakami's service*

I

NEW YEAR'S DAY

*January 1,
1861*

1

The *Star of Bethlehem*

Crossing an unknown river far from your domain, observe the surface turbulence, and note the clarity of the water. Heed the demeanor of the horses. Beware of massed ambush.

At a familiar ford near home, look deep into the shadows on the far bank, and watch the movement of the tall grass. Listen to the breathing of your nearest companions. Beware of the lone assassin.

SUZUME–NO–KUMO
(1491)

Heiko, feigning sleep, kept her breathing deep and slow, her muscles relaxed but not slack, her lips closed, at the very edge of parting, her eyes soft beneath unfluttering eyelids, her hooded gaze turned within, to the calm place at the center of her being. She sensed rather than felt him awaken beside her.

When he turned to look at her, she hoped he would see:

Her hair: the utter dark of starless night spilling across the blue silk undersheet.

Her face: pale as spring snow, glowing, with light stolen from the moon.

Her body: suggestive curvatures beneath the coverlet, also of silk, emblazoned with a finely embroidered pair of white cranes, their throats crimson with mating frenzy, dancing and dueling in midair, against a field of gold.

She was confident of starless night. Her hair—dark, lustrous, fine—was one of her best attributes.

Spring snow might be too far a stretch, even with generous metaphorical license. She had spent her early childhood in a fishing village in Tosa Domain. Those happy hours in the sun so long ago could never be completely erased. Her cheeks were ever so slightly freckled. Spring snow was not freckled. Still, there was that moonlight glow to make up for it. He insisted she had it. Who was she to disagree with him?

She hoped he was looking at her. She was an elegant sleeper, even when she was actually asleep. When she was performing, as she was now, the effect on men was usually devastating. What will he do? Will he remove the concealment, lightly, discreetly, and look upon her unconscious nakedness? Or will he smile, lean down, and wake her with a soft caress? Or will he watch, patient as always, and wait for her eyes to flutter open on their own?

Such conjecture would not have troubled her with any other man, would not even have entered her thoughts. This one was different. With him, she often found herself indulging in such reveries. Was it because he was truly unlike the others, she wondered, or was it simply because this was the one to whom she had so foolishly lost her heart?

Genji did nothing that she had anticipated. Instead he rose and went to the window overlooking Edo Bay. He stood there naked, in the dawn chill, and watched whatever he was watching with close attention. Occasionally, he shivered, but he made no move to dress himself. Heiko knew that in his youth he had undergone rigorous training with Tendai monks atop Mount Hiei. Those austere mystics were said to be masters of internal heat generation, able to stand naked beneath icy waterfalls for hours at a time. Genji prided himself on having once been their disciple. She sighed and moved, as if shifting slightly in her sleep, to stifle the giggle that almost escaped her. Obviously, he had not mastered the technique as well as he might have hoped.

Her sigh, as beguiling as she knew it was, did not distract Genji from his observation. Without so much as a glance in her direction, he picked up the ancient Portuguese telescope, opened it to its full extension, and focused again on the bay. Heiko permitted herself to feel disappointment. She had hoped... What had she hoped? Hope, small or large, was an indulgence, was it not, and nothing more.

She pictured him standing there by the window. She did so without actually looking again. Genji would not fail to notice her awareness if she pressed too much. She wasn't entirely sure he hadn't already. That would explain why he had ignored her earlier when he arose, and again when she sighed. He was teasing. Or perhaps not. It was hard to say. So she gave up thinking and pictured him.

He was rather too pretty for a man. That, and the way he habitually carried himself in an excessively casual and unsamurai-like manner, made him seem frivolous, fragile, even effeminate. External appearances were deceiving. Without clothing, the visible striations of his musculature testified to the seriousness of his martial dedication. The discipline of war was a near neighbor to the abandon of love. She felt herself warming with remembrance and sighed, this time involuntarily. It was too difficult now to maintain any pretense of sleep. She allowed her eyes to open. She looked at him and saw what she had pictured. Whatever was on the other end of that telescope must be truly fascinating. It held his full attention.

After a time, she said in a sleepy voice, "My lord, you are shivering."

He continued watching the bay, but he smiled and said, "A foul lie. I am immune to cold."

Heiko slipped from the bed and donned Genji's underkimono. She wrapped it close around her body, warming as much of it as she could, while she knelt and tied her hair loosely with a silk ribbon. It would take her maid, Sachiko, hours to restore her elaborate courtesan's coiffure. For now, this would have to do. She stood and walked toward him with the short, shuffling steps required of gracious women, then went to her knees and bowed when she was a few feet away. She held the bow for several moments, not expecting any acknowledgment from him, and not receiving any. Then she rose, took off the underkimono, warm now with the heat of her body and redolent with her scent, and put it around his shoulders.

Genji grunted and shrugged himself into the garment. "Here, look."

She took the offered telescope and scanned the

bay. Last night, there had been six ships at anchor, all warships from Russia, Britain, and America. Now there was a seventh, a three-masted schooner. The new arrival was smaller than the naval vessels, and lacked their paddle wheels and tall black smokestacks. There were no gun ports along her sides and no cannon visible on deck. As insignificant as it looked beside the warships, it was still twice the size of any Japanese ship. Where had it come from? West, from a Chinese port? South, from the Indies? East, from America?

She said, "The merchant ship wasn't there when we went to bed."

"It just dropped anchor."

"Is it the one you've been waiting for?"

"Perhaps."

Heiko bowed and returned the telescope to Genji. He hadn't told her what ship he was waiting for, or why, and of course she hadn't asked. In all likelihood, Genji himself wouldn't know the answer to those questions. He was, she assumed, awaiting the fulfillment of a prophecy, and prophecies were notoriously incomplete. Wherever her thoughts went, she kept her eyes on the ships in the bay. "Why were the outsiders making so much noise last night?"

"They were celebrating New Year's Eve."

"New Year's Eve is six weeks away."

"It is for us. The first new moon after the winter solstice, in the fifteenth year of the Emperor Komei. But for them, the New Year is already here." He said in English, "January 1, 1861," then shifted back to Japanese. "Time is more rapid for them. That's why they are so far ahead of us. Here it is, their New Year's Day, while we remain mired six weeks in the past." He looked at her and smiled. "You shame me, Heiko. Don't you feel the cold?"

"I am a mere woman, my lord. Where you are muscular, I am fat. That flaw keeps me warm a little longer." In fact, she was using all her discipline not to react to the chilly air. Warming the kimono, then giving it to him, was a moderately attractive gesture. If she trembled, she would be putting too much emphasis on what she had done, and all grace would be lost.

Genji looked at the ships again. "Steam engines that propel them whether the wind blows or the seas are becalmed. Cannon that can hurl destruction miles away. A handheld firearm for every soldier. For three hundred years, we have deluded ourselves with the cult of the sword, while they have been busy being efficient. Even their languages are more efficient. Because of that, so is their thinking. We are so vague. We rely too much on the implied and unspoken."

"Is efficiency so important?" Heiko said.

"It is in war, and war is coming."

"Is that prophecy?"

"No, only common sense. Everywhere they have gone, the outsiders have taken all they could take. Lives, treasure, land. They have seized the better part of three-quarters of the world from its rightful rulers, looted, murdered, and enslaved."

Heiko said, "How unlike our own Great Lords."

Genji laughed brightly. "It is our duty to ensure that all looting, murdering, and enslaving in Japan is done by us alone. Otherwise, how can we call ourselves Great Lords?"

Heiko bowed. "I am secure in the knowledge of such profound protection. May I draw a bath for you, my lord?"

"Thank you."

"For us, this is the hour of the dragon. What time is it for them?"

Genji looked at the Swiss clock on the table. He said in English, "Four minutes after seven A.M."

"Would you prefer to bathe, my lord, at four minutes after seven A.M., or in the hour of the dragon?"

Genji laughed again his free and easy laugh, and bowed, conceding her point. It was said among his many detractors that he laughed too frequently. This was, they said, evidence of a critical lack of seriousness in these perilous times. Perhaps this was true. Heiko wasn't sure. But she was sure that she loved to hear him laugh.

She returned his bow, took three backward steps, then turned to walk away. She was naked in her lover's bedroom, but her walk could not have been more graceful if she had been in full ceremonial attire in the Shogun's palace. She could feel his eyes on her.

"Heiko," she heard him say, "wait a moment."

She smiled. He had ignored her as long as he could. Now he was coming to her.

• • • • •

The Right Reverend Zephaniah Cromwell, humble servant of the Light of the True Word of the Prophets of Christ Our Lord, looked across the water to the city of Edo, the teeming pagan anthill of sin to which he had been sent to convey the word of God to the ignorant Japanese. The True Word, before these blighted heathens were totally ruined by the Papists, and the Episcopalians, who were only Papists in disguise, and the Calvinists and Lutherans, who were but profit-mongers hiding behind the name of God.

Heretical deviationists had beaten the True Word to China. The Right Reverend Cromwell was determined that they not triumph in Japan. In the battle to come, at Armageddon, how powerful these samurai will be, if they take Christ into themselves and become true Christian soldiers. Unafraid to die, born for war, they would be the most perfect of martyrs. That was the future, if future there was. The present did not look promising. This was a hellish land of harlots and sodomites and murderers. But he had the True Word to sustain him and he would triumph. God's will be done.

"Good morning, Zephaniah."

Her voice instantly melted his righteous rage, and he felt in its place that terrible, now-familiar heat rising inexorably in him, firing his brain and his loins. No, no, he would not yield to those evil imaginings.

"Good morning, Emily," he said. He fought to maintain a stern calm as he faced her. Emily Gibson, a faithful member of his flock, his student, his fiancée. He tried not to think of the fresh young body under her clothing, the rise and fall of her ample bosom, the beckoning curve of her hips, the length and shapeliness of her legs, the occasional flash of an ankle beneath the hem of her skirt. He tried not to imagine what he had not yet seen. Her unhindered breasts in naked repose, their fullness, the shape and color of her nipples. Her belly, rich with fertility and ready for his flooding seed. Her procreative mound, so sacred to the commandments of the Lord Our God, so profane with the Evil One's sweetest inducements of sensation, scent, and taste. Oh, the temptations and deceptions of the flesh, the ravenous hungers the flesh called forth, the raging flames of madness the flesh stoked with incendiary lust. "They that are after the things of the flesh do mind the things of the flesh; but they that are after the Spirit the things of the Spirit." He didn't realize he had spoken aloud until he heard Emily's voice again.

"Amen," she said.

Reverend Cromwell felt the world spinning away from him, and with it, the grace and salvation promised by Jesus Christ, the only begotten Son of God. He had to drive away all thought of the flesh. He looked again across the water at Edo. "Our great challenge. Sins in mind and body aplenty. Unbelievers in their vast multitudes."

She smiled that soft dreamy smile of hers. "I am sure you are up to the task, Zephaniah. You are a true man of God."

A blush of shame flowed over Reverend Cromwell. What would this innocent and trusting child think if she knew what foul hungers tortured him every moment he was in her presence? He said, "Let us pray for the heathens," and knelt down on the deck of the ship. Emily obediently knelt beside him. Too close, too close. He could feel her body heat, and despite his every effort not to notice, his nostrils were flooded with the natural perfume of her sex.

"Her princes within her are roaring lions," Reverend Cromwell said. "Her judges are evening wolves; they gnaw not the bones till the morrow. Her prophets are light and treacherous persons; her priests have polluted the sanctuary, they have done violence to the law. The just Lord is in the midst thereof; he will not do iniquity; every morning doth he bring his judgment to light, he faileth not; but the unjust knoweth no shame." Gaining confidence from the familiar cadences of the True Word, his voice grew stronger and deeper as he went on, becoming in his own ears like unto the very voice of God Himself. "Therefore wait thee upon me, saith the Lord, until the day that I rise up to the prey: for my determination is to gather the nations, that I may assemble the kingdoms, to pour upon them mine indignation, even all my fierce anger: for all the earth shall be devoured with the fire of my jealousy!" He paused to gulp down air. "Amen!" he screamed.

"Amen," Emily said, her voice as soft as a lullaby.

•　•　•　•　•

In the high seaward observation tower of Edo Castle, a Dutch celestial telescope the size of a main cannon from an English man-of-war nested atop a complex French tripod capable of the most minute calibrations. The telescope was a gift from the Dutch government to the first Tokugawa Shogun, Ieyasu, some two hundred fifty years ago. Napoleon Bonaparte had sent the tripod to the eleventh Shogun of the dynasty, Ienari, on the occasion of his own coronation as Emperor of France. That so-called empire lasted a mere ten years.

As the hour of the dragon gave way to the hour of the snake, Kawakami Eichi's eye was at the huge telescope. It was aimed, not at the cosmos, but at the palaces of the Great Lords in the Tsukiji district less than a mile away. His mind, however, was elsewhere. Contemplating the history of the telescope itself, he concluded that the present Shogun, Iemochi, was likely to be the last Tokugawa to hold that high honor. The question, of course, was who would come next? As head of the Shogun's secret police, it was Kawakami's duty to protect the regime. As a devout subject of the Emperor, presently powerless but endowed with the inviolable mandate of the gods, it was his duty to protect the nation. In better times, these two duties had been inseparable. Now it was not necessarily so. Loyalty was the most fundamental of samurai virtues. Without loyalty, there was nothing. To Kawakami, who had looked at loyalty from every possible angle—examining loyalty was, after all, his occupation—it had become increasingly clear that the days of personal allegiance were coming to an end. Loyalty, in the future, must be to a cause, a principle, an idea, not a man or a clan. That such an unprecedented thought had entered his mind was a marvel in itself, and yet another sign of the outsiders' insidious influence.

He shifted the telescope's focus from the palaces to the bay just beyond. Six of the seven ships at anchor were warships. Outsiders. They had changed everything. First, the arrival of the fleet of Black Ships, seven years ago, commanded by that arrogant American, Perry. Then the humiliating treaties with outsider nations, giving them the right to enter Japan and freeing them from the jurisdiction of Japanese law. It was like being tortured and raped in the most terrible ways, not once, but repeatedly, while being required to smile and bow and express gratitude. Kawakami's hand clenched as if gripping his sword. How cleansing it will be to behead them all. One day, without a doubt. Unfortunately that day was not this one. Edo Castle was the most strongly fortified place in all of Japan. Its mere existence had helped keep rival clans from testing the Tokugawa hold on power for nearly three centuries. Yet any one of those ships could reduce this great fortress to bloody rubble in a matter of hours. Yes, everything had changed, and those who would survive and prosper must change as well. The outsiders' way of thinking, scientific, logical, cold, was what allowed them to produce their amazing weapons. There had to be a way to use their thinking without becoming the stinking offal-eating demons that they were.

"My lord." The voice of his lieutenant, Mukai, came from outside the door.

"Enter."

Mukai, on his knees, slid the door back, bowed, entered on his knees, slid the door closed, and bowed again. "The new maritime arrival is the *Star of Bethlehem*. It sailed from San Francisco, on the western coast of America, five weeks ago, and ported in Honolulu, in the Hawaiian Islands, before proceeding here. Its cargo does not include explosives or any quantity of firearms, and none of its passengers are known agents of outsider governments, military experts, or criminals."

"The outsiders are all criminals," Kawakami said.

"Yes, my lord," Mukai agreed. "I meant only that none of them have actual criminal records so far as we know."

"Meaningless. The American government is exceedingly poor at keeping track of its people. It is to be expected, since so many of them are illiterate. How can sensible records be kept when half the record keepers themselves can neither read nor write?"

"Very true."

"What else?"

"Three Christian missionaries, with five hundred English-language Bibles."

Missionaries. That worried Kawakami. The outsiders were extremely ferocious in matters of what they called "freedom of religion." This was, of course, a totally nonsensical concept. In Japan, the people of every domain followed the religion decreed by their Great Lord. If the Great Lord subscribed to a particular sect of Buddhism, then the people were also of that sect. If he was Shinto, then they were Shinto. If he was both, as was often the case, they, too, were both. Every subject was also at liberty to follow any other religion he chose. Religion was concerned with the other realm, and the Shogun and the Great Lords were not concerned about any realm but this one. Christianity was an entirely different matter. That outsider doctrine had treason built into it. One God for the entire world, a God above the gods of Japan, and above the Son of Heaven, His Most August Imperial Majesty, the Emperor Komei. The first Tokugawa Shogun, Ieyasu, had wisely proscribed Christianity. He had expelled the outsider priests, crucified tens of thousands of converts, and that was that for more than two hundred years. Christianity was still officially forbidden. But it was a law that could no longer be enforced. Japanese swords were no match for the guns of the outsiders. So "freedom of religion" meant that every individual could practice the religion of his choice to the exclusion of all others. Besides encouraging anarchy, which was bad enough, this permitted the outsiders a pretext for intervention on behalf of their coreligionists. Indeed, Kawakami was certain that this was the real reason for "freedom of religion."

"Who is to receive the missionaries?"

"The Great Lord of Akaoka."

Kawakami closed his eyes, took a deep breath,

and centered himself. The Great Lord of Akaoka. Lately, he had been hearing that name far too often for his liking. The fief was small, distant, and unimportant. Two-thirds of the Great Lords held richer lands. But now, as always in times of uncertainty, the Great Lord of Akaoka assumed a prominence completely out of proportion to his true significance. It didn't matter if he was a wily old warrior and politician, like the late Lord Kiyori, or an effete dilettante like his boyish successor, Lord Genji. The centuries-old rumors elevated them above their rightful station. The rumors of their supposed gift of prophecy.

"We should have arrested him when the Regent was assassinated."

"That was an act by anti-outsider radicals, not Christian sympathizers," Mukai said. "He was not implicated at all."

Kawakami frowned. "You are beginning to sound like an outsider."

Mukai, realizing his error, bowed low. "Forgive me, my lord. I misspoke."

"You cite proof and evidence, as if they are more important than what is in a man's heart."

"My profound apologies, my lord." Mukai's face was still pressed against the floor.

"What is thought is as important as what is done, Mukai."

"Yes, my lord."

"If men, especially Great Lords, are not held accountable for their thoughts, then how will civilization survive the onslaught of the barbarians?"

"Yes, my lord." Mukai raised his head slightly to look at Kawakami. "Should I issue the order for his arrest?"

Kawakami turned back to the telescope. This

time, he focused on the ship Mukai had identified as the *Star of Bethlehem*. The powerful magnification provided by the Dutch device put him on deck with a man remarkably ugly even for an outsider. His eyes bulged as if there were too much pressure in the lumpy head. His face was grooved with lines of anguish, his mouth twisted in what appeared to be a perpetual grimace, his nose long and bent off to one side, his shoulders raised and hunched with tension. A young woman stood beside him. Her skin appeared exceptionally fair and smooth, no doubt an illusion caused by the curvatures and densities of the optical glass. Otherwise, she was a beast, like all of them. The man said something and knelt on the deck. A moment later, the woman knelt beside him. They were engaging in some kind of Christian prayer ritual.

Guilt at his own thoughts had made Kawakami react a little too strongly to the outsider taint in Mukai's words. Of course there could be no arrest. Akaoka was a minor fief, but the ferocity of its dedicated corps of samurai had been legendary for centuries. Any attempt at arrest would result in waves of assassinations, which could drag in other Great Lords, leading to all-out civil war, which in turn would provide too tempting an opportunity for outsider invasion. If the Great Lord of Akaoka was to be destroyed, it would have to be by less direct means. Means that Kawakami already had in place.

"Not yet," Kawakami said. "Let him proceed for now, and let us see who else we might net."

· · · · ·

The gun was in his right hand and the knife was in his left before his eyes were open. Stark snapped awake, screams of rage ringing in his ears. Dim morning light seeped into his cabin, casting vague, shifting shadows. His pistol followed his eyes as he swept the room. No one lurked there waiting for death. He was still alone. For a moment, he thought he had been having the bad dream again.

"Therefore wait ye upon me, saith the Lord, until the day that I rise up to the prey ..."

He recognized Cromwell's voice coming from the deck above. He exhaled and lowered his weapons. The preacher was at it again, spewing hellfire at the top of his lungs.

Stark got up from the bunk. His trunk was open, ready for final packing. In a few hours, he would be ashore in a new land. He felt the comforting heft of the big gun in his hand. The .44 caliber Colt Army Model Revolver with the six-inch barrel. He could draw the two pounds of steel and fire, all inside of one second, hitting a man's torso at twenty feet with the first shot three times out of five, and with the second shot the other two times. At ten feet, he could send the first bullet between a man's eyes, or into his right one or his left, take your pick, two times out of three. The third time, if the man ran, Stark could put the bullet through his spine, right at the base of the neck, and blow his head clean off his shoulders.

He would have preferred to keep the Colt on him, in an open holster slung low on his right hip. But now was not the time to wear a gun outside his clothes. Or a knife the size of a small sword. The bowie went back in its sheath and into the trunk between two sweaters Mary Anne had knit for him. He wrapped the Colt in an old towel and put it next to the bowie. He covered them both with folded shirts, and on top of the clothes he placed a layer of a dozen Bibles. In the hold of the ship was a crate with five hundred more. How the Japanese were going to read the King James Version, only God and Cromwell knew. It didn't matter to Stark. His interest in Scripture began and ended with the second line of Genesis. And the earth was without form, and void; and darkness was upon the face of the deep. He doubted he would be called upon to do any preaching anyway. Cromwell too dearly loved the sound of his own voice.

Stark had a second gun, a compact Smith & Wesson .32 caliber pocket pistol. It was small enough to hide under his jacket and light enough to keep in a reinforced pocket on the lower left-hand side of his vest, just above the belt line. To get it out, he had to cross-draw, reaching under his jacket and into the vest. He tried it a few times, practicing until his body remembered the movements, and he was as smooth and as quick as he was going to be. He didn't know how good the .32 was at stopping a man. He hoped it was better than the smaller bore .22 he'd had before. With the .22, five bullets could go into a man, and if the man was big enough and angry enough and afraid enough, he would keep on coming, blood spilling from his face and chest, the ten-inch blade of his bowie knife still hungry for your guts, and it could take a lucky swing of the empty gun fracturing the man's skull to finally bring him down.

Stark put on his jacket, picked up his hat and gloves, and went up the stairs. Cromwell and his fiancée, Emily Gibson, said their final amens and rose from their knees as he arrived on deck.

"Good morning, Brother Matthew," Emily said. She wore a simple gingham bonnet, a cheap cloth coat lumpy with cotton padding, and an old wool scarf around her neck to keep the cold away. A stray ringlet of golden hair fell out of the bonnet by her right ear. She reached up and tucked it back in as if it were something to be ashamed of. How did that line go? Neither cast ye your pearls before swine, lest they trample them under their feet, and turn again and rend you. Funny. She made him think of biblical verses. Maybe she was meant to be a preacher's wife after all. Worry briefly creased her brow before her turquoise eyes sparkled again, and she smiled at him. "Did our prayers wake you?"

Stark said, "What better way to wake than to the Word of God?"

"Amen, Brother Matthew," Cromwell said. "Is it not said, I will not give sleep to mine eyes, or slumber to mine eyelids, until I find out a place for the Lord."

"Amen," Emily and Stark said in unison.

Cromwell gestured grandly toward land. "There it is, Brother Matthew. Japan. Forty million souls doomed to eternal damnation but for the grace of God and our own selfless efforts."

Buildings covered the landscape as far as Stark could see. Most of them were low-lying structures of flimsy appearance no more than three stories tall. The city was vast, but it looked like it could all blow away in a strong wind, or burn at the touch of a single match. Except for the palaces along the shoreline and the towering white fortress with the black roofs about a mile inland.

"Are you ready, Brother Matthew?" Cromwell asked.

Stark said, "Yes, Brother Zephaniah, I am."

• • • • •

Sohaku, abbot of Mushindo Monastery, sat alone in his hojo, the ten-foot-square private meditation room of the temple's resident Zen master. He sat unmoving in full lotus posture, his eyelids closed to narrow slits, not seeing, not listening, not feeling. Birds twittered in the trees outside. A light breeze, rising with the sun, moved through the hall. In the kitchen, monks banged pots as they prepared the next meal. They should not be making so much noise. Sohaku caught himself thinking and sighed. Well, he lasted for a minute or two, that time. Getting better at it, anyway. Gritting his teeth against the pain, he lifted his right foot off his left thigh with both hands and placed it on the floor before him. He leaned back and lifted his left foot off his right thigh and let the leg stretch out next to the other. Ah. Such wonderful pleasure simply from straightening his legs. Life was truly a gift and a mystery. The pots banged again in the kitchen, and someone laughed. It sounded like Taro. That undisciplined lazy fool.

Sohaku, grim coldness in his eyes, rose to his feet and strode out of the hojo. He moved, not with the slow, mindful, deliberate steps of the Zen monk that he now was. His steps were long, aggressive, permitting no possibility of pause or retreat, the steps that were habitually his before he took the two hundred fifty vows of monkhood, when he was the samurai Tanaka Hidetada, commander of cavalry, sworn vassal in life and in death of Okumichi no kami Kiyori, the late Great Lord of Akaoka.

"Idiots!" He stepped over the threshold into the kitchen. With his arrival, the three burly men in the brown robes of Zen acolytes dropped instantly to their knees, their shaven heads pressed hard against the floor. "Where do you think you are? What do you think you are doing? May you and your fathers be damned as women in all your incarnations to come!" None of the three men moved or made a sound. They stayed as they were, pressing themselves as far downward as they could go. They would remain there, Sohaku knew, until he permitted them to rise. His heart softened. They were, in truth, good men. Loyal, brave, well disciplined. This business of being monks was difficult for them all. "Taro."

Taro raised his head slightly off the floor and peeked up at Sohaku. "Yes!"

"Take Lord Shigeru his breakfast."

"Yes!"

"And be careful. I don't want to lose another man, not even one as useless as you."

Taro smiled as he bowed down. Sohaku was no longer angry. "Yes! I will do so immediately."

Sohaku departed without another word. Taro and the other two, Muné and Yoshi, rose to their feet.

Muné said, "Lord Hidetada's mood has been consistently foul of late."

"You mean the Reverend Abbot Sohaku," Taro said, ladling bean curd soup into a serving bowl.

Yoshi snorted. "Of course his mood is foul, whatever name he chooses to use. Ten hours of meditation every day. No training with sword, lance, or bow. Who could endure such a regimen without becoming foul?"

"We are samurai of the Okumichi clan," Taro said, chopping a pickled radish into bite-sized pieces. "It is our duty to obey our lord no matter what he orders."

"True," Muné said, "but is it not also our duty to do so with good cheer?"

Yoshi snorted again, but he picked up a broom and began sweeping the kitchen.

" 'When the archer misses his target,' " Taro said, quoting Confucius, " 'he looks within himself for error.' It is not our place to criticize our superiors." He put the soup and the pickled vegetables on a tray along with a small pot of rice. When Taro left the kitchen, Muné was washing the pots, being very careful not to bang them together.

It was a beautiful winter's morning. The cold that penetrated his flimsy robe invigorated him. How refreshing it would be to wade into the stream beside the temple and stand under the icy flow of its small waterfall. Such pleasures were forbidden to him now.

He was certain it was only a temporary prohibition. While the present Great Lord of Akaoka might not be the warrior his grandfather was, he was still an Okumichi. War was coming. That was plain even to a simple man like Taro. And whenever there was war, the swords of the Okumichi clan were always among the first to redden with the blood of enemies. They had been waiting for a long time. When war came, they would not remain monks for long.

Taro stepped lightly on the small stones of the footpath between the main hall and the residence wing. When the stones were wet, they were treacherously slippery. When they were dry, they made the sound of a small landslide with every step. Reverend Sohaku had offered a year's exemption from stable duty to the first man to walk the path in silence for ten paces. So far, Taro had attained the best results, but he was nowhere near inaudible. Much practice was still required.

The twenty other monks would be sitting in meditation for another thirty minutes before Muné rang the bell for the first meal of the day. Nineteen monks, that is. He had forgotten about Jioji, whose skull was fractured yesterday while engaged in the very task now assigned to Taro. He made his way through the garden to the wall marking the perimeter of the temple grounds. Near the wall was a small hut. He knelt at the door. Before announcing himself, he brought his senses to full attention. He had no wish to join Jioji in a funeral pyre.

"Lord," he said, "it is Taro. I have brought your breakfast."

"We fly through the air in great ships of metal," came the voice from within. "In the hour of the tiger, we are here. By the hour of the boar, we are in Hiroshima. We have traveled through the air like gods, but we are not satisfied. We are late. We wish we had arrived even earlier."

"I am entering, lord." Taro removed the wooden rod that kept the door locked and slid it open. The heavy stench of sweat, feces, and urine immediately assailed his nostrils and twisted his stomach into a trembling knot. He rose and stepped away as quickly as he could without upsetting the food on the tray. With effort, he managed to keep the bile from rising all the way up into his mouth. He would have to clean the room before he served breakfast. That meant he would also have to clean its occupant. This was not something he could do alone.

"In our hands are small horns. We whisper to each other with them."

"Lord, I will return shortly. Please calm yourself."

In fact, the voice was calm, despite the insanity of the words it pronounced.

"We hear each other clearly, though we are a thousand miles apart."

Taro quickly returned to the kitchen.

"Water, rags," he said to Muné and Yoshi.

"By the Merciful Buddha of Compassion," Yoshi said, "please tell me he hasn't fouled his room again."

Taro said, "Strip down to your loincloths. There's no point in dirtying our clothing." He took off his robe, folded it neatly, and put it on a shelf.

When they came through the garden and could see the hut, Taro realized with a shock that he had left the door open. His two companions stopped abruptly as soon as they saw it.

"Didn't you lock the door before leaving?" Muné asked.

"We should get more help," Yoshi said nervously.

Taro said, "Wait here."

He approached the hut with extreme caution. Not only had he left the door open, the stench had been so repulsive to him that he had failed to look inside before going for assistance. It was unlikely that their charge could have escaped all the bonds that held him in place. After the incident yesterday with Jioji, they had not only tied Lord Shigeru's arms and legs tightly to his body, they had also tied him with four ropes that extended to each of the four walls. Shigeru could not shift more than a foot in one direction before at least one of the ropes prevented further movement. Still, it was Taro's responsibility to make certain.

The putrid odors were as bad as before, but he was now too worried to care.

"Lord?"

There was no answer. He looked in quickly without exposing himself to attack. The four ropes were still connected to the walls, but no longer to Shigeru.

Pressing himself against the outside wall to the left, he peered into the right side of the hut, then reversed his position and checked the other half of the small space. The hut was definitely empty.

"Inform the abbot," Taro said to Yoshi. "Our guest has departed his residence."

While Yoshi ran to spread the alarm, Taro and Muné stood close together and looked uncertainly around the immediate area.

"He could be gone from the temple grounds, on his way back to Akaoka," Muné said. "Or he could be hiding anywhere. Before his illness, he was a master of concealment. He could be in the garden with a dozen horses and cavalrymen and we wouldn't see him."

"He doesn't have horses or cavalrymen with him," Taro said.

"My point," Muné said, "is not that he does, but that he could, and we still wouldn't know where he is. Himself alone, how easily he can escape detection."

Taro was prevented from responding, first, by the look of horrified astonishment on Muné's face as he looked, not at Taro, but just past Taro's shoulder, and second, by what he later learned was a fist-sized rock that slammed into the back of his head just a moment later.

When Taro regained consciousness, Sohaku was attending to Muné's injury, an eye swollen completely shut. With his other eye, Muné fixed a baleful glare on Taro.

Muné said, "You were mistaken. Lord Shigeru was still in the hut."

"How can that be? I looked everywhere and no one was there."

"You didn't look up." Sohaku checked the dressing at the back of Taro's head. "You'll live."

"He was clinging to the wall above the doorway," Muné said. "He came leaping out when you turned your back to talk to me."

"Unforgivable, lord," Taro said, trying to bury his face in the ground. Sohaku prevented him from doing so.

"Calm yourself," he said in a mild voice. "Consider this valuable training. For twenty years, Lord Shigeru was the chief martial arts instructor of our clan. It is no shame to be defeated by him. Of course, that is no excuse for laxity, either. Next time, be sure he's secure before leaving him, and always lock the door."

"Yes, lord."

"Raise your head. You're aggravating the bleeding by groveling that way. And I am abbot, not lord."

"Yes, Reverend Abbot." Taro asked, "Has Lord Shigeru been found?"

"Yes." Sohaku smiled without humor. "He's in the armory."

"He has weapons?"

"He's a samurai," Sohaku said, "and he's in the armory. What do you think? Yes, he has weapons. In fact, he has all the weapons. We have none, except for what we are able to improvise."

Yoshi came running, still only in his loincloth, but now carrying a ten-foot staff freshly cut from the temple's bamboo grove. "He has made no effort to break out, sir. We've blocked the doors of the armory as best we can with logs and barrels of rice. If he really wants to leave, however . . ."

Sohaku nodded. There were three barrels of gunpowder in the armory. Shigeru could blow away any obstruction. Indeed, if he so chose, he could blow up the entire armory, with himself in it. Sohaku rose.

"Stay here," he said to Yoshi. "Take care of your companions." He made his way through the garden to the armory. There, he found the other monks all equipped as Yoshi had been with ten-foot staffs of green bamboo. Not the ideal weapon with which to face a swordsman who, despite his present condition of debilitating madness, was almost certainly the best in the nation. He was glad to see that his men had arrayed themselves properly. A thin screen of four observers at the closed back of the building, and three teams of five men each at the front, where Shigeru was likely to appear if he tried to escape.

Sohaku went up to the front door, blocked, as Yoshi had described, with logs and heavy barrels of rice. Inside, he could hear the swift movement of steel through air. Shigeru was practicing, probably with a sword in each hand. He was one of the few modern swordsmen strong enough and skilled enough to follow the legendary Musashi's two-sword style of two hundred years ago. Sohaku bowed respectfully at the door and said, "Lord Shigeru. It is I, Tanaka Hidetada, commander of cavalry. May I speak with you?" He thought his former name would cause less confusion. He hoped it would also elicit a response. He and Shigeru had been comrades in arms for twenty years.

"Air you can see," the voice within said. "Layers of color on the horizon, garlands for the setting sun. Beautiful, unbreathable."

Sohaku could make no sense of the words. He said, "May I be of assistance in some way, lord?"

The only answer from within was the hiss of swords slashing air.

. . . . .

The longboat knifed through the water toward the intricate network of wharves that formed Edo Harbor. Light sea mist rising from the bow wave touched Emily's cheeks with icy dew. Astern, a Japanese lighter hove to beside the *Star of Bethlehem,* ready to shift cargo from ship to shore.

"There is where we are bound," Zephaniah said, "that palace beside the shore. Its master calls it the Quiet Crane."

Brother Matthew said, "It looks more like a fort than a palace."

"A most excellent observation, Brother Matthew. It is well to bear in mind where we are going. Among the most murderous heathens on the face of the earth. Some trust in chariots, and some in horses; but we will remember the name of the Lord our God."

"Amen," Brother Matthew and Emily said.

Emily tried not to let her expectations get the better of her. Her destiny lay ahead. When it was revealed, would it match her hopes? She sat beside her betrothed, the Reverend Zephaniah Cromwell, and gave every appearance of peaceful quietude. He maketh me to lie down in green pastures; he leadeth me beside the still waters. He restoreth my soul; he leadeth me in the paths of righteousness for His name's sake. In her bosom, her heart thundered so loudly she was surprised to be the only one who heard it.

She turned toward Zephaniah and saw him staring at her. His cheeks and brow, as usual, were tight with a righteous concentration that caused his eyes to bulge, his lips to turn down, and the deep lines of his face to grow ever deeper. That fierce and knowing visage always made her feel his gaze deep in the most secret depths of her being.

"The name of the Lord is a strong tower," Zephaniah said. "The righteous runneth into it, and is safe."

"Amen," Emily said. She heard Brother Matthew's echoed amen behind her.

"He will not fail thee," Zephaniah said, his voice growing louder, his face redder, "nor forsake thee!"

"Amen," Emily and Brother Matthew said.

Zephaniah's near hand rose, as if to touch her, then he blinked and drew his bulging eyes back into his head. His hand dropped down onto his own thigh. He looked across the bow to the approaching pier. Gospel came from his throat in a choked whisper. "Be not afraid, neither be thou dismayed: for the Lord thy God is with thee whithersoever thou goest."

"Amen," Emily said.

In truth, she feared what was behind her more than what was ahead. Whatever dread she felt at the approach of the unknown had been polished and honed so much by anticipation, it had turned into hope long ago.

Japan. A land as unlike her own as any could be and still be of God's green earth. Religion, language, history, art—Japan and America held nothing in common. She had never even seen a Japanese man or woman, except in those museum daguerreotypes. And the Japanese, Zephaniah had told her, had seen almost no outsiders for nearly three hundred years. They had become incestuously ingrown, he said, feeling with hearts twisted by isolation, hearing with ears deafened by demonic gongs, seeing with eyes clouded by pagan delusions. We and they will look upon the same scene and see entirely different landscapes. Be prepared for this, he said. Guard yourself from disappointment. Abandon all that you have long taken for granted. You will be cleansed, he said, of all vanity.

She felt no fear, only anticipation. Japan. She had dreamed of it for so long. If there was a place where her infernal curse might be lifted from her, it was Japan. Let the past truly be past. That was her most fervent prayer.

The landing dock neared. Emily could see two dozen Japanese there, wharfmen and officials. In another minute, she would see their faces, and they would see hers. When they looked at her, what would they see?

Her blood thundered in her veins.

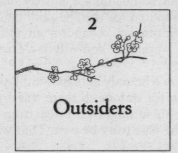

2

Outsiders

Some say there is no difference among the barbarians, that they are all the same offal-eating abominations. This is false. The Portuguese will trade guns for women. The Dutch demand gold. The English want treaties.

From this, you should know that the Portuguese and the Dutch are easily understood, and the English are the most dangerous. Therefore, study the English carefully and ignore the others.

SUZUME–NO–KUMO
(1641)

Okumichi no kami Genji, Great Lord of Akaoka, regarded himself in the mirror. He saw an anachronism sheathed in layer upon layer of antique clothing, topped with a complex coiffure, partially tied, partially stacked, partially shaved, more burdened with symbolism than the central icons of the simpler peasant religions.

"Lord." His sword bearer knelt at his side. He

bowed, raised Genji's short sword, the wakizashi, above his own head, and offered it up to him. When Genji had secured this in his sash, the sword bearer went through the same procedure with the second longer sword, the katana, the samurai's main weapon for a thousand years. There would be no need for one sword on this brief outing, much less two. They were, however, required by his status.

While elaborate, his overall appearance was at the same time extremely conservative, more appropriate for an elderly man than for a youth of twenty-four. This was because the clothing he wore had in fact belonged to an elderly man, his grandfather, the late Lord Kiyori, who had died three weeks earlier at the age of seventy-nine. The black-and-gray outer kimono, without adornment of any kind, radiated a kind of warlike austerity. Over this, the stiffly winged black jacket was likewise plain, lacking even the crest of his house, a stylized sparrow dodging arrows from the four directions.

This last omission did not find favor with Saiki, the chamberlain he had inherited from his grandfather. "Lord, is there a reason for you to be incognito?"

"Incognito?" The suggestion amused Genji. "I am about to go into the street in a formal procession surrounded by a company of samurai, all wearing the sparrow-and-arrows crest. Do you really think anyone will fail to recognize me?"

"Lord, you give your enemies an excuse to pretend they don't, and thus the freedom to insult you and instigate a crisis."

"I will refuse to be insulted," Genji said, "and you will prevent any instigation."

"They may not permit you to refuse," Saiki said, "and I may be unable to prevent."

Genji smiled. "In such case, I am confident you will proceed to kill them all."

Kudo, the security chief, bowed and entered the room. "Lord, your guest will leave the compound after you depart. Would it not be advisable to have her followed?"

"For what purpose?" Genji said. "We know where she lives."

"A simple precautionary measure," Kudo said. "Outside your presence, she may let down her guard. We may learn something of value."

Genji smiled. He had known Heiko for less than a month, and he already knew she never let down her guard.

"We should do as Kudo suggests," Saiki said. "We have never looked into the woman's background and past associations as thoroughly as we should have." What he meant, but did not say, was that Genji had forbidden any such inquiries. "Some rudimentary surveillance would surely be appropriate."

"Don't worry," Genji said, "I myself have investigated Heiko thoroughly, and find nothing to doubt."

"That is not the kind of investigation we need," Saiki said, a sour expression on his face. He found playful references to sex distasteful in the extreme. During two hundred fifty debilitating years of peace, many clans had crumbled because their leaders had allowed themselves to be distracted by prurient impulses. "We know nothing of substance about her. Not prudent."

"We know she is the most celebrated geisha in

Edo," Genji said. "What else do we need to know?" He held up his hand to cut off Saiki's response. "I have psychically examined her in the four directions of time and space. Rest assured, she is completely above suspicion."

"Lord," Saiki said, his face full of reproach, "this is not a matter for jest. Your life could very well be at risk."

"What makes you think I'm jesting? Surely you have heard the rumors. I have but to touch a person and I know their destiny." He could see by the way that Kudo and Saiki looked at each other that they had indeed heard the rumors. With a last dissatisfied glance in the mirror, Genji turned and left the room.

His two advisors followed him down the hall to the outer courtyard. Two dozen samurai awaited his presence, a palanquin and four bearers in their midst. Members of the household staff lined the way to the gate, ready to bow as he departed. They would be there, bowing again, when he returned. It was, all in all, a tremendous waste of human energy. His destination was only a few hundred yards away, and he would be back within minutes. Yet a rigid and ancient protocol of rank demanded that his every departure and arrival be treated with ceremonial seriousness.

He turned to Saiki. "No wonder Japan has fallen so far behind the outsider nations. They have science and industry. They produce cannons, steamships, and railroads. We, in pathetic contrast, have a superabundance of empty ceremony. We produce bows, kneelings, and more bows."

"Lord?" Saiki's expression was clouded with confusion.

"I could saddle a horse, ride there on my own, and be back in less time than it took to assemble this unnecessary crowd."

"Lord!" Saiki and Kudo both dropped to their knees on the hallway floor. Saiki said, "I beg you, do not even consider such a thing."

Kudo said, "You have enemies among both supporters and opponents of the Shogun. Going out without an escort is tantamount to suicide."

Genji gestured for them to rise. "I said I could. I didn't say I would." He sighed and went down the steps into the sandals that had been placed on the ground for him. He took five steps to the palanquin (which had by now been raised three feet by the bearers, making it possible for him to enter with a minimum of effort), removed the two swords (which he had just a minute earlier placed in his sash), and put them inside the palanquin, stepped out of the sandals (which the sandal bearer now bowed to before placing in the sandal compartment under the entrance of the palanquin), and seated himself within. He looked out at Saiki and said, "Do you see what I mean about empty ceremony?"

Saiki bowed. "Lord, it is my failing that I do not. I will study the matter."

Genji let out an exasperated sigh. "Let us proceed, then, before the sun sets."

"My lord jests again," Saiki said. "The sun has only just risen." He stepped forward, bowed, and slid the door of the palanquin shut. The bearers rose. The procession moved forward.

Through the front window, Genji could see eight samurai in a double column. If he cared to look behind, he would see twelve more. Two were to his left, and two, including Saiki, to his right. Twenty-four men, twenty-eight counting the bearers, were prepared to give their lives to preserve his. Such martial dedication imbued every act of a Great Lord, no matter how mundane and insignificant, with altogether too much drama. No wonder Japan's past was so bloody and its future so wrought with danger.

Genji's contemplation moved in another direction when he saw an elaborate coiffure among the bowing heads of the household staff. It was formed by the same lustrous hair that had so recently decorated his pillow like night itself spilling from the sky. Her kimono was one he had never seen before. He knew she wore it now for the sole purpose of bidding him farewell. It depicted dozens of pink roses cast about by white foam on a sea of deepest blue. Her white overcoat had exactly the same design, but without any additional colors. Three different textures of silk for white roses on white foam on a sea of white. It was evocative, daring, and extremely dangerous. Heiko's roses were of the variety sometimes referred to as American Beauty. The most rabid antiforeign samurai among the reactionary clans took offense at everything that came from outside. With the same simplistic arrogance that enabled them to style themselves Men of Virtue, it was entirely possible that one of them might think to kill her merely for wearing this design. Against such an attack, her only defense was her courage, her fame, her incredible beauty.

"Stop," Genji said.

Immediately, Saiki cried out the order. "Halt!" The leading contingent of samurai had passed through the front gate of the compound and was now stopped in the street. Genji's palanquin was just inside the gate. The rest of the bodyguard corps was still in the courtyard behind him. Saiki grimaced. "This position invites ambush, lord. We enjoy neither the protection within nor the freedom of movement without."

Genji opened the sliding door. "I have complete confidence in your ability to defend me at all times, in all circumstances." Heiko was still bowing deeply, like everyone else.

"Lady Mayonaka no Heiko," he said, using her full geisha name. Midnight Equilibrium.

"Lord Genji," she replied, bowing even lower.

How was it, he wondered, that her voice could be so soft and so clear at the same time? Were it as fragile as it seemed, he should not be able to hear her at all. The illusion was tantalizing. Everything about her was tantalizing.

"Such a provocative kimono."

She came out of her bow, smiling, and slightly spread her arms. The wide sleeves of her kimono opened like the wings of a bird about to take flight. "I am sure I don't know what Lord Genji means," she said. "These colors are so common I border on visual cliché. Surely only the most hopeless of idiots could be provoked by it."

Genji laughed. Even the steadfastly dour Saiki was unable to suppress a short chuckle, though he did a fair job of disguising it as a cough. Genji said, "The most hopeless of idiots are precisely the ones who worry me. But perhaps you are right. Perhaps the traditional colors will blind them to the foreign roses."

"Foreign?" A most beguiling look of query widened her eyes and caused her head to tilt. "I have been told roses, pink, white, and red, blossom every spring in the innermost garden of the famous castle,

Cloud of Sparrows." She added pointedly, "I have been told, though I have never been invited to see for myself."

Genji bowed, not too deeply. Protocol forbade a Great Lord from bowing low to anyone below him in rank, which was practically everyone but the members of the Imperial Family in Kyoto and the Shogunal Family in the great castle that towered over Edo. With a smile, he said, "I am certain that oversight will be remedied in a day not distant."

"I am less certain," she said, "but I am heartened by your confidence. In any case, is that castle not one of the most ancient in all of Japan?"

"Yes," Genji said, playing along with her. "It is."

"Then how can these flowers be foreign? By definition, what blooms in an ancient Japanese castle must be Japanese, must it not, Lord Genji?"

"It is obvious I was wrong to worry about you, Lady Heiko," Genji said. "Your logic is certain to deflect all criticism."

The household staff was still bowing. Outside the gate, passersby who had dropped to their knees at the appearance of a Great Lord's procession remained on their knees, their heads pressed to the ground. This was less out of respect than out of fear. A samurai could cut down any commoner who failed, in the samurai's opinion, to display the proper humility, which generally meant groveling until the samurai and his lord had passed by. During the entire conversation, all activity in the vicinity had come to a halt. Seeing Heiko, Genji had forgotten about everyone else. His lack of consideration embarrassed him now. With a quick farewell bow to her, he gave the signal to proceed.

"Forward!" Saiki ordered. As the procession

finally departed, Saiki shot a glance at Kudo, who remained behind.

Genji observed this exchange and knew right away what it meant. The two were disobeying his order to let Heiko be. When she left the compound minutes later, she would be accompanied by her maidservant at her side, and behind her at a discreet distance, Kudo, the surveillance specialist among his senior advisors. There was nothing he could do about that now. Nor was there much reason for concern. Events had not yet taken such a turn that he had to worry about his bodyguards killing his mistress. The situation would deteriorate soon enough. He would worry about it then.

"Saiki."

"Lord."

"What transportation awaits our guests?"

"Rickshaws, lord."

Genji said nothing more. Rickshaws. Saiki knew they would be more comfortable in carriages, so he had arranged for rickshaws instead. This clear signal of his vassal's disapproval didn't upset Genji. He understood the dilemma.

Saiki was bound to him by honor, history, and tradition. Yet the code history and tradition had created, the code from which all honor flowed, was itself under attack by the very actions Genji now took. Foreigners threatened the hierarchical order of lord and vassal upon which their society was built. While the most decisive lords sought their expulsion, his own lord went out of his way to befriend them. And not just any foreigners, but Christian missionaries, the most politically provocative and practically useless of them all.

Genji knew Saiki was not alone among his

tradition-bound vassals in doubting his judgment. Indeed, of the three generals he had inherited from his grandfather—Saiki, Kudo, and Sohaku—there wasn't one whose adherence was utterly certain. Loyalties were coming into conflict in a way never foreseen. When those loyalties could no longer be reconciled, would they follow Genji, or would they turn against him?

Even with prophecy as a guide, the road ahead was uncertain.

•   •   •   •   •

A dozen roughly dressed Japanese dockworkers awaited the arrival of their longboat. At the base of the pier, three men in much more elaborate attire sat at a table. Stark could see that all three wore two swords in their sashes. They must be what Zephaniah had said were samurai, the warrior caste that ruled Japan. All of the Japanese regarded their approach without expression of any kind.

"May God in heaven watch over you," Captain McCain said, "because it's for certain He's not anywhere ashore." The skipper of the *Star of Bethlehem* went with them to arrange for his ship's provisions. Unlike his passengers, he had been to Japan before, and his opinion of the place and its inhabitants was not high.

"God is everywhere," Cromwell said, "and in everything. He watches over all without exception."

McCain grunted. The wordless syllable made his thoughts on the matter clear. He stepped out onto the pier with the longboat's mooring rope in hand and passed it to one of the waiting Japanese dockworkers. This man bowed deeply as he accepted it. No words passed between them, since McCain spoke no

Japanese, and none of the Japanese wharf men spoke English.

"The *Star* sails for Hong Kong in a fortnight," McCain said. "If you're not back aboard by then, it will be six weeks before we return on our way back to Hawaii."

"We will see you in six weeks, then," Cromwell said, "to bid you a good journey. This is where we will remain, doing God's work, for the rest of our lives."

McCain grunted again and stalked off toward the dockside warehouses.

"Prior arrangements have been made," Cromwell said to Emily and Stark. "Permissions have been granted. We face only formalities here. Brother Matthew, if you will keep Sister Emily company and watch over our luggage, I will deal with the Shogun's officials."

"I will do so, Brother Zephaniah," Stark said.

Cromwell hustled off to the table where the three officials sat. Stark offered his hand to Emily. She took it and stepped from the boat onto the pier.

The obvious fact that all the workers were Japanese didn't cause Stark to relax. Men could do a task because they were driven to it. They could do it because they were afraid not to do it. And they could do it because they were paid to do it. Anyone among them could be such a man. He had no intention of dying as soon as he stepped ashore, stopped before he could even begin.

"You seem taken by the appearance of the Japanese, Brother Matthew," Emily said. "Do you find them so unusual?"

"Not at all," Stark said. "I was only admiring their efficiency. They have removed our belongings from the longboat in a quarter of the time it took our own seamen to place them there."

They followed their luggage to the table where the three officials sat. Cromwell had become engaged in a rather heated discussion with them.

"No, no, no," Cromwell said. "Do you understand? No, no, no."

The official in the center was apparently chief among them. His face remained bland, but his voice, too, rose as he said, "Must yes. Yes, yes. Understand you?"

"They're insisting on searching our luggage for contraband," Cromwell said. "That is expressly forbidden by treaty."

"No yes," the official said. "No Japan come."

"What harm is there in allowing a search?" Emily said. "We carry no contraband."

"That's not the point," Cromwell said. "If we yield to arbitrary interference now, there will be no end to it. Our mission will be destroyed before it can begin."

A samurai came running up to the table. He bowed to the chief official and said something in Japanese. His tone was urgent. All three officials jumped to their feet. Following a quick exchange among them, the two junior officials went running off with the samurai who had brought the message.

The stubborn look was gone from the remaining official's face. Now he appeared agitated and extremely worried. "Please to wait," he said with a bow, suddenly polite.

In the meantime, samurai who had apparently been in readiness poured from the dockside armory onto the pier. A good number of them carried firearms as well as swords. Stark recognized them as muskets of an earlier era. Antique, but still capable of killing at a good distance in the hands of marksmen. Distance, in this case, would not be an issue. Even as they ordered themselves in ranks, another group of samurai arrived, about two dozen of them, wearing uniform clothing of a different color and pattern. Four bearers in the center of the group carried a palanquin on their shoulders. The new arrivals came onto the pier and stopped less than five paces away from the front rank of the Shogun's men. Their attitude was not friendly.

• • • • •

"Make way!" Saiki declared. "How dare you obstruct the passage of the Great Lord of Akaoka."

"We were not informed that any Great Lord would grace us with his presence." Saiki recognized the speaker as Ishi, the fat and pompous commander of the Shogun's harbor police. If it came to violence, his would be the first head Saiki would take. "We are therefore not authorized to allow such a presence."

"Mannerless creature!" Saiki took a step toward Ishi, his right hand on the hilt of his sword. "Lower yourself to your proper level!"

Without any order being given, half of the Akaoka samurai arrayed themselves in battle line alongside their commander, their hands like his on the hilts of their swords. Though there were four times as many men wearing the Shogun's colors, they were not nearly as well organized. The musketeers were at the back, where their weapons could not be employed without potentially decimating their own ranks. That is, if they had been prepared to fire, which they were not. The swordsmen in the front rank were equally unprepared for conflict. When

Saiki stepped forward, they staggered backward as if they had already been struck.

"Our lord needs to inform wharf rats of nothing!" Saiki was ablaze. Another insolent remark from Ishi and he would cut the oaf down where he stood. "Remove yourselves from our path or we will assist you in your departure."

Inside the palanquin, Genji listened with grim amusement. He had come to the harbor to greet visitors. It would not seem to be a difficult undertaking. Yet here he was, on the verge of becoming involved in a life-and-death struggle over simple access to the pier. Enough. He slid open the door of the palanquin with a sharp clack of wood on wood.

"What is the problem?"

"Lord, please don't expose yourself." One of his bodyguards knelt beside the palanquin. "There are musketeers nearby."

"Nonsense," Genji said. "Who would want to shoot me?" He stepped out. As his feet went toward the ground, his sandals were quickly placed beneath them.

In the back rank of the Shogun's men, Kuma, in the guise of a musketeer, saw Genji step into the open. He saw also that there was no identifying crest on Genji's clothing. This was the opportunity he had been warned to expect. Because Genji wore no crest, it could be claimed that he was suspected of being an impostor involved in some plot against the recently landed missionaries. No one would believe this, nor was it meant to be believed. It was an excellent excuse, however. Kuma stepped back where he would not be seen by his fellow musketeers, raised his musket, and sighted in at the center of Genji's right shoulder joint. As he had been instructed, he would administer a crippling wound, not a mortal one.

Saiki rushed to stop Genji from proceeding any farther. "Lord, please go back. There are thirty musketeers not ten paces away."

"This is too ridiculous." Genji brushed past Saiki and stepped out beyond the front rank of his own men. "Who is in charge here?"

Kuma pulled the trigger.

The musket did not fire. Kuma looked at it. He should have been more careful when he had rushed out of the armory. He had grabbed someone else's empty weapon instead of his own loaded one.

"You there, what do you think you're doing?" The gunnery captain strode up to him. "No one ordered you to raise your musket." He looked sharply at Kuma. "I don't know you. What is your name and when were you assigned to this unit?"

Before Kuma could answer, Ishi said, "Lord Genji," and fell to his knees. His men, including Kuma and the angry gunnery captain, were forced to follow suit.

"So you recognize me?" Genji said.

"Yes, Lord Genji. If I had known you were coming, I would have properly prepared for your arrival."

"Thank you," Genji said. "May I greet my guests, or must I go elsewhere first to secure permission to do so?"

"Get out of Lord Genji's way," Ishi said to his men. They moved swiftly to the side without standing completely and dropped right back down to their knees. "Forgive me, Lord Genji. I could not let your men proceed without knowing you were really among them. There are so many plots these days, and the Shogun is especially concerned about plots against outsiders."

"Idiot!" Saiki was still on the verge of exploding. "Are you suggesting I would undermine the best interests of my own lord?"

"I am sure he is not," Genji said. "Are you?"

"Not at all, Lord Genji," Ishi said, "I was merely ..."

"There," Genji said to Saiki, "all settled. Now may we proceed?" He walked down the pier toward the missionaries.

Saiki watched him go, his heart filled with admiration. With a hundred potential assassins at his back, he walked away as casually as if he were strolling in the innermost garden of his own castle. Genji was young and inexperienced, and perhaps lacked sound political judgment. But there was no doubting the strength of the Okumichi blood in his veins. Saiki's hand left his sword. With a final glare at Ishi, he followed his lord's lead.

• • • • •

Emily didn't realize she had stopped breathing until she exhaled with a gasp.

Moments earlier, a bloody fight had seemed inevitable. Then someone had stepped out of the palanquin, spoken a few quiet words, and the tension had immediately dissipated. Emily watched with a high degree of curiosity as that someone now walked toward them.

He was a young man of striking appearance, with dramatically dark features that stood out vividly against his pale skin. His eyes were long, rather than wide. They would have attracted more notice than admiration in a Western face. In the oval of his Eastern one, they were perfect complements to the high arches of his brows, his delicate nose, the mild rise of his cheekbones, the suggestion of a smile that held his lips in a small curve. Like the other samurai, he wore a jacket with stiff winglike extensions at the shoulders, had the same elaborately styled hair with partially shaved sections, and like all of them, wore two swords in his sash. Despite the weapons, his manner seemed distinctly unwarlike.

As he neared, the official who had been giving Zephaniah so much trouble fell to his knees and pressed his head to the wooden planks of the pier. The young man said a few words in Japanese. At this, the official came quickly to his feet.

"Genji Lord, come, he," the official said, nervousness causing his English skills to deteriorate even as he spoke. "You, he, go, please."

"Lord Genji?" Cromwell said. When the youth bowed in affirmation, Cromwell introduced himself and his party. "Zephaniah Cromwell. Emily Gibson. Matthew Stark." God help us, he thought. This effeminate child is the Great Lord of Akaoka, our protector in this savage land.

Now a second samurai approached. This one was more mature, and much more ferocious in appearance. Genji said a few soft words. The ferocious one bowed, turned, and made a small circular gesture with an upraised hand.

Genji said something to the official. The official bowed to the three missionaries and said, "Genji Lord say, welcome Japan."

"Thank you, Lord Genji," Cromwell said. "We are most honored to be here."

Clattering noises came from the land end of the

pier. Three small two-wheeled carriages came their way, pulled, not by horses, but each by a single man.

"They have slavery here," Stark said.

"I had thought not," Cromwell said, "but it appears I was mistaken."

"How terrible," Emily said. "Human beings used as beasts of burden."

"It's the same in the slave states," Stark said, "and worse."

"Not for long, Brother Matthew," Cromwell said. "Stephen Douglas awaits inauguration as President of the United States, and he is pledged to abolition."

"It might not be Douglas, Brother Zephaniah. It might be Breckinridge or Bell or even Lincoln. This past election was full of uncertainty."

"The next ship will bring the news. But it matters little. Whoever is President, slavery is finished in our country."

Genji listened to their conversation. Here and there he thought he recognized a word. Human. United States. Pledged. He couldn't be sure. He had practiced conversational English with tutors since he was a child. But the flow of the language from the mouths of native speakers was another matter altogether.

The rickshaws stopped in front of the missionaries. Genji gestured for them to step aboard. To his surprise, all three adamantly refused. The ugliest of the three, their leader, Cromwell, gave a long explanation to the harbormaster.

"He says their religion does not permit them to ride in rickshaws." The harbormaster nervously wiped the sweat from his brow with a handkerchief.

Genji turned to Saiki. "Did you know this?"

"Of course not, lord. Who would ever think rickshaws had anything to do with religion?"

Genji asked the harbormaster, "In what way do rickshaws offend them?"

"He's using many words I don't understand," the harbormaster said. "Forgive me, Lord Genji, but my usual task is dealing with freight. My vocabulary is limited mostly to trade items, landing permits, fees, prices, and the like. Religious doctrine is far beyond my ken."

Genji nodded. "Very well. They will have to walk. Load the luggage into the rickshaws. We've paid for them. We might as well put them to some use." He gestured for the missionaries to proceed on foot.

"Good," Cromwell said, "we have won our first victory. We have made our host understand how firmly we stand for Christian morality. We are the people of His pasture and the sheep of His hand."

"Amen," Emily and Stark said.

Amen. There was a word Genji recognized. His ears were so poorly attuned to the actual sound of the language, he had completely missed the prayer that had preceded it.

Saiki moved closer to him as they walked. He spoke quietly, as if the missionaries could understand his words if they overheard him. "Lord, we cannot let the woman walk along with us."

"Why not? She appears to be in good health."

"It is her appearance that concerns me, not her health. Have you taken a good look at her?"

"Frankly, I have tried to avoid doing so. She is singularly uninspiring."

"That is a kind understatement, lord. She dresses like a ragpicker, she's the size of a draft animal, her coloration is shocking, her features excessive and grotesque."

"We're walking with her, not marrying her."

"Ridicule can cut as deeply as a blade, and as fatally. In this degenerate age, alliances are fragile, resolve is weak. You should take no unnecessary chances."

Genji looked back at the woman. The two men, Cromwell and Stark, flanked her gallantly, as if she were a precious beauty. The pretense was admirable. She was without question the most difficult woman to look upon that he had ever encountered. Saiki was right. The ridicule she would bring down on them could be extremely damaging.

"Wait." They had come alongside the palanquin. "What if she rode in my place?"

Saiki frowned. If Genji walked, he was more vulnerable to assassination. If he didn't, the woman would display herself among the Okumichi samurai for all of Edo to see. There was no good choice, only one less bad. It would be easier to protect Genji than to live with the ridicule. "Yes, that is the best solution."

While Genji and his aide talked, Emily glanced at their host's small troop of samurai. They were all staring at her, their faces seeming to register varying degrees of distress. She quickly looked away, her heart racing. Perhaps it was not her they found distressing, but Zephaniah or Brother Matthew, or the difficulties their arrival had caused. She should not let her hopes rise only to be dashed. She told herself to leap to no conclusions. Not yet. But, oh, could it be? Yes, it could. It could.

Cromwell said, "Emily, I believe Lord Genji is offering you the use of his palanquin."

"How can I accept, Zephaniah? Surely it is four times more evil to be held aloft by four slaves than to be pulled along by one."

Cromwell looked again at the bearers. "I doubt these are slaves. Each man carries a sword at his waist. No armed slave would be permitted to be so close to his master."

Emily saw that Zephaniah was right. The men were armed, and they held themselves as proudly as the samurai. It was probably a position of great honor to serve as bearer to their lord. She noticed that these men, too, were staring at her, aghast. Despite her caution, she felt joy welling in her heart. "Still, I would not be comfortable, Zephaniah, to be carried while you walk. That would be unseemly and most unwomanly."

Genji smiled. "Palanquins are apparently also a religious issue."

"Yes, lord," Saiki said, but his attention was on his men. "Control yourselves! Your thoughts are naked on your faces."

Emily knew the fierce one had said something about her because all of the samurai now affected bland expressions and avoided looking in her direction.

"I cannot disagree with you, Emily. But in the circumstances, it might be best to acquiesce with good grace. We must adapt ourselves as we can, insofar as our morality allows, to the customs of this country."

"As you wish, Zephaniah." Emily curtsied to Lord Genji and obediently stepped up to the palanquin, where she was immediately stymied. The entryway was exceedingly small. She would have to engage in a sequence of unladylike contortions to pass through it. And once inside the compact box, her thickly padded coat and voluminous skirt and petticoats would consume all the space not taken by her body. There would be almost no breathing room.

Zephaniah said, "Let me take your coat, Emily. The palanquin will keep you from the cold."

Emily clutched the coat possessively to her chest. "I prefer to wear it, thank you." It was another layer between her body and the world. The more layers the better.

"She doesn't know how to get in," Saiki said. "Her intelligence matches her appearance."

"How would she know?" Genji said. "She's never done it before." He bowed politely to her and went up to the palanquin. He took off his swords and placed them inside. Then he bent his body, and as he entered, turned, so that when he completed the movement, he was properly seated. To exit, he first brought his legs outside, then followed with the rest of his body. He made every move with deliberate slowness, so Emily could clearly observe. As he stood, he smoothly placed the swords back into his sash. His demonstration complete, he bowed again and gestured for Emily to board the palanquin.

"Thank you, Lord Genji," Emily said, genuinely grateful. He had saved her from making a disgraceful spectacle of herself. She followed his example and boarded the palanquin without incident.

"Can you carry so huge a creature?" one of the samurai said to the bearers.

"Hidé!" Saiki said. "You're on stable duty for one month. Are there any other dung-shoveling jesters?" No more remarks were made. The bearers lifted the palanquin without noticeable effort. The company left the harbor and entered the streets of Edo.

. . . . .

San Francisco was the largest city Stark had ever visited. There, at the mission, he had heard fabulous stories about Japan from men who said they had sailed there aboard naval frigates, merchant ships, and whalers. They told him of strange customs, stranger sights, and even stranger food. Most fantastic of all, they told him of people, of vast populations in the millions, even in one city alone, the Shogun's capital of Edo. Stark had listened without believing. His informants, after all, were drunks, derelicts, fugitives. No others came to the mission house of the True Word. Yet the wildest ravings he had heard had not prepared him for the shock of actual immersion into the multitudes of Edo.

People were everywhere. In the streets, in the shops, in the windows of the apartments above. Though the hour was early, the crowds were such that movement itself seemed impossible. Human life filled his eyes and ears.

"Brother Matthew, are you well?"

"Yes, Brother Zephaniah. I am stunned, but I am well." Perhaps he was not so well. He had grown to manhood in the open rangelands of Texas and the Arizona Territory. He had found home there. There was where he was at ease. Cities were not to his liking. Even San Francisco made his chest tight. And San Francisco was a ghost town compared to this.

Before them, people cleared the road and without exception dropped to the ground like prairie grass blown flat by a northern wind. One man, finely dressed, attended by a trio of servants and astride a beautiful white horse, dismounted hurriedly and threw himself down, heedless of the dirt that now stained his rich silk garments.

Stark asked, "What has Lord Genji done to command such respect from the people?"

"He was born, that is all." Zephaniah frowned his disapproval. "Members of the warrior caste are at liberty to cut down anyone who fails to show them proper respect. A daimyo, that is the native term for a Great Lord like Lord Genji, has the right to execute a family, even an entire village, for the failing of one individual."

"I can hardly believe such barbarism exists," Emily said from within the palanquin, alongside which Stark and Cromwell walked.

"That is why we are here," Cromwell said. "He saveth the poor from the sword, from their mouth, and from the hand of the mighty."

Again the missionaries said amen. Genji walked a few paces ahead of the palanquin. He had been listening as closely as he could, yet he had once more missed whatever prayer had been said. Apparently, Christian prayers could be as brief as the mantras of the Pure Land Buddhists or those of the Lotus Sutra sect.

Suddenly, Saiki threw himself on Genji and yelled, "Danger!"

At the same moment, a shot rang out.

• • • • •

"If you have any questions," Kuma said, "address them to Lord Kawakami."

The gunnery captain blanched at the mention of the secret police chief's name. He turned abruptly and walked away. While Genji and Saiki went to greet the missionaries on the pier, Kuma returned to the armory. He retrieved his own weapon and placed it inside a black cloth case, which he strapped to his back. Then he departed without further delay.

He knew there was only one road between the harbor and the Okumichi clan's palace in the Tsukiji district big enough to comfortably accommodate Genji's retinue. Scouting there the previous night, he had selected a building that stood at one of the curves in the road, a narrow two-story structure squeezed in among others of its kind in the unplanned congestion typical of commoners' dwellings in Edo. He went there now and climbed to the roof from an alley in the back. No one saw him. If anyone had, that person would have doubted his own eyes. Kuma went straight up the wall like a spider.

The location was ideal. From here, Kuma could sight his target as it approached, shortening the distance and minimizing any adjustments that might be needed. Furthermore, the curve would cause the procession to slow slightly, and any reduction in movement made aiming easier. He checked his musket. This time, he would be sure to pull the trigger on a loaded weapon.

It was the hour of the horse before Genji appeared at the far end of the street. The townspeople receded and fell to the ground as the Great Lord passed by. All the easier for Kuma. He rested the first inch of the musket's barrel on the edge of the roof. So little would be visible from below, it was unlikely that even the most diligent observer would notice it. There was Genji walking unconcernedly among the leading group of bodyguards. Kuma aimed at his elegant head. How simple it would be. But the moment for a shot to cripple or disfigure had passed. The idiot harbor policeman, Ishi, had conceded Genji's identity. Anything close to an assassination of Genji now would point too obviously back to Edo Castle.

Kuma shifted his aim, steadied, and fired.

* * * * *

"Lord!"

"I'm unhurt," Genji said.

Saiki pointed at a nearby roof. "There! Hidé! Shimoda! Take him alive!"

The rest of the men, their swords drawn, formed a ring of bodies and blades around Genji. The townspeople had disappeared, running for cover at the first sign of violence.

"The missionaries!" Genji said. He rushed to the palanquin. A bullet had torn a hole in the closed right-side window. A passenger's torso would normally be on the other side, in the middle of the bullet's trajectory. Genji slid the door open, expecting to see the outsider woman, Emily, bloody and dead.

But she was not. Trying to find a bearable position in those tight and unfamiliar confines, Emily had fallen into a temporary slouch. Stuffing fell out of the front of her coat where the bullet had ripped it open. Otherwise, it had benignly passed her by.

"Lord!" One of his bodyguards called out from the other side of the palanquin. Cromwell lay on the ground, blood pouring out of a wound in his lower abdomen, struck by the same bullet that had torn through the palanquin.

"We cannot linger here," Saiki said. "Move!"

The bearers hoisted the palanquin. Four men lifted Cromwell's unconscious body to their shoulders. Swords flashing in the morning light, they ran at high speed to the palace in Tsukiji.

• • • • •

When Heiko left the palace shortly after Genji's departure for the harbor, Kudo himself followed her. It was too important a task to be left to someone less experienced, less able. This wasn't conceit on Kudo's part. He was the best covert watcher among the Okumichi samurai. Thus the work was his. That was all.

Heiko and her maidservant meandered slowly inland from Tsukiji. Like all women of the Floating World, she was officially licensed to reside exclusively in the gated pleasure district of Yoshiwara. Had that been her destination, she would most likely have taken a water taxi up the Sumida River. Instead, she was heading in the direction of her country cottage in the woods of Ginza, at the eastern edge of Edo. This second residence was not strictly legal. There was considerable laxity in the enforcement of Floating World regulations, however, particularly in the case of the most famous and most beautiful courtesans. Mayonaka no Heiko was arguably the most famous of the current crop. There was no question she was the most beautiful. In that sense, she was an excellent companion for Lord Genji. Saiki's concern, and Kudo's as well, was that they knew nothing about her beyond her public geisha persona, which was, as everyone knew, a highly polished performance.

His initial investigation, hampered by Lord Genji's prohibition against it, revealed only that her contract was held by the banker Otani. This was a man well known as a proxy. Ordinarily, a combination of bribes and threats would have been sufficient to pry information from Otani, perhaps even the identity of Heiko's secret patron. Not in this case. Otani adamantly refused, saying his life and the survival of his family depended upon his silence. Even allowing for overacting on the man's part, this suggested that the patron was a Great Lord of equal or greater power than Genji. Among those who had survived the Battle of Sekigahara two hundred sixty years ago, only sixty were truly great. Heiko was the friend of a powerful man. Or was the tool of one. Without knowing which, Genji was at risk with every assignation. Kudo was determined to discover the truth. If he could not, then he was prepared to kill her as a precaution. Not today, but in due course. Civil war was coming. Uncertainties had to be reduced in order to improve the clan's chances of survival.

Kudo watched as Heiko stopped to chat with yet another shopkeeper. How was it possible for someone to have a destination and yet progress so slowly toward it? He left the main street and cut through a narrow alleyway. He would move ahead and observe Heiko as she approached. If she suspected someone was following her, her suspicion would more easily be visible from an unexpected viewpoint. That in itself would confirm deception on her part, for a geisha without hidden motivations would never be wary of surveillance.

Two men were carrying refuse from the back of a shop as Kudo turned the corner. They saw him and dissolved in fear. Their burdens fell to the ground, and they dropped down, faces in the dirt, groveling. On hands and knees, they scrambled backward out of his path, struggling to make themselves as inconspicuous as possible.

Eta. Kudo's face twisted into a grimace of disgust.

His hand went to the hilt of his sword. *Eta*. Filthy out-casts whose fate it was to do the foulest, most disgusting tasks. To even permit themselves to be seen by one of Kudo's rank warranted their immediate death. But if he killed them, it would cause a commotion, attracting attention, and defeating his purpose. He left his sword sheathed and hurried past. *Eta*. The very thought of them made him feel unclean.

Kudo reentered the main street a hundred paces ahead of where he had last seen Heiko. Yes, there she was, still wasting time with the same shopkeeper.

Some chattering women momentarily obscured Kudo's view of his subject. When they passed, neither Heiko nor her maid was anywhere to be seen. He ran to the shop where she had last dallied. She wasn't there.

How had that happened? One moment he had been looking at her. The next moment she was gone. Geisha did not move that way. Ninja did.

Kudo turned to retrace his steps to the palace in Tsukiji, more uneasy than ever. And nearly collided with Heiko.

"Kudo-sama," Heiko said. "What a coincidence. Are you shopping for silk scarves, too?"

"No, no," Kudo said, fumbling for an explanation. He was not at his best when taken by surprise. "I am going to the temple at Hamacho. To make offerings for ancestors fallen in battle."

"How laudable," Heiko said. "My interest in scarves is shallow and useless in comparison."

"Not at all, Lady Heiko. For you, scarves are as important as swords for a samurai." The idiocy of his words made Kudo cringe inside. The more he talked, the more foolish he would seem. "Well, I must be on my way."

"Will you not tarry a few moments to take tea with me, Kudo-sama?"

"Nothing would give me more pleasure, Lady Heiko, but my duties require a speedy return. I must hurry to the temple, and hurry back to the palace." With a quick bow, Kudo strode swiftly west in the direction of Hamacho. If he had been paying attention, instead of hallucinating that Heiko might be a ninja, he would have saved himself this lengthy detour. When he looked back, he saw her bow to him. Since she was watching, he had to continue on for quite a way before it was safe to change course.

Gritting his teeth, he silently berated himself all the way back to Tsukiji.

3

Quiet Crane

*Mists shroud the forest ahead and the sea behind.
At the same time, the faraway peak of Mount Tosa
is as vivid as a spring sky. Ahead, snipers hide
among the trees and shadows. Behind, submerged
assassins close in, hanging on driftwood.*

    What use is distant clarity?

SUZUME–NO–KUMO
(1701)

Cromwell woke from dream to dream. Now Emily's face hovered above, her golden curls drifting toward him. She seemed weightless, and so did he. Was it a dream of shipwreck, then? They were underwater. The *Star of Bethlehem* had gone down and they were both drowned. He tried to look for flotsam, but his vision would not leave Emily.

"The *Star* is unharmed," Emily said. "It lies at anchor in Edo Bay."

So in this dream she perceived his thoughts. The world outside of dreams would be a better place if all minds were as open books. Then there would be no need of pretense or of shame. Sin, repentance, and salvation could occur at once, in the same moment.

"Rest, Zephaniah," Emily said. "There is no need to think of anything at all."

Yes. She was right. He tried to touch her hair, but he had no arm to raise. Cromwell felt himself grow lighter. How was that possible, if he was already weightless? Thoughts did not adhere. His eyes closed and he left this dream for another.

• • • • •

Emily paled. "Is he dead?"

"He's drifting in and out of delirium," Stark said.

They had brought Cromwell into the guest wing of the palace. He lay on a bed of thick cushions spread on the floor. A middle-aged Japanese man, whom they presumed to be a doctor, examined Cromwell, applied a strong-smelling salve to the wound, and bandaged it. Before he left, the doctor called a trio of young women over to the bedside. Showing them the salve and the bandage, the doctor gave brief instructions, then bowed to Emily and Stark and departed. The young women retreated to the edge of the room and waited there on folded knees, still and quiet.

Emily sat at Cromwell's right side on a cushion three feet square. Stark sat on a similar cushion to the left. Neither of them was comfortable on the floor. They lacked the arts of seated posture in which their Japanese hosts were clearly well practiced. Stark could make his legs bend, but he couldn't keep them there for long. He shifted from one position to another every few moments. For Emily, her long skirt and voluminous petticoats made it that much more difficult to arrange her limbs in an acceptable posture. Finally, she settled herself on one hip and extended her legs out to the side, careful to keep them covered with her skirt. It was how she used to sit at picnics in her childhood, not entirely appropriate here, but the only way she could manage.

"We bring nothing with us but the word of Christ," Emily said. She wiped the sweat from Cromwell's face with a cool, wet towel. "Why would anyone wish us harm?"

"I don't know, Sister Emily." Stark had seen the glint of metal on the roof an instant before the assassin fired. He dove for the ground before the sound of the gun reached his ears. If he had not done so, the bullet would have struck him instead of Cromwell. Stark's alertness was the preacher's misfortune. That and enough bad luck of his own. After missing Stark, the bullet went in one side of the palanquin and out the other. It should have struck Emily, but somehow it had not. Instead, upon exiting, it bore a hole straight into Cromwell's belly. Gutshot. Men sometimes took weeks to die when they were gutshot.

"He looks so peaceful," Emily said. "His brow is unfurrowed and he smiles as he sleeps."

"Yes, Sister Emily, he looks very peaceful." The more Stark thought about it, the more likely it seemed that he had been the assassin's target. Money would have changed hands. A hireling would have gone on the roof to kill a man he had never seen. Mutually incomprehensible languages posed no barrier. Stark had no doubt money bought death in Japan as easily as it did in America.

He stretched his legs for a few moments, to keep them from cramping. Every time he moved, the four samurai on guard became more alert. They knelt in the hallway outside the room. It was not clear if they were there to protect the missionaries or to imprison them. Ever since the shooting, they had been watching him closely. Stark didn't know why.

· · · · ·

"The bandages will have to be changed frequently," Dr. Ozawa said. "I have given him medicine that will reduce the bleeding, but it cannot be stopped altogether. Major arteries were severed. The bullet itself is lodged against the base of his spine. It cannot be removed."

"How long?" Genji asked.

The doctor shook his head. "Hours if he is fortunate. Days if he is not." He bowed and made his exit.

"How inauspicious," Genji said. "The American consul will have to be informed. Harris. A most unpleasant individual."

Saiki said, "Lord, that bullet was meant for you."

"I doubt that. My enemies would not send such a poor marksman. How could he aim at me and hit a palanquin ten feet away?"

A maid entered with a fresh pot of tea. Saiki impatiently waved her off, but Genji accepted another cup. The hot brew took the edge off the winter chill.

"I have examined the palanquin," Saiki said. "Had you been in it, as everyone would expect, you would have been killed instantly. Only her barbaric posture saved the outsider woman's life."

"Yes, I know. I saw that for myself." Genji smiled at the maid. She colored, embarrassed to receive his attention, and bowed deeply to the floor. She was charming, Genji thought, and pretty enough, though a little old to be unmarried. Twenty-two or

-three, he guessed. What was her name? Hanako. He considered the men of his bodyguard. Which one of them was in need of a wife, and was of the proper age to appreciate this maid? "I was not in the palanquin, however. I was in plain sight outside of it."

"Precisely my point," Saiki said. "An assassin who does not know you would not think to find you on foot. What Great Lord walks while a female outsider rides? Also, you were not wearing the crest of your house. That, too, is unheard of. So he expected you to be where you should have been, and put his bullet there."

"Tortured reasoning," Genji said.

Hidé and Shimoda arrived at the door, breathing hard. They were the bodyguards Saiki had sent after the assassin.

"Forgive us, lord," Hidé said. "There was no sign of him anywhere."

Shimoda said, "No one saw anything. It was as if he disappeared into thin air."

"Ninja," Saiki said. "Accursed cowards. They should all be put to the sword, down to the last woman and child."

"The building belongs to a grocer named Fujita," Hidé said. "A simple man. No involvement with unsavory characters, no connections to any clan, no debts, no daughters in bondage in the Floating World. He is unlikely to be involved. Of course, he is terrified of your retribution. Without being asked, he insisted on supplying all the provisions for our New Year's festivities."

Genji laughed. "Then he would be bankrupt, and he would be forced to sell all his daughters into the Floating World."

"That would not bring him much credit, lord," Hidé said with a smile. "I have seen the daughters."

Saiki slapped the floor. "Hidé! Remember your place!"

"Yes, sir!" The chastised samurai pressed his head to the floor.

"We need not be so harsh," Genji said. "This has been a trying morning. Hidé, how old are you?"

"Lord?" Hidé was taken aback by the unexpected question. "Twenty-nine, lord."

"How is it that you are unmarried at such an advanced age?"

"Uh, lord, uh . . ."

"Speak up," Saiki said, "and stop wasting our lord's time." This was all a waste of time as far as he was concerned. What frivolity was Genji engaging in now? With his life in danger and the existence of the clan itself threatened, he was playing some silly game.

"The opportunity has never presented itself, lord," Hidé said.

Saiki said, "The truth is, Hidé has an excessive fondness for women, wine, and gambling. His debts are such that no one of good family would even consider the burden of marriage with him." Saiki gave the information to hurry things along. Then perhaps they could return to more pressing matters. The extremely suspicious outsider Stark, for example.

"What is your debt?" Genji asked.

Hidé hesitated. "Sixty *ryo*, lord." That was a massive sum for one of his station. His annual stipend was ten ryo.

"Undisciplined idiot," Saiki said.

"Yes, sir." Hidé pressed his head to the floor once more, genuinely mortified.

"Your debts will be discharged," Genji said. "See to it that you do not accumulate new ones. In fact, now that you are solvent, I advise you to immediately find a wife. Someone with household experience, so she may guide you in remaining solvent, and show you the ways of domestic bliss."

"Lord." Hidé remained down in the deepest possible bow. Lord Genji's generosity astounded him.

"In fact, I myself will look into it for you," Genji said. "Will you trust me in this matter?"

"Yes, lord. Thank you."

"Hanako," Genji said, "show these men to another room where they may recover from their recent exertions. Remain there to serve them."

"Yes," Hanako said. Bowing gracefully, she led Hidé and Shimoda from the room.

When they were gone, Saiki made a deep formal bow of respect to Genji. At last he understood what had taken place. In the midst of a crisis that could take his life, Lord Genji had not ceased to think of those in his care. The housemaid, Hanako, was an orphan. Despite her good manners and womanly charm, she was highly unlikely to find a worthy match on her own. She had no family connections to offer, and no dowry. Hidé, an excellent samurai in most respects, needed the weight of responsibility in order to fully mature. Left to himself, he would continue to squander his time and his money on worthless diversions. In the end, he would be a useless sot, like so many of the samurai of the other, degenerate clans, and not a few of their own. All this Lord Genji had cured with a single stroke. Tears came to the gruff warrior's eyes.

"What's this, Saiki? Have I died and become a deity?"

"Lord," Saiki said, too deeply moved to speak further, unable even to bring his head from the floor. Once again, he had misjudged the depth of his lord's character.

Genji reached for his teacup. The other maid, Michiko, bowed and refilled it. She was already married, so Genji smiled at her, but gave her no further thought. He drank his tea and waited patiently for Saiki to recover. Samurai were strange creatures. They were expected to endure the most atrocious physical tortures without a single complaint. Yet they felt free to weep when they witnessed nothing more serious than the beginnings of a marriage arrangement.

After a time, Saiki raised his head and roughly brushed away his tears with a single sweep of his kimono sleeve. "Lord, you must consider the possibility that the missionaries are somehow involved in the plot against you."

"If there is a plot."

"The one called Stark anticipated the firing of the assassin's gun. I saw him diving for cover before I called out. That means he knew the man was there."

"Or it means he is highly observant." Genji shook his head. "It is good to be on guard against treachery. But there is such a thing as seeing too much treachery everywhere. We must not let our imaginings distract us from real danger. Stark has only just arrived from America. There are assassins enough in Japan. Who would go through the complication of bringing one from outside?"

"Perhaps someone who wishes to obscure any hint of his identity with an additional veil of confusion," Saiki said. "Someone who you would not otherwise suspect."

Genji sighed. "Very well. You may look into the matter further. But please, do not intrude too much on Stark. He is our guest."

Saiki bowed. "Yes, lord."

Genji said, "Let us see how they fare."

On their way down the hall, Saiki thought to ask about the grocer whose building the assassin had used. "What shall we do about Fujita's offer?"

"Convey our thanks and say we will permit him to supply the New Year's sake."

"Yes, lord," Saiki said. That will be costly enough to relieve the grocer's fear, but not so costly as to be destructive. A wise decision. Saiki followed his lord with ever-increasing confidence.

• • • • •

The Dutch celestial telescope took Kawakami's eye onto the rooftops above Genji's procession. Although his angle of view prevented him from seeing that particular street, he knew where the entourage was by the behavior of people at the one intersection not obstructed by buildings. When they threw themselves to the ground, the lord was approaching. When they rose and resumed their activities, he had passed.

Kawakami was greatly amused to see Monzaemon, the rich merchant banker, hastily stumble from his famous white horse and grovel in the dirt like any other peasant, despite his sartorial finery. Many of the Great Lords were in Monzaemon's debt. The Shogun himself owed the insufferable little man vast sums. Yet there he was, face pressed against the ground at the passage of his betters. Money was one thing. The privilege of wearing two swords and the right to use them freely, that was quite another. No matter how much and how rapidly the world changed, Kawakami was certain of one thing. The power to buy would never match the power to kill.

Kawakami thought he heard the sound of a single distant gunshot. As he watched through the telescope, Monzaemon jerked his head up from the ground, a look of fear on his fat peasant's face. The white horse beside him reared in panic. Only the quick action of one of his servants prevented him from being trampled to death.

Something had happened. He would have to wait to find out what. He stepped away from the telescope.

"I will be in the garden cottage," he said to his assistant, Mukai. "Do not disturb me unless the matter is urgent."

Kawakami went to the cottage alone. It was not much more than a simple shed in one of the smaller gardens of the vast castle. Yet it provided him with the greatest pleasure of his life.

Solitude.

It was a rarity in a place like Edo, filled with nearly two million people, and for a man like Kawakami, a Great Lord himself, usually surrounded by a small crowd of attendants of various ranks and kinds. Indeed, a key motivation for becoming the Shogun's chief spy was that it gave him an excuse to be alone. Whenever he needed relief from the suffocating weight of social responsibilities, he could always invoke the need for secrecy and disappear. At first, he had done so mainly to get away from his wife and concubines and visit his various mistresses. Later, it allowed him to avoid his mistresses as well. Eventually, he warmed to the task of freely prying into private lives. Now he truly had little time for wives, concubines, mistresses, or any other of the frivolous pursuits he had once enjoyed.

It was the waiting that was now so precious. A rare time to be alone with the small fire, the boiling water, the scent of tea, the feel of the heated cup in his hands. But today, the water had barely begun to boil when there was a familiar voice at the door.

"Lord, it is I."

"Enter," Kawakami said.

The door slid open.

• • • • •

Heiko departed from the palace immediately after Genji did. She was accompanied only by her maid, Sachiko. Great Lords could go nowhere without a troop of bodyguards. The most fearsome men in the land, they were also the most fearful. They dealt out death as freely as a happy child offered laughter. So by the Buddha's law of inescapable karma, death they also received. Unlike the powerful warlords, courtesans were feared by no one. Weakness, in fact, was what they so artfully embodied with the exquisite fragility of their beauty, their grace, their youth. Thus, they could go where they wished without fear. This, too, followed the Buddha's law.

"Lady Heiko," Sachiko whispered, "we are being followed."

"Ignore him," Heiko said. The lane through which they passed was lined with cherry trees. In the spring, they would be full of the blossoms so celebrated in paintings and poems throughout the ages. Now these trees were black and barren. Yet were they not as beautiful? She paused to admire a single bare branch that caught her eye. The light dusting of morning snow had nearly melted completely away, leaving icy water drops. Only a few flakes remained in the shadowed crook of the branch. In a moment, she would continue on her way. Sunlight would reach into this shadow. Well before she arrived at her destination, these snowflakes would be gone. The thought tightened her chest. Unwelcome tears welled in her eyes. Namu Amida Butsu, Namu Amida Butsu, Namu Amida Butsu. Veneration to the Compassionate Buddha, who saves all sufferers. Heiko breathed from deep within her center and kept her tears from falling. It was truly a terrible thing to be in love.

"We should not tarry," Sachiko said. "You are expected in the hour of the snake."

"I should not make appointments so early," Heiko said. "It is unsoothing to begin the day in a rush."

"True, true," Sachiko said. "Yet what can a woman do? She is told, and she obeys." Sachiko was nineteen, the same age as Heiko, but acted as if much older. In an important sense, that was her job. By taking on all the practical considerations, she freed Heiko from the mundane burdens of daily life.

The two women resumed walking. It was Kudo who followed them. He fancied himself an expert in surveillance. How he had acquired that conceit, Heiko couldn't guess. Like most samurai, Kudo was impatient. His entire training taught him to seek the single decisive moment that determined life or death. A lightning slash with his sword. Blood and life running out onto the earth. It almost didn't matter who was vanquished and who was victorious. The decisive moment. That's what counted. Following two women who strolled so leisurely, and who stopped so often to admire a tree, or examine goods, or simply to rest, this was extreme duress for him. So of course, Heiko made sure she took even slower steps than usual, and made more than the normal number of stops, and engaged in the most unhurried of conversations. By the time they reached the Tsukiji district's main shopping area, Kudo was scurrying around like a trapped rat.

"Now," Heiko said. Several neighborhood women passed by, temporarily shielding her from Kudo. She walked beside them to a shop across the street, while Sachiko simply squatted down and devoted her full attention to a basket of dried squid. She watched from an alleyway as Kudo came running up. He looked frantically here and there, not even noticing Heiko's maid at his feet. When his back was turned, Heiko recrossed the street and stood behind him. She acted surprised when he nearly walked into her.

"Kudo-sama. What a coincidence. Are you shopping for silk scarves, too?" Throughout their brief conversation, Heiko had to struggle mightily not to break down in laughter. When Kudo was gone, angrily striding toward Hamacho, Heiko summoned a rickshaw. The hour of the dragon had already yielded to the hour of the snake. She no longer had time to proceed on foot.

· · · · ·

Kawakami Eichi, Great Lord of Hino, Presiding Inspector of the Office of Shogunate Internal Regulations, awaited his visitor's entry into the cottage. He cloaked himself with the weighty dignity appropriate to his importance and his titles.

Which evaporated as soon as the door slid open.

Though he thought he was prepared, in fact he was not. He was never prepared. He should know that by now. There was an elusive quality to her. Whenever she was out of sight, the details of her face and form blurred, as if neither mind nor eye had the strength to hold a vivid image of such awesome beauty.

He saw her and gasped, a sigh in reverse.

To regain some illusion of composure, he admonished her.

"You are late, Heiko."

"My apologies, Lord Kawakami." Heiko bowed, naturally exposing the fine curve of her neck. Again she heard Kawakami's sharp intake of breath. She kept all expression from her face. "I was being watched. I thought it prudent not to let him know I saw him."

"Surely you didn't let him follow you here?"

"No, lord." She smiled, amused at what she recalled. "I allowed him to blunder into me. After that, he could no longer follow."

"Well done," Kawakami said. "Was it Kudo again?"

"Yes." Heiko removed the kettle from the fire. Kawakami had let the water boil too long. If it was poured over the tea now, all subtleties of flavor would be ruined. It would have to cool to the proper temperature.

"He is their best man at this sort of thing," Kawakami said. "Perhaps you have caused questions to arise in Lord Genji's mind."

"That is doubtful. I am quite certain Kudo is acting on his own initiative. Lord Genji is not of a suspicious nature."

"All lords are of a suspicious nature," Kawakami said. "Suspicion and survival cannot be separated."

"I wonder," Heiko said, tilting her head at an angle Kawakami found quite fetching. "If he can see the future, then he has no need of precautions. He knows what will happen, and when. Suspicion becomes quite meaningless."

Kawakami snorted. "Preposterous. His family has traded on that ridiculous pretense for generations. If any one of them could ever have seen the future, the Okumichi would be the foremost clan in the Empire, not the Tokugawa, and Genji today would be Shogun instead of the keeper of a backwater domain like Akaoka."

"No doubt you are right, lord."

"You seem uncertain. Have you discovered any evidence of this reputed mystical gift?"

"No, lord. At least, not directly."

"Not directly." Kawakami grimaced as if the words tasted sour.

"Once, when Kudo and Saiki were discussing Lord Genji, I overheard mention of *Suzume-no-kumo*."

"Suzume-no-kumo is the name of the main castle of Akaoka Domain."

"Yes, lord, but it was not a castle of which they were speaking. It was a secret text."

Kawakami was having difficulty paying attention to Heiko's report. The more Kawakami looked at her, the more he wished for sake to drink instead of tea. The time of day as well as the circumstances made that highly inadvisable. It was just as well. The social distance appropriate between master and servant had to be maintained. He felt himself growing irritated. Was it because he couldn't do what he wanted to do with Heiko? Certainly not. He was a samurai of ancient lineage. His base desires did not control him. What, then? The issue of knowing more than others knew. That was it. Kawakami was the one who saw, the one who knew, with vision based on reports from a network of a thousand spies. Yet in the popular mind Genji was endowed with the ability to see even further than Kawakami. He was believed to possess the gift of prophecy.

"It is not uncommon for clans to have so-called secret teachings," Kawakami said. "Usually, they are books of strategy, often simply plagiarized from Sun Tzu's *The Art of War*."

"This one is said to contain the visions of every prescient Lord of Akaoka since the days of Hironobu, six hundred years ago."

"Such rumors have long swirled around the Okumichi family. Supposedly, one in every generation is born a prophet."

"Yes, lord. So it is said." Heiko bowed. "With your permission." She poured the hot water into the teapot. Fragrant vapor rose into the air.

"And you believe it?" Kawakami's anger caused him to take the tea too quickly into his mouth. He swallowed without letting the pain show on his face. The hot liquid seared his throat on the way down.

"I merely believe that if such things are said, perhaps truth of some kind lies behind the rumors. Not necessarily prophecy, lord."

"Just because something is said doesn't make it so. If I believed everything I heard, I would have to execute half the population of Edo and imprison the rest."

This was as close to wit as Kawakami could get. Heiko giggled politely, covering her mouth with a sleeve of her kimono. She made a playful mock bow of deep reverence.

"Not including myself, I hope."

"No, of course not yourself," Kawakami said, somewhat mollified. "About Mayonaka no Heiko only the highest praise is ever heard."

Again, Heiko giggled. "Unfortunately, just because something is said doesn't make it so."

"I will try to remember that." Kawakami smiled broadly, gratified to hear himself quoted so soon and so playfully by a woman of such grace and charm.

Heiko never ceased to marvel at how easy it was to deflect men. All it took was a little show of silliness. They heard giggles, they saw smiles, they inhaled soft scents rising from the folds of silken cloth, and they never noticed the hard glint in the eyes behind the girlishly fluttering lids. This was true even of Kawakami, who of all people should know better. He was the one who had created Mayonaka no Heiko. Yet here he was, as vulnerable as all the others. All the others, that is, except Genji.

"Lord Genji's grandfather, the late Lord Kiyori, was also said to have cognition of future events." Kawakami accepted more tea from Heiko. This time, he sipped more carefully. "Yet he died suddenly, three weeks ago, the probable victim of poisoning. Shouldn't he have foreseen that, and avoided the fatal dose?"

"Perhaps not everything can be foreseen, lord."

"A convenient excuse," Kawakami said, once again growing heated. "It helps keep the myth alive. All of it is empty propaganda put out by the Okumichi clan. We Japanese are a hopelessly superstitious and gullible lot. The Okumichi cleverly exploit this. Because of these children's tales about prophecy, they are treated with an importance they do not deserve."

"Is it certain that poison was the cause of Lord Kiyori's death?"

"If you are asking me whether I ordered it, the answer is no."

Heiko dropped herself to the floor in a full bow. "I would not dare be so presumptuous, Lord Kawakami." Her tone and manner were completely serious. "Forgive me for having given you the wrong impression." The man was a buffoon, but a dangerous and clever one. In her eagerness to know what he might have in store for Genji, she had pushed too far. Unless she was more careful, he might sense that her interest was going beyond the bounds of duty.

"Oh, get up, get up," Kawakami said expansively. "I take no offense. You are my trusted retainer." Women, of course, could not have that status. But it was just a word. It cost him nothing to say it.

"You honor me beyond my worth."

"Nonsense. You must know what I am doing so you can act in accordance. I was not fond of Lord Kiyori, it is true, but he did not lack for enemies. His friendliness toward outsiders, especially the Americans, angered many. And many more were angered by his interest in Christianity. He did not enjoy enthusiastic support even within his own clan. You yourself reported to me that Saiki and Tanaka, two of his most senior vassals, both strenuously objected to the presence of missionaries in the fief. Indeed, Tanaka was so upset, he resigned his office and retired to the Mushindo Monastery six months ago."

"Yes, lord, that is so. He has taken the Buddhist precepts, and the believer name Sohaku."

"Religious fanaticism can be deadlier than the

political variety. Tanaka, or Sohaku if you prefer, is the likeliest assassin, in my opinion."

"How tragic," Heiko said, "to be struck down in old age by one so close."

"Those who are close are the most dangerous," Kawakami said, watching Heiko for her reaction, "because we too often neglect to truly see them. You share Lord Genji's bed, for example, yet at any moment, you might slit his throat. Is this not so?"

Heiko bowed, being careful that her smile was just right, acquiescent without being eager. "Yes, that is quite so."

"You would have no difficulty in overcoming your affection for him?"

Heiko laughed gaily. "You toy with me, Lord Kawakami. I am in his bed because you put me there, not because of any supposed affection for him."

Kawakami frowned. "Be careful, Heiko. When you are with him, that truth must remain unknown even to you. You must love him, completely, even hopelessly, or he will know you for what you are, and you will be useless to me."

Heiko bowed down to the floor. "Yes, lord. I hear and obey."

"Good. Now what about Lord Genji's uncle? Have you discovered his whereabouts?"

"Not yet. Since Lord Shigeru left the castle, he has not been seen at any other lordly dwelling place within Akaoka Domain. It is possible he is a fugitive from his own clan."

Whatever the cause, that would be good news indeed. The uncle was much more dangerous than the nephew. Shigeru was a fanatical practitioner of all the ancient samurai arts. He could kill with and without weapons, and had. It was widely known that he had engaged in fifty-nine duels and won them all, only one short of the record established by the legendary Miyamoto Musashi two hundred years in the past. The sixtieth and sixty-first duels were set for the last day of the old year and the first day of the new, but it was unlikely now that they would ever take place. Shigeru had disappeared.

"Tell me what you have learned."

Heiko began doing so without delay. If she thought too much about what she was saying, she would be unable to continue. Pieces of information had come to her from several different sources. She believed she had put the story together correctly, but she hoped with all her heart she was wrong.

· · · · ·

The small Buddhist temple on the grounds of Suzume-no-kumo Castle was built in the long-ago thirteenth year of the Emperor Go-hanazono. Unlike all others, it was not dedicated to a particular sect. This was because Lord Wakamatsu had built it to atone for his destruction of three dozen Jodo, Nichiren, Tendai, and Shingon monasteries, and the slaughter of five thousand monks, together with their families and supporters. The heavily armed faithful had ignored the lord's command to cease their religious quarrels and political machinations.

Shigeru knew about the temple in considerable detail. Ever since his childhood, it had figured prominently in the most gruesome of his recurring dreams. Knowing that these dreams were fraught with omens, and understanding none of them, he had spent years studying the history of the temple in the hope of finding guidance from past events and personages. None had been forthcoming.

Now, too late, he understood. That was the way omens always unlocked for him. Too late. He knelt in the dim light of a single lamp and lit the one hundred fifth stick of incense. With a reverent bow, he placed it on the funerary altar of his father, Kiyori, the late Lord of Akaoka.

"I am sorry, Father. Please forgive me."

For the one hundred fifth time, he said the same words. Then he lit the one hundred sixth stick. Fumes from the overabundance of burning incense filled the temple with a smokey miasma. He ignored the searing pain in his eyes and lungs.

It was said the realms of hell were sixteen in number. He knew better. One hundred and eight were the afflictions that man brought on himself through his endless greed, hatred, and ignorance. One hundred and eight were the repentances that brought lost souls to the light of Buddha. One hundred and eight was the number of lives Shigeru would live in one hundred and eight hells for his unthinkable crimes. When one hundred and eight sticks of incense had been lit, he would begin.

"I am sorry, Father. Please forgive me."

But he would not be forgiven, this he knew. Lord Kiyori's spirit might forgive him for his own murder. But not for the others. No one would forgive him.

"I am sorry, Father. Please forgive me."

Shigeru was amazed. Somehow, he had kept count. Despite the monstrous visions that kept him from sleep, that filled his head with such pressure he expected his skull to burst open at any moment, that mocked his very existence, he had kept count. This was the one hundred eighth stick of incense.

"I am sorry, Father. Please forgive me."

He pressed his forehead to the floor. The incessant

thumping of wingless flying machines filled his ears. Behind his closed eyes, great lanterns burning without fire blinded him. His throat choked with the acrid taste of colorful, visible air.

He was, he knew, completely mad.

One person in every Okumichi generation was cursed with the gift of foreknowledge. In the previous generation, it had been his father. In the next, it was Genji. In his own, the misfortune had befallen Shigeru himself. The one who saw always suffered, because seeing did not always lead to understanding. For him, it never led to understanding at all, only suffering. The event occurred, unrecognized by him until it slipped from future to past. And suffering was followed by more suffering.

If he were mocked only by prophetic dreams, life would be bearable. But then the waking visions began. A samurai truly disciplined in the martial ways could endure much, but the relentless flow of consciousness unrelieved even by sleep could be endured for only so long.

The sky turned to fire and fell to the ground, burning screaming children. Swarms of metallic insects crawled over Edo, stuffing their bellies with human flesh, spewing fumes noxious with the stench of their prey. Dead fish floated in their millions in the poisoned silver waters of the Inland Sea.

What he saw in his mind overlay what he saw with his eyes. Always. There was no relief.

Shigeru paused at the entrance of the temple. He bowed to the bodies of the two slain nuns, taking care not to slip in the twin pools of their coagulating blood as he stepped past. The full moon had been high above the castle when he crossed the courtyard earlier. Now, returning to his family's quarters, he saw the night still brightened by moonlight, but the orb itself was out of sight behind the walls of the castle.

His wife's bed was empty, the coverlet thrown hastily aside. He checked the children's rooms. They, too, were gone. This he had not foreseen. A grim smile distorted his face. Where were they? There was only one possibility.

He went to his personal armory and dressed himself.

A metal helmet with a red horsehair plume and wooden horns.

A lacquered face mask to protect his cheeks and jaw.

A *nodowa* to shield his throat, and two *sodé* to do the same for his shoulders. *Donaka, kusazuri,* and *haitaté* made with steel plates solid enough to deflect musketballs girded his torso, loins, and thighs. In addition to his swords, he stuffed five single-shot English flintlock pistols into his sash.

Shigeru was commander of this night's watch. He had no difficulty getting his horse from the stable. No one questioned his appearance. When he ordered the gate opened, it was opened, and he rode swiftly from the castle.

The compound of his father-in-law, Yoritada, lay in the mountains to the east a short distance away. When Shigeru arrived there, he found Yoritada and a dozen of his retainers waiting for him outside the walls. They were dressed as he was, in full armor. Six of the samurai held muskets at the ready.

"Approach no closer," Yoritada said, "or you will be shot down."

"I have come for my wife and children," Shigeru said. "Send them out and I will leave in peace."

"Umeko is your wife no longer," Yoritada said. "She has returned to my house and begged protection for herself and her children."

Shigeru laughed as if the notion were utterly ridiculous. "Protection? From what?"

"Shigeru," Yoritada said, his voice gentle with sadness, "your mind and spirit are unwell. I have seen this for many weeks. Tonight, Umeko came to me in tears. She says you have taken to whispering constantly, day and night, of the bloodiest tortures of hell. The children tremble in your presence. I beg you, ask Lord Kiyori for guidance. Your father is a wise man. He will help you."

"He will help no one," Shigeru said, watching closely for an opening. "Lord Kiyori was poisoned tonight with blowfish bile."

"What!" Yoritada stumbled forward a step, stunned by Shigeru's revelation. The news had a similar effect on the other samurai. Now. This was the decisive moment.

Shigeru spurred his horse into a charge, firing his pistols and discarding them as rapidly as he could. He was not a good shot and hit no one. His intention was only to further distract Yoritada's men.

In this he was successful. Only two of the musketeers came close to their target. Both balls struck his horse, causing the animal to fall.

Shigeru leaped from the saddle, landed on his feet at a run, and decapitated his father-in-law with the first stroke of his katana. Slashing with the katana in his right hand and stabbing with the *tanto* in his left, Shigeru killed or mortally wounded everyone who opposed him before the dust had settled from his horse's fall.

Inside the gate, his mother-in-law, Sadako, waited

with four of her attendants. Each held a *naginata*, the long-blade lance favored as a weapon by samurai women.

"Accursed demon." Sadako spit out the words. "I warned Umeko against marrying you."

"She should have listened," Shigeru said.

He found Umeko and his children in the teahouse of the inner courtyard. When he leaned forward toward the door, a child-sized katana came stabbing through the rice paper that covered the wooden frame. The blade sliced open his left brow, barely missing his eye.

"Enter and die!" a brave little voice declared, without the slightest waver of fear. It was the youngest child, their six-year-old son, Nobuyoshi. Shigeru could picture the scene inside. Nobuyoshi guarded the door, his katana extended in front of him, its point at eye level. Behind him, Umeko and their daughters, Emi and Sachi.

Shigeru used the tip of his katana to open the door. Nobuyoshi saw him and gasped. The child quickly retreated. It would have been better strategy to hold his ground, since the small doorway limited Shigeru's freedom of movement when he entered. But he could not blame the child. He knew he must look horrible. He was drenched from head to foot with the blood of eighteen people. Nineteen, if he counted himself. Blood dripped from the wound in his neck where his mother-in-law had struck him. If she had cut an inch lower, she would have killed him.

Shigeru's heart filled with pride as he looked at his son. In his short life, he had learned his lessons well. His sword was held at the proper angle, with the proper poise. His posture was balanced, allowing for movement in any direction. And, most important, he placed himself where his own life stood between the attacker and his mother and sisters.

"Well done, Nobuyoshi." Shigeru had said the same words many times before, after hard practice sessions with sword, spear, and bow. Nobuyoshi said nothing. His attention was focused entirely on Shigeru. His son was looking for an opening, seeking that decisive moment. He deserved to die like the true samurai that he was. Shigeru allowed himself to stumble as he stepped into the small space.

"Aaaiiii!" With a loud shout expressing full commitment, Nobuyoshi lunged at the gap in the armor at Shigeru's throat. His son did what every samurai must do. He vanished into the attack, without a single thought of self. In that liberating instant, Shigeru cut so swiftly, Nobuyoshi's body continued forward in midstride while his head fell to the floor behind him.

Emi and Sachi cried out and clutched each other, tears streaming down their childish cheeks. "Why, Father, why?" Emi said.

Umeko held a dagger in her left hand. In her right hand was a derringer. She raised this and fired. The ball rang against the steel of his helmet and bounced off. Umeko dropped the pistol and replaced it with the dagger.

"I save you from further sins," she said. With two swift movements, she slit her daughters' throats. Their blood gushed onto the pale silk of their bedroom kimonos. Then Umeko looked straight into Shigeru's eyes. "May the Compassionate Buddha lead you safely to the Pure Land," she said, and plunged the dagger into her own throat.

Shigeru sat on the floor of the teahouse, in the bloody ruins of his life, a sword in each hand. He watched the small doorway. Soon he would hear the sound of horses bearing troops from the castle. He began to laugh. He was still doomed. But he had freed his beloved wife and children. They would be untouched by the coming horrors promised by his prophetic dreams and visions.

II

BEAUTIFUL DREAMERS

4

Ten Dead Men

Doubts assail you. Confusion reigns. You know not yesterday from tomorrow. Listen to your heart and find guidance. Beating, like a drum. Roaring, like winter rapids. Finally, sound and silence indistinguishable.

    Listen.

    Listen.

    Listen.

    Blood, not water.

    Your blood.

SUZUME–NO–KUMO
(1860)

Emily's anticipation of her wedding night had been imbued with hope and dread. The latter condition found its chief cause in the complete physical repugnance she felt for Zephaniah; the former in the equal and relentless aversion he displayed toward her. Had either of these qualities been absent, she would have given no consideration to his proposal.

Combined as they were with a promise of escape from America, they made him an irresistible suitor. Their relationship as husband and wife could not be so perfectly devoid of intimacy. It was unreasonable to expect a total absence of the brute animal coupling attendant upon marriage. Happily, a bare minimum of it seemed highly probable. Occasional agony was a small price to pay for the opportunity he offered.

Now both hope and dread were gone, destroyed by an assassin's bullet. When Zephaniah died, Emily would be alone, and alone she could not remain in Japan. Without the protection of father, brother, or husband, a woman had no respectable place in a foreign land. She would be forced to return to America. Or was there perhaps an alternative? Could she continue the mission with Brother Matthew?

She turned a furtive glance upon him. He was looking out at the garden. Neither his face nor his posture nor any aspect of his demeanor suggested what he might be thinking. He was, as always, an enigma to her.

He had come into their lives for the first time only four months earlier. That was at the San Francisco mission of the True Word. She had been serving soup to the poor and the homeless when she noticed a man standing at the entrance of the dining hall.

His trail rider's clothes were filthy. The black hat on his head looked like it might once have been white. Hair streamed down his back and over his shoulders like a savage Indian's. The face was gaunt, with sunken cheeks and dark circles under the eyes. The stubbly growth of beard was uneven, as if he'd hacked at it with a knife. In his obvious need, he seemed like any other of the dozens of unfortunates to whom she daily tendered care. Except that he did not eagerly push into the serving line, nor gulp hungrily, nor fix his whole attention upon the food she dispensed. He was stillness itself there in the frame of the doorway. The only movement was in his eyes. They slowly scanned the men seated at the tables and standing in line. His arms hung loosely at his sides, in readiness somehow, rather than inert. That's when she noticed the bulge at his right hip under the jacket caked with dirt.

She asked Sister Sarah to take her ladle at the soup pot and went up to the stranger.

As she neared, he removed his hat politely and nodded to her. "Ma'am."

"You are most welcome to join us for supper, Brother Christian." Emily used the mode of address followers of the True Word applied to all newcomers. Brother, because, as Zephaniah said, are not all men brothers? Christian, because, though they may not realize it, are not all men, be they sinner, saint, or heathen, Christians in the grace and forgiveness of the Lord our God?

"Obliged, ma'am," the stranger said, nodding again in a kind of short bow. "Grateful to you." His words had a fluid twang to them. Texas, she guessed, or somewhere near there.

"This place is blessed with the peace of the Lord, Brother Christian." She held out her hand to him. "Violence shall not enter here."

He looked at her and blinked several times before comprehending. "No, ma'am," he said. He undid the leather cord that held the bottom of the holster to his thigh, unbuckled it from his waist, and handed it to her with the gun still in it.

She almost dropped it. " 'I commend you to God,

and to the word of His grace.'" The gun was very large, and very heavy.

"Thank you," he said.

"We say 'amen' to the words of the Gospel," she said.

"Don't know the Gospel, ma'am. Don't know what to amen."

"I commend you to God, and to the words of His grace. These are true words. Acts 20:32."

"Amen," the stranger said.

She smiled. His meekness was promising. No doubt he had done wrong, probably with the very weapon she now held. And perhaps with the other, whose handle she saw tucked at the left side of his belt. Yet no one was beyond the mercy and protection of the Lord. "And that," she said, gesturing with her chin.

He looked down at the handle of the weapon, as if surprised to see it. "Forgot about it." For the first time, he smiled. "Haven't had it long." It was more of a small sword than a big knife. He put it down on top of the gun and holster Emily held in her arms.

"Your money is better spent on instruments of peace," Emily said.

"Amen," the stranger said.

"Those were merely my own words," she said, "not Gospel."

"Didn't buy it, either." He smiled again, an odd smile. His lips curved up and his eyes narrowed.

"Where, then, did it come from, Brother Christian?" Won at gambling, Emily thought, or worse, stolen. She was offering the stranger an opportunity to make a small confession, and so take the first step at beginning life anew in the mercy and grace of the Lord.

"Bowie knife with a ten-inch blade," he said. Then, realizing he had explained nothing, added, "Was a parting gift."

Very well, there would be no confession for the moment. She had done her duty by opening the way for one. She said, "What is your given name?"

"Matthew," he said.

"I am Sister Emily, Brother Matthew. I am pleased to welcome you to sup with us, in the protection of the Lord."

"Thank you, Sister Emily," Brother Matthew said.

The memory of those more promising times brought tears to her eyes so suddenly, she was unable to keep them from spilling onto her cheeks.

· · · · ·

Reaching over Cromwell, Stark gave Emily his handkerchief. She covered her face with it and wept in near silence, her shoulders trembling with barely suppressed sobs. He was surprised to see such emotion coming from her. Her demeanor with the preacher had always been distantly polite. One who didn't know otherwise would never guess they were betrothed. It just went to show how little he knew about women. Not that it mattered. Not that he cared. Stark's heart pumped blood through his body, that was all. Otherwise, it was a dead man's heart.

Stark said, "You ought to take rest, Sister Emily. I'll watch over Brother Zephaniah."

Emily shook her head. After several deep breaths, she was able to speak. "Thank you, Brother Matthew, but I cannot go. My place is with him."

Stark heard the rustle of clothing in the hallway. Someone was approaching. The four samurai outside bowed low. Moments later, Lord Genji appeared in the doorway with the captain of his bodyguard. He looked at Emily and Stark, then said a few words to the samurai. The four men bowed again, uttered a single syllable that sounded like "*Hai!*" and rushed off. Stark noticed that everyone around Genji said that word frequently. He guessed it meant yes. People were unlikely to say no much to someone who could exterminate them and everyone they knew on the slightest whim.

Genji smiled and greeted them with a slight bow. Before they could struggle to their feet, he was seated beside them on his knees, apparently in complete comfort. He said something and waited. It seemed to Stark that he was looking at them as if he expected a reply.

Stark shook his head. "I'm sorry, Lord Genji. Neither of us speaks Japanese."

Amused, Genji turned to Saiki and said, "He thinks I spoke to him in Japanese."

Saiki said, "Is he a fool? Doesn't he recognize his own language?"

"Apparently not the way I speak it. My accent must be even worse than I thought. However, I did understand him. That's something to be glad of." Genji switched again to English and said to Stark and Emily, "My English is not good. I apologize."

Stark shook his head again. All he could think of to say was what he had already said. "I'm sorry," he began. Then Emily interrupted him.

"You're speaking English," she said to Genji. Or he was trying to, at least. Her eyes, still wet with tears, widened in surprise.

"Yes, thank you," Genji said. He smiled like a child who had pleased an important adult. "I regret the offense to your ears. My tongue and my lips have great difficulty with the shapes of your words."

What Emily heard was a string of strange syllables in the general rhythm of English. "Yeh-su, san-kyu. I lee-glet-to zah offen-su to yo-ah ee-ah-su. My tahn-gu ahn my rip-su ha-bu glate difficurty with zah shay-pu-su of yo-ah wod-zuh."

She struggled to separate one blurred sound from the next. If she could puzzle out even a few words, she might have some idea of what he was talking about. Had he used the word "difficulty"? She thought it might be a good idea to repeat the word in her reply.

Enunciating carefully, she said, "Any difficulty can be overcome if people try hard enough."

Ah, so that's how the word was pronounced, Genji thought. "Difficulty," an "el" with a flip of the tongue toward the upper palate, not an "ur" with a soft growl in the throat.

"Difficult but not impossible," Genji said. "Sincerity and persistence go a long way."

His accent was strange and severe, but there was a consistency to it that made the words clearer the more of them she heard. He was also a quick learner. This time, his "difficult" was much closer to hers.

"Lord Genji, how on earth did you learn our language?"

"My grandfather required me to study it. He believed it would be useful." In fact, Kiyori had told him it was an absolute necessity. He had seen Genji in conversations with English speakers in prophetic dreams.

Those conversations, Kiyori had said, will one day save your life.

Genji had been seven years old. He had said, If

your dreams are true, why should I bother to study? Prophecy says I will speak English, so when the time comes, I will speak it.

Kiyori had laughed loudly. When the time comes, you will speak it, because now, today, you will begin learning it.

The Shogunate's prohibition against outsiders was still in force in those days. Native speakers were unavailable as tutors. So Genji's studies had been confined almost entirely to books. Words on paper were one thing. On the tongue and in the ear they were quite another.

Stark said, "You understand him."

"Yes, with an effort. Can you not, Brother Matthew?"

"Not at all, Sister Emily." For Stark, Genji spoke in strings of indecipherable syllables. What Emily heard as English came more slowly, with utterances in smaller groups, more murmured than clipped. It was a difference leading to no increase in comprehension for him, no matter how closely he listened.

Genji spoke very slowly. "Perhaps if I speak very slowly?"

Stark heard, "Pah-ha-pu-su i-fu-aye su-pee-ku-be li-shrow-ree?" All he could do was shake his head again.

"I'm sorry, Lord Genji. My ears are not as wise as Sister Emily's."

"Ah," Genji said. He smiled at Emily. "It's ironic, I know, but you will have to translate my English for Mr. Stark into English he can understand."

"It will be my privilege," Emily said, "and a temporary one, I'm sure. It is only a matter of becoming accustomed to each other's idiosyncrasies."

Genji blinked. "You have sped up your speech a

little too much for me, Miss Gibson. I could not follow that time."

"My apologies, Lord Genji. I was carried away by my enthusiasm." She considered rephrasing her statement using simpler words. Looking into the gentle warlord's eyes, she decided against it. She thought she saw there a soul of high sensitivity. Condescension would not escape his notice. He would be insulted. Worse, he would be hurt. Emily repeated her previous words with care.

Saiki knelt at the doorway a short distance away. He was far enough not to intrude on the discussion. He was also just one stride away from inserting himself between his lord and the outsiders, and decapitating Stark, if it became necessary. The need did not appear imminent. Nevertheless, Saiki maintained his readiness. Though the woman seemed harmless, he watched her as well.

A small crowd stood behind Saiki. The four guards had returned carrying a Western-style bed. With them were Hidé and Shimoda, bearing additional furnishings. The maid, Hanako, arrived with a silver English tea service upon her tray. They all looked with amazement at the scene before them.

"Lord Genji is speaking the outsiders' language," Hidé whispered.

Saiki maintained his watch. Without turning, he said softly, "Keep losing discipline, Hidé, and you will spend your coming nuptials in the stables instead of in your bride's embrace."

Nuptials? Hidé wanted to laugh. That would never happen. Their lord had made an offhand comment, nothing more. Only a humorless old coot like Saiki would take it seriously. He turned to share his amusement with Shimoda. His friend was smiling quite a different kind of smile. Next to him, Hanako, her usually pale cheeks crimson, stared down at her tray. Hidé's jaw dropped open. Why did he never know what was going on until it was too late?

Saiki shuffled forward on his knees. "Lord, the appurtenances for the outsiders."

"Bring them in." To Emily and Stark he said, "Let us move aside while this room is furnished more suitably." Both of them, he saw, had considerable difficulty rising. They had to bend into vulnerable positions and push themselves from the floor with their hands, somewhat like toddlers just learning how to stand. Stark was up first and quickly went to Emily's assistance. Did all outsiders treat their women with such excessive deference? Or was it only missionaries? In any case, it was admirable of the man to behave with such gallantry toward a woman so difficult to look upon. It was easy to be kind to beautiful women. Ugly ones required considerably more willpower.

Bed, chairs, and tables were installed sooner than it took Stark to get full circulation back into his legs. Cromwell remained unconscious when they lifted him into the bed. The blankets on the floor were soaked black, and blood still flowing now stained the fresh linen beneath the wounded man. The color of the fluid as well as its odor told Stark the bullet had torn through Cromwell's intestines as well as his stomach. Poisons and acids from those organs were even now spreading into his living flesh.

"Shall we retire to the next room?" Genji asked. "These maids will attend Mr. Cromwell. They will call us if there is any change."

Emily shook her head. "If he wakes, it may comfort him to see me."

"Very well. Then let us be seated." Genji sat on the edge of the chair. Just as when he was on the floor, he used his posture to hold his spine erect. Emily and Stark immediately leaned onto the back of the chair and let it do the work of holding them up. That seemed rather unhealthy, but Genji was open-minded. He tried it. Within a few seconds, he felt his abdominal organs shifting out of correct alignment. He looked at Cromwell. The man might live another hour, perhaps two. Genji wasn't sure he could bear sitting atop this outsider device that long.

Stark, too, was looking at Cromwell, but he wasn't concerned about the preacher's demise. His thoughts were on the mission house the True Word had established in Yamakawa Domain northwest of Edo. Eleven missionaries had gone there from San Francisco a year ago. Among those eleven was someone Stark wanted to see very badly.

Stark, Emily, and Genji sat by Cromwell's bedside and waited for him to die.

· · · · ·

"There was no opportunity to shoot Genji at the harbor," Kuma said. He wasn't about to tell his client he had grabbed an empty musket. For a freelancer, reputation was the most valuable of all attributes. Why damage it for nothing?

"I find that difficult to believe," Kawakami said.

"Nevertheless, such was the case."

"Explain again why you shot that particular missionary."

Another error, though a less important one. The one he had aimed at, the cold one walking on the near side of the palanquin, had tripped at precisely the moment Kuma fired. It almost seemed as though the man had looked in his direction, seen him, and dived out of the way. But that was most improbable. Even a trained ninja would not so easily have detected Kuma's presence. He must have tripped. Kuma kept the confident look on his face. There was no way Kawakami could know his shot was entirely fortuitous.

He said, "He was the older of the two men. I assumed he was the leader. His loss will be more painful for Genji and other Christian sympathizers. I thought you would be pleased."

Kawakami contemplated the situation. It would not do to have Kuma making critical decisions on his own. At the same time, he was most effective if he was free to act should promising circumstances develop. "Take no further action against Genji. If an opportunity to attack the missionaries arises, do so, but only while they are supposedly enjoying the full protection of the Okumichi clan." Such a humiliating event was pleasant to imagine.

"Do you mean while they are inside Quiet Crane Palace?"

"Yes."

"That will not be easy."

Kawakami placed ten gold ryo on the table and pushed them toward Kuma. "Continue to watch Heiko. I am not so sure she remembers what she should remember."

Kuma bowed, finished his tea, and slipped out the door. It had gone more easily than he had expected. Kawakami usually asked many more questions. Today he seemed distracted. No matter. Kuma was ten ryo richer. More important, he was still assigned to watch over Heiko. He would have done so anyway. To be paid for it was a blessing indeed. Namu Amida Butsu.

Kuma the Bear walked briskly, but not too briskly, toward the market section of Tsukiji. Anyone who bothered to notice him would see a fat, balding, middle-aged peasant with the vaguely cheerful expression typical of those who are not too bright. No one would see the deadliest ninja in the Home Provinces.

No one ever did. At least, not in time.

· · · · ·

Kawakami had a hard time paying attention to Kuma. He couldn't stop thinking about Heiko's report. Such devastating carnage. Father and son killed in the same wretched hour. Root and the branch destroyed, and not by an enemy's hatred but by one's own madness. Could such a horror be true? Until there was confirmation from additional sources, Kawakami could only hope. If it was so, Kuma's failure to maim Genji was most fortunate. Far better that the Okumichi clan collapse from within than be destroyed from without.

Kawakami closed his eyes and dropped into deep contemplation. In the fourteenth year of the Emperor Go-yozei, two and a half centuries ago, Reigi, Lord of Minato, had followed Nagamasa, Lord of Akaoka, into battle against the Tokugawa armies. Reigi had believed in Nagamasa's gift of prophecy. The Tokugawa clan is doomed, Nagamasa said. I have seen it in a visioning. Nagamasa died, and good riddance to the false prophet. Reigi, at Nagamasa's side, also died. As did his wife, his concubines, and all his children but one, a daughter who had married into a junior line of the Tokugawas. Kawakami's revered ancestress. For generations, from grandmother to mother to daughter, the story had been passed, and grandmothers, mothers, and daughters had told the story in their nurseries to their grandsons and sons.

If not for Nagamasa, Kawakami and his ancestors would have been Lords of Minato, a truly great domain, instead of Hino, great in name more than reality.

Now the continuation of Nagamasa's bloodline depended on one man.

Genji.

Dwelling in silence, Kawakami considered how he could further nurture the most painful, most humiliating ways in which that line might be cut.

· · · · ·

Stark was a guest in the palace of a Japanese warlord on New Year's Day, 1861, because of ten dead men.

The second dead man was Jimmy So Fast. His real name was James Sophia. He was called So Fast because he didn't like to be called Sophia, and because he was so fast with cards no one could catch him cheating. The third reason he was called So Fast was because he was faster with a pistol than seven men. Those were the seven men he'd shot dead, none of whom was among the ten who eventually brought Stark to Japan.

Stark didn't know any of this until Jimmy So Fast was dead. One of the reasons Jimmy So Fast was dead was because Stark, unlike any of the other men Jimmy So Fast cheated at cards, saw him cheating.

"Hold on," Stark said. "You just palmed the bottom card, you son of a bitch." He was seventeen then, a runaway from an Ohio orphanage on his first cattle drive in west Texas. His head hurt, his balls hurt, his back hurt, his hands hurt, his knees hurt, his ass hurt, his feet hurt. He had a bad sunburn and a worse hangover. But his eyes were as sharp as ever and he saw the son of a bitch palm the card. The ace of spades.

Jimmy So Fast gave him a cold look. "You know who you talkin' to, boy-o?"

"Yeah, I do," Stark said. "I'm talkin' to a card-palming, cheating son of a bitch. Put down that ace of spades, you fuckless shitheel, or I'll beat your goddamned head in for you." The night he left the orphanage, Stark had done exactly that for Elias Egan, the night supervisor. For years, Egan had abused and brutalized many of the boys, including Stark. After he had his head beaten in, he didn't do it anymore. Elias Egan was the first dead man.

Jimmy So Fast lived up to his name. His pistol was in his hand and pointed at Stark's chest before Stark's pistol was out of its holster. He would have made Stark his eighth dead man instead of becoming Stark's second if not for his fascination with newfangled inventions.

Instead of a black-powder muzzle-loading revolver like everyone else had at the time, Jimmy So Fast carried a Volcanic Pistol, which fed revolutionary rimfire cartridges into the firing chamber, six of them one after another, with a hand crank. That was the other reason he was dead. The Volcanic Pistol jammed. When the cartridge in the chamber didn't fire, Jimmy So Fast tried to crank in the next one, but the crank wouldn't budge. While he was pulling and pushing at it, Stark drew his old muzzle-loader, pressed it against Jimmy So Fast's cheek, and pulled the trigger. Jimmy So Fast was much faster on the draw than Stark, but Stark's old muzzle-loader fired, and Jimmy So Fast's Volcanic Pistol didn't.

The third, fourth, and fifth dead men were gunslingers who thought it would increase their price in the killer's marketplace by gunning down the man who had gunned down the famous Jimmy So Fast. The first of them would have killed the old Stark easily. The new Stark was something else. When he found out who he'd shot, he realized he'd done something more than blow the brains out of his second dead man. He'd also made himself a target for everyone looking to make a name as a fast gun.

The best thing would have been to undo Jimmy So Fast's death. Stark couldn't do that, so he did the next best thing. He practiced drawing his pistol, aiming, and firing. He practiced being alert to shifty eyes, tense shoulders, unnatural breathing, too much noise, and too little. He practiced not staying in one place too long. He practiced carrying a second gun in case his first one jammed.

When the third dead man found him in Pecos, Stark was faster than Jimmy So Fast had ever been. Five cowboys and two whores watched the third dead man die with his gun barely in his hand. Five cowboys and two whores can spread a story far and wide in not much time. They can also exaggerate like nobody's business. By the time Stark rode into Deadwood, his reputation was so frightening that dead men four and five teamed up to face him together. Two things went wrong for them. First, they started firing at twenty feet, and they couldn't hit a herd of cattle at that distance. Second, it so happened Stark did his target practice at twenty feet, and he shot targets every day since he had killed Jimmy So Fast.

No one else looked to face Stark after Deadwood. Who had a chance against a man whose gun hand moved faster than the eye could see? Who pulled the trigger so quick the second man was dead before the first man even started to bleed? Who could hit an eyeball at a hundred paces? Deadwood had its share of tale-spinning cowboys and whores, too.

For a long time after that, Stark didn't shoot anything except targets. His reputation got so big, he hid inside of it. Stark the fast gun was six foot eight, scarred across his right eye with a knife cut, mean as a rabid sow, drank whiskey and never ate, liked beating women more than fucking them, and fucked them only after he had beaten them to within an inch of their lives. Stark started saying his name was Matthews and no one recognized him. They were looking for somebody a lot bigger and a lot meaner.

Two years passed before Stark met the sixth dead man. He was a whoremaster in El Paso who didn't know how to let go. After that, Stark didn't think about dead men for almost a year. He even stopped shooting targets. He was happy and he thought he would always be happy from then on. He was wrong. He said good-bye to Mary Anne and the two girls and went looking for dead men seven, eight, nine, and ten.

He found the seventh dead man four days' ride north of the Mexican border in a dust hole with the highfalutin name of la Ciudad de los Angeles. It wasn't close to being a city, and if any angels called it home, those divine beings were extremely well disguised. Before he died, the seventh dead man told Stark that the others had fled north with plans to take ship across the Pacific. He told Stark not because he hated his former companions, or because he was dying from the pulsating hole in his stomach, or because he wanted to atone for any pain he might have caused innocent parties. He told Stark because Stark had shot him in both knees after shooting him in the stomach, and was promising to shoot him in the groin next.

The eighth dead man tried to run out of a bar in Sacramento, and Stark put a .44 caliber bullet into the back of his neck and took his head clean off.

The ninth dead man caught Stark off guard. He was waiting behind the door in a San Francisco hotel room. How a five-hundred-pound man could hide behind a door was a mystery Stark didn't have time to ponder. He came out stabbing with a huge bowie knife and almost buried the ten-inch blade in Stark's back. Stark's .44 got knocked out of his hand, so he pulled his concealed .22 revolver and pumped five bullets into the ninth dead man. He kept on coming, that bowie knife flashing in front of him. Stark swung the .22 like a hammer, got lucky, and bashed the ninth dead man's temple in.

The tenth dead man was one of two people. He was the man who took ship to Japan as a True Word missionary one year earlier. If it wasn't him, then the tenth dead man was Stark himself.

One of them had to die.

· · · · ·

The monk they called Jimbo returned to Mushindo Monastery late in the afternoon. Sohaku could hear children's happy voices well before anyone came into view. Wherever Jimbo went, he was followed by a flock from the nearby village.

"Don't go back yet, Jimbo!"

"Yeah, don't go!"

"It's still early!"

"What are those weeds for? You're not going to eat them, are you?"

"My grandmother said you can have dinner with us, Jimbo. Don't you want to do that? Aren't you sick of monk's gruel?"

"Tell us one more story! Just one!"

"Jimbo, tell us again about how Buddha's angels came from the Pure Land and showed you the Way!"

"Jimbo! Jimbo! Jimbo! Jimbo!"

Sohaku smiled. The last voice belonged to Goro, the slow son of the village's idiot woman. He was big, even bigger than Jimbo, who was a head taller and fifty pounds heavier than any other man in Yamakawa Domain. Before Jimbo arrived, Goro moaned, groaned, cried, and screamed, but he didn't speak. Now he had a one-word vocabulary and he used it constantly.

"Jimbo! Jimbo!"

"Stop." Jimbo arrived at the gate. He saw the monks, armed with bamboo staffs, deployed around the armory. Abbot Sohaku sat in meditation beside the barricaded doorway. "Go home," he said to the children.

"What's happening?"

"Let me see, let me see!"

"It's the crazy man, I bet. He must have got loose again."

"Jimbo! Jimbo! Jimbo!"

"Shut up, stupid! We know his name."

"Go home now," Jimbo said, "or tomorrow I won't come to the village."

"Oh, if we leave now, we'll miss all the fun!"

"Yeah, last time the crazy man threw people over the wall!"

Jimbo looked sternly at the children. "I won't come to the village the day after tomorrow either."

"Oh, all right. Come on, let's go."

"But you'll come tomorrow?"

"You promise?"

"I promise," Jimbo said.

The two littlest girls each took one of Goro's hands. If he'd resisted they wouldn't have been able to budge him. But Goro always obeyed women. Old women, young women, little girls. Perhaps some lesson harsh or gentle his mother had taught him had comfortably lodged in his porous mind. When the little girls pulled, he went along with them without resistance.

"Jimbo!"

He stood and watched until the children disappeared down the narrow path to the valley below. He didn't turn away until the last one was gone. Daylight faded with the hour of the monkey. It was time to prepare the evening gruel. He proceeded directly to the kitchen. He had no curiosity about the extraordinary situation. If it was necessary for him to know, the abbot would tell him.

With care and gratitude, he washed the wild grasses he had collected in the mountains. Soon, the long green blades would be chopped into tiny slivers. They would garnish the gruel, adding a small portion of celebratory flavor and color to the simple meal. During his time at the monastery, he had lost track of the months and days. Seasons were easier to recognize. It was winter now. Christmas was in winter. This very day, perhaps. Jimbo was no longer a Christian, but he saw no harm in remembering Christmas. The words of Buddha and Christ were very different, but how different were their messages? Not so different, he thought.

"Jimbo, the abbot wants to see you." Taro looked in through the doorway. He was dressed for travel, with leggings and a riding jacket in place of monk's robes. Two swords were in his sash. Outside, a horse whinnied.

Jimbo followed Taro to the armory. The abbot motioned for Jimbo to join him. To Taro he said "Go." Taro bowed, leaped on his horse, and galloped out of the gate. Nightfall was near. Taro would ride through darkness into the hostile territory of neighboring Yoshino Domain. Jimbo said a silent prayer for his friend's safety.

"Great metal beasts spitting gouts of flame." Shigeru's voice came from the barricaded building. "The smell of burning human flesh is everywhere."

Sohaku said, "Do those words sound like prophecy to you, Jimbo?"

"I don't know what prophecy sounds like, Reverend Abbot."

"I thought Christianity was a religion of prophets."

"I wouldn't know. I am not a Christian."

"But you were," Sohaku said. "Listen to him. Is that prophecy?"

"Prophets are sometimes madmen," Jimbo said, "but not all madmen are prophets."

Sohaku snorted. "I am neither mad nor a prophet. That's my problem." Lord Genji had left explicit instructions. When his uncle began prophesying, he was to be summoned without delay. How he knew his uncle would begin prophesying at all was undoubtedly also a matter of prophecy. Or madness. How much simpler life would be as the vassal of a lord who only saw yesterday in the past, today in the present, and tomorrow in the future. The late Lord Kiyori at least had the virtue of being a disciplined warrior. His grandson and heir spent far too little time, in Sohaku's opinion, studying the ways of the samurai.

"No Shogun," Shigeru said. "No swords. No topknots. No kimono."

"I have decided this is prophecy," Sohaku said, "and I have sent word to Lord Genji. Taro will reach Edo in a night and a day. He will be back with our lord within seven days' time. You will meet him then."

"I wonder if I deserve such an honor. I am not necessarily the outsider of Lord Kiyori's prophecy."

The prophecy Jimbo spoke of was the one that said that in the New Year an outsider would appear holding the key to the survival of the Okumichi clan. It was a prophecy Sohaku put little stock in. He put little stock in any prophecy. After all, if Lord Kiyori could see the future so well, why had he not prevented his own assassination? He was not required to believe any prophecies, however. He was only required to follow the commands of his liege lord. And even that was somewhat open to question. How open, Sohaku had not yet decided.

Sohaku said, "You are the only outsider known to our clan. The New Year is nearly upon us. Who else can it be?" Right now, he was far more interested in Shigeru. There was a chance Sohaku could take him by surprise and recapture him. Otherwise, they would be in a most awkward position when Lord Genji arrived. They were supposed to be the clan's best cavalrymen. Yet, here they were, locked out of their own armory by one insane and babbling man, a man they had been entrusted to guard.

"I will prepare Lord Shigeru's meal." Jimbo bowed and made his way back to the kitchen. He had learned their ways remarkably well in a short time. Sohaku was most impressed with how he had grasped their language. The American consul, Townsend Harris, had been resident in Japan for over four years and still could not speak more than a few poorly enunciated words of Japanese. Sohaku had witnessed this for himself when he accompanied Lord Kiyori on a visit to the diplomat's new Edo lodgings. After only one year, Jimbo sounded almost Japanese.

"Deformity everywhere. By birth, by accident, by design." Sohaku listened to the continued muttering from within. If he failed to recapture Shigeru now, he would certainly do so during the next day or two. Even madmen had to sleep.

· · · · ·

Miracles followed unceasingly one upon the other, miracles of visions, understandings, and powers.

He walked with Jesus upon the waters.

He stood with Moses before the burning bush.

He flew with Gabriel above the battlefield of Armageddon.

Reinvigorated with holy zeal, he awoke to another place and found bestowed upon himself the ability to decipher the Japanese tongue. When the effeminate warlord next spoke, Cromwell was blessed with comprehension.

"Shall we retire to the next room?" Genji said. "These maids will attend Mr. Cromwell. They will call us if there is any change."

Emily shook her head. "If he wakes, it may comfort him to see me."

"Very well," Genji said. "Then let us be seated."

Accustomed as he had become to miracles, Cromwell was astounded by what he heard. He didn't know which surprised him more. That Emily, like him, found meaning in the mutilated alien syllables, or that the warlord understood the English words that came from her lips. Of great signs and portents, was not the undoing of Babel's curse among the greatest? Cromwell opened his eyes.

Emily smiled at him. Why did tears roll down her cheeks? She said, "Zephaniah."

He tried to say her name. Instead of words, hot liquid filled his mouth.

"Oh, God," Emily said. Her hands, balled tightly into fists, shot to her mouth. She would have fallen backward out of her chair if Stark hadn't caught her.

"Sit him up," Stark said, "or he'll drown in his own blood."

Genji took Cromwell in his arms and lifted the shuddering torso from the bed. Where his arm crossed the wounded man's chest, the sleeve of his kimono was already black with the dark gouts spewing from the spasm-wracked throat.

"Lord!" Saiki sprang forward. "Please don't touch him! The outsider's foulness will pollute you!"

"It is his life's blood," Genji said, "no different from yours or mine."

Stark felt Emily's body, already tight with fear, grow ever tighter. She was going into shock.

"Emily," he said. He rested her head on his shoulder and turned her away from Cromwell. He felt her soften. Her arms went around him. She buried her face against his chest and wept. Stark walked with her from the room. A short distance away was a small garden. He would take her there. "Come. There is nothing more we can do."

In the hallway leading to the garden, Stark and Emily crossed paths with two men hurrying toward the room they had just left. Both wore the two swords of samurai, but the second man's head was shaven, and his clothing was rough and simple. He must have come some distance in a great hurry. Dust mixed with sweat turned to mud on his face.

"No, Brother Matthew," Emily said. "I cannot leave Zephaniah alone."

"Brother Zephaniah is no longer alone," Stark said. "He is with the hosts of the righteous in his Savior's home."

· · · · ·

Saiki was horrified. The outsider had coughed out his bloody guts all over Lord Genji. Worse, he had died in his arms. Shinto priests would have to be called immediately to cleanse the lord. Then, as soon as the body was removed, the room would have to be exorcised as well. Sheets, bedding, furniture, tatami mats, all must be removed and burned. Saiki himself didn't care. All religions were fairy tales to him. Some of the men, however, were vulnerable to old superstitions.

"Lord," Saiki said, "the outsider is beyond your help. Please let others deal with his body."

"He's not dead," Genji said, "only sleeping."

"Sleeping?" Impossible. Saiki leaned closer. The awful odors rising from the outsider nauseated him. But he saw the chest slowly rising and falling, and he heard the faint whistle of air moving through the huge nose.

Genji turned Cromwell over to Hanako and the other maid. "Keep him sitting up until Dr. Ozawa returns. If he begins to choke again, do whatever is necessary to clear his throat, including reaching in with your hand if you must."

"Yes, lord," the two maids said. They struggled not to gag at the foul reek rising from the outsider's body. To show displeasure at anything in their lord's presence would be an unforgivable breach of etiquette.

"Look at the calm in his face," Genji said to Saiki. "He dreams healing dreams. I believe he will survive."

"That would be a miracle."

"He is a Christian. His religion is a religion of miracles."

"He's not yet dead, lord, but that hardly means he will survive. All about him is the stench of death."

"Perhaps not. I doubt he bathed during his entire sea voyage. That is probably the source of the stench."

A samurai from the perimeter watch waited at the door. When Genji glanced in his direction, he bowed.

"Lord, a rider has brought an urgent message."

"Bring him." He would have preferred to strip himself of these bloody clothes and bathe immediately. It would have to wait.

Despite the rough clothing and the shaven head, the messenger was familiar. His name was Taro. Six months ago, he and two dozen more of Akaoka Domain's best cavalrymen had taken holy orders with their former captain. Taro could only have come from his present station, Mushindo Monastery, and coming from there, he could have only one message to deliver. Genji did not have to hear it to know what it was.

"Lord," Taro said. He stopped for a moment to catch his breath. "Captain Tanaka..." He stopped again and bowed apologetically. "That is, Abbot Sohaku requests instructions."

Genji nodded. "What is the situation in the countryside?"

"Much movement of troops in Yoshino Domain, lord. I was forced to leave the road for concealment several times."

"Be more precise, Taro," Saiki said sternly. "Were you trained as a scout or not?"

"Yes, sir." Taro calculated quickly in his head. "Five hundred mounted musketeers with four siege cannons went south on the main highway toward the Inland Sea. Three thousand troops on foot, in three brigades, traveled by night in the same direction."

"Very good, Taro. Take refreshment and be ready to ride in one hour."

"Yes, lord."

Saiki hissed. "Yoshino is an ally of Kurokawa. That domain is separated from yours by the narrowest stretch of the Inland Sea. They may be plotting to take advantage of your grandfather's recent death."

"I doubt it. The Shogun would not give his permission for an attack on Akaoka. He's too worried about outsiders to risk any unnecessary internal distractions."

"The Shogun is a joke," Saiki said. "His title of Great Barbarian Subduing Generalissimo is more weighty than himself, a fourteen-year-old boy with cowards and idiots for advisors."

"He may lack the power of his ancestors," Genji said, "but no lord would dare flaunt his authority in such a blatant way. The Shogun's army is still the strongest in Japan. And no one else has any navy to speak of." He paused thoughtfully. "This is actually good news. With so much attention to the west, travel to the north will be less hazardous."

"Lord, surely you don't intend to go to the monastery yourself?"

"I must. 'Abbot Sohaku requests instructions' means something has arisen that requires my personal attention. Don't worry, Saiki. I won't travel in state. That will attract too much attention. I'll go incognito, with Taro." Genji looked around the room. "Hidé and Shimoda, too."

The two men bowed. "Yes, lord. Thank you. We will prepare for the journey."

"Bows but no firearms," Genji said, "and no armor. A casual hunting expedition. No crests on your clothing."

"Yes, lord. We understand and obey." Hidé and Shimoda hurried from the room.

Saiki shuffled forward on his knees and bowed low. "Lord, please reconsider. An attempt was made on your life not an hour ago. An outsider guest of yours has been seriously wounded. All Edo knows this by now. Who would choose such a moment to go hunting? It is most implausible. No one will believe it."

"I disagree. My reputation as a frivolous dilettante practically demands such an act."

Saiki said, "Lord, at least permit me to accompany you."

"I cannot. Your very presence will make us appear excessively serious. That is the opposite of what we want."

One of the samurai began to laugh at this, but stifled himself when Saiki turned and glared.

"Besides," Genji said, stifling laughter of his own, "you are needed here to protect our guests against any further attack." He looked at Cromwell. Behind his closed lids, his eyes danced a dreamer's dance.

"Where are the other two?"

"In the inner garden, lord," one of the guards said.

"Paper," Genji said. When it was brought, he penned a brief note in English. "Dear Miss Gibson and Mr. Stark, I regret that I must leave for a short time. I will send a friend to stay with you. Her English is even worse than mine, I am sorry to say, but she will see to it that your needs are met." He signed it in the outsider fashion, with his given name before his family's. "Sincerely, Genji Okumichi."

． ． ． ． ．

After meeting with the Shogun's spymaster, Heiko returned to her cottage in the Ginza woods on the eastern outskirts of Edo near the New Bridge to the Tokaido Highway.

"Your bath is ready," Sachiko said in greeting.

"Thank you." Heiko undressed quickly, threw on a simple cloth robe, and walked out to the bathhouse. She always bathed after meeting with Kawakami, no matter what the time of day. Today she felt more in need of cleansing than usual.

The report she had given forced her to recall images she would have preferred to forget. She had met Genji's uncle Shigeru on several occasions. There had never been a hint of anything out of the ordinary. What madness drove him to slaughter his entire family, including his only heir, a fine boy six years of age? Was the malady an individual affliction, or did it signify a fatal taint in the entire bloodline? Would her beloved Genji, too, go mad one day?

"Can you verify everything you have told me?" Kawakami had asked.

"No, lord."

"Then this is all conjecture."

"The deaths are not conjecture, lord, only the manner of their occurrence. Shigeru's father-in-law, Yoritada, was reportedly killed in an avalanche near Mount Tosa along with his entire household, including his visiting daughter, Umeko, and her three children. While they were gone, a fire said to be accidental burned down their residence. Unlikely in the first instance, and extremely convenient in the second, if bloodshed did take place."

"Coincidences do occur from time to time," Kawakami said.

"Yes, lord."

"Is that all?"

"No, lord. There is more. The arrival of an outsider ship this morning excited Lord Genji's interest. The *Star of Bethlehem*. He didn't say what cargo it carries." Heiko was not concerned about giving anything away. By now, Kawakami's other spies would have told him all this and more. "He left for the harbor in the hour of the dragon."

"Human cargo," Kawakami said. "More Christians of the True Word sect. This may signal Lord Genji's involvement in a Christian plot of some kind."

Heiko giggled. "It's so ludicrous, the idea of

someone like him involved in any plot at all. He's only interested in women, wine, and music. If there was a plot, then surely it would have been the late Lord Kiyori's. And with his demise, the plot must also be dead."

"He has an interest in hunting, too, does he not? That is part of our martial tradition."

Again Heiko giggled. "Part of your martial tradition, perhaps, Lord Kawakami, for you are a true samurai. When Lord Genji goes hunting, he invariably returns empty-handed."

"Don't be swayed so easily by appearances," Kawakami cautioned. "That could be a performance for our benefit."

She bowed, contrite in appearance. "Yes, lord." She doubted that he believed what he said. More likely, he thought the Okumichi clan, like that of the Shogun's, was in the terminal stage of its decline. The grandfather, Kiyori, was the last of them who bore any resemblance to the Great Lords of yore. The son, Yorimasa, had been a degenerate opium addict who died young. The grandson, Genji, appeared to be much as Heiko had described. And Shigeru, the only truly dangerous Okumichi left alive, was insane. Perhaps this was enough to preserve Genji's life. If he was not a threat to anyone, there would be no reason to order his death.

She came out of her reverie a few short steps from the bathhouse. Goose bumps flashed across her skin under the thin cotton robe, and not from the chill of the day. Steam rose from the hot water within the tall rectangular tub. A lone bird called from the woods. Nothing was out of the ordinary. So what had brought her to full attention? A name came to her, by chance or instinct.

"Come out, Kuma," she said, "and I won't kill you. Not today, anyway."

A roar of big-bellied laughter came from the bathhouse. Kuma stepped out and bowed.

"Don't look so angry, Hei-chan," Kuma said, using the friendly diminutive "chan." "I was just testing your alertness."

"And would you have kept testing while I disrobed?"

"Please," Kuma said, affecting an aggrieved expression. "I am a ninja, not a degenerate peeper." Then a huge grin widened his broad face. "I would have continued to observe from my hiding place, but only for testing purposes."

Heiko laughed as she passed Kuma and entered the bathhouse. "Turn around, please." When Kuma complied, she removed her robe and began to bathe. She stood beside the tub, drew water with a small bucket, and poured it over herself. The extreme heat of the water made her shudder with pleasure.

"Two weeks ago, Kawakami told me to shoot Genji at the first opportunity," Kuma said, scrupulously keeping his back to the bathing woman. "It almost came this morning." He could tell from the sounds when the water splashed on Heiko's body, and when it splashed on the ground. He thought he could also tell which parts of the body. Now, from the sudden cessation of splashing, he knew his words had unsettled her.

"That's a surprise," Heiko said. When she spoke, her voice was as careless as ever, and she resumed bathing after only the slightest pause. "He has given me the impression that the assignment will be mine to carry out."

"He's too devious to ever tell anyone more than a

small part of the truth," Kuma said. "Perhaps he is even too devious to really know what he himself is doing. When I met with him today, he didn't order me to try again. I think he still hasn't decided whether he wants Genji dead or not."

"It makes things more confusing than they have to be," Heiko said.

Kuma could hear the relief in her voice. That told him what he had long suspected. Heiko was playing her role as Lord Genji's lover a little too well.

"I hope you haven't begun fooling yourself as well as your target."

"What do you mean?"

"You care for him," Kuma said.

"Of course I do," Heiko said. "If I didn't, he would know. There is no way to pretend with one so sensitive, especially in such intimate circumstances."

"But you are ready to kill him, if necessary?"

"Only a fool acts out of love," Heiko said. "You did not raise a fool."

"I hope not," Kuma said, listening to softer sounds coming from the bathhouse. Heiko was soaping herself. "Anyway, I think Kawakami has another, completely different plan underway, and that one has taken precedence over the one that calls for Genji's immediate demise."

"Oh? What plan?"

"I don't know yet," Kuma said. "It must involve you. Don't you know?"

"No." Heiko rinsed the soap off. Clean, she stepped into the deep wooden tub. The water was very hot. She lowered herself slowly until she sat on the bottom with the water up to her neck. "You can turn around now."

Kuma did. Heiko's face scrubbed free of makeup,

124 · Takashi Matsuoka

her long hair wet and unbound, she looked like the little girl he once knew. How unpredictable fate was, how inclined toward tragedy.

Heiko said, "Kawakami's change of heart might have something to do with Genji's grandfather's death and his uncle's disappearance."

"Perhaps," Kuma said. "If those reports are true, then the Okumichi clan is on the brink of disaster. A perfect situation for the cruel kinds of mischief our present employer favors. And speaking of our employer, don't take him lightly. He doesn't trust you."

"He doesn't trust anyone. That's his purpose in life. Distrust."

"He told me to watch you. I think that means he distrusts you more than usual. Be careful, Hei-chan."

"And is someone watching you to make sure you are watching me?"

Kuma laughed. "It's you he distrusts, not me."

"Are you so sure? He's not in the habit of announcing his suspicions to those he suspects." Heiko poured water over her head. "You did check to make sure you weren't followed?"

Kuma jumped to his feet. "Damn. You're right. I should be more careful. I'd better backtrack. Take care of yourself, Hei-chan."

"You, too, Uncle Kuma."

He was in a nostalgic mood all the way back to Edo. How swiftly time passed. The little girl put into his charge fifteen years ago was now a woman of almost unbearable beauty. Uncle Kuma, she called him. She should know the truth. She was old enough now. That would violate his orders, but orders be damned. Kuma smiled to himself. Only a fool acts out of love, she said. Then call me a fool, Kuma thought. During fifteen years of training, he had grown to love Heiko like the daughter he never had. In any conflict between his duty and his love, he had no doubt which would triumph.

Yes, she should know the truth. The next time they were together, he would tell her. It would be difficult for her, very difficult. In a better world, she would never have to know. In the best of worlds, it would not matter at all. But this world was not better, and it was certainly not the best of the countless many. That was Sukhavati, the Pure Land of Amida Buddha. One day, they would all dwell there.

But not today.

• • • • •

Heiko soaked for several minutes after Kuma left. How fragile life was, she thought, how unpredictable. We flatter ourselves, thinking we are actors on a stage, geniuses who write our own plays, extemporize our words, and shift major plot lines and the most subtle of nuances at our every whim. Perhaps wooden Bunraku puppets feel the same way. They do not notice the puppeteers who guide their every move.

Steam rose from the water that immersed her. But she felt a painful coldness in the marrow of her bones. Genji could have died today, and she would not even have known until it was too late.

After her bath, she left her hair down in a long ponytail. She dressed in farmer's clothing, being careful to cover every inch of skin so that her fairness would not be compromised even by the weak winter sunlight. Then she went out into her garden and tilled the soil around the winter melons. When she worked in her garden, she thought of nothing but what she was doing. There were no thoughts of slaughter, or treachery, or love.

The sun was well past midpoint in the sky when she saw four riders approaching from the south.

• • • • •

Genji looked down from his horse. "Honorable farm woman, I was told a famous Edo beauty lives hereabouts. Can you direct me to her abode?"

"Edo is far away," Heiko said, "beauty so fleeting, any abode all too impermanent. May I not instead interest you in some hot soup to ward off the present chill?" She gestured at the garden. "I have made it with these very winter melons." She would never have dressed in such unglamorous fashion had she thought there was the slightest possibility of his coming her way. Outsiders had his complete attention this morning. Genji had gone to the harbor especially to meet them. It was entirely reasonable to expect him to be occupied in the city for the rest of the day. Yet here he was in the afternoon, to all appearances heading into the hills on a hunting expedition, with nary an outsider in sight. Though her embarrassment was great, so was her joy. Genji lived, so did she, and here they were together. After what Kuma had told her this morning, she felt the preciousness of these unexpected moments.

"Your skill with the earth is most impressive," Genji said. "Surely in a world with greater balance and harmony, a woman possessed of such farming arts would be treasured more than one adept merely in the arts of the bedchamber."

"You are too kind, good sir." Heiko bowed deeply to conceal the color that came to her cheeks.

"But let me detain you no longer. Surely you are eager to keep your assignation with your famous lady."

"Winter melon soup or storied beauty," Genji said, "a difficult choice indeed." Her discomfort amused him. She was always so sure of herself. Now here she was out of her finery, hoe in hand, tilling soil like a common peasant. Was this the first time he had ever caught her off guard? He thought it was. He was determined to enjoy it for as long as he could.

"A wise man would always choose the soup," Heiko said, "especially on such a cold day." Genji's smug expression irritated her no end. To let him see that would please him even more. She was not about to increase his satisfaction.

"I wonder. True wisdom would lead to beauty, would it not? What can warm the body and spirit more?" He had caught her in farmer's garb and without makeup, it was true. But was the triumph his? Her lustrous hair flowed down her back like a Heian-era princess's of a thousand years ago. The lack of powder, rouge, and other cosmetic artifices did not diminish her. Instead, her usually concealed natural self emanated a vitality and brightness that astounded him even more than her obvious physical allure.

"I beg to suggest your lordship is misinformed," Heiko said. "Beauty can be colder than the harshest winter's day. It is love, not beauty, that warms."

"Well said, good farm woman." Genji calmed his horse, which grew impatient with the long standstill. "Never have I heard such true words from the mouth of any Edo courtesan. Save one."

"Your lordship is too kind." Heiko smiled at Genji. With that simple compliment, he had restored her dignity.

"It is you who are too kind," Genji said, returning her smile, "and too beautiful to hide yourself away in these Ginza woods. A cavalry captain will shortly come this way with two spare mounts, one for you and one for your maid. I plead with you to go with him to Edo, where you will find a better setting for your talents."

"How can I refuse such generosity?" Heiko said.

"I wonder how long you will think me generous. Among the talents we need is your facility with the English language."

Oh, no! It was all very clear to her now. Some emergency was taking Genji away from his outsider guests. He intended her to be their translator and companion in his absence.

"Farewell, Heiko." He pulled the reins, turning his horse's head in the direction of the New Bridge. "I'll be back within the week."

"Wait! Lord Genji!" Heiko took several steps in his direction. "I have never spoken but a few words of English, and that only with you. How can you leave me alone with outsiders?"

"You are too modest." He smiled. "I have long believed you possess greater facility than you have demonstrated. Now you will have an opportunity to prove me right."

"Lord Genji!"

But he bowed from the saddle, spurred his mount, and was gone at a gallop, followed by his three companions.

When Saiki arrived with two extra horses, Sachiko had already helped Heiko restore her proper appearance. The gruff old samurai said not a word to either of them on the ride back to Edo. It was just as well. Heiko was in too foul a mood for idle conversation.

· · · · ·

That night, Genji and his men took shelter in a farmhouse at the northern edge of the Kanto Plain. The next day, they would enter Yoshino, the territory of Lord Gaiho, one of Genji's sworn enemies.

They had no personal antagonism. Indeed, Genji wasn't sure he would recognize Gaiho on sight. If he strained his memory, he generated a hazy image from which all details were absent. A stout cheerful man about sixty years of age. Or seventy. Was his nose sharp or blunt? His hair dark or gray? Dark, Genji thought, through the use of dye. That would suggest a certain vanity. So Gaiho was vain as well as stout and cheerful. When had they last seen each other? It was nearly three years ago, on the occasion of Tokugawa Iemochi's installation as Shogun. They had been on opposite sides of the room, so Genji had caught no more than a passing glimpse of Gaiho. In truth, he wasn't sure the man he had in mind was Gaiho at all. Yet this stranger would kill Genji on the slightest pretext if he could.

Nothing had happened between their families in their lifetimes, or in the lifetimes of their fathers or their grandfathers or even their grandfathers' fathers. No insults had been given or received, no lovers tragically entangled, no battles fought over territory, influence, or pride. The problem was simple and unitary. It was the same problem for all the clans that ruled the two hundred sixty domains of the nation. The problem was Sekigahara.

Sekigahara was a small village in western Japan of no particular importance. Yet an event that had taken place there in the fourteenth year of the Emperor Go-yozei continued to dominate their lives. On a late autumn morning, as frost fell and fog lifted, two hundred thousand samurai divided into two huge opposing armies collided in a valley near the village. Half of them followed Tokugawa Ieyasu, Great Lord of Kanto. The other half rallied behind the banners of Ishida Mitsunari, Regent of Western Japan.

Genji's ancestor, Nagamasa, sided with Ishida. A month before the battle, it had been revealed to him in a dream that the Tokugawa clan would be shorn of all powers and privileges, including their hereditary Great Lord status. By nightfall, Nagamasa and eighty thousand other samurai were dead, and Ieyasu reigned supreme. He soon became Shogun, and the title would remain in his family to the present day. Genji did not doubt the validity of his ancestor's dream. He had simply not gotten the timing right.

Though Nagamasa died, and the Okumichi clan was on the losing side, they were not utterly destroyed. Enough opponents of the Tokugawas survived to prevent their complete annihilation. For two hundred sixty-one years, they had endured and contemplated revenge. At the same time, the Tokugawa partisans, Gaiho's ancestors among them, had plotted their final destruction. This is what the Japanese had been doing for so long while the outsiders created science and conquered the world. And now, perhaps, while the Japanese continued to fight and refight the same ancient battle, the outsiders would also conquer Japan.

"Sir lord." The farmer came crawling into the room on his knees, his head pushing against the floor like a plow. "Your honorable bath is ready." The man's thin body trembled with fear.

Genji wanted to tell him to get up. This was his home after all, and Genji was no more than an uninvited guest. But he could not say that, of course. He, like the farmer whose house he had requisitioned for the night, was bound to an ancient, unyielding etiquette.

"Thank you," Genji said.

The farmer, still bowing, quickly shuffled out of the way so that the lord could pass without the bother of stepping around his own lowly body. Two hopes filled his fearful heart. The first was that the lord would not find his simple peasant's tub offensive to his person. His wife and daughter had bloodied their hands in the hour since the lord's arrival scrubbing it clean. He offered a silent prayer to Amida Buddha that it was clean enough. His second hope was that the lord, accustomed to the legendary courtesans of Edo, would not take an interest in his daughter. She was fifteen, in the first blossoming of womanhood, and thought to be the beauty of the village. He wished now that she were as homely as Muko's daughter. He offered another silent prayer to Amida Buddha, begging the Compassionate One for protection and mercy through this dangerous night.

Outside, the farmer's youngest son, sweating profusely, wiped down and fed the four horses while Taro watched. There was no suitable food here for the mounts of a lord, so he had run to the neighboring village and begged the headman there for hay. He returned with a fifty-pound bale on his back. He wished his older brother, Shinichi, were here to help. But a month earlier, he had been conscripted into Lord Gaiho's army. Who knew where he was or when he would return home? War was coming. Everyone said so. War against the outsiders. War between the Shogun's supporters and his enemies. Foreign war and civil war at the same time. Thousands, hundreds of thousands, even millions would die. Perhaps Shinichi would be safer in the army than they would be on the farm. Genji stepped from the house. The boy dropped to the ground and buried his face in the dirt.

Hidé and Shimoda stood guard around the bathhouse. Genji found the farmer's wife and daughter inside. They, too, knelt with their heads pressed against the ground. Like the farmer, their bodies trembled fearfully. Had he been a demon from hell, they could not have been more afraid. Come to think of it, to a farmer what difference was there between a demon and a lord?

Genji heard a sob escape from one of the women. Without looking, he knew it was the mother. She assumed, quite naturally, that he would require their assistance in bathing, would notice how nubile the daughter was, and would take her into his bed for the night. That is, if he was possessed of a patient nature. If not, he might take her here, on the ground, even before cleaning himself.

"You may go," Genji said. "I prefer bathing in solitude."

"Yes, sir lord," the mother said, with her daughter echoing a moment after her, "Yes, sir lord." Still on their knees, the two women backed out of the bathhouse.

Late that night, as the family huddled together in the storage shed, they speculated on the nature of the visitor in their house.

"He must be a courtier from the Imperial Capital," the farmer whispered. "He seems too refined to be a warrior."

"Those horses are warhorses," the son said. "They barely tolerated my presence. If that bald-pated samurai hadn't controlled them, they would have kicked me to death when I tried to feed them."

"They may be joining Lord Gaiho's army," the mother said. "I hope they are. The more men he has, the safer our Shinichi will be." She silently repeated a string of mantras to Amida Buddha, counting them off as if she held her precious sandalwood prayer beads in her hands. She missed them, but she was happy about where they were. A holy talisman around her firstborn child Shinichi's neck. Surely they would ward off all evil, attract all good, and keep him safe. He was only sixteen and away from home for the first time.

"It's possible," the father said. "This young lord won't be much help in battle. But his men look strong."

"He could be a prince," the daughter said. "He's handsome enough."

"Silence!" her father hissed, slapping into darkness and connecting with her face.

"Ow!"

"Whoever he is, he's used to taking what he wants. You stay in here until they leave in the morning."

But their four visitors were gone before the sun rose. When the farmer returned to his home, he found a scarf of saffron silk neatly folded and placed on the altar of the family's humble household shrine. When he took it to Edo the next week, he found it was worth more than his share of the previous year's rice harvest.

·   ·   ·   ·   ·   ·

Genji and his men were astride strong horses and they rode them hard. At this pace, they would reach Mushindo Monastery by midday. They had managed to cross nearly the entirety of Yoshino Domain without encountering any of Gaiho's troops. Beyond the next stream was the territory of Genji's friend, Hiromitsu, Great Lord of Yamakawa. Hiromitsu was another man Genji would have trouble recognizing. He was a friend in the same sense, and for the same reason, that Gaiho was an enemy. Hiromitsu's long-ago ancestor had also been on the losing side at Sekigahara.

Rounding the last bend in the road before the border, they encountered five mounted samurai at the head of a column of forty pikemen. These, too, were moving southwest like the others Taro had seen.

Genji slowed to a walking pace, giving the band of soldiers time to move to the side of the road. Though he wore no crest and flew no banner, his mode of dress, the quality of his mount, the demeanor of his companions, all clearly identified him as a lord. Social convention required those of lower rank to yield.

But these men did not. Their leader shouted, "Make way, there!"

Genji reined his horse to a halt. Had he seen the soldiers earlier, he could have led his men out of sight and gone on when the way was clear. But it was too late for that. He could not honorably surrender the right-of-way to an oaf of such low breeding. He sat quietly in the saddle and waited for the obstruction to be cleared.

Hidé spurred his horse forward until he was directly in front of the troop leader. He said, "A man of rank, traveling incognito, honors you with his passage!"

The samurai laughed. "A man of rank? I see no such person. Only four bedraggled wanderers far from where they belong. Leave the road! We travel under orders from Lord Gaiho. We have priority."

"Descend to your proper level!" Hidé was outraged. "Do you not know a lord when you see one?"

"There are lords, and there are lords." Sneering, the samurai put his hand on the double-barreled flintlock pistol in his sash. "Times are changing. The strong rise. Degenerate vestiges of the past will be swept aside."

What happened next happened very quickly.

Hidé didn't say another word. Blurred steel flashed in his hands and traced a thin red line in the leader's body from the left side of his neck to his right armpit. A moment later, the man's torso split in two and blood spewed into the air in every direction.

The blood-splattered samurai next to the falling corpse reached for his sword. Before an inch of blade showed in his scabbard, Shimoda's arrow whirred into his heart and he, too, fell from the saddle.

"Aaaiiiii!" Taro, sword out to the side like a scythe, kicked his horse into a charge at the opposing formation.

One of the remaining mounted samurai waved his sword in the air and called out commands. "Form battle ranks! Form bahhhgghhh...!" He clutched the arrow that suddenly blossomed in his throat, dropped his sword, and toppled from his horse.

The column of pikemen broke, flinging their weapons aside and screaming in panic. Most of them fled into the woods. A less fortunate handful turned and ran down the road. These were the ones Taro pursued. He whipped his blade to the left and right of his horse's head as he galloped through their midst. Dirt turned to bloody mud in his wake.

Another samurai, fleeing, took an arrow high in his spine.

Hidé crashed through the remaining horseman's weak parry and sliced open his jugular vein.

Taro wheeled and charged back the way he had come. The last man standing threw up his arms to shield himself from death and screamed a final time.

Genji sighed. It was over. He urged his horse past the bodies littering the road. All these lives squandered. For what? A breach of etiquette? A congested road? An accident of history? Even without the assurance of a prophetic vision, Genji was certain such senseless violence would not be part of the world to come. It couldn't be.

Shimoda glanced at the first dead man. He said to Hidé, "What did he say that made you cut him down so swiftly?"

"He said, 'Times are changing.'" Hidé wiped his blade clean. "Then the wretch made an insulting remark about 'vestiges of the past.'"

Shimoda said, "Times aren't changing, they're decaying. Such arrogance from men of low birth. Only seven years ago, this disgrace could not have occurred." Seven years ago was when the American Commodore Perry had sailed into Edo Bay with his steamships and cannons.

"We did them a favor." Taro shook off the bloody gristle clinging to his sword. "We saved them a futile journey. Wherever they were going, whomever they were fighting, they would have been defeated. What useless cowards."

Hidé said, "The outsiders are destroying us

without a battle. Their mere existence makes us lose our way."

Genji looked at each of the dead as he rode by. The last one, the tenth, stared lifelessly at the clear winter sky, his skull split open. His right forearm remained connected to his elbow by some shattered bone and a stringy tendon. His left arm ended at the wrist. The hand had fallen near his feet. He wasn't really a man at all. The face belonged to a youth barely past childhood, no more than fifteen or sixteen. Around his neck was a string of wooden prayer beads. An amulet of hope. Into each small piece of sandalwood was carved a *sauvastika,* the Buddhist symbol of infinity.

"The outsiders aren't at fault," Genji said. "The blame is ours alone."

The incident was unfortunate, but it had its good side. Hidé, Shimoda, and Taro had shown their mettle. Genji was pleased to be such a good judge of character.

5

Visionaries

Knowledge may hinder. Ignorance may liberate.
Knowing when to know and when not to know, this
is as important as a fluent blade.

SUZUME–NO–KUMO
(1434)

After five days with the outsiders, Heiko understood them much better. Especially Mr. Stark.
He spoke with a drawl that lengthened the vowels
and slowed the flow of words, making the language
easier to follow. Miss Gibson's words were more
clipped and rapid. And Reverend Cromwell, well,
even when Heiko recognized the words, she often
didn't understand the way they were put together.
Mr. Stark and Miss Gibson both responded as if he
made sense, but Heiko thought it likely they were
only being polite to the wounded man.

Reverend Cromwell slept most of the time, his
closed eyes twitching madly. When awake, he tended
toward frenzy, and would not be calmed without

Miss Gibson's constant and most gentle ministrations. Dr. Ozawa's visits seemed particularly disturbing to him. Perhaps the doctor's demeanor revealed the meaning of the Japanese words.

"Half his intestines and stomach have rotted away," Dr. Ozawa said. "The damage to his vital organs is grievous. Poisonous bile pollutes his blood. Still, he breathes. I must admit, I am at a loss."

"What does the doctor say?" Miss Gibson asked.

"He says Reverend Cromwell is very strong," Heiko said. "Though he cannot predict what will happen, his condition is stable, which is promising."

Cromwell pointed at the doctor. "Ye ought to say, If the Lord will, we shall live, and do this, or that."

"Amen," Miss Gibson and Mr. Stark said.

Dr. Ozawa gave Heiko a questioning look.

"He expressed gratitude for your care," Heiko said, "and said a prayer of his own religion for your well-being."

"Ah." Dr. Ozawa bowed to Reverend Cromwell. "Thank you, honorable outsider priest."

"Thou child of the devil, thou enemy of all righteousness."

Heiko's opinion, which she expressed to no one, was that Reverend Cromwell had been driven mad by his injuries. That would explain why he said what he did. No sane person would curse someone who was doing his best to care for him.

While Heiko understood the outsiders much better after five days, she still didn't understand why Genji had sent her to be with them. The apparent purpose was obvious; she was to keep them company, translate for them, reduce their isolation in his absence. It also left her free to thoroughly investigate them in a way that would otherwise have been impossible. That was the part she didn't understand. Only a person Genji trusted completely should be in this position. But trust had to be based on knowledge, and he knew almost nothing about her. Heiko had a fully elaborated past waiting to be discovered. A place of birth, parents, childhood friends, older geisha mentors, key events, significant locales. Facts expertly layered to hide the most important one—that she was an agent of the Shogun's secret police. Everything awaited serious inquiry. Yet Genji had shown no interest except in who she seemed to be. In the devious world of Great Lords, only very young children were who they seemed to be. If he really trusted her, he was showing suicidally poor judgment. Since that was highly unlikely, she came back to the same conclusion again and again.

Genji knew who she was.

How he knew, she had no idea. It could be that the rumors about the Okumichis were true, that one in every generation foresaw the future. If he was the one, then he would know something she didn't— whether she would betray him or not. Did his trust mean that she would not? Or that she would and he fatalistically accepted this outcome?

The irony did not escape her. Her suspicion and confusion were heightened by the apparent lack of the same on his part. Did some truly arcane deception lie hidden under the appearance of his trust? For five days, Heiko pondered the matter, and not even the shadow of an answer appeared. She was completely baffled.

"A penny for your thoughts." Miss Gibson smiled at her. They were sitting in a room facing the inner courtyard. Since the day was unseasonably mild, all the sliding doors were open, almost making the space into a kind of garden pavilion.

"A penny?" Heiko said.

"A penny is our smallest coin."

"Our smallest coin is the sen." Heiko knew Miss Gibson wasn't actually offering to pay her for her thoughts. "You are asking me what I am thinking?"

Again Miss Gibson smiled. In Japan, homely women smiled more often than pretty ones. It was a natural, ingratiating effort that apparently was practiced by homely American women, too. Miss Gibson smiled very freely. Heiko thought that was a good habit. It emphasized her personality and took attention away from her awkwardness. "Awkward" hardly began to describe the American woman's unfortunate lack of physical gifts. But as Heiko had gotten to know her, she had begun to develop an affection for the kind, gentle person inside the repulsive, unwieldy husk.

"That would be impolite," Miss Gibson said. "When I say 'A penny for your thoughts,' I acknowledge that you appear thoughtful, and I offer to listen if you wish to speak. That is all."

"Ah, thank you." Heiko herself also smiled very freely. That was the secret of her charm. While the rest of Edo's famous geisha maintained a haughty air, Heiko, the most beautiful of them all, smiled as often as the plainest farm girl. But only for those she favored. It was as if, in their presence, she felt her beauty to count for nothing, that her heart, undefended, undisguised, was theirs. It was all an act, of course, and everyone knew it. The act was so effective, however, that men were happy to pay for it. Only with Genji was it not an act. She hoped he didn't realize it. If he did, then he would know she loved him, and if he knew that, all balance would be gone. Perhaps he did know, and that is why he trusted her. Back to that again. What was Genji thinking?

Heiko said, "I was thinking how hard it must be for you, Miss Gibson. Your fiancé is injured. You are far from home and family. A most difficult situation for a woman, yes?"

"Yes, Heiko. A most difficult situation." Emily closed the book she had been reading. Sir Walter Scott had been her mother's favorite author, and among his books she had practically worshipped *Ivanhoe*. Apart from her locket, it was the only possession of hers Emily had kept when the farm was sold. How often since then had she read her mother's treasured passages, recalled her voice, and wept, in the solitude of school, mission, ship, and now, here in this lonely place so far from the graves of her loved ones. She was glad she had not been crying when Heiko appeared. "Please, call me Emily. It is only fair, since I call you Heiko. Or you can tell me your family name and I will call you Miss, too."

"I have no family name," Heiko said. "I am not of noble birth."

"I beg your pardon?" This took Emily by surprise. It was like the condition of the bondsmen in *Ivanhoe*. But that was hundreds of years ago, during the blighted Dark Ages of Europe. "Didn't I hear a servant calling you another name, a longer one?"

"Mayonaka no Heiko, yes. That is my full geisha name. It means 'Midnight Equilibrium.' "

"What is a geeshaw name?" Emily asked.

"Geisha," Heiko said slowly.

"Geisha," Emily repeated.

"Yes, that is right," Heiko said. She thought

about what she had read in Genji's English dictionary. "Your closest word is probably 'prostitute.' "

Emily was so shocked she couldn't even speak. *Ivanhoe* fell from her lap. She bent down to pick up the book, grateful for an opportunity to look away from Heiko. She hardly knew what to think. All along, she had assumed her hostess was a highborn lady, a relative of Lord Genji. It seemed to her that all the servants and the samurai treated Heiko with the greatest deference. Had she missed something mocking in their behavior?

"Surely there is some error in the translation," Emily said, her cheeks still flushed with embarrassment.

"Yes, perhaps," Heiko said. Miss Gibson, or Emily, as she now asked to be called, had surprised her as much as she had apparently surprised Emily. What had she said that was so unsettling?

"I knew there had to be." Emily felt greatly relieved to hear this. To her, a prostitute was one of those alcohol-drenched, disease-ridden slatterns who had occasionally taken refuge at the mission house in San Francisco. This elegant young woman, barely more than a child, could hardly be more different.

When Emily dropped her book, Heiko had been seeking the right English words to explain the different classes of female companions. There was one for every stratum of society. At bottom were the artless purveyors of simple sexual relief. The barred warrens of the Yoshiwara pleasure district were full of these, mostly peasant girls indentured to pay off family debts. At the top were a select few geisha like herself, nurtured from childhood, who carefully chose with whom they spent their time and in what manner; her company and her favors could be paid for, but only if she was willing, for neither could be compelled. In between, there were nearly infinite gradations of cost, services, talent, and beauty. Seeing Emily's continuing discomfort, Heiko hesitated. She had assumed that everything in Japan had its counterpart in America, and vice versa. The words would be different because the languages were different, but the underlying essence would be the same. People everywhere were driven by the same needs and desires. So she had thought.

"In America, some well-bred ladies become governesses," Emily said, still struggling against the implications of Heiko's words. "A governess instructs the children of a household in manners, looks after their welfare, even sometimes tutors them in certain subjects. Might this not be what you meant?"

"A geisha is not a governess," Heiko said. "A geisha is a female companion of the highest order. If I did not use the right word, then please teach me, Emily."

Emily looked into Heiko's open gaze. It was her Christian duty to be honest, no matter how painful the truth. She said, "We have no equal word, Heiko. In Christian countries, such work is not considered honorable; indeed, is against the law."

"There are no prostitutes in America?"

"There are," Emily said, "because of human frailty. But prostitutes must hide from the police and rely upon vicious criminals for protection and sustenance. Their lives are shortened by violence, addictions, and diseases." She took a deep breath. Any cohabitation outside of marriage was a sin, but surely there were degrees of wrongdoing? She couldn't believe that Heiko actually meant to say she was a prostitute. "Sometimes a rich and powerful man will have a mistress. A woman whom he loves, but who is not his wife under the law or in the eyes of God. Perhaps 'mistress' is a closer word than 'prostitute.' "

Heiko thought not. "Mistress" and "concubine" were much alike, and neither was quite as close to "geisha" as "prostitute." There was something strangely hesitant in Emily's whole attitude toward the subject. What was the cause? Was it possible that she herself had been a prostitute, and was ashamed of her past? She could not have been the equivalent of a geisha, of course. No matter how great her skills and charms, they could not overcome her dreadful appearance.

"Perhaps," Heiko said. "Let us ask Lord Genji when he returns. His understanding is deeper than mine."

Emily was saved from having to reply to this outrageous suggestion by Brother Matthew's arrival.

"Brother Zephaniah is asking for you," he said.

* * * * * *

"You mean to tell me my uncle has been in the armory for the past four days?" Genji did his best to keep from smiling. Abbot Sohaku's embarrassment was plain to see.

"Yes, lord," Sohaku said. "We made three attempts to recapture him. The first time, I got this." He pointed to the raised welt across his forehead. "If he had used a real sword instead of a wooden one, I would have been spared the dishonor of living to give you this report."

"Don't be so hard on yourself, Reverend Abbot."

Sohaku glumly went on. "The second time, he

seriously injured four of my men, rather, the monks. One of them is still in a coma, and will probably not recover. The third time, we went in with bows and arrows made of green bamboo. Not the best, but good enough, I thought, to sufficiently disable him. He perched there on the powder barrels, grinning, with a lit fuse in his hand. We made no further attempts."

Genji sat on a small dais under a tent fifty paces from the armory. The monks who were not on guard sat in ranks before him, looking less like monks and more like samurai awaiting his command. Six months ago, his grandfather had secretly ordered his best cavalrymen into the monastery. They supposedly left the world behind in protest against his befriending of True Word missionaries. The idea, of course, was to keep his enemies guessing. Who, seeing these men of obvious martial mien, would ever be fooled into thinking they had become world-leaving monks?

"Well, I suppose I should go and talk to him." He rose from the dais and went to the armory, followed by Hidé and Shimoda. Mutterings came from the other side of the barricade. "Uncle, it's Genji. I'm coming in." He gestured at the barricade and his men began removing the obstructions. The inside of the armory became very quiet.

"Lord, please be careful," Hidé said softly. "Taro told us Lord Shigeru is completely deranged."

Genji slid the door open. A hot miasmic stench flooded from the interior and washed over him. He reeled backward.

"Forgive me," Sohaku said, offering a perfumed scarf. "I have grown so accustomed to his condition, I didn't think to warn you."

Genji waved off Sohaku's offer. He would have liked to use it, but with his face covered, Shigeru might not recognize him. Disregarding the way the foul odors twisted his stomach, he stood again in the doorway. Shigeru squatted like a monkey deep in the shadows of the shuttered space, covered in his own filth. Only the long blades he held in his two hands were pristine. They gleamed so brightly, they could have been emitting their own light.

"I am very disappointed to see you in such unclean condition." Genji spoke very gently. "On the one hand, I am only your nephew. On the other, I am your liege, Great Lord of Akaoka Domain. As your nephew, I am obligated to visit you where you are. As your liege, I cannot permit myself to tolerate such filth. As your nephew, I beg you to look to your health. As your liege, I command you to present yourself to me within the hour, with an explanation for this highly inappropriate behavior."

He turned away from his uncle and slowly went down the steps. If Shigeru didn't attack him during the next heartbeat or two, there was an excellent chance his command would be obeyed.

Genji's form, silhouetted in the doorway, began to shrink. His back was exposed! Now! It was time to complete the purification of the Okumichi bloodline. Shigeru's muscles tensed and released. He leaped forward silently and at high speed. Or at least, his body did. His fractured mind, filled with leakages as it was, went elsewhere, and at its own distorted pace.

Shigeru was with his father. They were astride horses on the edge of the cliffs at Cape Muroto. Lord Kiyori was younger than the Shigeru in the armory, and Shigeru was as young as his own son at the time of his death.

"You will speak of things to come," his father said. "You will see them as clearly as you see the waves below."

"When, Father?" Shigeru asked. He could hardly wait. His older brother, Yorimasa, might rule Akaoka Domain after their father, but if Shigeru was the one with the vision, he was the one who would be respected the way Lord Kiyori was. Yorimasa wouldn't be so arrogant then, would he?

"Not for a long time, and be glad of it."

"Why should I be glad?" Shigeru pouted. This was not what he wanted to hear. It only meant Yorimasa would continue to lord it over him. "The sooner I can see the future, the better."

His father looked at him for a long time before speaking again.

"Don't be impatient, Shigeru. What will happen will happen, whether you know of it or not. Believe me, it is not always better to know."

"Knowing must be better," Shigeru said. "Then no one can take you by surprise."

"Someone will always take you by surprise, because no matter how much you know, you can never know everything."

"When, Father? When will I see things to come?"

Again his father looked at him in silence. Shigeru thought he wasn't going to say another word, but he did.

"Cherish the days before then, Shigeru. You will be very happy. In the flower of your manhood, you will fall in love with a woman of great virtue and resolve. It will be your good fortune that she will fall in love with you as well." His father continued to smile, though tears now streamed down his face.

"You will have a strong, brave son and two beautiful daughters."

Shigeru didn't care about any of that. He was six years old. He didn't dream of love. He didn't dream of sons and daughters. He dreamed of being a real samurai like his glorious ancestors.

"Will I win many battles, Father? Will other men fear me?"

"You will win many battles, Shigeru." His father wiped away his tears with the wide sleeve of his kimono. "Other men will fear you. They will fear you very much."

"Thank you, Father." Shigeru was very happy. He had received a prophecy! He promised himself he would always remember this propitious day, the sound of the waves, the feel of the wind, the movement of the clouds across the sky.

"Listen to me, Shigeru. This is very important." His father reached over and gripped his shoulder. "When your visions begin, someone will come to visit you. Your first impulse will be to kill him. Do not strike. Stop. Look into your mind. Pay attention to what is there." His father's grip tightened. "Will you remember to do this?"

"Yes, I will, I promise," Shigeru said, frightened by his father's intensity.

Now, with his sword thrusting at Genji, that promise made long ago illuminated Shigeru's being. In the next instant, a keen blade the length of a man's arm would plunge into Genji's back, sever his spine, perforate his heart, and burst out of his chest. Shigeru looked into the sudden brightness of his mind and saw what he least expected.

Nothing.

Shigeru stopped. He had taken just one step

toward the doorway. Genji had just turned away. An instant had passed, no more.

Shigeru listened. He heard nothing except the slight sound from Genji's footsteps and the songs of the birds in the woods. He looked. He saw only the inside of the armory, Genji's back, the doorway-framed view of the monastery's courtyard.

The visions were gone.

Was it coincidence, or had Genji's presence somehow canceled them out? He didn't know. He didn't care. His killing drive had vanished with the visions.

He let the swords fall from his hands and walked out the front door. The two samurai on each side moved back a few paces and bowed. He noticed they kept their hands on the hilts of their swords and their eyes on him as they did so. Shigeru began stripping off his clothes as he walked around to the back of the kitchen, where the bathhouse was.

"Where's Sohaku?" Shigeru asked the samurai who followed him. "Tell him I need to borrow clothing appropriate for an audience with Lord Genji."

The samurai said, "Yes, sir," but kept following him.

Shigeru stopped and the samurai stopped. "Go ahead, do as I say." He dropped the last of his clothes onto the ground. They would be burned. No amount of washing would make them clean again. Shigeru spread his arms. "What do you think? That I'm going to run away like this, naked and covered with shit in the middle of winter? Only a madman would do that." He laughed and continued on. He didn't look back to see if the samurai followed.

When he got to the bathhouse, he was not surprised to see the tub already filled with steaming water. Genji had always been an optimistic lad.

Shigeru washed himself thoroughly three times outside the tub. Only when he was certain of his cleanliness did he lower himself into the water with a sigh of pleasure. He had not had a bath for how long? Days, weeks, months? He couldn't remember. It would have been extremely enjoyable to soak in the soft heat for a length of time. Under other circumstances, that is exactly what he would do. But his lord awaited him. Shigeru heaved himself out of the water.

Steam rose from his body as if he were a volcanic vent in the earth. New sandals had been placed on the ground. He put these on his feet, threw a towel around his body, and went into the residence wing of the temple. There, two monks helped him into his borrowed clothing. Extending from his shoulders were the stiff wings of the *kamishimo* jacket he wore over his kimono. Over the bottom of the kimono, he wore wide-legged *hakama* pants. The formality of the attire was just right for an audience with his lord in the field. He was almost ready.

"Where are my swords?"

The two monks looked at each other.

At last, one of them said, "Lord, we were not told to bring you weapons."

Both monks were tense, as if they expected a violent reaction. But Shigeru just nodded meekly. Of course, after all that he had done, he would not be permitted anywhere near Genji with weapons. He followed the monks out to where his lord waited.

"Stop," Genji said.

Shigeru halted. Perhaps he was not even to enter the tent. He did not see another place set up for his execution. That didn't necessarily mean anything. Genji may have decided against a formal act. The two samurai who had accompanied the lord from Edo might simply cut him down here and now.

Genji turned to Sohaku and said, "How dare you allow an honored retainer into my presence half naked."

"Lord Genji," Sohaku said, "I beg you to be cautious. Five of my men have been killed or maimed at his hands."

Genji stared straight ahead in silence.

Sohaku, having no other choice, bowed to him, then nodded to Taro. Taro ran off to the armory and returned with two swords, the long katana and the shorter wakizashi. He bowed to Shigeru and presented the weapons to him.

As Shigeru placed them in his sash, Sohaku shifted his seated posture ever so slightly. When Shigeru drew his sword against Genji, Sohaku would throw his body in harm's way. This would give Hidé and Shimoda, the only other armed samurai in attendance, a chance to kill Shigeru, if they could. At least, they would impede him, and the monks could swarm him en masse before he reached Genji. Although Sohaku was abbot of a Zen temple, he did not find much comfort in Zen. Zen taught one how to live and how to die. It said nothing about the afterlife. Now that he was about to leave this world for the next, Sohaku said a prayer of the Honganji Buddhist faith in the silence of his heart. Namu Amida Butsu. May the blessings of the Buddha of Infinite Light be upon me. May the Compassionate One show me the way to the Pure Land. Even as he prayed, Sohaku watched Shigeru's every step toward their seated lord.

Shigeru knelt upon the mat before the dais and bowed deeply. This was the first time he had seen his nephew since the rule of Akaoka Domain had passed into his hands. Normally, such a meeting would be a highly formal one, in which there would be an exchange of gifts, and Shigeru, like every vassal, would pledge his life and the lives of his family to the service of the lord. But this was far from a normal occasion. For one thing, Genji was now lord because Shigeru had poisoned the previous one, his own father. For another, he had no family to pledge, since he had butchered them all three weeks earlier. He kept his head pressed against the mat. He didn't know what else to do. This was a trial. It had to be. He kept his head down and awaited the sentence of death.

"Well, Uncle," Genji said softly, "let's get this over with so we can really talk." In a louder, more regal voice, he said, "Okumichi Shigeru, for what reason did you seize control of the armory of this temple?"

Shigeru raised his head. His mouth dropped open in astonishment. Why was Genji talking about such a trivial matter?

Genji nodded as if Shigeru had spoken. "I see. And what led you to believe the arms were not properly secured?"

"Lord." Only the one choked word came out of Shigeru's throat.

"Well done," Genji said. "Your zeal in protecting our weapons is an inspiration to us all. Now, for the next matter. As you know, I have received the high honor of ascending to the sovereignty of our ancestral domain. All other vassals have sworn their allegiance to me. Do you do so now, or do you not?"

Shigeru turned to the assembly. Their faces were as astonished as his own. Sohaku in particular looked as though he were in the throes of a heart seizure.

Genji leaned forward. Again he spoke softly. "Uncle, make the usual move and we can finish."

Shigeru bowed down to the mat again. Then he lifted his head and reached for his swords.

The entire gathering rose to its feet as one, and as one leaned in his direction. All but Genji.

His voice was angry. "You men came here to practice the ways of the Zen masters of old, to clear your minds of delusion, and to see the world as it really is. Yet you twitch and jump around like lice-infested outcasts. What have you been doing for the past half year?" He glared at them until they resumed their seats.

Shigeru pulled his swords from his sash, scabbards and all. Bowing and raising his weapons above his head, he walked on his knees to the foot of the dais. It was all he had to offer in the way of a gift. He could think of nothing to say, so he said nothing.

"Thank you," Genji said. He took the swords and placed them on the dais to his left. Then he turned to the right and picked up another set of swords. Shigeru recognized them right away. They had been crafted by the great sword smith Kunimitsu, late in the Kamakura period. No one had worn them since the carnage at Sekigahara, when they were recovered from their ancestor Nagamasa's dying hands.

"A time of great danger is upon us." Genji held the swords out to Shigeru in both his hands. "All karmic debts will be paid. Will you stand with me in the battles to come?"

Not since he was a child had Shigeru's hands

shaken when holding a weapon. They shook now as he accepted the totem blades.

"I will, Lord Genji." Shigeru held their ancestor's swords high, and bowed low.

Dread chilled Sohaku's blood. His lord had just accepted the allegiance of a man who, with his own bloody hands, had brought their ancient lineage to the brink of extinction. A murderer of father, wife, and offspring. The most unpredictable, most dangerously volatile lunatic in all the domains of Japan.

With one inexplicable act, Lord Genji had doomed himself and all who followed him.

. . . . .

Emily sat at Zephaniah's bedside. His hand in hers was cold and heavy. It was also more rigid than it had been an hour ago. His face was as smooth and carefree as a sleeping infant's, and as gray as a stone carving of one. Perfumed sheets enfolded him. In the four corners of the room, sandalwood incense burned constantly. They did not diminish the putrid fumes rising from the decaying flesh. The malodorous presence was made heavier instead, more cloying, more suffocating, by the futile aromatic cloak. She trembled, on the verge of nausea, and fought down the bile that rose in her throat.

"It has been given to me in a visioning," Cromwell said. He no longer felt any pain. Indeed, he no longer felt his body at all. His senses had been reduced from five to two. He saw Emily floating above him, radiant. Her hair, bright as spun gold, formed a halo around her exquisite face. He heard the rolling thunder of the approaching angelic host. "I shall not die of this wound."

"You are blessed, Zephaniah." Emily smiled at

him. If the thought brought him comfort, she was glad for him. He had spent the previous night screaming in wordless agony. His present calm was a welcome change.

"Angels are not like us," Cromwell said, "better humans in form, with white wings. No, not at all. They are inconceivable. Brighter than the sun. Explosive. Deafening." At last the words of Revelation were being made clear to him. "By fire, and by smoke, and by brimstone. As it was written, so shall it be. Murders, sorceries, fornications, thefts. This place is cursed with them. When the angels come, the righteous shall be lifted up, the unrepentant burned, torn apart, buried."

Emily marveled at the quiet conversational way in which Zephaniah said these wild words. His normal manner, before the shooting, had been considerably more strident and hysterical. Then sweat burst full and sudden upon his brow; his bulging eyes bulged out yet more; veins in his neck and forehead filled up, in appearance near bursting; spittle flew from his lips, along with loud words and hot breath. Now he was at peace.

"Then let us pray that all repent," she said, "for who among us has not cause for it?"

• • • • •

Lucas Gibson owned a farm in Apple Valley, fifteen miles north of Albany, New York. He met Charlotte Dupay, a distant cousin from New Orleans, at his grandfather's funeral in Baltimore. Lucas, handsome, stolid, reliable beyond his years, was twenty-two at the time. Charlotte, who, like many Southern girls of her generation, read far too much Scott for her own good, was a feverishly romantic golden beauty of fourteen. Thinking she had met her Ivanhoe, she went as a virgin bride to one hundred fifty acres of apples, pigs, and chickens. Their first child, Emily, was born nine months and a day after the wedding. By then, Charlotte had already given up on her good Saxon knight and was beginning to dream, almost against her will, of the evil but wildly passionate Templar, de Bois-Guilbert.

When Emily herself was fourteen years old, her father was killed in an accident in the apple orchard. He had fallen from a ladder. This was rather curious, since he was famed for his balance among the pickers and had never fallen before, not once, in Emily's memory. Also curious was the condition of his body. The back of his skull had been crushed with such force that the shattered bones were driven inward. While it was conceivable that a man could die in a fifteen-foot fall, it was hard to believe that his head would hit the ground so hard. Yet there it was. Her father was dead, her mother was widowed, she and her two younger brothers were half orphaned.

Before grass sprouted over her father's grave, the farm foreman began spending his nights in her mother's bedroom. The wedding itself didn't take place until six months of mourning had passed. By then her mother's belly was swollen with child. The beatings began soon after. The loud cries of passion that had punctuated the night became screams of pain and terror.

"No! Jed, please! Jed! Don't! Don't! I beg you!"

Emily and her brothers huddled together in her bed and wept. They never heard a sound from their stepfather, only their mother's terrified voice. Sometimes, in the morning, her mother's face would be bruised. At first, she tried to hide her injuries from her children, with powder, or a bandage, or a tale of a misstep in the darkness.

"I'm so clumsy," she would say.

But it grew worse, and no powder, bandage, or story could conceal the truth. Her nose was broken, and broken again. Her lips were smashed and swollen. She lost her front teeth. There were days she couldn't walk without a limp and days when she couldn't rise from bed. The baby was delivered stillborn. In one agonizing year, her beautiful mother became a crippled old hag.

They were no longer invited to community gatherings. The neighbors stopped coming to call. The best pickers would not work for them. Their orchard, which had once produced the sweetest apples in the valley, began to die.

Then their stepfather started on them.

Her brothers were whipped with a thick leather razor strop until their buttocks bled. If their legs weakened and they couldn't stand, he would tie them over an apple barrel, and whip them more. They were punished for not doing their chores, or doing them poorly, or not feeding the chickens, or feeding them too much, or leaving bad apples in a barrel of good ones, ruining them all. It was hard to say what the punishments were for. Their stepfather never said.

Emily alone remained untouched. When she treated her brothers' injuries, they asked her why. Why were they beaten? Why was she not? She didn't know. Fear and guilt tore at her heart with equal ferocity.

On the eve of her fifteenth birthday, Emily was alone in the children's bedroom. Her brothers had been locked in the cellar for a week, sentenced there for an unknown infraction. She had heard them crying until two days ago. Her mother was abed, delirious from an infection of an old, unhealed wound. Emily had just changed into her nightgown when she saw her stepfather standing in the doorway. How long had he been there? Long enough to have seen her unclothed? More and more often, she found him behind her when he should not have been. His eyes were bright and staring, as if inflamed with fever.

"Good night," she said, and climbed into bed. He had asked her to call him by his given name, Jed. Though it was dangerous to disobey him in any way, she couldn't bring herself to say his name. She closed her eyes, praying silently that he would leave, as he had always done so far.

This time, he did not.

When it was over, he clutched her hard and wept. Why did he weep? She didn't know. She hurt in a strange way. But she didn't cry. She couldn't. She didn't know why.

She must have fallen asleep, because she awoke to flickering candlelight and her mother's grotesquely deformed face.

"Emily, Emily, my dearest Emily." Her mother was crying.

Emily looked down at herself and saw that she was lying in blood. Was she killed? Somehow, that prospect did not frighten her. It would be a deliverance.

Her mother cleaned her with a warm towel and clothed her in her Sunday best. She had not worn the dress in a long time. They no longer went to church. It was too tight now around her hips and bosom, but she was glad to wear it. Her father had always said it was her prettiest dress.

"Go to the Partons' farm," her mother said. "Give Mrs. Parton this letter."

Emily begged her mother to come with her, to rescue her brothers from the cellar, to flee together and never return.

"Tom and Walt," her mother said, shaking her head. "I must pay for my sins. God forgive me, I never meant harm to befall the innocent. It was love. I was blinded by love."

Her mother wrapped Emily in her own best coat and sent her on her way. It was very late. The moon had set. Only the bright spring starlight lit her way.

When she reached the Partons' farm, the sky behind her was brightening. She wondered why dawn was breaking in the west, and turned. Plumes of flame consumed her home and rose high into the air.

The Partons took her in. They were a kindly old couple who had grown up with her grandfather. They had known her father from the day he was born until the day he died. She never asked about her mother's letter, and they never spoke of it to her. But not long after, she overheard their conversation.

"I always knew it was no accident," Mr. Parton said. "That boy could climb as sure as an African ape before he could walk."

"She was too passionate," Mrs. Parton said. "She had too much emotion in her."

"And she was too beautiful, too. They say beauty is in the eye of the beholder, and so should it be. When a woman's beauty is so obvious that everyone can see it, it is not a good thing. Men are weak, easily tempted."

"That is a danger we have adopted," Mrs. Parton said. "The daughter is like the mother. Have you seen the way the men look at her? Even our own good sons?"

"And who is to blame?" Mr. Parton said. "She is but a child, yet has the face and form of a Babylonian harlot."

"The curse runs through the female line," Mrs. Parton said. "What are we to do?"

One night, a dream of fiery death awakened her. She saw shadows looming in the darkness, and thought the vengeful demons had followed her from her sleep. When they crept closer to her bed, she recognized the Partons' three sons, Bob, Mark, and Alan.

They moved swiftly then, before she could rise or speak. Hands were everywhere. Holding her down, covering her mouth, tearing at her clothes, touching her.

"It's not our fault," Bob said. "It's you."

"You're too beautiful," Mark said.

"This is nothing you haven't done before," Alan said. "You have no virtue to lose."

"Put the gag in her mouth," Bob said.

"Tie her," Mark said.

"If you're quiet, we won't hurt you," Alan said.

It was her fault. It was all her fault. Her father's death, her mother's destruction, her brothers' innocent suffering. She stopped struggling.

They sat her up and lifted off her nightgown.

They pushed her down and pulled away her underpants.

"Harlot," Bob said.

"I love you," Mark said.

"Don't make a sound," Alan said.

The door burst open and the room filled with

light. Mrs. Parton's staring eyes burned more brightly than the lantern she held.

"It's not our fault," Bob said.

"Get out," Mrs. Parton hissed.

The three slouching boys gave her a wide berth as they went from the room.

When they were gone, Mrs. Parton stepped up to the bed. She drew her hand back and slapped Emily so hard her ears rang and her vision went white. The old woman spun on her heels and left without a word.

Mr. Parton returned from a trip to Albany the next day. The following week, Emily was sent to a parochial school in Rochester with the proceeds from the sale of her family's farm. No one came to visit her. On holidays, she alone among the girls remained at the school. She rarely left the campus. On excursions, she did her best to remain hidden within the group. Still, she was unable to escape the gaze of men. She saw them looking at her with those eyes. Her stepfather's eyes. The Parton boys' eyes. The eyes of men seizing her.

Once, during a school visit to the museum, a young man came up to her. He was very polite. He bowed and said, "May I say, miss, you are more beautiful than any treasure in these collections." He seemed surprised when she fled. She knew what it was. He wasn't to blame. None of them were. The fault was hers. There was something in her appearance that eroded men's restraint.

Was it really beauty, as they always seemed to say? Mary Ellen was more beautiful than she. All the girls agreed. Men thought she was beautiful, too, and paid her much attention. Except when Emily was present. Then they looked only at her.

Mary Ellen didn't like Emily. None of the girls did. If not for the headmaster, Mr. Cromwell, her life at the school would have been utter misery. He protected her with the power of his intimidating personality and the words of the prophets.

"Let none of you imagine evil against his brother in your heart," he would say, his fearsome eyes bulging.

"Amen," the girls would answer.

"The wolf and the lamb shall feed together, and the lion shall eat straw like the bullock."

"Amen."

"Thou shalt love they neighbor as thyself."

"Amen."

"Mary Ellen."

"Yes, sir?"

"I didn't hear you."

"I said 'amen,' sir."

"I heard you in my ear, not in my heart. Speak it with your very soul, girl. The word said truly is your salvation! Mouthed like a hollow thing, it is your eternal damnation!" His voice would grow louder and louder, the veins would rise in his forehead and neck, and his arms would wave like the wings of an avenging angel. "Mary Ellen, say 'amen'!"

"Amen, sir! Amen!"

"Did not He that made me in the womb make him?!"

"Amen!" the girls would reply, their voices, too, more frantic.

"Have we not all one Father? Hath not one God created us?!"

"Amen!"

"Behold, how good and how pleasant it is for brethren to dwell together in unity!"

"Amen!"

Mr. Cromwell never stood too close to her. He never tried to touch her. He never told her she was beautiful. He never looked at her the way other men did. His eyes would bulge and his veins would pop up, the same way they did whenever he was thinking of the words of the prophets. He was the one man she trusted, because he was the one man who did not desire her.

That day in the museum, it was Mr. Cromwell who came looking for her after she ran from the handsome stranger's compliment. He found her huddled in a corner among a display of artifacts from some faraway Asian land.

"Get up, child, get up."

He didn't try to force her to her feet. When she failed to rise right away, he turned his attention to the exhibit.

"Japan," he said. "A heathen land of murderers, idolaters, sodomites." The tone of his voice surprised her. Though his words were harsh, he spoke them with affection rather than condemnation. "They are ripe for conversion, Emily, ready to hear the True Word, I know they are. I will publish the name of the Lord; ascribe ye greatness unto our God." He looked down at her, waiting.

"Amen," she said.

"Hear the word of the Lord, O ye nations, and declare it in the isles afar off."

"Amen."

"These are the isles afar off of which the Old Testament speaks. The isles of Japan. There are none more distant than these."

Emily stood and came timidly to his side. On the wall was a map, not of the land, but of the great

Pacific Ocean. There, far to the left, at the very edge of the waters, were four larger islands and many smaller ones. The letters of the word "Japan" stretched along their eastern shores.

"The kingdom was sealed for two centuries and a half," Mr. Cromwell said, "until Commodore Perry forced open its gates five years ago. Our own Reverend Tuttle has opened a mission house there, under the protection of one of their warlords. Next year, I shall be ordained and follow, to build another."

"You're leaving Rochester?" Emily's heart plummeted.

"My name shall be great among the Gentiles, saith the Lord of hosts." When there was no amen from Emily, Mr. Cromwell turned a harsh gaze upon her.

"Amen," Emily whispered. Without Mr. Cromwell, it would begin again. She could bear the girls' enmity. Such cruelties as they could devise were insignificant. But the men. Who would hold them away once he was gone?

Mr. Cromwell did not usually let such weakly uttered amens pass unrebuked. Perhaps Emily's very visible discomfiture caused him to make an allowance this time. He paused by a series of tinted daguerreotypes.

"These are ladies of that land," he said.

Through eyes blurry with tears, Emily saw figures as dainty as porcelain dolls, hair piled high in elaborate coiffures, wearing wide-sleeved gowns with wide sashes that flattened their torsos. Long, narrow eyes looked out of faces childishly round and shallow.

Emily pointed at one of the ladies, whose slightly

open smile revealed a dark and toothless mouth. "She has no teeth, sir."

"Not so, Emily. Their highborn women blacken their teeth."

She looked at the placard explaining the daguerreotypes. It was entitled "Famous Beauties of the City of Yokohama." When she turned back to Mr. Cromwell, she saw him staring at her with his hard, unblinking eyes.

"In Japan, you would be considered homely at best," Mr. Cromwell said. "More likely outright hideous. The gold of your hair, the blue of your eyes, your height, your size, your shape. All wrong, all very, very wrong."

Emily stared at the ladies' narrow eyes, at their blackened teeth, at the flat bodies that displayed none of the gross feminine swellings and protrusions with which she was cursed. Mr. Cromwell was right. Two women could not be more unalike than Emily and any famous beauty of Yokohama.

"Take me with you," Emily said. She didn't know which surprised her more. Her sudden plea or Mr. Cromwell's calm reaction.

"I have long thought of it," he said, nodding. "We were brought together for a purpose, you and I. And that purpose, I believe, is Japan. We will bear forth the True Word, and we will be exemplars of that word with our very beings. If you truly wish it, I will write to your guardians without delay."

"I truly wish it, sir," Emily said.

"Outside the classroom, you should call me Zephaniah," Mr. Cromwell said. "It is excessively distant for one affianced to call her future husband 'sir.' "

And so it was done. Without intending to do so,

she had given herself away. Mr. and Mrs. Parton freely gave their consent. Emily and Zephaniah agreed to wed in the new mission house they themselves would build in the domain of the warlord of Akaoka Province. The imminence of the marriage she had not thought of did not trouble her in the least. There was no other way for her to reach Japan. The engagement, the journey, the destination, became the treasury of her only hope, the hope of sanctuary from her own accursed beauty.

She was two months shy of her seventeenth birthday when the *Star of Bethlehem* sailed west from San Francisco. She took only three things with her, and they were everything. Her mother's copy of *Ivanhoe,* her locket, and a heart full of the past.

. . . . .

Emily was disappointed to hear the fading sound of Brother Matthew's boots. She had thought he might keep her company. Conversation with Zephaniah was punctuated by long periods of silence as he passed in and out of sleep. When he was unconscious, as he was now, there was nothing to distract her from the hopelessness of her situation. This was the man who would have been her husband. Because of him, she was here, in this strange land that, miraculously, blessedly, showed every sign of being the place of deliverance for which she had prayed. During her five days in this palace, not a single man had looked at her with those eyes she feared. In every face that displayed expression, male or female, she saw only disdain, pity, disgust. It was as Zephaniah had promised. They saw her as hideous.

Yet she had found safety only to lose it. When

Zephaniah was gone, she, too, would have to go. Back to America.

The prospect horrified her. Once there—she did not think of it as home—she would have nowhere to go. She could not return to the mission house in San Francisco. During the last weeks before sailing, her situation there had grown increasingly perilous. A dozen new missionaries had arrived from Boston to prepare for posting in China. Several among them took far too much interest in her. At first, the polite veneer was maintained. But it didn't last. It never did. Finally, their faces grew hungry when they looked at her, and their eyes began to wander too freely over her person. She found herself bumped, or touched, or pressed against, in the hallways, in the dining room, on her way to chapel, or on her way back. Neither the commandments of the True Word, nor her betrothal to Zephaniah, nor her consistent coldness toward them was sufficient defense. Not for long. Sooner or later, whatever restraint they had would dissolve. She could see it in their eyes.

Zephaniah sighed in his sleep. She took his hand in hers and squeezed it gently. The smile she gave him held back her tears.

"Bless you, Zephaniah. You did your best. No one can do more."

6

Lord Genji's Death

That year, Lord Shayo froze in the icy winter sea; a branch laden with spring blossoms crushed his successor, Lord Ryoto; the next heir, Lord Moritake, was immolated by summer lightning. Koseki then became lord of the domain.

He said, "I can do nothing about the weather."

During the early autumn rains, he executed the entire bodyguard corps, sent every concubine into a nunnery, banished the cooks, married the stablemaster's daughter, and declared war against the Shogun.

Lord Koseki ruled for thirty-eight years.

SUZUME–NO–KUMO
(1397)

Sohaku was past all argument and worry. When Genji asked to be left alone with Shigeru in the abbot's meditation hut, Sohaku said "Lord," bowed, and withdrew. The inevitability of disaster gave him an inner peace six months of Zen effort had not come close to delivering. In a place where generations of monks had attained satori, a boyish dilettante and a homicidal maniac were deciding the future of the Okumichi clan. Perhaps both of them would come out alive. Perhaps not. It hardly mattered. They might live through this day, and tomorrow, and the day after that. But someday soon, both Genji and Shigeru would die. There could be no other outcome. The only matters in doubt were how they would die, and who would do the killing.

Sohaku felt a strange chill in his bones as he walked away from the meditation hut. This surely signaled the onset of an ailment, probably a serious one. The possibility made him smile. What would be the perfect bodily metaphor for this outrageously dismal situation? Perhaps cholera, a revival of the epidemic that had swept through the nearby villages a few months ago. No, something worse. The Festering Plague? Then he realized what the strangeness was, and why it drained the heat from the core of his being.

For the first time, his footsteps on the small stones of the pathway were utterly silent. Without trying, he was accomplishing a feat that had so far eluded the most skillful of his samurai. His body had known this before his mind, and knowing, a deeper realization had penetrated to his marrow. In a sudden flash of insight, Sohaku saw a possible assassin he had never thought of before.

Himself.

If the Okumichi clan was doomed, as it surely was, then his true responsibility was to the survival of his own family. Unless he could become the vassal of another lord, he and his descendants would be extinguished along with all the others who maintained their ancient loyalty. Sohaku considered the possibilities. The only lord who could guarantee a smooth transition in these uncertain times was the Shogun. Or rather, the people around him. The actual occupant of the office, Iemochi, was a sickly boy of fourteen. Clearly, the person with whom to make contact would have to be Kawakami, the head of the secret police.

Before he did that, he had to make sure of his own men. Which ones could he rely on? Which would he have to eliminate? And what of his old comrades at the palace in Edo, Saiki and Kudo? He would sound them out at the first opportunity. The danger would be much less if they joined with him.

If Lord Kiyori were still their leader, these thoughts would never have come to him. But the wily old warrior was dead.

Sohaku saw the future as clearly as in a vision. Saiki and Kudo would join with him, or they, too, would die.

With his next step, his full weight came down on the pathway. The stones clattered beneath his sandals. Lost in the multitude of things to come, Sohaku heard nothing.

· · · · ·

After pouring tea for Lord Genji and Shigeru, Hidé bowed and began to back out of the abbot's meditation hut. He didn't think it was such a good idea for his lord to be alone with Shigeru, especially now that he was armed once again. Of course, even without a sword, Shigeru could easily overpower Lord Genji, so the weapons didn't really make a significant difference. It made him wonder, not for the first time, whether the young lord was frivolous and impetuous, or brilliant and determined. In the course of a single hour, Shigeru had undergone an incredible transformation. He was once again behaving like the clan martial arts instructor he had been before the onset of his madness. How had it happened? The only thing that had changed, as far as Hidé could see, was that Lord Genji had arrived and given him back his swords. It was difficult to fathom, impossible, in fact, for someone as limited as himself. The only decision he was competent to make was to decide whom to obey, then to obey without question. Since the old lord's death, this was a matter that never left Hidé's mind for long. Who was really in charge of the clan now? Saiki, the chamberlain? Kudo, the chief of security? Sohaku, the commander of cavalry? Or could it be the young lord? That seemed most unlikely of all. Surely he was no more than a figurehead. And yet, here he was, to all appearances completely at ease with a man who had recently slaughtered more than a dozen of his kinsmen. On the surface, it seemed like exceedingly poor judgment. But under one specific set of circumstances, it would be judgment of the clearest kind. If Lord Genji knew what would transpire, then there was no risk at all. And if he knew, then he was without doubt the one to follow, for who was superior to a Great Lord with mystical foresight?

"Stay with us for a time," Lord Genji said. He gestured at a teacup.

Hidé bowed deeply, took the cup from the tray, and kept bowing as Lord Genji filled it. That the lord himself should pour tea for him was astonishing. Only those in the innermost circle were treated with such intimacy.

"Thank you, lord."

"Your conduct on our journey here was exemplary," Lord Genji said. "I was impressed by your skill and your courage. But, most especially, I was impressed by your decisiveness. In these uncertain times, a samurai who does not hesitate is a true samurai indeed."

"I am unworthy of such praise," Hidé said, bowing again. Despite his modest words, he couldn't help but feel a surge of pride in his breast.

"That is not for you to say," Shigeru said. "When your lord speaks, you have only to be silent, thank him, apologize, or obey, as the case may be. That is all."

"Yes, sir. Forgive me my discourtesy, Lord Genji. I am better suited to the stables than to your presence."

Shigeru slapped the floor with such force that the walls of the hut shook. "What did I just say? Offer thanks, apologies, silence, obedience. Did you not hear me? I said nothing about mouthing excuses. Never make excuses. Never. Do you understand?"

"Yes, sir." Chastened, Hidé pressed his forehead to the floor.

Lord Genji laughed. "We need not be so formal, Uncle. We are only three comrades sharing tea and discussing plans for the future."

A shuffling of footsteps rapidly approached the door to the hut.

"Lord," a tense voice said, "is everything in order?" The explosive slap had undoubtedly brought the assembled company to the door with their swords drawn.

"Yes, yes. Why would they not be? Leave us."

"Yes, lord."

Lord Genji waited until the retreating footsteps faded away before continuing.

"As I was saying, your actions have led me to a decision." He looked hard at Hidé and stopped speaking. He was silent for so long, Hidé began wondering whether a response was expected from him. If so, was it thanks or an apology? He glanced furtively at Shigeru, hoping to see some indication, but the young lord's fearsome uncle sat stonily, his eyes hooded as if in meditation. Hidé was saved from yet another verbal blunder when Lord Genji spoke again just as he opened his mouth to thank him. "No doubt you have heard talk about my supposed prescience."

"Yes, lord."

"What I say now, you must never divulge to another."

"Yes, lord."

"It's true."

Chilly winter air rushed into Hidé's lungs. He couldn't say a word. That Lord Genji could see the future was not particularly shocking. Most of the men were of the opinion that whoever was Lord of Akaoka had the gift, and most of the time Hidé shared that view. Like everyone else, his confidence had been badly shaken when Shigeru poisoned Lord Kiyori and went on his rampage. Who, foreseeing such a tragedy, would allow it to happen? His friend Shimoda turned the tide back in favor of the mystical view when he pointed out that no one knew what else Lord Kiyori had seen. Unimaginable though it was, perhaps the alternatives had all been worse. And was it not a fact that the greatest triumphs often arose from the worst disasters? Consider the founding of Akaoka Domain itself, six hundred years ago, with the omen of the sparrows. No, what surprised

Hidé so much was that the lord was sharing the clan's most treasured secret with him, one of the lowliest of retainers.

Exhaling at last, too stunned by the revelation to be embarrassed by the sound of his breathing, Hidé bowed deeply all the way to the floor. "Lord Genji, you honor me with your trust. I will not fail you."

"I know you will not, Hidé, for I have seen your future."

Hidé swayed on his heels, dizzied by what he was hearing. Only the discipline he had built through a lifetime of martial training kept him from hyperventilating and toppling over.

"You will be loyal to me unto death," Lord Genji said. "Since I know there is no one more trustworthy, I appoint you captain of my bodyguard. I will make the announcement to the assembly after my uncle and I discuss some other matters. In the meantime, consider whom you will want as your lieutenants. They will help you select the rest of your men."

Hidé felt his chest tightening with emotion. At this most dangerous time, when the fate of the nation as well as the clan was in doubt, his lord had chosen him above dozens of more accomplished, more senior retainers—him, Hidé, the buffoon, the gambler, the drunkard—to be his shield! He could restrain himself no longer. Tears of gratitude fell to the mat, plopping loudly like the start of a winter squall.

"Thank you, Lord Genji."

Hidé left the meditation hut in a daze. He took his place among the other samurai awaiting Lord Genji's reappearance. Uncharacteristically, he neither smiled nor exchanged pleasantries with his companions. How unexpectedly, how suddenly, how irrevocably his life had changed within this very hour.

Loyal unto death.

Hidé's greatest fear had always been that he would make the wrong choice in some complicated crisis and betray his lord, not by cowardice, but out of stupidity. Now that fear was gone. Lord Genji, who saw the future, guaranteed it. He would be loyal unto death. He could feel himself grow stronger and steadier from this certainty alone.

"You were in there for a long time," Shimoda said. "What did they want?"

"It's not for me to say," Hidé replied. Turning inward once again, he knew he had found his first lieutenant. Though Shimoda was only fair with a sword, and downright pathetic in unarmed combat, no one in the clan could outshoot him with bow, musket, or pistol, from a stationary position or from horseback. And, equally important, he was honest to the core. If he gave his word, he would keep it, though it cost him his life.

Shimoda sat back, surprised by Hidé's reticence and even more surprised by his serious demeanor. What had happened in the meditation hut? His carefree friend seemed like someone else entirely.

"So, what's up?" Taro sat down next to Shimoda. He rubbed the stubble of new growth on his scalp. It itched. Like all the other temporary monks, he had stopped shaving his head as soon as it was known that Lord Genji would be called to the monastery. That was the long-awaited signal for their return to duty. All of them had already changed into their former clothing and once again wore their two swords in their sashes. The erstwhile monks were notable only by their lack of hair. It was an embarrassing distinction, one that would be even more embarrassing once they returned to Edo. The samurai's elaborate coiffure was an important part of his wardrobe. But it couldn't be helped. Sometimes it was necessary to endure the unendurable. Taro rubbed his head again. "What did Hidé tell you?"

"Nothing," Shimoda said testily.

Taro was taken aback. "I thought we were friends. If he told you, you should tell me."

"I'm telling you," Shimoda said. "He said nothing."

"Really?" Taro looked past Shimoda. He saw a samurai sitting with spine erect, eyes half closed, in alert quietude, as still as a stone Buddha. Taro had to look twice to be sure it was really Hidé.

• • • • •

Genji smiled at Shigeru. "Aren't you going to ask?"

"Ask what?"

"The obvious."

"Very well," Shigeru said. "Why did you say those things to Hidé?"

"Because it's the truth?"

Genji and Shigeru both laughed.

Immediately growing serious, Shigeru said, "I think you've made a mistake. Hidé is a frivolous wastrel. All his peers have gone on to greater responsibility. He alone is still among the rank and file with men ten years his junior. Moreover, his appointment will offend Sohaku. He was my father's chief bodyguard, and he no doubt expects to continue as yours."

"Your words are very wise, Uncle," Genji said, "and this in itself could be considered baffling. Not an hour ago, you were naked, covered in your own excrement, and making faces like a trained monkey.

One might wonder how such a sudden transformation is possible, and whether it is to be trusted. How would you advise me?"

Shigeru colored and stared at the floor.

"Ah, well, we can deal with that later. I have some thoughts on the matter I will share with you. You may find them salutary. As for Hidé, you are certainly right about his past performance. And without doubt, many in his situation would be crushed by the weight of such unexpected responsibility. But I believe the opposite will happen with this man."

Shigeru gave Genji a questioning look. "You believe? You don't know?"

"Why would I know?"

"In every generation of our family, one person inherits the curse of foresight. My father in his, I in mine. In yours, it must be you. There is no one else."

"There's no one else now," Genji said. "There were three others. Your children, my cousins. One of them might have been the one."

Shigeru tried not to remember when he last saw them. He shook his head. "They were spared. They saw no more than what was in front of them, and in their normal childish dreams."

Genji said, "My father was a drunkard and an opium addict. He could easily have had unacknowledged offspring without even knowing it."

Again Shigeru shook his head. "Alcohol and opium in the quantities in which he consumed them have a highly suppressive effect on sexual desire. It is remarkable that he sired you." Shigeru smiled, though his eyes were sad. "There is no use denying it. You know."

"Are you sure there are no others?" Genji said. "Grandfather was extremely virile, was he not?

Could you have brothers or sisters you don't know about? And they children of their own?"

"My father was virile, yes, but he was also very aware. He would have done nothing to send the curse out of the family line."

"You keep saying 'curse.' It's usually thought of as a gift."

"Is that how you think of it?"

Genji sighed and leaned on his armrest. "Having it didn't make Grandfather happy. Not having it destroyed my father. And you, look what it's done to you. No, you're right, it's no gift. I was hoping someone else would bear the burden. I still do."

"I don't understand," Shigeru said. "If you have it, you know it. You can't help but know it. How can you have any hope of escape?"

"Grandfather told me I have it," Genji said. "Beyond that, I have no certain evidence."

"You've had no visions?"

"I hope not," Genji said.

.   .   .   .   .

They were walking deep in the woods outside the castle, hunting for shiitake mushrooms on the shaded bark of the oldest evergreens when Grandfather told him.

"I don't want it," Genji said. "Give it to someone else."

Grandfather tried to keep a stern expression, but he couldn't quite manage it. Genji saw the old man's eyes twinkling, a sure sign of mirth.

"You're talking like a baby," Grandfather said. "This has nothing to do with wanting or not wanting."

"I don't want it anyway," Genji said. "If my father can't have it, then give it to Uncle Shigeru."

"It's not mine to give or withhold," Grandfather said. "If it were..." Genji waited, but Grandfather didn't finish what he was saying. His eyes had stopped twinkling, too. "Shigeru already has it. You in turn will have it, too."

"If Uncle has it, then why must I? I thought it was supposed to be only one of us at a time."

"One in each generation," Grandfather said. "I in mine, Shigeru in his, you in yours."

Genji sat down on the grass and began to cry. "Why, Grandfather? What wrongs did our ancestors do?"

Grandfather sat down next to him and put his arm around his shoulders. The touch surprised Genji. Grandfather didn't usually show much affection.

"One ancestor is responsible," Grandfather said, "all the rest of us have only reaped his karma. Hironobu."

Genji dragged his sleeve across his face, wiping away tears and sniffing to keep the mucus from running down his face. "Hironobu is our first ancestor. He founded this domain of Akaoka when he was six years old. I'll be six tomorrow."

"Yes, Lord Genji." Grandfather bowed to him.

Genji laughed at the mock formality, his tears quickly forgotten. "What did Hironobu do? I thought he was a great hero."

"No one's being excludes every possibility." Grandfather often said things Genji didn't understand. He was doing it again. "Birth and death occur and reoccur from moment to moment. Some rebirths are better left unborn. But we never know until it's too late. Hironobu fell in love with the wrong woman. A witch's granddaughter."

"Lady Shizuka? I thought she was a princess."

Grandfather smiled at him and said what he'd said before. "No one's being excludes every possibility." Saying it twice didn't help. Genji still didn't understand. "She was a princess. She was a witch's granddaughter. If she'd stayed in the convent where she belonged, she would have had no issue, and no Okumichi would ever have had a single vision, or spoken a single prophecy, or suffered from knowing what is to come. Of course, then there might also be no Okumichi clan by now. Visions have saved us time and time again. Good and evil are indeed not two."

Grandfather bowed in the direction of the clan columbarium, which was in the northeast tower of Cloud of Sparrows Castle. It wasn't visible from this point in the forest, but they both knew where it was. They had to know in case of an attack. Genji respectfully followed his example.

"If she was a witch, why are we bowing to her, Grandfather? Shouldn't we scatter her ashes to the four winds and erase her memory?"

"Then she'd be everywhere. This way, we know where she is. Safely trapped in an urn and guarded night and day by fearless warriors."

Genji leaned closer to Grandfather and quickly took his hand. The forest shadows had suddenly lengthened.

Grandfather laughed. "I'm joking, Gen-chan. There are no such things as ghosts, or demons, or invisible spirits. Lady Shizuka, witch and princess, has been dead for six hundred years. Do not fear her. Fear instead the living. They are the only danger."

"Then I'm glad I have the gift," Genji said, still clutching Grandfather's hand as tightly as he could. "I'll know who my enemies are, and I'll kill them all before they can do me harm."

"Killing brings killing," Grandfather said, "yet otherwise changes surprisingly little. You will not ensure your safety that way."

"Then what use is knowing?" Genji said, pouting.

"Listen carefully, Genji. This is not a matter of use or no use, of good or evil, of choice or no choice. Those are only labels, not the thing itself. They obscure, not clarify. Listen well and strive to understand my meaning. Gift or curse, wanted or unwanted, you have it. You cannot ignore it any more than you can ignore your own head. Either you use it, or it will use you. Do you understand?"

"No, Grandfather. You're talking like old Abbot Zengen. I don't understand him either."

"It doesn't matter now. You have the Okumichi memory. You'll remember what I've said, and later you'll understand. Hear me. Visions come in different ways. Shigeru will have many. In your life, you will have only three. Pay close attention. Examine them without fear or desire. Then you will see clearly and those three visions will show you all you need to know."

Three visions, Genji thought. Only three. That's not so bad. Maybe they'll come and go and I won't even notice. He saw Grandfather looking at him. Everyone said Grandfather could read minds as well as see the future. Genji didn't believe that, not really. But it was always better to take precautions. He concentrated hard on the clouds in the sky and tried to remember his mother's face. She had died when he was three. With every passing year, her image grew fainter and fainter. When he tried to remember, there was often only the trying, no more, so that was all Grandfather would find in his mind, if he looked there.

· · · · ·

"I understand," Shigeru said through a tight smile. "If you haven't had one yet, you think you'll escape entirely. None of us has been so lucky. Nor will you. Prepare yourself. If my father said you'll have three, you will. He was never wrong about visions."

"That's not the only reason," Genji said. "I hope what I saw was not a vision, because if it was, I know something no one should know."

"I know a thousand things no one should know," Shigeru said.

"Do you know the moment of your own death?" Genji said.

· · · · ·

Genji doesn't recognize the place. He's retrieved the vision repeatedly, examined it as carefully as a swordsman examines the stance of his opponent, seeking that critical opening, to no avail. It's not yet a place he knows. That he will know it and be known there is clear by the roaring voices of the assembled multitude. Which are louder and more numerous, the cheers or the curses? It's impossible to say. If he had to guess, he would guess the curses.

"Damn you to hell!"

"Traitor! Traitor! Traitor!"

"*Banzai!* You've saved the nation!"

"Death to cowards!"

"You shame us all! Show honor and kill yourself!"

"May all the gods and all the Buddhas bless you and protect you!"

He walks down the central aisle of a great hall unlike any he has seen. Though it is night outside, it is as bright as midday within. The numerous lamps along the walls emit not the slightest smoky discharge. Their light is steady, evenly incandescent, without a flicker of flame. (A new wick has been invented, or a new source found for a superior oil?) Instead of cushions arranged in rows, there are perhaps two hundred chairs of the outsider pattern facing the raised podium. In the back, a large balcony holds another hundred chairs. No one is sitting. All are on their feet, shouting, gesturing, full of emotion. Perhaps the chairs are symbolic and not for actual use. (That seems likely. Genji, having so recently used one of them for the first time, now knows what excruciating displacements those devices can cause one's inner organs.)

He sees not a single head with a topknot, nor anyone with the obligatory two swords of the samurai. Like madmen or prisoners, everyone displays an unruly mess of hair, and no one is armed. All the faces are Japanese, but all the bodies are dressed in the graceless clothing of the outsiders. It reminds him of the puppet shows of little children and clumsy peasant pantomimes. He wonders again if anything this ridiculous can truly be a vision.

At the podium, an elderly man with thin white hair strikes the tabletop with a small wooden hammer.

"Order! Order! The Diet will come to order!"

No one pays the slightest attention. (What is the Diet?)

Most of the cheers are coming from his left, most of the curses from his right. Genji raises his right hand to acknowledge the cheers. Just as he does so, a young man comes rushing at him from among the cursers. He's dressed in a plain dark blue uniform with no emblems or insignias. His hair is cut very close to his scalp. His hands are wrapped around the hilt of a sword.

"Long live the Emperor!"

With that shout, the young man drives his sword deep into Genji's torso just below the sternum. Genji feels the sudden jolt of contact, a sharp stinging sensation as if a wasp has stung his chest, a sudden relaxation of all his muscles.

An explosion of blood drenches the young man's face.

Then everything goes white.

Silence descends, followed by darkness.

But the vision isn't over.

Genji opens his eyes. Worried faces peer down at him. From the angle of their bodies, and the sight of the ceiling behind them, he knows he's lying on the floor.

He feels blood pulsing from his chest. His entire body feels cold and wet. He feels no pain.

The crowd of faces parts and an extraordinarily beautiful woman appears. Heedless of the blood, she takes him in her arms, cradles his head, and holds him close against her breast. Tears flow down her cheeks and drop onto his face. Sobbing, she presses her cheek against his. For several moments, their heartbeats are synchronous, then his, slowing, drifts away.

"You will always be my Shining Prince," she says. A play on his name. Genji. The same name as an ancient fictional character.

Two burly men, bodyguards or police, kneel down next to him. They, too, weep shamelessly.

"Lord Genji," one of them says. "Lord Genji." These are the only words he can choke out.

"Hold on, my lord," the other says. "Help is on the way." The man takes off his coat and presses it against the wound. Genji sees, in a holster high up against his ribs, a flat pistol formerly concealed by the coat. Ah. Pistols replace swords. It makes sense. He wonders whether samurai carry a single pistol, or two. He wonders, too, why the weapon is worn concealed. He would like to ask, but he lacks the strength, the will. He has begun to feel very light.

The woman smiles at him through her tears. She says, "I finished the translation this morning. I wonder whether we should use the Japanese name, or translate the title into English as well. What do you think?"

"He can't hear you, Lady Shizuka," one of the men says. "He is unconscious."

Lady Shizuka was the witch and princess who enchanted the clan's founder. This can't be her, unless she has returned in a rebirth. No, Genji doesn't believe in rebirth. Like firewood once burned does not return from its ashes, a person once dead does not return to life. So this is another Lady Shizuka, namesake of the first.

"He hears me," Lady Shizuka says.

Genji sees now that her beauty is not entirely Japanese. Her eyes are hazel, not black, and her hair is light brown. Her features are rather sharper and more dramatic than usual, more outsider than Japanese. He doesn't recognize her. But each time he examines this vision, she seems more familiar. She reminds him of someone. Who? He still doesn't know. What he knows is this: Lady Shizuka is the most beautiful woman he has ever seen. (Or, more accurately, the most beautiful he will ever see.)

"English," Genji says. He means to ask what she has translated into English, but only that one word passes his lips.

"English it is, then," Lady Shizuka says. She smiles through her tears. "It will be another scandal. 'Genji again,' people will say, 'and that terrible Shizuka of his.' But we don't care, do we?" Her lips tremble, her eyelids flutter, but her smile holds, and for the moment no more tears fall. "She would be so proud of us," Lady Shizuka says.

Genji wants to ask, Who would be so proud, and why? But he has no voice. Something sparkles at her long, smooth throat. He looks. He sees what it is. Then where he had heard his heart, he hears nothing, and sees no more.

· · · · ·

"Abandon any hope of escape," Shigeru said. "There can be no doubt but that you have had a vision."

"What I have described is familiar to you?"

"Some of it. The clothing. The hair. The absence of weapons. There is only one possibility. We will be defeated by the outsiders and become a nation of slaves."

"What about the Diet? What is it?"

"I have not seen it in my visions. It may be what will replace the Shogun's Council when we have been reduced to servitude. The outrageous conduct of those present could only be possible once all order and discipline have been lost. Can you imagine a single voice raised to a disrespectful volume, much less an entire unruly crowd in the Shogun's presence?"

"No, Uncle, I admit I cannot."

"Your assassin? You don't recognize him?"

"No. Nor anyone else. There isn't one familiar face there."

"Then your retainers have all been killed, for I would not permit you to enter such a place unprotected. Nor would Saiki, Kudo, or Sohaku."

"Who are the men with the concealed pistols, then? They seem to be extremely solicitous of my welfare."

"Guards, perhaps. You may be in someone's custody." Shigeru closed his eyes. He breathed deeply in silence for several moments. When he opened his eyes again, he bowed to the floor. "Forgive me for failing you so miserably, my lord."

Genji laughed. "You haven't failed me yet, Uncle. Perhaps we may find our way to an alternate result."

"We can do nothing to prevent it. We can protect our loved ones from suffering such a fate. But we cannot stop the future from coming and devouring us and all who remain."

"Is that why you did it?" Genji's voice was very gentle.

Shigeru stiffened. He began to tremble, slightly at first, then more and more violently, until he appeared to be in the throes of a monstrous convulsion. At last, a strangled cry came from his throat and he collapsed in a sobbing heap.

Genji sat quietly. He neither said nor did anything. After several minutes passed, Shigeru managed to restore himself to a semblance of normality. Genji poured tea. Shigeru accepted it.

"This is painful, Uncle, but it cannot be avoided. I must learn as much as I can of your visions. It is the only way I will gain insight into the meaning of mine."

"I understand, my lord." Shigeru's behavior was once again highly formal. He was relying on protocol to hold himself together. "From time to time, as you require, I will answer as many of your questions as I can."

"Thank you, Shigeru," Genji said. "For now, I think we have both had enough of visions. Let us address another matter. When I turned to leave the armory, you were going to kill me. Why didn't you?"

"The silence stopped me," Shigeru said. "The sights and sounds that had assailed me without pause for so long, ceased in your presence. I remembered my father's words from long ago. He said it would happen as it did, and when it did, he said I must not act on that impulse."

"Lord Kiyori was wise," Genji said. And, he thought, a true visionary as well. Yet he had not prevented his own death at the hands of this his madman son. Why? Perhaps it was as Shigeru said. We are powerless to prevent what must be.

Shigeru waited as long as he could. But when Genji did not continue, he had to ask. "What did you see? What sparkled at the woman's throat?"

"That is one memory I can never bring with me from the vision," Genji said. It filled his eyes as vividly now as it had the first time, but he thought it wise not to burden his uncle further. It was enough to deal with what he had already shared.

"Too bad. It could be an important guiding omen."

"Yes," Genji said, "it could be."

*   *   *   *   *

Shigeru didn't pay much attention while Genji addressed the assembly. Instead, he thought about Genji's vision. Many events must occur before the conditions he had foreseen could arise. No matter how degenerate the samurai or powerful the outsiders, surely it would take several years at least for Japan to fall to any conquerers. Some had not lost the ancient martial virtues and would fight to the death. Apparently, Genji was not one of them. In his vision, he was called a traitor. Shigeru hoped it was calumny and not an accurate description.

Despite this concern, Shigeru felt hope. For the first time in months, his visionary inundation had ceased. In the hours since Genji's arrival, he had seen nothing but what others saw. Perhaps the maddening flood was being staunched by the same mystical mechanism that allowed Genji only three visions. He didn't think he was permanently cured. That would be too much to expect. The visions would return. But if they ceased even briefly every few days or so, he was confident he could use that time, as he was using it now, to revive his self-control. He had trained in the martial arts for his entire life in order to defend himself against attack. What were these visions, after all, but an attack from within? They were no different from any other attack, except in their point of origin. He would not be defeated by them.

He heard Hidé's name and saw him bowing deeply to Genji. The announcement of his appointment had been made. Shigeru noted which faces among the assembly revealed dissatisfaction. They were men who would have to be watched. He glanced at Sohaku. He expected to see shocked dismay on his face. But the abbot of Mushindo Monastery, who had been and would once again be commander of cavalry, listened to the announcement with complete equanimity. Shigeru knew from this that he would have to kill his old friend. The only reason Hidé's appointment would not anger Sohaku was if he had already decided to betray the young lord. If only Sohaku knew what he knew: Until the outsiders conquered Japan, Genji was invulnerable.

And when the moment came, even then Genji would be fortunate. He would die without fear, drenched in his own heart's blood, in the embrace of a beautiful woman, and she would weep for him.

What samurai could hope for more?

III

DAIMYO

7

Satori

Every battle is not won by advance. Every retreat is not loss. Advance is strategy. Retreat is also strategy.

Retreat must be orderly. It must not always appear orderly. Retreat is strategy. Appearance in retreat is also strategy.

SUZUME–NO–KUMO
(1600)

Jimbo is not your real name," Genji said.

"What name is a real name?" Jimbo said.

Genji laughed. "You are an outsider, yet you've shaved your head, donned the patchwork robe of a Zen monk, and speak in the same riddles that old Abbot Zengen used to use. Was it he who taught you our language?"

"No, my lord. Abbot Zengen saved my life during the cholera epidemic; the village children who nursed me afterward taught me how to hear and speak."

"How unexpected. I doubt any of them can read a single character."

"And I, too, cannot, my lord."

"Then your linguistic accomplishment is all the more impressive. There is not a man among us who, spending a year in the American countryside among unlettered peasants, would learn your language half so well."

"I thank you, my lord, on behalf of my teachers. They deserve all the credit."

A momentary winter breeze briefly fluttered the fabric of the tent above them. Genji glanced at the pale winter sky. The sunlight was already fading. Before the hour of the ram was past, they could begin their return to Edo. They would reach the border after nightfall and traverse the hostile territory of Yoshino Domain in darkness. This conveyed one distinct advantage: They were far less likely to encounter hostile troops than during the day. One senseless slaughter per journey was more than enough.

Genji said, "When you arrived in Japan, you were a Christian missionary. Now you are a Zen monk. Then you called yourself James Bohannon. Now you say you are Jimbo. Tell me, what did you call yourself before you became James Bohannon?"

"Ethan Cruz," Jimbo said.

"And before that?"

"Before that I was just Ethan."

"I assume such name changes have nothing to do with the Christian religion."

"That is correct, my lord."

"Nor with Zen."

"That, too, is correct, my lord."

"Then, why?"

Before answering, Jimbo lowered his gaze and inhaled from his abdomen, taking the long slow breath deep into the *tanden*, the center of his being. With his exhalation, he let go of all fear, hatred, and desire.

"I was running away," Jimbo said.

"From whom?"

"From myself."

"A difficult endeavor," Genji said. "Many have attempted it. None that I know of has succeeded. Did you?"

"Yes, my lord," Jimbo said. "I did."

• • • • •

Tom, Peck, and Haylow had ridden with him before. They were personable enough and had never caused any problems on any of the jobs, but Ethan didn't like them because he didn't trust them. It was a habit Ethan had learned from the old man. It was a good habit, especially in his trade, which was robbing, stealing and rustling.

Never like anybody you can't trust, Cruz said. You might think you're a smart boy, you can like somebody and still keep your eyes open. But there's something about liking that dismays your attention, I don't know what it is. You allow yourself to like somebody you don't trust, and one night soon enough, you'll wake up to find an ax cleaved in the back of your skull, and you'll have your own foolish liking to thank for it.

Ethan supposed Cruz was speaking from exact experience, since he had an ax-shaped dent in the back of his own skull marked with a long white scar where the hair hadn't grown back.

It's bad enough liking the untrustworthy, Cruz said, try loving them. That's women I'm talking about, boy. Don't ever love a woman you can't trust. No, don't sit there nodding and agreeing. I know damn well you will. We all do. You know why? Because there is no woman ever you can trust. Every one of them, first to last, is a lying, cheating, treacherous whore.

The company Cruz kept surely influenced his viewpoint. A whoremaster spent most of his time with whores after all, and lying, cheating, and treachery were a whore's stock in trade, aside from her parts, that is.

Ethan never knew whether a man or a woman was responsible for the axing Cruz had suffered. He supposed if a woman was involved, then a man was, too. It was usually that way. Cruz blamed his dizzy spells, fits of violent anger, memory lapses, and alcoholism on the head wound.

Can't even remember how it happened, Cruz said. The bone healed pressing in, in the selfsame axly shape. It's there prodding at the soft innards of my head, reminding me always and forever, never like much less love whomsoever you can't trust. You hear me, boy? That's women I'm mostly meaning, but you keep a close watch on men, too, especially where women and money are involved. And you know what? There're always women and money involved. That's why the world is a vale of larcenous mayhem. Women's love of money.

It wasn't women's love of money or an ax that finally did Cruz in. It was a whore named Mary Anne. She was nothing special, older than the others, with two young girls to feed and clothe, girls too young to be in the trade themselves, since Cruz didn't abide pederasts. Nobody fucks anybody under twelve years old in my establishment, he said, and meant it. He'd shot two men dead for trying the day Ethan met him. The two men had been trying to fuck Ethan at the time. They weren't doing it in Cruz's establishment, but Ethan was under twelve, under ten in fact, and Cruz happened to wander into the stable, his attention attracted by the sound of Ethan's screams, saw what he saw, and extended the reach of his rule enough to disabide those two pederasts on a permanent basis.

Your parents aren't doing such a wonderful job of upraising you, boy, Cruz said. You want a little more looking after than they've been giving you. Might be I should go have a talk with them about it.

Ethan told him to let him know who they were once he found them.

So you're an orphan, are you?

What's an orphan?

Cruz was an orphan, too. He took Ethan back to his whorehouse, had Betsy wash him up, and gave him a job cleaning rooms, mopping floors, pouring whiskey, and feeding the garbage to the pigs out back. There's something about the smell of pigs that makes a man want to fuck and keep on fucking, Cruz said. Pigs are good for business. Ethan said he didn't like the smell of pigs. You'll change your mind once you're here for a while, boy. What kind of a world is it where a child is safer working in a whorehouse than in a stable? But here we are, aren't we?

What's your name, boy?

Ethan.

Ethan what?

Just Ethan. What's yours?

Manual Cruz.

Manuel Cruz.

No, goddammit. Manual, like manual labor. Not

Manuel, like a fucking starving Mexican dirt scratcher. Do I look like a fucking dirt scratcher? He gestured at his immaculate clothing. Do I look like I'm starving? He patted his prominent belly. Do I look like a fucking Mexican?

That was a harder question to figure the right answer to, since Cruz was Mexican. Sticking with what had been working so far, Ethan shook his head no again.

Cruz laughed and cheerfully slapped him on the back. I better look like a fucking Mexican because that's exactly what I am. But I'm not starving and I'm not scratching dirt. My parents did enough of that, and died before their time.

Cruz died before his time, too, and that was the reason Ethan Cruz was sitting by a campfire in the hills north of Austin with Tom and Peck, waiting for Haylow to come back with word, which he presently did, and the word was that he'd found Matthew Stark's hiding place.

"Small ranch, twenty, twenty-five miles north. He ain't there, though." Haylow got off his groaning horse. He'd need to steal himself a new one soon. Horses didn't last long under the hard-riding three-hundred-pound man. "Word is, he's off to Arizona Territory, get him a commission from the governor as a Arizona Ranger. What's to eat?"

Tom said, "I thought the only rangers was Texas Rangers."

"Me, too," Haylow said, spooning beans into his mouth straight from the pot. "But that's the word in town."

"They hiring murderers for rangers over there in Arizona?" Peck said.

"That's all they ever hiring for laws anywheres

these days," Haylow said, finishing the beans and digging in the pack for jerky. "They wanting experience for the job."

"Well, then, let's we go over there and get us commissions, too," Tom said. "We murderers."

"Only by incidence," Haylow said. "They wanting purpose experience."

"Who's at the ranch?" Ethan said.

"Just the whore and her two little bitches," Haylow said.

Ethan got up and threw his saddle on his horse. The three others caught up with him just before dawn, on the rise above Stark's ranch.

"We gonna wait for him?" Peck said. "Ambush-like, when he gets back?"

"Word is, he'll be back any day now," Haylow said. "Could be a good idea."

"Does he love the whore?" Ethan said.

"He came and took her," Haylow said. "There must be a fondness."

"Does he love her?" Ethan said.

"Who knows but him?" Haylow said.

A first puff of smoke came out of the ranch house chimney. Somebody was awake. Ethan put his heels to his horse and rode down the hill.

When they were finished, Ethan didn't much feel like waiting for Stark. He didn't feel much of anything but sick to his stomach. There was no point in going back to El Paso. The whorehouse was still there, but with Cruz dead, it was just a whorehouse, and Ethan never had gotten to like the smell of pigs.

They drove Stark's small herd across the border and sold it in Juarez for half of what it was worth. They didn't know for sure that Stark would come after them, but they all assumed he would.

"I would," Peck said, "for damn sure."

"Not me," Tom said. "Not over a whore."

"What about the two little bitches?" Haylow said. His appetite had gone up since they'd been to Stark's ranch. He weighed close to four hundred pounds now. His horse, a new one he'd bought in Juarez, was already making those wind-broken groans.

Tom and Peck didn't say anything, but they both looked over their shoulders, which was answer enough. Haylow looked over his shoulder, too.

Eventually, they knew Stark was looking for them because sometimes they'd go into a town just a day or two after he'd been there. Neither they nor he were traveling in a straight line. Meandering, they were bound to run into each other eventually.

"I'm done with this shit," Haylow said. "I'm going home."

"What the fuck for?" Peck said. "You think he won't find you in El Paso?"

"Not El Paso. Hawaii." Haylow's real name began with He'eloa and kept on going and going.

"What you got there?" Tom said. "You told us your family, your town, your whole nation was about dead of the pox."

"The mountains still there. The rivers still there. The ocean still there. Lately, been missing all that."

They stayed together until they reached la Ciudad de los Angeles. Peck said, Fuck it, if he wants to find me, let him find me here. Tom stopped in Sacramento, where his uncle owned a bar, and offered Tom a job keeping watch over the whores. I didn't really do nothing that bad, Tom said. Might be he let it pass with a sorry from me and a small beating from him. Haylow rode with Ethan to San

Francisco, where he was going to catch a ship to Hawaii, but he changed his mind once he saw the ocean. The big man—closing in on five hundred pounds by now and using a two-horse carriage instead of a saddle—sat there and cried as the waves lapped against the pilings of the wharf. Too many graves back home, he said.

Ethan stayed in San Francisco, too. Until one day, on his way out of a bar, he heard a streetcorner preacher. I am not come to call the righteous, the preacher said, but the sinners to repentance. When someone standing nearby said amen, something clenched in Ethan's heart let go, and he fell to his knees, weeping. That very night he was welcomed into the shelter of the Light of the True Word of the Prophets of Christ Our Lord. A month later, the new missionary, James Bohannon, was on his way to Japan.

Ethan took the new name because he felt himself reborn as a totally new man. But this didn't really happen until he and the other dozen missionaries reached Kobayashi Village in Yamakawa Domain, the site of their new mission house. The day they arrived, a cholera epidemic broke out. Within a month, Ethan was the only one of his party left alive. The villagers, too, were dying, and they blamed it on the arrival of the missionaries. Ethan only survived because the abbot of nearby Mushindo Monastery, an old man named Zengen, took him in and nursed him. He must have been a person of some influence, because the villagers soon changed their attitude. They began bringing food to him, and changing his clothing, and bathing him. The children especially were numerous among his visitors, their curiosity aroused by his strange appearance. They had never seen an outsider before.

Somehow, in his delirium, barriers fell away. When his fever broke, he found he could understand much of the children's vocabulary, and could speak a few words as well. By the time he was back on his feet, he was having conversations with Zengen.

One day, Zengen asked him, What was your face before your parents were born?

He was about to tell Zengen that he had never known his parents when up and down, inside and outside, disappeared.

Since then, Jimbo had worn the robes of Buddha instead of the suit of a Christian missionary. This was out of respect to Zengen more than anything else. Clothing was like names. There was no real meaning to them.

Jimbo had been James Bohannon, and Ethan Cruz, and he still was. At the same time, he was none of them anymore.

· · · · ·

Jimbo related none of this to Genji. He was about to begin when the lord smiled and said, "Truly? You have succeeded in escaping from yourself? Then you must share the enlightenment of Gautama Buddha himself."

"Enlightenment is a word whose meaning I don't know," Jimbo said. "I know the meanings of fewer and fewer words with every breath. Soon the only sensible thing I will be able to say is nothing at all."

Genji laughed and turned to Sohaku. "He is a more suitable successor to Zengen than you ever were. It's just as well you're leaving and he's staying."

"Is he not the outsider for whom you have been waiting, my lord?"

"I think not. That one is presently at Quiet Crane Palace."

"You have welcomed more outsiders?" Sohaku frowned, unable to keep his displeasure from showing.

"It was our late lord's recent policy to offer hospitality to missionaries of the True Word. I am only continuing what he began." Genji turned to Jimbo. "That is why you are here, is it not?"

"Yes, my lord."

"You will be together with them shortly," Genji said. "They came to help construct the mission house. It will be a difficult task. Your companions here have perished, and of the three who came, it is likely only two are still alive."

"One is ill, my lord?"

"I am sorry to say he was accidentally struck by an assassin's bullet meant for me. He may be a friend of yours. Zephaniah Cromwell."

"I don't know him, my lord. He must have arrived in San Francisco after I departed."

"A shame to come so far only to die a senseless death. Is there anything you need, Jimbo?"

"No, my lord. Abbot Sohaku has provisioned the temple well."

"When your former coreligionists arrive, what will you do?"

"I will help them build the mission house," Jimbo said. "Those who cannot hear the words of Buddha may hear the words of Christ and come to the same salvation."

"A healthy attitude. I wish you well, Jimbo. Or do you prefer James? Or Ethan?"

"A name is just a name. Any will do as well as none."

Genji laughed. "If more of us felt that way, the history of Japan would be far less bloody than it has been. And will be, still."

Genji stood. The assembled samurai all bowed and maintained their bows until the lord left the tent, escorted by Shigeru, to prepare for his departure.

Sohaku said, "Will you be well here alone?"

"Yes, Abbot, I will," Jimbo said. "And I will not always be alone. The children will not permit it."

"I am not abbot any longer," Sohaku said. "You are abbot now. Perform the rites. Maintain the meditation schedule. See to the spiritual needs of the villagers, to their births and deaths, their mournings and celebrations. Can you do that?"

"Yes, lord, I can."

"Then it is indeed fortunate that you entered among us, Jimbo, and became who you have become. Otherwise, with Zengen's death and my departure, this temple would be abandoned. It is never good to abandon a temple. Bad karma always follows."

Sohaku and Jimbo exchanged bows, and the cavalry commander rose. "Recite the sutras for me as well. I enter a time of much peril, and am more likely to fail and die than succeed and live."

"Those who succeed and those who fail are both destined to die," Jimbo said. "Nevertheless, I will recite sutras for you daily."

"My thanks," Sohaku said, "for those true words." He bowed again and departed.

Jimbo remained seated where he was. He must have slipped into meditation without knowing it, for when he next had a conscious thought, he was alone, enveloped by the deep darkness. The cry of a single distant night bird passed through him.

Above, the winter stars moved across the sky in their set orbits.

• • • • •

Though the doors were open to allow the passage of air, there was no escaping the fetid atmosphere of the room. The two maids, Hanako and Yukiko, sat stolidly at the edge of the room. They had requested permission to wear scented scarves across their faces two days ago, but Saiki had forbidden it.

"If the outsider woman can stand it, then you can stand it. You will shame us if you appear weaker than she is."

"Yes, lord."

But when was the last time Saiki had visited this breathing corpse?

Hanako and Yukiko watched the outsider woman speaking to the unconscious man. She sat close to the source of the foul emanations and showed no signs of gagging. Should they admire her for her self-discipline, or pity her for her desperation? She was so repulsive, Hanako and Yukiko conjectured, she must despair of ever finding another husband. Who could deny that her fears were well justified? That must be why she clung so pathetically to a man who was already as good as dead.

"What about the other?" Hanako had asked. "Might he not step forward after this one dies?"

"No," Yukiko had replied. "He does not look at women."

"He prefers his own sex?"

"He does not look at men or boys, either. Not in

that way. I believe he is a true monk of their religion. He seeks only souls to save, not bodily gratification."

The other had looked in on the woman and the dying man. Hanako did not recall seeing any passion in his eyes. Yukiko was right. He was intent on another purpose. After a few moments, he had walked away, perhaps to pray or to study their sacred text.

Heiko knelt beside the two maids. "My, my. This odor truly tests resolve, doesn't it?"

"Yes, Lady Heiko," Hanako said. "It's terrible."

"I would think some of our brave samurai should be in attendance, strengthening their will," Heiko said, "yet only we weak women are here."

The two maids giggled behind their hands.

"Just so," Yukiko said.

"You may go for now," Heiko said. "Return at the end of the hour."

"Lord Saiki ordered us to remain," Hanako said reluctantly.

"If he complains, tell him I asked you to leave, in order that I might fully follow Lord Genji's command to put the outsiders at ease."

"Yes, Lady Heiko." The two maids bowed gratefully, and withdrew.

Heiko shut down her sense of smell. She could do this because she had been trained since childhood to control the balance of her senses. How, she wondered, did Emily manage? She bowed to her and took the adjoining chair. If she perched on its very edge, she could just touch the floor with the tips of her toes.

"How is he?" Heiko asked.

"Brother Matthew believes sometime today, Zephaniah will fall asleep and not awake again."

"I am sorry."

"Thank you," Emily said. "I am sorry, too."

Cromwell's eyes snapped open. He looked past Emily, past the ceiling of the room, to somewhere far distant. He took a deep breath and half rose from the bed.

"The angels of resurrection and damnation are come," he said, a blissful smile brightening his face. "To whom will ye flee for help? And where will ye leave your glory?"

"Amen." Emily leaned forward to comfort him.

And the room exploded with white light and thunder.

The force of the blast lifted Cromwell from the bed and flung him skyward through the disintegrating roof.

As he had prophesied, he did not die of the gunshot wound.

· · · · ·

"He seems completely normal now," Taro said.

"Three days of peacefulness prove nothing," Abbot Sohaku said. "Even a madman can restrain himself for three days."

The small party threaded its way through Edo toward Quiet Crane Palace. Taro and Sohaku were at the rear. Hidé and Shimoda led the way, with Genji and Shigeru in the center. They wore no crests and flew no banners, and shadowed their faces with large basketlike hats of woven reeds. By the conventions of incognito travel, this meant they were unrecognizable, so the crowds in the streets were not obligated to cease all activity and prostrate themselves as they were required to do with any appearance of a Great

Lord. Passersby simply bowed as they would to any samurai.

"I've never seen him this quiet," Taro said. "Perhaps Lord Genji's presence has a curative effect on him."

"You don't believe those stories, do you?" Sohaku said.

"Which ones?" Taro said. "There are so many of them."

Sohaku snorted. "About our lord's supposed magical powers. His ability to control the thoughts of others."

"Maybe not everyone's thoughts," Taro said, "but look at Shigeru. You can't deny he's changed since he's been with Lord Genji."

"Three days of peacefulness prove nothing," Sohaku said again. He looked ahead to where Genji and Shigeru rode together, separated enough from the others to allow them to speak privately. As if it mattered what they said. More babble, Sohaku thought, more useless babble.

"As you predicted, Hidé chose Shimoda as his lieutenant," Shigeru said. "And Taro will be chosen next?"

"It wasn't that kind of prediction," Genji said. "Hidé is unimaginative in the extreme. Not necessarily a defect in a bodyguard. I simply assumed he would do the natural thing, which is to select his best friends."

"You shouldn't allow him to name Taro. He's Sohaku's direct vassal. His father and Sohaku were comrades in arms during the time of the peasant uprisings. He himself took almost all his advanced martial instruction from Sohaku. You can't trust him."

"If Hidé trusts him, then I trust him," Genji

said. "It is important to know when to delegate authority."

"It is error to take too much comfort in your first prophecy," Shigeru said. "For all you know, you might be in a coma for the next ten years, thanks to an attack by Taro, then wake up to be killed in that place you envisioned."

"I realize that."

"Do you? Then why have you so lightly dismissed the possibility that Jimbo could be the outsider to whom Lord Kiyori alerted you? He may be the one yet to save your life."

"An outsider met in the New Year has already done so."

"Only if you were, in fact, the target of the attack," Shigeru said, "and it is not yet the New Year."

"It is for the outsiders. You doubt that I was the intended victim?"

"I am certain you were not."

"Oh? You were not there, yet you know? Through a vision of your own, perhaps?"

"No, my lord," Shigeru said, responding to Genji's irritated manner with increased formality. "I am convinced by the nature of the attack. You were walking in plain view, yet it was the palanquin that was struck, not any person walking near you."

"We Japanese have not yet mastered firearms, yet we insist on using them, even when a bow would be the more effective weapon. We have always been easy prey for foreign fads."

"The assailant not only escaped capture but disappeared unseen."

"He was a considerable distance away. By the time the men got there, he was gone. Nothing unusual about that."

"It bears all the marks of a ninja act," Shigeru said. "He shot whom he intended to shoot. The leader of the missionaries."

"To cause unrest and heighten suspicion?"

"Exactly."

"Possible. Perhaps I will look into it."

Further conversation was prevented by loud noises echoing out of Edo Bay. It sounded like huge tree trunks were being snapped in two. Then the shoreline ahead of them exploded.

"Cannonade!" Shigeru shouted. "Ships are firing on the palaces!"

Genji spurred his horse through the panicking crowd and sped toward Quiet Crane at full gallop.

"Wait!"

"Lord!"

Genji ignored them. Shigeru, Hidé, and Shimoda kicked their horses and dashed after him.

Taro looked to Sohaku for orders.

"Is this the best we can do?" Sohaku said. "Rush into the muzzles of the outsiders' cannons?"

"Sir!" Taro worked hard to restrain his horse, which was eager to join its galloping companions.

"Our leaders are going in the wrong direction," Sohaku said.

"Sir, your orders!" Taro was as eager to go as his horse. Six months posing as a monk had not made him one.

Sohaku nodded.

Taro released the restraining pressure on the bit and his horse bolted forward. Taro sped away, a monk with two incongruous swords in his sash, poised in his saddle like a charging cavalryman.

Sohaku was alone in the street. The populace had fled indoors. A wise reaction when warfare was a matter of swords and arrows. Potentially suicidal now. Almost as suicidal as riding into cannon fire. Sohaku kicked his horse and chased after his lord.

•   •   •   •   •

Stark hadn't fired a gun in over a year. After he joined the True Word Mission in San Francisco, he told Emily and Cromwell he'd thrown his weapons into the Pacific Ocean. That put an end to target practice. Since he couldn't shoot, he concentrated on drawing his guns as fast as he could. He did this in his room at the mission and, on the voyage, in his cabin aboard the *Star of Bethlehem*. His aim was probably off some by now. There was only one way to stay sharp, and that was actually firing bullets. Feeling the gun kick backward as the gunpowder exploded and the lead went flying. Not letting the movement or noise or flash or smell or smoke distract him. He was confident he could still hit the center of a man's chest at ten paces. Twenty might be a stretch now. His speed was definitely up, though. He was a notch or two quicker than he had been before, when he was famous for a time out in west Texas.

For the five days they'd been in Lord Genji's palace, he hadn't touched his guns at all. Half the walls were literally made of paper, and people were always around. The only place he could be sure of privacy was his own mind. So that's where he practiced.

Draw.

Cock the hammer on the upswing.

Sight the heart.

Squeeze the trigger.

Cock the hammer on the recoil.

Sight the heart.

Squeeze the trigger.

There was an advantage to this. His mind was a portable room, he could practice anywhere he was, anytime.

The samurai who kept watch over him thought he was engaged in prayer or meditation, communing with his God or letting his consciousness release all thoughts, silently repeating mantras like the followers of Amida Buddha, or being one with the void like the practitioners of Zen. Whatever he was doing, it kept him motionless for long stretches of time. The samurai had never before seen an outsider so quiet. He was nearly as still as the rocks he stood among, there in the courtyard garden.

Draw, cock the hammer, sight, fire. Over and over and over. Stark was hard at it in his head when he heard a sharp whistling sound coming his way. He didn't hear the explosion.

When he opened his eyes, he was in complete silence. It was night. He stood by the doorway and looked into the bedroom. Mary Anne cradled the two children in her arms. Becky and Louise were still little girls, but not as little as they used to be. It was time for the girls to go to their own bed and let him get into his. But mother and daughters looked so serene in their sleep, he couldn't bring himself to wake them. They were his three beautiful dreamers.

Mary Anne's eyelids fluttered open. She saw him and smiled. Softly, she said, "I love you."

Before he could answer, the next explosion knocked him awake. He was flat on his back. More whistling, more blasts followed in quick succession. Shrapnel and debris sliced through the air.

A rain of blood splashed on the ground beside him. Stark looked up. The upper half of the samurai who had been watching him was tangled in the branches of the willow tree. The lower half remained kneeling on the polished wooden walkway.

The smart move was to cover up and stay put. There was no use trying to escape. Which way was safety? But Stark didn't think about that. He jumped up and ran toward Cromwell's room. That's where he had taken Emily only minutes ago, and that's where Heiko was going when he passed her in the hallway. Emily was the only person left in the world whom he could even call an acquaintance. Without her, he was completely alone. Why Heiko was also on his mind, he didn't know.

One of the four buildings that had enclosed the courtyard was gone, and a second disintegrated into fire and splintered wood as Stark ran by.

He found the entire guest wing of the palace smashed and burning. Someone had gotten there before him, a burly man already searching intently for survivors.

Kuma, who was the man Stark saw, was interested in only four people. Heiko, to save her if he could. And the three outsiders, to finish them off. The bombardment gave him an opportunity to enter the palace he would not otherwise have had. He didn't know whose cannons had done the damage, but he was sure it wasn't the Shogun's. The Sticky Eye, Kawakami, would have told him in advance if that was the case. So who had dared commit such an act of war without the Shogun's knowledge or permission? Kuma wondered about it idly as he probed in the rubble. Perhaps the civil war everyone had anticipated for so long had begun at last. Odd, though, that it would commence here at the palaces of the Great Lords in Edo instead of with attacks on castles, key passes, and the two great national highways, the Tokaido along the coast and the Nakasendo through the center of the country. The explosions were moving away to the east, ravaging the palaces of supporters and opponents of the Shogun alike. What a confused time to live in.

Kuma lifted away a fallen beam. Ah, there she was.

"Hei-chan," Kuma said. Heiko opened her eyes and blinked. Her color was good. A quick check revealed no major bones out of place, and no bleeding. She was probably only dazed. "You're not hurt, are you?"

"I don't think so," Heiko said.

Kuma didn't realize how much tension was in his body until his shoulders relaxed in relief at Heiko's words. He had watched her at Sticky Eye's behest ever since she was brought to the village when she was three years old. Then it had been a job. Through the years, it had become something else. He had decided some time ago that if Sticky Eye ordered him to kill her, he would kill Sticky Eye instead. Indeed, he was ready to kill anyone who was a threat to her. Genji, Kudo, even the Shogun himself. Not a very professional attitude, nor a loyal one, he admitted, but what was he to do? He loved like his most precious child this young woman who was no more than a tool he had helped create.

"Did you set off a bomb?" Heiko asked.

"No. Cannons, I think from the sea."

"Why? Has war come?"

"I don't know. Don't struggle. I'm getting you out." He carefully shifted the heavy beam away from her. When he did so, he saw strange pale hair spilled across one of Heiko's arms. The outsider woman. He pulled out his dagger. An inconspicuous slit at the side of her throat and her death would be certain.

Stark was still twenty paces away when he saw the blade. The man appeared ready to cut away some obstruction. Then he turned in Stark's direction and their eyes met. Stark recognized the look. That was how eyes focused when they sighted down the barrel of a gun.

Kuma let the knife fall from his hand as soon as he saw Stark. He reached for a *shuriken*, a star-shaped throwing knife, hidden in his sash. Twenty paces was somewhat beyond perfect range, but if he missed with the first one, he would connect with the second. He dashed toward Stark, closing the distance between them as he threw.

At the same moment, Stark reached for the .32 caliber revolver concealed in his shirt at his left waist. The constant imaginary gunfights had set a pattern in his body that movements followed without thought. He cross-drew with his right hand and fired less than a heartbeat before the shuriken left Kuma's hand. Lack of live firing took its toll on his aim. His bullet ricocheted off a rock to the right of Kuma.

The unexpected crack of gunfire disturbed Kuma just enough to make him miss, too. His first shuriken went spinning by Stark's left shoulder. Still moving toward his target, he drew his second shuriken.

Kuma was far more practiced in his arts than Stark was in his. But it took him a full second to draw his arm back from the first throw, pull another shuriken from his sash, and fling it at Stark. It only took Stark half as long to cock the hammer on the re-coil, aim, and squeeze the trigger a second time.

The bullet tore through Kuma's chest and threw

him on his back. The shuriken went high into the air and fell harmlessly in the remnants of the garden.

Stark walked toward the fallen man, ready to fire again. But as he stood over him, Stark saw that he wouldn't have to use another bullet. He put his gun away and began digging the two women out.

The bombardment was over. In the new dead silence, Stark heard approaching footsteps. He almost drew on the two samurai before he saw who they were.

· · · · · ·

Genji rode through where the front gate had been. He leaped from his saddle and ran into the rubble toward the center of the palace. Reverend Cromwell had been placed in a room bordering the central garden. Heiko would likely have been nearby.

He was surprised that his first concern was for her. He should be thinking about defense or evacuation. Such a short barrage could easily be followed by the landing of an invasion force. Or he should be thinking about the outsiders, specifically Matthew Stark. He had told Sohaku that the dying preacher, Zephaniah Cromwell, was the one whose arrival was prophesied by his grandfather, but of course, that was not at all what he thought. Genji had known as soon as he'd seen Stark that he was no missionary. He had to be the one his grandfather meant. But searching through the ruins of Quiet Crane, Genji could think of nothing but Heiko.

How dull his life would be without her. Quite apart from the prophecies of his grandfather and his own, as yet unconfirmed, gift of foreknowledge, everyone else he knew was so drearily predictable. The three advisors he had inherited, Saiki, Kudo, and Sohaku, could always be counted on to advocate the least dynamic course of action. Saiki, the eldest, was not yet forty, yet all three behaved like old men. And if a man was to be judged by his enemies as well as his friends, how inadequate must he be to have as his main foe a blithering incompetent like Sticky Eye Kawakami, the Shogun's spymaster? Did Kawakami really believe Heiko could enter Genji's bed without arousing suspicion as well as desire? He didn't have to follow her to know who employed her. It could be no one else. As for love, well, the most beautiful geisha in Edo would hardly let herself fall in love with him unless she had an ulterior motive. Of the sixty truly great Great Lords, at least fifty were richer and more powerful than Genji.

And yet, here he was, his breath shallow, his heart cold, his body numb, fearing the worst, a world without Heiko. How and when had it happened? He hadn't noticed. The most important person in his life was a woman who was surely a spy, and almost surely an assassin as well.

"Lord!" Saiki stumbled out of a half-collapsed room, bleeding from a small cut on his forehead. "You should not be here. The enemy may resume firing at any time."

"Where's Heiko?" Genji said. The pounding of the blood in his ears was as loud as cannon fire. He ran toward the shattered guest wing and climbed over a collapsed walkway just in time to see a fat man he didn't recognize fling two spinning star blades at Stark. Stark drew a hidden pistol, fired even faster than the ninja threw, and dropped the fat man with his second shot.

"Was that gunfire?" Saiki scrambled up next to him.

"Come on," Genji said, "I think Stark found her."

•   •   •   •   •

"Hei-chan." Heiko heard her name and opened her eyes. She saw Kuma's comforting face looking down at her. Behind him was the open sky. "You're not hurt, are you?"

"I don't think so," Heiko said.

Kuma smiled and began shifting pieces of the building off her.

"Did you set off that bomb?" Heiko asked.

Kuma's eyes lost their gentleness. His smile disappeared and he pulled out his dagger.

Heiko knew his intentions right away. She could feel Emily's head resting on her shoulder.

"No, Kuma, don't."

Kuma abruptly looked away, dropped his dagger, and leaped out of Heiko's field of view. Two gunshots followed in quick succession, then nothing, until Matthew Stark stood over her where Kuma had been. He began digging her out without saying a word. Then he, too, stopped suddenly, his hand going to his left waist. He was the one who had fired the gun, Heiko realized, which was now hidden in his shirt. Stark must have recognized whoever was coming because he left the gun where it was and resumed his rescue efforts.

"Don't move her," Genji said. "She might be hurt. Wait until Dr. Ozawa arrives."

Heiko sat up. "I might be bruised, lord, nothing more. When the doctor arrives, he will be needed elsewhere." She could hear cries of anguish coming from every direction, near and far. Kuma must have set more than one bomb. Why had he not warned her? That was very unlike him. Indeed, it was so unlike him, someone else must be responsible. Kuma would never have put her life at risk. Unlikely though it seemed, perhaps it had been cannons after all. She would question him when they next met and learn the truth. Kuma was a good liar, but not with her. She stood and tested her footing.

"Be careful, please." Genji put his arm around her waist to support her. "You could be seriously injured and not know it." His face, usually so placid under the most trying of circumstances, was tense with worry. Furrows lined his forehead. His brows bunched together. The small, slightly disdainful smile that always seemed to grace his lips was gone.

Genji's unconcealed concern surprised Heiko more than the explosion that had blown the room apart. Sudden joy flooded her heart and she smiled without thinking. Then Genji surprised her even more. His arms went around her and he embraced her tightly.

His lord's flagrant emotional nakedness stunned Saiki. Embarrassed, he turned away and saw Hidé and Shimoda staring openmouthed at Genji and Heiko.

"Why are you standing there like two fools?" Saiki said. "Check the perimeters. Prepare for an assault."

"The ships are sailing away," Hidé said. "No troops came ashore."

"Ships?"

"Yes, sir. In the bay. Three warships under steam, flying red, white, and blue tricolor flags. They raked the entire Tsukiji district with their cannons."

"Outsiders did this?" Saiki's voice shook with outrage.

"Yes, sir," Hidé said.

"What was the pattern of the flags? The Dutch, French, English, and Americans all use red, white, and blue."

"There were more than three bars of color, I think," Hidé said, "weren't there?"

Shimoda tipped his head noncommittally. "I thought, yes, perhaps so."

"How observant," Saiki said. "Now all we know for sure is that the Russians and the Germans were not involved. It's not likely to be the Dutch. So French, English, or American."

"Or perhaps all three," Shimoda said. "There might have been more than one kind of flag."

"Give a hand," Stark said.

Hidé and Shimoda understood what he wanted without understanding his words. They both bowed to Saiki and went to the outsider's assistance.

"Slowly," Stark said. He and the two samurai moved the heavy beam that lay across Emily's back. Most of its weight rested on a partially collapsed wall. If it had hit the wall before it hit Emily, she shouldn't have been hurt too badly. He couldn't tell right now because she was still lying facedown and unconscious. She hadn't moved since he'd found her. He knelt and ran his hand slowly down her back, feeling for breaks. When he neared the base of her spine, her eyes snapped open with violent suddenness. She took in a short, sharp breath, spun around, and kicked Stark in the stomach, knocking him on his back. She was on her feet in a flash, eyes wild and confused, looking for a place to run.

"Emily, we're safe." Heiko slipped out of Genji's embrace. She moved slowly toward the frightened woman. "Lord Genji and his samurai are here. No one can harm us."

"Heiko." Emily's eyes cleared. The tension that had clenched her body dissolved and she melted into Heiko's arms, sobbing. "I thought . . ." She didn't finish what she was saying, but Heiko understood. It was the past clawing at her. So it was with so many women. The past, always the past. That which was and could not be undone.

"May all the Buddhas and all the gods save us," Saiki muttered. He turned away from yet another outrageous, inappropriately public display of emotion. The outsider woman's behavior was of no consequence. She was a barbarian like any other outsider. But Heiko should know better. The perfected expression of appropriate behavior was the essence of a geisha's being. If it had not been clear to Saiki before, it was utterly clear now: The outsiders were a deadly pollution that must be completely expunged, and the sooner the better. Their very presence caused the ancient ways to deteriorate with shocking rapidity. Before his eyes was the proof. His own lord, the heir of one of the most venerable clans in the realm, clutching at a woman like a drunken lout in the Yoshiwara pleasure district. The most renowned geisha of Edo embracing an outsider woman as if the two were unnatural lovers.

All the Buddhas and all the gods may not be enough to save us, Saiki thought. We are supposed to be a nation of warriors. Yet we have permitted ourselves to grow so weak, the outsiders can smash the palaces of the Great Lords in the Shogun's capital and we can do nothing to defend ourselves. His hand went to his sword in frustrated rage. But he didn't draw it. There was no one to draw it against.

Smiling, Stark said, "Never knew you packed such a wallop, Emily."

"I'm so sorry, Matthew. I was confused."

"No harm done." He bent down and picked up the dagger Kuma had dropped.

Saiki instantly drew his sword.

"Unnecessary," Genji said to him. Then to Stark he said, "Who was he going to kill? Heiko or Emily?"

Stark and Genji looked down at Kuma's body. Stark shook his head.

"Do you know him?"

"No," Genji said. He turned to Heiko. "Do you?"

When she'd heard the two shots and nothing more, she'd assumed Kuma had gotten away. All her life, he always had. At the sight of his body, she lost her balance. She closed her eyes and leaned against Genji, feigning a lesser weakness to cover the greater one that took away the strength in her legs. Kuma was dead!

"No, my lord," Heiko said.

Saiki said, "Surely, as weak as they are, not even the Shogun's advisors will let this insult pass unpunished."

Genji looked around at the ruins of Quiet Crane.

"There is no insult here," he said. "We have been asleep for three centuries, dreaming an ancient warrior dream. Now we are awake. That is all."

8

Makkyo

Some believe victory comes from superior strategy.
Others trust valor.
Yet others rest their hopes on the favor of the gods.
Then there are those who place their faith in spies, assassins, seductions, betrayals, corruption, greed, fear.
These are all delusory paths for one simple reason. One thought of victory and you lose the real while clutching the false.
What is the real? When the blades of your enemies are slashing ferociously at you, and your life hangs in the balance, you will know.
If you do not, you have lived your life in vain.

SUZUME–NO–KUMO
(1599)

Saiki said, "You were remiss, Reverend Abbot, in not bringing the other outsider back with you. According to the prophecy, an outsider will save our lord's life in the New Year. We do not yet know which one."

Sohaku ignored the sarcastic edge in Saiki's voice when he pronounced his former ecclesiastical title. "I urged Lord Genji to do so. He refused, saying the outsider of the prophecy has already been met, and his life already saved."

"We three were entrusted by our late Lord Kiyori to safeguard his grandson," Kudo said. "This sometimes means we must be adamant, even against the express views of the young lord. His life is more important than whether we win or lose his favor."

"I am well aware of that," Sohaku said, "but I can hardly order actions in direct contradiction to his commands."

"A weak argument," Saiki said. "You could have arranged for the outsider to come to Edo on his own, perhaps as a result of a 'misunderstanding.' Our lord would have accepted that."

"Thank you for your instruction," Sohaku said. Heat rising, he bowed with excessive submissiveness. "Please guide me further. What 'misunderstanding' might I have used to keep him from returning Lord Shigeru to duty?"

"Thank you for raising another important issue," Saiki said, returning Sohaku's exaggerated bow with one of his own. "Perhaps you would be so kind as to tell us in detail how that happened. My poor understanding fails to grasp how such a dangerous and preposterous turn of events could possibly have occurred."

"May I suggest we converse in lower tones," Kudo said. "Voices tend to carry from our present location." In fact, both Saiki and Sohaku were speaking in a subdued manner. The rapidly escalating level of politeness, however, was a clear danger signal. It was the customary prelude to many a sudden duel. Kudo's warning was his way of defusing the situation.

The three men were in the wreckage of one of the rooms that had faced the central garden. Remarkably, the garden itself had survived the bombardment intact. Not even the pattern raked into the sand had been touched. The same could not be said of the room. The roof, walls, and most of the floor were gone. Saiki, Sohaku, and Kudo sat in a remnant corner, their attendants on guard where the doorway had been. The change in circumstances was not reflected in anyone's posture, demeanor, or formality.

"There is much confusion, fear, and speculation," Kudo said. "No one knows who perpetrated the attack, or why. We are leaders. Everyone will look to us for answers. Should we not be seeking those answers instead of allocating blame?"

"Answers are unimportant," Saiki said. "What matters is our behavior. If we are confident, those who follow us will be confident as well, whether they—or we, for that matter—know anything or not."

Sohaku leaned forward. "We shouldn't quibble over meaningless details about the outsider or Shigeru. The real question is much more serious."

"I agree," Kudo said. "We should reach a decision on the critical matter."

"I do not believe an obvious conclusion has yet presented itself," Saiki said.

Sohaku and Kudo looked at each other in surprise.

"Am I missing something?" Sohaku said. "When last we met, you were the strongest among us in contemplating the appointment of a regent to wield actual power in the domain. If my recollection is correct, you said the young lord was a dilettante who would lead our clan to ruin."

"Perhaps I should have characterized him as somewhat too refined, rather than as a dilettante."

"What of his infatuation with the Christian outsiders?" Kudo said. "Surely you have not changed your mind about that?"

"No, I continue to see danger there," Saiki said. He recalled the display of unconcealed emotions he had just lately witnessed. "If anything, the danger is greater than ever. Actions against them may have to be initiated in the future, covertly and without the permission of the young lord, if necessary."

Kudo nodded, reassured. "Taken together with everything else, his behavior toward his uncle is decisive."

"I wonder if it is," Saiki said. "It appears questionable on the surface, I agree. However, put in the context of prophetic visions, it could be an extremely wise move."

"Prophetic visions?" Sohaku was outraged. "Since when do you believe in that fairy tale? I never saw any evidence Lord Kiyori could foretell the future, and I served him for twenty years. As for Lord Genji, the only interest he has in the future is which geisha he will sleep with tonight and which sake he will acquire for his next moon-viewing party."

"Shigeru is a complete madman," Kudo said. "I was among those who took him into custody. Had you been there, you would not be so complacent. He sat laughing, drenched in the blood of his own clansmen, the slaughtered bodies of his wife, his daughters, and his heir lying before him. I will never forget it. I wish I could."

"I hear and understand," Saiki said.

Sohaku and Kudo looked at each other again, this time with resignation. Saiki had spoken his favorite catchphrase, the one that indicated that his mind was made up and would not be changed.

Saiki continued. "However, as cogent as your observations undoubtedly are, my view of the young lord has undergone a certain transformation. While I remain uncertain about his visionary ability, I am now open to the possibility of its existence." He pointed off to the eastern end of the garden, where the innermost part of the palace had been.

Sohaku looked. "I see nothing but ruins. Undeniable evidence of the need for drastic change."

"I, too, see ruins," Saiki said, "but I see something you fail to see."

"Which is?"

"Those are the remains of Lord Genji's quarters."

"Yes, I know. So?"

"He would have been there when the bombardment took place had he not traveled to Mushindo Monastery." Saiki was gratified to see the dawning of understanding in his comrades' faces.

"He couldn't have known," Kudo said. But his voice was shaky.

"Yet it appears he did," Saiki said.

"Nothing is proven," Sohaku said.

"Nor disproved," Saiki said.

"If he knew, why didn't he warn us?" Sohaku said.

"I don't pretend to understand the workings of mystical foresight," Saiki said. "Clearly, we must defer a decision on this matter to a later date. In the meantime, prepare for travel. This location is no longer safe."

"You mean to recommend evacuation to Cloud of Sparrows," Sohaku said.

"I do."

"Logistically alone, a very difficult undertaking," Sohaku said. "Most of the domains between Edo and Akaoka are hostile to us. The Inland Sea is not itself a significant barrier. Its waters, however, are patrolled by the Shogun's naval forces. Crossing to our home island under such conditions will be hazardous."

"I prefer hazardous to fatal," Saiki said. "We cannot remain where we are."

"There is another consideration," Kudo said. "The Shogun has not given permission for anyone to withdraw from Edo."

"My loyalty is to Okumichi no kami Genji, Great Lord of Akaoka," Saiki said, "not the usurper who boasts the Shogun's title and occupies the Shogun's palace." He bowed and rose to his feet. "If my lord orders me to obey that person, I will. If he orders me to kill that person instead, then only my own death will prevent me from carrying out the command. I know who I am. I trust you do, too." Without waiting for a reply, he turned away and proceeded toward the wreckage of his lord's quarters.

"He's a stubborn old man," Kudo said.

Sohaku snorted. "He was a stubborn young man. Why would the years diminish his salient attribute?"

"It's very clear he'll never agree to a regency now. He's convinced himself Genji can see the future."

No more words were spoken. After a lengthy

silence, Sohaku and Kudo looked at each other, eye to eye, bowed, and rose as one.

• • • • •

"I'm sorry, Emily," Stark said. "I can't find the slightest trace of him."

"Perhaps the angels transported him as he thought they would," Emily said, then smiled a sad smile to show she didn't believe it.

"What will you do now?" Stark asked.

"What I must. I will gather as much of our things as I can find, pack them, and await the next ship returning to America." The very thought convulsed the muscles of her chest and brought fresh tears to her eyes. She sat down hard on the ground beside the debris of her former room and wept shamelessly. She had found the haven she had not dared to believe existed, a paradise where she escaped her beauty so completely she was considered positively repulsive. She had found it, and with a single gunshot, she had lost it. It was too much for her. She was strong, but she was not that strong.

Stark knelt down and took her into his arms, resting her head against his chest. Misunderstanding the cause of her sorrow, he said, "You will feel better when you're home," which only served to increase her agony. Helplessly, he held her as she clutched at him and sobbed. "You're young, Emily. Your life has just begun. Heaven will smile on you. You will find love anew. I know you will."

Emily wanted to tell him it wasn't love she wanted to find, it was peace. The words couldn't find their way out through her devastating sorrow.

• • • • •

As soon as the cannons stopped firing, Shigeru went to the perimeter of the palace grounds, where the outer walls had been, and stood guard. There was no danger within. But if anyone intended to take advantage of the confusion to make an attempt on Genji's life, they would do so now, in the moments immediately following the attack. Shigeru was certain Sohaku was not yet ready to take action. He would have to sound out Saiki and Kudo first. So the only present concern was external enemies. He hoped they would come. It would be good practice. He would worry about Sohaku later, and about Saiki and Kudo, too, if it became necessary. It was unfortunate that, with danger all around, there was also the possibility that the three senior commanders of the clan must be killed. Even if Saiki and Kudo remained loyal, the loss of Sohaku would be a severe blow. He was the best strategist of the lot, and the best fighter after Shigeru himself.

The sound of approaching horses focused Shigeru's attention. Two horses. Followed by between forty and fifty men on foot. The steady, disciplined pace of the runners' footsteps told him they had to be samurai. Shigeru felt his shoulders relax and his breathing slow. He was ready.

Moments later, Sticky Eye Kawakami, chief of the Shogun's secret police, entered the street fronting the palace astride a black horse. Beside him, also mounted, was his assistant, Mukai, on an appropriately inferior gray mare. Behind them was a brigade of forty running samurai. Kawakami reined his horse to a halt, a surprised look on his face as he recognized Shigeru.

"Lord Shigeru, I was unaware of your presence in Edo."

"I have only just arrived, Lord Kawakami, and have not yet had the opportunity to inform you of my whereabouts."

"Not to put too fine a point on it, but I was also unaware of your previous location."

"Oh? A terrible lapse on the part of my subordinates." Shigeru bowed without taking his eyes off Kawakami. "I will be sure to chastise the guilty parties."

"I am sure you will," Kawakami said. "In the meantime, please permit me to enter the grounds and make an inspection."

"We were not informed that an inspection was to take place. Therefore, I must regretfully decline your offer."

"I am not making an offer." Kawakami spurred his horse forward and his men followed closely. "By the command of the Shogun, I am to inspect every damaged palace and interview every surviving lord. Please stand aside, Lord Shigeru."

Shigeru's swords came out of their scabbards as smoothly and lightly as the unfolding of a crane's wings. One moment, he stood empty-handed. The next, the longer katana was in his right hand and the shorter wakizashi was in his left. He held the weapons to either side of his body, in a stance that presented neither defensive posture nor offensive preparation. Indeed, to the untutored eye, it would seem that Shigeru was preparing to surrender, so unready for combat did he appear to be.

Kawakami, of course, knew that this was not the case. Like every good samurai, he had studied the *Go-rin-no-sho*, Miyamoto Musashi's classic treatise on swordsmanship. Shigeru's stance was the ultimate one in the moment before combat—*Ku*, emptiness.

Far from being unready, he was open to anything, anticipating nothing, accepting everything. Only one man in ancient times had dared to use the stance, and that was Musashi himself. Since then, there had been only one other. Shigeru.

Kawakami gave the signal and forty blades left their scabbards. His men quickly moved into position to attack the lone swordsman from three directions. They did not go behind him. That would require them to cross the line between the Edo street and the grounds of the Okumichi palace. Kawakami had not yet ordered them to do so.

Kawakami did not draw his own sword. He kept his horse at what he judged to be a safe distance from the likely confrontation. "Are you so ungrounded in reality that you dare to defy the direct commands of the Shogun?"

"As you know, I do not have the privilege of serving the Shogun," Shigeru said. "Unless my own lord conveys those commands to me, they do not exist." He could tell from the way Kawakami held his saddle that he was not an expert horseman. That meant that he could reach him before the man could turn the horse and escape. He estimated the distance between them at five heartbeats. It would be necessary to cut down a dozen intervening men first, but that would be no problem. All of his potential opponents were tense with fear. They were already as good as dead.

"Lord Kawakami, what a surprise." Saiki approached the taut arrangement of adversaries in a casual manner. He seemed unaware of the drawn swords. "I would invite you within for refreshment. However, as you might have noticed, our ability to offer hospitality is somewhat restricted at present. Perhaps another time?"

"Saiki, talk some sense into Lord Shigeru, if you can." He stroked the mane of his jittery mount. "He refuses to permit my entry, which is commanded by the Shogun."

"Forgive the contradiction, Lord Kawakami," Saiki said, walking right up to the semicircle of glittering blades. "I believe Lord Shigeru is correct to deny you entry."

"What?"

"According to the Osaka Protocols, the Shogun must inform a Great Lord of any inspection at least two weeks prior to the scheduled date. As chief administrator of Akaoka Domain, I must inform you that my lord has received no such notice."

"The Osaka Protocols are two hundred and fifty years out of date."

"Nevertheless," Saiki said, with a deep bow and a deeper smile, "they are still in effect."

A clever look came onto Kawakami's face. "As I recall, the Protocols make exception in time of war."

"That is correct. But we are not at war."

A burning building collapsed behind Kawakami, and his horse, panicking, reared up on its hind legs. It was several moments before he was able to fight it back under control.

"If this is not war, it is a remarkably good imitation of it," Kawakami said.

"I was thinking in terms of an actual declaration," Saiki said, "to which the Protocols make specific mention. Has the Shogun declared war on someone?"

Kawakami frowned glumly. "No, he has not."

He turned his horse and abruptly rode off, leaving

Mukai to order his men to cover their weapons and withdraw.

"As diplomatic as ever," Shigeru said, putting his swords away.

"Thank you," Saiki said, though he knew Shigeru had not meant it as a compliment. "You seem quite yourself again, Lord Shigeru, and just in time, too."

• • • • •

"My lord," Hidé said, "Stark carries a hidden firearm."

"Yes, I know," Genji said. "Don't worry. He's not a danger to me."

"Are you certain, my lord?"

"I am."

Hidé relaxed. If this was a matter of foreknowledge, then it was outside his realm of responsibility.

Genji smiled. It was comforting to have as chief bodyguard a man whose mind he could read as well as if he could truly read minds. He said, "Is Hanako well?"

"I don't know, my lord."

"Have you not found her?"

"I haven't looked."

"Why not?"

"My responsibility is to ensure your safety. I can't wander off with personal concerns."

"Hidé, you're speaking of your betrothed, the future mother of your son and heir, your lifetime friend and companion."

"Yes, lord."

"Go find her. Shimoda will protect me in your absence, won't you, Shimoda?"

"Yes, lord."

Hidé bowed down to the ground. "I will return quickly."

"You will return tomorrow morning," Genji said, "after breakfast. And one more thing. Reduce the depth of your bows. As chief bodyguard, it is incorrect for you to take your attention away from our surroundings, even momentarily."

"I hear and obey, my lord."

"Good. Go find your bride."

Heiko waited until Hidé was gone and Shimoda had withdrawn to a discreet distance. They sat on cushions beneath a large tent erected near the shoreline wall, the only section of wall to survive the bombardment intact. A mild onshore wind carried the sea scent to them.

"How much you have changed in such a short time," Heiko said. She touched the side of the sake flask. Satisfied that it contrasted appropriately with the ambient temperature, she filled Genji's cup.

"What do you mean?"

"One week ago, you were a figurehead. A nonentity merely tolerated by your hereditary vassals. Now you are truly their lord. A most remarkable transformation."

"Crisis changes people," Genji said, filling Heiko's cup in turn. "If they are fortunate, crisis shows them what truly matters."

She turned away, dizzied by his frank gaze. How difficult it had been to be in love with him. How much more difficult it was now that he returned her love. If only they were farmers or shopkeepers or fisherfolk, they could give life to their feelings freely, without concern for hidden consequences.

"You are overwhelmed by the emotions of the

moment," she said. "I will not remember anything you say to me today."

"You will always remember," he said, "and so will I. It's not the moment that overwhelms me. It's you, Heiko, you alone."

"It is unnecessary to say sweet words to me," she said. Tears rolled down her cheeks, but a soft smile was on her lips, and her breathing remained calm. "I love you. I have loved you from the moment I met you. I will love you with my life's last breath. You don't have to love me in return."

He smiled that careless smile that always melted her heart. "For me to love you with equal passion is boringly symmetrical, I know. Perhaps, in time I will learn to love you less. Will that please you?"

With a laugh, Heiko fell into his arms. "With my charms? I am afraid you are doomed to love me more over time, not less."

"Confident, aren't you?"

"No, Gen-chan," she said, "I'm not, not at all. Love is a woman's weakness, not her strength. And no matter how beautiful she is, her time of fullest flowering is brief. I don't expect you to love me forever. But please, if you can, please be kind."

He thought of slipping his hand through the wide sleeve of her kimono to caress her. But the day was chilly and his hands were cold. It wouldn't be pleasant for her, so he refrained. Even as these thoughts arose, she moved in such a way that her hand and his found their way into each other's kimonos at the same time. The instant he felt the warmth of her bosom was the same instant he also felt the sharp chill of her fingertips against his own body. Heat and cold were one. Who, he wondered, was the real mind reader here?

"How can I be anything other than kind? When I am with you, when I even think about you, all the cruel edges of the world fall away, and my heart, my entire being, grows soft."

"Not your entire being."

"Well, no, perhaps not my entire being."

They gave no thought to undressing. Even had they been within the confines of Genji's innermost rooms, they would not have done so, not for a midday tryst. Their clothing was too complex, particularly Heiko's.

Her kimono was silk, of the *omeshi* style of heavy crepe. Over it, she wore a long *haori* outer coat, padded against the cold. The kimono was secured by a wide, embroidered *obi* sash, which was tied in a *fukura suzume* bow and accented at the top edge by an *obi-age* bustle sash tucked under it.

There were over three hundred different bows to choose from, and every day Heiko spent considerable time deciding which one to tie. She had chosen the fukura suzume pattern—the plump sparrow—because she had thought it likely that Genji would return home today, and wanted to celebrate the occasion with a subtle visual reference to the clan totem. As it turned out, she had estimated his arrival day accurately. Had she been wrong, she would not have tied the fukura suzume again. That would have been graceless. Instead, if her timing had been off, she would have missed the opportunity and accepted the fact.

An *obi-jime* cord held the obi itself in place. Between the kimono and the obi, she wore an *obi-ita* stay, which served to keep the kimono from wrinkling along the obi line. A *makura* pad beneath the bow helped keep its shape. An *obi-dome* brooch attached to a cord somewhat narrower than the obi-jime cord decorated the front of the obi.

Beneath the kimono, obi, makura, obi-age, obi-jime, and obi-dome, she wore a *nagajuban* full-length underkimono, also of silk. The cords attached to the collar ends were passed through the loops of the *chikara nuno* collar and tied in such a way as to create the appropriate fist-sized opening at the nape of the neck. A *date-maki* undersash was tied around the nagajuban.

Beneath the nagajuban was the *hadajuban* undershirt and *susoyoke* half slip. Beneath these were various pads at the collarbone, stomach, and waist. Since the kimono was cut in straight lines, these pads were necessary to conform the shape of the body to the gown's natural flowing outlines. She would normally also have worn a sash around her upper torso to suppress her bustline. But since she expected Genji's return, she had not wrapped herself this morning.

Though both Genji and Heiko remained clothed, there were more than enough openings in their attire to permit intimacy of the highest and closest order. Indeed, just as heat and cold were one, so were being dressed and the state of utter nakedness.

Breathing hard, Genji said, "If love is your weakness, I shudder to imagine what your strength might be."

Doing her best not to pant, Heiko said, "You will, I think, shudder anyway, my lord."

Keeping his eyes politely averted, but unable to keep a smile from his face, Shimoda silently lowered the flaps of the tent.

· · · · ·

Once he began searching for Hanako, the full extent of the destruction finally struck Hidé. A ferocious earthquake had devastated Edo when he was a child, followed as earthquakes often were by a fire that immolated half the city. Quiet Crane Palace had been reduced to similar smoking rubble, with crushed and dismembered bodies strewn everywhere, and the air acrid with roasting human flesh. Hidé's stomach churned as he imagined what the odor burning his nostrils could signify. He fought back nausea and tears with equal effort.

At the wreckage of the outsiders' rooms, he saw a bright shred of a woman's kimono caught under a fallen beam. Kneeling, he picked it up and held it gently with both hands. Was it hers? She had worn a similar fabric when he had last seen her, he thought, but he couldn't be sure. Why wasn't he more observant? How could he deserve to be chief bodyguard when he couldn't even identify his intended wife's kimono?

No sooner did Hidé have this thought than he rejected it. He could no longer indulge in such self-doubt. His lord had appointed him to this post. To doubt his ability to carry out his duties was to doubt his lord. Loyalty demanded that he believe in himself because his lord believed in him. When he experienced one of his many faults, he must now endeavor to correct himself, to become the man his lord saw within him. Such was his obligation. He stood. His posture straight and confident.

But the shred of silk was still in his hand and tears welled in his eyes. What good were status and accolades with no one to share them? Where was the sweetness in triumph, the comforting presence in defeat, the celebration and mourning even in a perfect samurai's death?

Hidé was sixteen years old and wearing his first full-sized katana when he met Hanako. She was then an orphan nine years of age, just brought into the palace by Lord Kiyori on old Abbot Zengen's recommendation. He blushed as he remembered the first words he had spoken to her.

•   •   •   •   •

"You, fetch me some tea."

The little girl in the faded cotton kimono raised her chin and said, "Fetch it yourself."

"You will bring me tea, girl."

"I will not."

"You are a servant. I am a samurai. You will do as I command."

The little girl laughed.

"Lord Kiyori is a samurai," she said. "Lord Shigeru, Lord Saiki, Lord Kudo, Lord Tanaka, they are samurai. You, you're just a brat with a new unblooded sword."

Angry embarrassment brought him to his feet, his hand on the hilt of his katana.

"I am a samurai. I can cut you down right now."

"You cannot."

"What?" Hidé was stunned yet again by the girl's brazen and unexpected responses. "A samurai has the power of life and death over any peasant like you."

"Not you."

"And why not me?"

"Because I am in the household service of your clan. You are duty-bound to protect me. With your own life, if necessary."

And with that, the little girl walked away, leaving a shamed Hidé standing openmouthed and speechless behind her.

· · · · ·

He looked around at the ruins of the palace. Yes, was it not, in fact, right on this very spot that it had occurred, so many years ago? He stared at the ground, as he had stared at it then. She had been only a child, but she had reminded him of something he should never have let out of his thoughts. A samurai was a protector, not an arrogant bully.

That brazen little girl had grown up to be a woman of merit and virtue, and so, naturally, he had avoided her over the years as he drank and gambled his life away.

What a perfect wife Lord Genji had chosen for him. And now she was lost forever.

"Hidé!"

He turned at the sound of Hanako's surprised voice.

She stood where a walkway had been, a tray with a tea service in her hands.

Overwhelmed by happiness, Hidé moved to embrace her, but caught himself just before doing so. He bowed instead.

"I am relieved to see you uninjured."

She returned his bow.

"I am honored that you have some small concern for such an unimportant person."

"You are not unimportant," Hidé said, "not to me."

Though it was impossible to determine who was more surprised by his words, Hanako or Hidé himself, Hanako's reaction was clearly more dramatic.

Stunned by his directness, she teetered and almost dropped the tray. Only Hidé's quick assistance prevented it. When he grabbed the tray, he inadvertently brushed against one of her hands. Unexpectedly, she felt herself softening at this, their first touch.

Hidé said, "Lord Genji has commanded me not to return until the morning. After breakfast."

Hanako blushed, understanding his meaning. "Our lord is very generous," she said, keeping her eyes demurely averted.

Hidé had so much to say, he couldn't keep it all in any longer. "Hanako, we fought a battle against Lord Gaiho's troops on the way to Mushindo Monastery. On the basis of my actions, Lord Genji has appointed me his chief bodyguard."

"I am so happy for you," Hanako said. "There is no doubt you will conduct yourself with great courage and honor." She bowed low once again. "Please excuse me for a time. I must attend upon Lord Shigeru and Lord Saiki. I will return to you, my lord, as soon as my duties permit."

It wasn't until he was watching her walk away—not on the shortest route across the ruins, but properly where the interior corridor had been, as if nothing had changed—that Hidé realized she had referred to him as "my lord," and that he was now entitled to be so called. Chief bodyguard was a landed rank. Though Lord Genji had not specified this, he surely would during his official New Year's proclamations.

Hidé recalled the warmth he had felt when their hands had touched a few moments ago. It was the first physical contact they had ever had. He realized he had loved Hanako for a long time without knowing it. Yet Lord Genji knew. Once again, Hidé was moved to tears by the gratitude he felt. How blessed he was, they all were, to serve a prescient master.

He went to examine his room, to see if it still existed. He hoped at least a wall remained so that he and his bride would have some measure of privacy tonight.

·　·　·　·　·

Hanako tried to focus all her attention on her footing. The wreckage encouraged missteps. To clumsily trip and fall in view of her future husband on the eve of their first intimacy, could anything be more mortifying? But her efforts to concentrate on the here and now were in vain. Her thoughts drifted back a dozen years, to the sound of Lord Kiyori's voice.

·　·　·　·　·

"Hanako."

"My lord." She fell to her knees and pressed her forehead to the ground. Her body shook with fear. Walking proudly, chin held high, she had been so pleased with herself for deflating that smug, handsome boy, she had failed to notice the presence of the Great Lord himself.

"Come with me."

Shivering uncontrollably in the mild spring sunlight, she followed with downcast eyes, certain she was being led to her doom. Why else would the Great Lord deign to speak to her, an orphaned nobody in this wondrous palace only because of the kindness of old Zengen, the village priest?

Was the boy the lord's relative, a favorite nephew, perhaps? Had she foolishly insulted the wrong person so soon after her arrival? Tears welled in her eyes and spilled down her cheeks. How ashamed she was for letting Zengen down. He had gone out of his way to help her after her parents' deaths, and she had wasted the chance. All because of her pride. Had not Zengen told her time and time again, Do not think so highly of yourself, Hanako; the self is but an illusion. Yes, Abbot Zengen, she had said, time after time. But she hadn't taken the lesson to heart, and now it was too late.

Ahead, she could hear the sound of samurai clashing in the practice compound. There was no doubt. She was about to be executed. How could she face her parents in the Pure Land? But no, she wouldn't have to worry about that. She was not worthy of Amida Buddha's salvation. She would descend to some hell realm instead, to work off her evil karma, with Kichi the hermaphrodite witch, and Gonbe the rapist, and Iso the leper. Perhaps in that terrible place she would become Kichi's slave, and Iso's wife.

"Eeeeehhhh!"

The fierce battle cries terrified her so much she couldn't make herself look up, and walked right into Lord Kiyori, who had come to a halt just inside the compound. She recoiled fearfully, but he paid no attention to either the collision or her retreat.

"My lord!" The armored samurai who called out dropped to one knee and inclined his torso forty-five degrees, the abbreviated bow used in the field of battle. The others quickly followed suit.

"Continue," Lord Kiyori said.

They rose and resumed their mock combat. At first, Hanako couldn't understand why no one was dropping dead. Then she saw they were wielding swords of heavy black oak instead of steel.

"The other clans use bamboo shinai for their training," Lord Kiyori said. "Shinai does no damage, and so is useless. In the hands of an accomplished swordsman, black oak can break bones, and sometimes kill, even when the blow lands on armor. We train this way so there is always an element of real danger. Training without danger is not training at all." He looked down at her. "Why do we train?"

"Because you are samurai, my lord."

"What is a samurai?"

She was surprised he was asking her questions instead of having her killed immediately. She was grateful for the delay. A wave of nausea washed over her at the thought of being dragged into Iso's leprous, hellish nuptial bed.

"A warrior, my lord."

"And when was the last war?"

"Over two hundred years ago, my lord."

"Then what is the use of practicing these violent arts? We live in peace."

"Because war may come at any time, my lord. Samurai must be prepared."

"Prepared for what?"

There it was. They had come to it. The ritual was over. Now she would die. She bowed her head and said, "Prepared to kill, my lord," and waited for the blade to sever her neck.

Then Lord Kiyori surprised her again. He said, "No, Hanako, that is not it. Killing doesn't require so much practice. Observe carefully."

She looked up. Men bashed at each other. That's all she could see. At first. But as she continued to watch, she noticed a difference in the bearing of the samurai in the melee. Some moved with focused determination even as blows rained down on them.

Others shifted and jumped about to avoid being hit, and were hit anyway. In the confusion of so many men fighting each other in so small a space, it was impossible to avoid blows, no matter what they did. If the swords had been steel, as they would be in a real battle, few of them would still be alive. And with that realization, the answer came to her.

She said, "They must be prepared to die, my lord."

Lord Kiyori smiled at her. "Such is the fate of a samurai, Hanako. It is not easy to live with such constant fear."

"But a true samurai has no fear, has he, my lord?" She could not imagine the Great Lord afraid of anything.

"Lack of fear is not the mark of courage. It is the mark of idiocy. Courage is knowing fear and overcoming it." Lord Kiyori patted her head. "Sometimes, especially when he is young, a samurai will cover his fear with arrogance. A virtuous woman will forgive him. She will do whatever she can to make him stronger. She will do nothing to weaken him. Do you understand?"

"Yes, my lord."

"You may go."

As soon as she left Lord Kiyori, she hurried to the kitchen. From there, she went back to the courtyard where she had exchanged words with the haughty young man. To her great relief, he was still there, sitting where she had left him. Was it her imagination, or were his shoulders discouragingly slumped? She felt a blush of shame heat her cheeks.

She went up to him, bowed, and knelt. "Your tea, sir samurai."

"Oh," the young samurai said, surprised and flustered. "Thank you."

His shoulders, she thought, straightened as he took the cup. She was glad. She was very, very glad.

• • • • •

Shigeru and Saiki sat on two woven straw tatami mats placed in the center of where Shigeru's main room had been. The original tatami had been blown to infinity by the cannonade. These were slightly damaged survivors from elsewhere. Shigeru was immobile, eyes hooded. He didn't move when Hanako knelt where the doorway had been, bowed, and came forward as if entering a room.

Saiki politely acknowledged her. "I am happy to see you survived the attack, Hanako."

"Thank you, lord." Having heard the horrible rumors, she neared Shigeru with some trepidation, but displayed nothing beyond calm politeness as she poured his tea.

"Have you had a chance to speak with Hidé?" Saiki said.

"Yes, lord."

"Then you know his good news. He has certainly come up in the world in a short time, hasn't he?"

Hanako bowed low. "Undeservedly so, and only because of the great kindness of Lord Genji." In her betrothed's absence, the obligation to be humble fell upon her.

"Our lord is kind without a doubt. But if he has faith in Hidé, then so do I." Saiki did not look at Shigeru, though these words were said more for his benefit than for Hanako's. "Have you decided where you will want to establish your household?"

"No, lord. I have only just learned of his promotion." In truth, she had already envisioned the empty officer's quarters in the west section of the palace furnished modestly yet tastefully. There was just enough room for a nursery. Of course, since that part of the palace had been totally obliterated just hours earlier, the move would have to wait until the rebuilding was completed. A more important action would not wait. Since Hidé was to be chief bodyguard as well as her husband, she was more determined than ever to give him an heir as soon as possible.

"Then you have much to discuss with him. You need not attend upon us. Go join him. He will surely appreciate your presence more than we will."

"Thank you, lord." Hanako gratefully took her leave.

Saiki smiled. How sweet life is when you're young and in love. Not even crisis and tragedy can diminish it. Perhaps they even provide a certain elevation of feelings. For a time, as he waited patiently for Shigeru to begin their discussion, he was lost in reverie, thinking of his own youth and days gone by.

"If he has faith in Hidé, then so do I," Shigeru said, echoing Saiki's words.

Saiki bowed. "I thought perhaps you were too deep in meditation to have heard me."

"I was in meditation, Saiki, not in a coma."

"I am glad of it, Lord Shigeru, for now is not a time for comas."

"Agreed." Shigeru sipped his tea. "The final phase of the Battle of Sekigahara is close at hand."

Saiki considered the inner meaning of those words. For two hundred sixty-one years, the losers in that battle had persistently thought of it as inconclusive. Inconclusive, despite the utter collapse of the Western Regency, the total annihilation of the then-ruling Toyotomi clan, the deaths of nearly one hundred thousand warriors in a single day, and the seemingly permanent elevation of the Tokugawas to Shogun. Inconclusive, because of the absolute unwillingness of any living samurai to accept defeat. What was conclusive? Only death. When the matter was viewed dispassionately, it was clearly insane. It was, however, a viewpoint Saiki shared, despite his awareness of its irrationality. What else could he do? He, too, was a living samurai.

Saiki said, "I am filled with gratitude that it comes in my lifetime." The depth of his emotions brought tears to his eyes. How blessed he was to be fated for war. His father and grandfather, far worthier warriors than he, had lived and died in peace. He was the one being given the opportunity to redeem the honor of his ancestors.

"I, too," Shigeru said.

For several minutes, neither man said anything further. Saiki poured tea for Shigeru. Shigeru poured tea for Saiki.

The day was unseasonably mild for winter. Saiki contemplated the sky. Stratospheric winds, unfelt here below, brushed streaks of white against a pale blue field. In that one eternal moment, he felt the great vividness of life with every cell of his being.

Shigeru, for his part, recalled the feeling of drawing the ancestral swords. Saiki's inopportune intervention had prevented him from testing their sharpness on that idiot, Sticky Eye Kawakami. Yet merely taking them from their scabbards was an enlightening experience. At the very instant he freed the blades, he knew he would be the last Okumichi to wield them in combat. He didn't know when that would be. He couldn't see that clearly. Nor did he know the identity of his ultimate opponent, or the outcome of that combat. All he knew was that he would be the last, and this brought a great heaviness to his heart.

In the debilitating peace that followed Sekigahara, the Tokugawa Shogun had decreed a compilation of the condition and ownership of the realm's most famous swords, called *meito*. The swords in Shigeru's possession, the Sparrow's Talons, were not included because the Lord of Akaoka at the time, Uenomatsu, had refused to participate in any Tokugawa-sponsored project involving swords, the soul of the samurai. Uenomatsu's statement on the subject, duly recorded in the secret scrolls of the clan, was known to every Okumichi.

Let those who prefer tea to combat, the lord said, compile a list of famous teacups.

Though nothing concrete had yet been discussed, the essence of the meeting had already taken place. Shigeru and Saiki had reaffirmed their commitment to Genji as Great Lord of Akaoka; they had pledged to help him bring down the Tokugawa Shogun though it cost them their lives; they had agreed to set aside whatever differences they might have—in the matter of the missionaries, for example—until the more important matter was settled. None of this was explicitly stated. Yet all was understood.

"The situation at Mushindo Monastery was not as it should have been," Shigeru said.

Saiki knew he wasn't speaking about his own recent incarceration, but about Sohaku's reliability as one of Lord Genji's key retainers. "Nor is the situation at Quiet Crane."

Shigeru nodded. So Kudo would have to be eliminated as well as Sohaku. Nothing more needed to be said on that subject. The time for action was not yet. Conditions would ripen, and when they did, actions would unfold as they should. Covert assassination was not a concern in this case. Neither Sohaku nor Kudo could hope to retain the loyalty of their own vassals if they used devious means to kill Genji. Such treachery would taint them beyond redemption. They could only triumph through open rebellion and victory on the field of battle. They would, of course, choose a time and place to their greatest advantage. One such opportunity would occur very shortly.

"You will recommend withdrawal from Edo?"

"There is no other choice," Saiki said.

Shigeru considered the possible routes. The ocean passage was impossible. The outsider fleet that had bombarded Edo might easily choose to begin sinking Japanese ships as well, no questions asked. Even without the threat they posed, there was the Shogun's navy to worry about. It wasn't much, compared to the outsiders' forces, but it was strong enough to easily destroy anything Akaoka could put to sea. The fastest land route was along the Inland Sea. Unfortunately, the domains there were loyal to the Shogun. That left only the mountain trails.

"The way home is long and fraught with peril," Shigeru said.

Saiki said, "I sent a messenger to Cloud of Sparrows within an hour after the attack. Five thousand men will be poised on the eastern border of the domain within two weeks, ready to strike out in our direction, if necessary."

"That would mean war."

"Yes."

Shigeru nodded. "Very good. I assume we start in the morning."

"With our lord's approval."

• • • • •

According to Heiko, the other True Word missionaries were at a place called Mushindo, a monastery in another province north of the city. There had been a plague there soon after their arrival a year ago. She didn't know how many of them had survived, or who they were.

You have friends among them?

Someone I have to see.

Then I hope that person is still among the living.

So do I.

If he is not, what does your religion say?

I don't understand what you mean.

If someone you care about dies, do you ever see them again? According to your religion?

Christians believe life after death is life everlasting. The good go to heaven, the evil to hell. Who you see again depends on where you go.

Stark considered stealing a horse and riding alone to Mushindo.

Heiko told him it took Lord Genji three days to get there. It was his country, he knew the way, and he was a lord. Despite those advantages, he had encountered resistance and had to fight his way through. Stark realized his chances of getting there on his own were slim.

He had waited for a long time. He would have to wait a little longer. Unless the attack triggered an expulsion order by the Shogun. In that case, slim was better than none. He should have paid more attention when Cromwell gave his shipboard lectures on the geography of the country. There were four main islands, he remembered, and the one they were on, the largest, was called Honshu. Honshu was where the True Word Mission was to be built. At least he was on the right island. That was a start.

Heiko had excused herself a short while ago to join the warlord, leaving Stark free to comb the wreckage for his most valued possession. He had just recovered the big .44 revolver from beneath some scattered Bibles, thankfully undamaged, when Emily unexpectedly appeared. He quickly slipped the gun back under the Good Book. He was afraid she had seen it, but she said nothing.

"May we speak frankly, Matthew?"

"Of course." He looked around. There was no chair to offer her.

"I am quite comfortable standing, thank you." She paused and looked down at the ground. Her hands were tightly clenched together. Worry pulled her lips into a frown. She took a deep breath and then it all came out in a rush. "I must remain in Japan. I must go forward, as you and I and Zephaniah had planned, and finish building our mission house here. I must, Matthew, I must. And the only way I can is with your help."

Emily's fervor impressed him. She was as determined as he was. But her determination was based on faith, and his, on its absence.

"I'm always ready to help you, Emily, as much as I can. But what you ask may be impossible now. The bombardment is certain to cause anger against us, because we are foreign, like the ships that did this. It won't be safe. And we may have no choice in the matter. The Japanese government may order us to leave."

"If that happens, will you go?"

"No," Stark said. "I won't. I came to Japan with a purpose, and I won't leave without accomplishing it."

"Then you understand me, because I feel exactly the same way."

Stark shook his head. How could he explain? He couldn't. All he could say was, "I expect I'll die here."

"I am ready to do the same."

No, Stark wanted to say, it isn't the same. You came to spread the word of God. I came to take a man's life.

．　　．　　．　　．　　．

Stark stopped before he rode over the last rise to the ranch and pinned on his shiny new tin star, five points, with the words "Arizona Ranger" embossed in a circle at its center. The governor's commission was in his saddlebag, along with ten gold pieces, what the governor called a signing-on bonus. He didn't understand why the governor would want to pay anyone just for signing on to a job, before he did any work at all, but he didn't argue with the man, said thank you, and took the money along with the star and the commission. Probably the troubles they were having out there with Apaches, renegades, bandits, and unwholesome troublemakers were worse than even he'd heard, which sounded bad enough. It was an opportunity, though, and he'd make the most of it.

He put the star on his jacket before going over the rise because sometimes, especially when the weather was as mild as it was today, Becky and Louise wandered a ways away from the cabin when they played, and he wanted them to see the star as soon as they saw him. They were all excited when he'd left, their stepdaddy about to be a ranger and all. Not a famous Texas Ranger, true, but a ranger was a ranger.

The girls were getting to where they needed companions their own age, and schooling, and Tucson had both. He'd had a good life on the ranch, better than good, this year with Mary Anne and the two girls. But it was time for it to end, and for the four of them to begin again a new and better life in Arizona.

Something made him stop halfway up the rise. He couldn't say what it was, exactly, just an uneasiness. He pulled the carbine from the pack behind him and listened. That's what it was. He didn't hear anything. His herd was small, nothing like the rolling rivers of livestock they had outside Dallas and Houston. But like any other, it made a sound you could hear from a good ways off, a soft murmuring rumble of a lot of bellies and not much brain. He knew by the silence the cattle were gone, so he wasn't surprised by the first thing he didn't see when he crested the ridge, namely his herd.

What he didn't see next sucked the heat from his skin and drained the color from his sight. He didn't see anything moving except dust, brush, and ironwoods in the wind, and not a sound came from the cabin.

Stark kicked his horse into a downslope gallop, his mind blank, his heart emptying fast. Halfway down the hill, he saw his two dogs lying just outside the fence, gutshot and bloating with rot. No varmints had come to feast on their carcasses. There could only be one reason for that. There was something better close by.

He jumped from the saddle, switching the carbine to his left hand and drawing his .44 with his right. He stood where he was for a long time before he began walking toward home. He held both guns up at shoulder level, ready to fire. He knew they were useless against what he would face. He did it because he couldn't do anything else.

He was still a dozen paces away when the wind shifted and the stench hit him. What was left of his mind stayed focused tightly on keeping the gun barrels aimed in the right direction. He barely noticed the clenching of his stomach, the acid sourness of the liquid that worked its way up his throat and into his mouth, the way the joints of his bones loosened and his muscles went slack.

"Mary Anne."

He thought someone else was there, calling her name, until he recognized his own voice.

He moved forward, stepped across the threshold of the doorway, and made no sense of what he saw. They were alive, they had to be, because they were moving, or the blankets covering them were, anyway. Mary Anne must have bought them from Mexican traders while he was gone. They had that geometric pattern weavers favored south of the border. The spring weather didn't call for so many blankets, not in the daytime for sure. Maybe they'd caught a chill. They must have, because under the blankets they were bundled in furs.

Then a piece of fur separated from the rest, and the blanket nearest to it moved and covered it.

Even when he heard them, he didn't know what he was hearing until it was almost too late. During the weeks that followed, the sound sometimes came to him out of nowhere, as clear as the first time, and hearing it, he would wish he'd died there among the diamondbacks. He'd never seen so many snakes in one place, never heard a rattling like that, like the bones of the dead shaking themselves awake. They had come to a banquet, some already so engorged they couldn't coil. The rats, gluttons for rotting flesh, were too fat to run. All they could do was squeal while the diamondbacks rattled and swallowed them.

They could have burned the cabin. Most who'd done what they'd done would have. There was only one reason they hadn't. They wanted him to see. That didn't happen, thanks to the snakes and the rats. Stark would have to imagine what had been done to the only three people in the world he'd ever loved.

He stepped back out, slowly. Inflamed by the sound of their own rattling, the snakes began striking at each other. Stark closed the door and shuttered the windows. He lit the roof first. When it fell in, he threw torches on the hay bales he'd set against the walls. He spent the rest of the day and all of the night walking around the fire, shovel in hand, ready to cut in two any vermin he saw. But none came out.

The next morning, a low mound of charred wood and stone stood where the cabin had been.

Nothing moved.

Stark got on his horse and headed for El Paso to find Ethan Cruz.

· · · · ·

Emily saw Matthew hiding the pistol under the Bibles. It was big, as big as the one he'd had when he'd first come to the True Word Mission. In all likelihood, it was the very same gun, the one he'd said he'd thrown into San Francisco Bay. She saw it, but she said nothing. It was not her place to judge. That was Zephaniah's role, and Zephaniah was gone. She had only one mission now, and that was to stay in Japan at all costs.

"Besides all that," Matthew said, "I don't know how I can help. I have no authority."

There was no way to say it except in plain words. She said, "A woman alone, without husband or family, cannot stay in a foreign land. The only way I can remain here is if you will be my family."

"Be your family?"

"Yes. My betrothed."

Emily expected her proposal to shock Matthew. If it did, he didn't show it.

"It's a little soon for you to be thinking along those lines, isn't it, Sister Emily?"

She felt heat rise to her cheeks. "It is what we will say. Not what will be."

Matthew smiled. "Are you suggesting we lie to our hosts?"

She raised her chin. "Yes."

Now he would ask her that question: Why? And what would she tell him? The truth? Tell him her beauty made it impossible for her to return to the land of her birth; her perfect ugliness here made it impossible for her to leave? No. It would make her seem the vainest woman on earth, or the maddest. Her faith. She would tell him the strength of her faith made the small lie acceptable in order to propagate the greater truth, the truth of our eternal salvation in Christ's name. It was blasphemy, but she didn't care. She would not return to America. If Matthew didn't help her, she would stay alone, somehow.

"They'll think it odd," Matthew said. "One

minute, you're weeping over Zephaniah. The next, you're set to marry me instead. We could get away with it, though. We're strange to them, as strange as they are to us. So they'll believe us."

It was Emily's turn to be shocked. "You'll do it?"

"Yes." He reached under the Bibles and took out the gun she'd seen him hide. He looked her in the eye and didn't look away. She met his gaze with a steady one of her own. "But I'm unlikely to walk the earth much longer. Before too long, you really will be alone, in this foreign and dangerous place. Are you prepared for that?"

"I am."

She watched him wrap the gun in a sweater, along with a box of what she thought was probably ammunition.

"I'll do the agreeing. You'll have to do the explaining." He moved a fallen section of wall aside and found his giant knife.

"I'll tell them ours is to be a marriage of faith, as Zephaniah's and mine was to be. Not one of earthly love. The Japanese have religion, as we do, though our beliefs are different. They will understand."

"We're partners, then," Matthew said.

"Thank you, Matthew."

He didn't ask why. She didn't say anything about the gun. Yes, they were partners indeed.

· · · · ·

Genji, Shigeru, Saiki, Sohaku, Kudo, and Hidé sat in a square in the main room of the maids' quarters. It was the only part of the palace to completely escape damage. Heiko and Hanako served tea. Everyone waited for Saiki to speak. He was lord chamberlain. As a matter of protocol, it was his duty to establish the context out of which a decision would arise.

With such sensitive matters to discuss, Saiki would have preferred that no women be present. Genji had overruled his objection, pointing out that if Hidé's bride and his own lover could not be trusted, then they were already doomed. Saiki restrained himself and did not point out that there was still time to put an unreliable party to the sword. Genji was clearly beyond reason where Heiko was concerned. If it became necessary, he would have to take action without the young lord's permission. This he was prepared to do, on the journey from Edo, if appropriate conditions arose.

Saiki said, "Lord Senryu's palace escaped damage. He has agreed to accommodate our seriously injured until they can be properly evacuated. The necessary cremations have been arranged. The ambulatory wounded will go with the main group."

"This will provoke a response from the Shogun," Kudo said. "Even in his weakened state—indeed especially because of it—he cannot allow such a flagrant dismissal of his authority."

"Agreed," Saiki said. "But we have no choice. What will the outsiders do next? We don't know. Perhaps they will return for another bombardment. Perhaps they will land troops the next time. This could be the eve of an invasion. Beyond these uncertain perils, there is the certain one. With the walls of our palace breached, we are highly vulnerable to domestic enemies. Two assassination attempts have already taken place. One against our lord before the bombardment, and one against Lady Heiko, or perhaps the missionary woman, immediately after it. The assailant was killed. His identity, and therefore his master, remains a mystery. In these confusing times, the motivations and aims of others are not always easy to fathom. Which only serves to exacerbate the danger."

"I agree we must evacuate," Sohaku said. "I also agree that the Shogun will respond. We must be prepared. Our cached firearms and ammunition should be dispensed immediately. All possible routes out of Edo and through the interior in the direction of Akaoka must be examined. Particular attention must be paid to where it is most likely the intercepting forces will attack. Because we refused entry to Kawakami, we are undoubtedly under watch, which means we may not even get out of Edo before we face hostile forces in number."

Kudo said, "A diversion would be useful. If a dozen volunteers were to attack Edo Castle, they might sufficiently draw attention away from here."

"A dozen men against the Shogun's fortress?" Saiki said. "They would all be dead within a few seconds."

"Not if they attacked individually and randomly," Kudo said, "at different times and from different directions. The garrison would have to remain on alert for an extended period. Our men could wear banners protesting the Shogun's inaction in the face of the outsiders' bombardment. That will add to the confusion."

Genji turned to Shigeru. "What do you think?"

Shigeru hadn't been listening. He'd been thinking about the ancient swords now in his possession. More specifically, he had been thinking about his most recent vision, the one that caused him to know he would be the last Okumichi to wield them in battle. The precognition made complete sense, and was unaccompanied by confusing visual and auditory pyrotechnics. This had never happened to him before. Did it signal a shift in him, or was this another side effect of his nephew's proximity? Or was it yet another form of *makkyo*—a delusion sent by demons? Unless he knew for sure, there was no point in saying anything to Genji.

"The plans put forth all have specific merits," Shigeru said. He knew without listening that the obvious options had been laid out. An overt and undisguised movement of the household in one body. A diversion, followed by the escape of the young lord with a core of the best cavalrymen. The dispensing of firearms. "The safe evacuation of our lord will best be accomplished by a combined approach. This will confer the most benefits while reducing the risks. Where is the cremation of our dead taking place?"

"Nakaumi Temple," Saiki said.

"Continue to transport bodies there."

Saiki shifted impatiently. "The task continues without further direction, Lord Shigeru, and is nearly complete."

"Continue to transport bodies there," Shigeru said again. "The living have been carrying the dead. Now let the living carry the living. Continue until half our men are at the crematorium. In the meantime, Lord Genji and a small party will proceed to the eastern marshes to observe the cranes in their winter plumage. This will come as welcome relief from the tensions engendered by the recent attack. Once there, he will proceed into the mountains and travel by back trails to Akaoka Domain. Those remaining here at the palace will wait until nightfall. Then our stealthiest men will eliminate the Shogun's spies and the evacuation of the palace will be completed in secrecy."

Saiki's frown, already apparent when Shigeru began, now deepened appreciably. "It's true our lord has a reputation for refined artistic sensibilities. But viewing cranes? After his palace has been blown to smithereens? When dozens of his retainers lie dead and wounded? Intolerable!"

"I will not really be viewing cranes," Genji said mildly.

"No, my lord, you will not," Saiki said. "But to have others believe it, even briefly, is beneath your dignity. You are the Twenty-sixth Great Lord of Akaoka. Your ancestors have brought down Shoguns and raised them up, and you and your descendants will do so as well. You would never even consider viewing cranes at such a time."

"Yet, inexplicably, I find myself with an irresistible desire to do that very thing." Genji smiled at Heiko. "Certain cranes, they say, even mate in winter."

Saiki closed his eyes for a moment. When he opened them, things had not changed. "My lord, please reconsider. The risks for such a course of action are incalculably high."

"With the other scenarios, how likely is violent confrontation?"

"Very likely."

"If our crane viewing is successful, no violence will impede my departure. Is that not so?"

"Only if it is successful, my lord."

Genji said, "My family has always been fortunate where birds are concerned."

Sohaku said, "There are other reasons to question

this strategy. You intend us to separate into three groups?"

"That is correct," Shigeru said.

"We are few as it is. In reduced numbers, we will be much more vulnerable to attack. And you propose to send the fewest men, armed most lightly, with our lord, to travel the most difficult and most lengthy way home."

"Yes," Shigeru said, "and for good measure, I think the missionaries should go with him."

"What?" Saiki, Kudo, and Sohaku cried out nearly in unison.

"If our lord wishes to show his new guests the beauty of the countryside, it is understandable. Otherwise, it will be difficult to explain why the outsiders are abroad at such a time."

"Why must we burden ourselves with them?" Kudo said. "Let them take shelter with Harris, the American consul."

"You are aware of the prophecy," Shigeru said. "An outsider will save Lord Genji's life. We don't know which one. So for our lord's sake, we must protect them as if their lives are his."

Kudo said, "That one has already served his function by taking a bullet and dying. These two are useless to us."

Saiki sighed. "That is not certain." Much as he hated to admit it, he now tended toward Shigeru's view, that the bullet had hit the person for whom it was intended—the leader of the missionaries. "I agree with Lord Shigeru. They must be safeguarded."

Kudo looked at Sohaku, who pretended not to notice. Silently, Sohaku cursed his accomplice for his superstitious nature. They would succeed in killing

Genji, or fail, depending on their own fates, not on some ridiculous prophecy about outsiders.

Sohaku said, "Who will lead the three units?" Shigeru's answer would tell him whether he was suspected or not.

"You are commander of cavalry," Shigeru said. "Obviously, you will take charge of the main force. Skirmish if necessary, but avoid pitched battles. Before you depart, we will confer, and see where along the way we might be able to join you."

"Very good, lord." Sohaku bowed. So he was still trusted; otherwise he would not be given the principal command.

"Kudo, the best assassins we have are among your household vassals." Shigeru paused. His expression did not change. A close observer, however, would have noticed the narrowing of his pupils as he looked at Kudo. "Therefore, you will organize the men left here. First, dispose of the spies watching us. Then join with Sohaku as quickly as you can."

"Yes, lord." Kudo, too, was relieved to receive an important assignment. The reference to assassins did unsettle him, but there seemed nothing sinister in Shigeru's words. If there was the least suspicion, neither he nor Sohaku would be given the responsibilities they had been given, and they would certainly not be ordered to join forces.

Saiki listened, horrified. Shigeru was turning over all of their available power to the two men he knew to be plotting against their lord. He was surely as mad as ever, though he seemed rational enough on the surface. Within a few days, somewhere in the high forests in the mountains along the spine of Japan, Sohaku and Kudo would find Genji and put him to death. His mind raced, struggling unsuccessfully to find a solution.

Shigeru said, "Lord Chamberlain, you will depart this night for our domain at top speed. Taro and Shimoda will accompany you. Once home, prepare our army for war. Be ready to move in any direction in three weeks' time."

"Yes, lord." Saiki bowed. In a flash, Shigeru's plan became clear. While Sohaku and Kudo were held in place by their commands, Saiki would be free to dash for Akaoka and ensure the loyalty of the main army by ruthlessly purging all questionable elements. In the meantime, Shigeru would guide Genji through the least likely pathways of the hinterlands in an attempt to evade the pursuit that would surely come from both the Shogun and these two traitors. Shigeru's task would be certain suicide for anyone but Shigeru. With him, Lord Genji had a good chance of survival.

Sohaku asked, "How many men will Lord Genji take with him?"

"Myself," Shigeru said, "and Hidé. Naturally, Lord Genji would never think to view winter cranes without Lady Heiko. And the two missionaries. No others are required."

"My lord." This was most excellent news. But Kudo felt it necessary to protest as a demonstration of his loyal concern. "Your prowess is beyond question, and Hidé has recently demonstrated his own high level of competence. But two men? To protect our lord on a journey mainly across domains pledged to his ancestral enemies? At least a troop should go with you. If there is an attack, those men can gain time for our lord by laying down their lives."

"Our only hope for survival is avoidance," Shigeru said. "If we engage in any battle, with or without a troop or two or even ten at our backs, we will fail."

"I also believe the risk is too high," Sohaku said. "Might it not be most prudent if the lord traveled with either Kudo or myself? We will have the manpower to protect him against all but a main force, and a main force cannot move fast enough to catch cavalrymen." As he spoke, a new idea came to him, one that would greatly simplify their plans. "He would travel in disguise. In the meantime, you would proceed as you have outlined, but with a false Lord Genji to draw attention. Our lord's safety will thereby be doubly ensured." With Genji in their hands and Shigeru out of the way, the victory was as good as won.

"A promising suggestion," Shigeru said, "and one with notable merits. What do you think, my lord?" He asked the question of Genji, not to get an answer, but to give himself time to regain control of his raging emotions. He was on the verge of beheading both Sohaku and Kudo on the spot. Arrogant, treacherous fools! But if he killed them now, his reputation for madness would be his nephew's undoing. Their clan would disintegrate. Calm. He needed to find that calm place within. If it still existed.

"Truly brilliant, Reverend Abbot," Genji said. "The dual deceptions you suggest are so clever." He and Shigeru had already decided on their course of action before the meeting. By pretending to consider Sohaku's proposal, Shigeru was showing his respect. If his uncle was able to take politesse into account, then perhaps his madness was truly behind him. This was cause for genuine optimism. Genji favored Heiko with another smile. "The more I think about it, the more it seems to be the most amusing way to leave Edo after all. Don't you agree, Heiko?"

"Amusing, perhaps." Heiko hoped Shigeru was not seriously considering placing Genji's fate in Sohaku's hands. This morning, before dawn brightened the hour of the hare, her maid, Sachiko, had observed a messenger slip out of the compound. He had come from Sohaku's quarters. Sachiko had followed him long enough to determine his likely destination. Edo Castle. "Lonely, without a doubt."

"Lonely? Will we not be sufficient company for each other?"

"We would if we were together," Heiko said, "but surely it will be necessary for me to accompany the false Lord Genji. If I did not, the deception would most likely fail at the outset."

Genji laughed. "Nonsense. We will both disguise ourselves, and a false Heiko will go with the false Genji. It will be great fun." He was thoroughly enjoying playing with the ridiculous notion. At some point, either Shigeru or Saiki would overrule them, so there was no danger that the plan would actually be carried out. "You do a fair imitation of a farm woman. A maid's guise should be well within your abilities."

"Thank you, lord." Genji's reminder revived her irritation at her earlier embarrassment. "Please excuse me. I will begin preparations by cutting my hair." She bowed and began to withdraw from the room. She hoped Genji would come to his senses before she actually did any cutting.

"Lady Heiko, please remain with us," Saiki said.

He had found the obvious flaw in Sohaku's suggestion, thanks to Heiko's words. "It would be a sin against heaven for you to mar your beauty in furtherance of such a ridiculous plan."

"To succeed in this difficult time," Sohaku said, "we must not be afraid to think outside the usual boundaries. It is not helpful to denigrate as 'ridiculous' every idea that does not come directly from *The Art of War*." The prize was on the verge of falling into his hands. All he needed to do was to deflect this rigid old fool.

Genji said, "I must confess, I see no flaw in the Reverend Abbot's plan. Do you?"

"None," Saiki said, "so long as Lady Heiko herself actually accompanies your impostor."

"That won't do," Genji said. "The fun in it is we can pretend to be other than who we really are. In our daily lives, such pretense is completely beyond us." Despite the obvious irony of his statement, Genji saw no revealing expressions pass across any of the faces in the room. The self-control of samurai was great, indeed. "An impostor can take her place as well."

Saiki said, "My lord, perhaps it is possible for you to disguise yourself as a low-ranking man at arms. Perhaps, too, Lady Heiko can use her arts to conceal her identity and pose as a household attendant. Perhaps one of our men can pretend to be you. But who can convincingly pass herself off as Lady Heiko?"

All the men in the room looked in her direction.

Heiko bowed humbly. "I am sure a substitute can easily be found."

Sohaku stared at her. The long eyes, sleepy and

alert at the same time. The perfect line of her nose and chin. The seductive shape of her tiny mouth. Her delicate and graceful hands. The way her body so correctly displayed the flowing lines of the kimono. His heart sank. It was true. No imitation of Heiko was possible.

"Saiki is right," Sohaku said. "A glance, even from a distance, will reveal the truth. If Lady Heiko does not accompany the false Genji, the plan will not work."

"Lady Heiko will accompany no one but the real me," Genji said. "I will not spend three weeks in the wilderness without her. What would I do then? Hunt?"

"No, my lord," Saiki said, relieved to have avoided disaster. "We are well aware hunting is not among your favorite pastimes."

"Are we agreed?" Shigeru said.

The assembly bowed in assent.

Shigeru's rage had passed. The Sparrow's Talons would stay in their scabbards until a more appropriate occasion. May the gods soon bring it forth.

・　・　・　・　・

Kawakami, the Shogun's Sticky Eye, was experiencing the euphoria that always came over him when he knew what others didn't. Since, by the very nature of his occupation, his knowledge never failed to exceed that of others, it could be said he was to some degree in a permanent state of bliss. Be that as it may, he felt exceptionally joyful this morning. He had just spoken with his second messenger of the day, and the sun had not yet risen. Sohaku, abbot of Mushindo and former commander of the Okumichi clan's cavalry, urgently sought a meeting. "Under the most discreet circumstances," according to the messenger. That signaled only one possibility. Sohaku was ready to betray his lord. He did not yet know whether Kudo and Saiki, the other two senior commanders, were part of the conspiracy. It didn't matter. Sohaku would never move without having taken them into account. Either Kudo and Saiki were with him, or he had made plans to dispose of them.

"My lord." His adjutant, Mukai, was at the door.

"Enter."

"The messenger still won't answer our questions."

Mukai was talking about the first messenger, not the emissary from Sohaku. This one was presently a resident of an interrogation chamber, from whence he would shortly go to a nameless grave. He had been intercepted attempting to leave Edo shortly after the bombardment. Kawakami knew him to be a member of Saiki's staff.

"Perhaps you are not asking him urgently enough," Kawakami said.

"We have broken the major bones in his arms and legs, my lord, and we have cut off—"

"Good," Kawakami said, quickly preventing a fuller description. "I will speak with him again. He may be amenable to a more normal conversation by now. Make him presentable."

"It has already been done, my lord."

Kawakami nodded. In many ways, Mukai was the perfect assistant. He was intelligent enough to anticipate Kawakami's needs, without being intelligent enough to plot against him. He was of sufficiently high birth to complement Kawakami's status, but not high enough to aspire to replace him. He was related to Kawakami by marriage, being the husband of his sister's husband's stepaunt's daughter. Furthermore, his family had been direct hereditary vassals of the Kawakami clan for nearly three hundred years. And then there were the intangible, personal factors. Mukai was a physically powerful man, but one who emitted not the dimmest ray of personality. He always dressed appropriately, yet clothing which would have been manly and correctly conservative on another appeared positively dull draped over Mukai. This may have been a consequence of his face, which was singularly homely, with a big, round nose, tiny eyes set too close together, a large mouth with extremely thin lips, and a receding chin. It was his appearance more than any other single factor that gave Kawakami the most confidence in his loyalty. A man like Mukai needed someone like Kawakami to serve, a samurai possessed of fine appearance, sophistication, charm, and a charismatic nature, in order to enjoy the inner light he could not generate on his own.

"Thank you, Mukai. You have done well, as always." It did not cost him anything to compliment the man, and the response never failed to gratify.

"I am unworthy of such praise, my lord." Mukai bowed deeply.

They walked to the interrogation chamber in silence. As usual, Kawakami's mind was filled with vivid thoughts of a self-congratulatory nature. Who could blame him? His future prospects appeared even more excellent than he had dared hope. He wondered if the man beside him was thinking anything at all. Not that he really wanted to know.

Often, as now, he seemed merely to be present in a dull, inactive sort of way. Only the gods and Buddhas knew what was in his mind, if they cared to look, which they probably did not. How unfortunate to be such a nonentity. At least he was blessed in terms of employers.

All obvious evidence of violence was gone. The messenger, a middle-aged samurai named Gojiro, was dressed neatly in the clothing he had been wearing when he was apprehended. He sat on a cushion on the floor in the usual position, with his legs folded under him. A wooden brace was placed behind him for support. Since his legs were broken, it would otherwise have been impossible for him to maintain his position. His face was contorted with pain, his breath came in short gasps, sweat dripped profusely from his face. Almost against his will, Kawakami looked at the man's hands, expecting to see missing fingers. All the digits of both hands were still there, however. Something else had been cut off.

"There is no point in maintaining your silence," Kawakami said. "We know what your mission was. To mobilize the army of Akaoka Domain. We merely ask you to confirm it."

"What you know concerns me not at all," Gojiro said.

"It should," Kawakami said, "for my knowledge will lead to the death of your lord, the abolition of his house, and the death or enslavement of every member of your family."

Gojiro's body began to shake. His face contorted. A strangled, choking sound made its tortured way from his throat. Kawakami thought he was suffering a seizure of some kind before realizing the man was laughing.

"You are the Sticky Eye," Gojiro said. "Everything everyone knows, you can know. Everything except what is most important."

"Which is?"

"The future," Gojiro said, "known to only one man. Lord Genji."

"Idiot!" Kawakami controlled himself. It would not do to strike a crippled captive. "You are willing to die in agony for a fairy tale?"

"I will die here, Sticky Eye, yes. But my sons live to serve the same prescient lord. They will piss on your rotting corpse." He laughed again, though at an obvious cost in pain. "It is you who are truly doomed."

Kawakami stood and left the chamber without another word. He was too angry to trust himself to speak. Mukai hurried after him.

"Shall I put him to death, my lord?"

"No. Not yet. Continue questioning him."

"He will not speak, my lord. I am certain of it."

"Continue nevertheless. Proceed in great detail, so no possibility is left unexplored."

Mukai bowed. "Yes, my lord."

Kawakami departed for his teahouse.

Mukai returned to the interrogation chamber. As he predicted, Gojiro would divulge no information, even as external parts of his body were broken, crushed, and removed, and various of his inner organs were exposed to his sight. He screamed and wept. Not even a hero could do otherwise. But he said nothing.

It was in the darkest depths of the hour of the ox before his lungs collapsed for the last time. Mukai bowed to the corpse and silently asked forgiveness. Gojiro's spirit would surely grant it. They were both samurai. Each served his lord as he must. Mukai gave instructions for the respectful, though secret, disposal of the remains.

When he left the chamber, he headed in the direction of his quarters, but he did not go there. As soon as he was certain he was not being observed, he slipped through a hidden doorway. Within minutes, he was outside the walls of Edo Castle and walking briskly in the direction of the Great Lords' palaces in the Tsukiji district.

9

Bitoku

The lord chamberlain said, "There have been arguments of late about whether virtue is inborn or acquired. What is your lordship's view?"

Lord Takanori said, "Pointless."

The chamberlain said, "If virtue is inborn, then training will avail us naught. If it is acquired, then an outcast can become the equal of a samurai."

Lord Takanori said, "The virtuous shit. The unvirtuous shit."

The chamberlain bowed respectfully and withdrew.

Lord Takanori returned his full attention to the scene before him and continued painting A View of Trees Obscuring Lady Shinku's Bath.

SUZUME–NO–KUMO
(1817)

The sound of stealth woke Heiko. Whoever was approaching was doing his best to minimize the sound of his footsteps. It was probably no one it shouldn't be. But the walls were down. A more sinister arrival was a distinct possibility. Genji's two swords were on a stand near his head. She was about to move into position to grab the shorter wakizashi when Genji reached for the katana. Until he did so, she didn't realize he had also awakened.

"Lord." Hidé's voice came from the other side of the door.

"Yes?"

"Forgive me for disturbing you. A visitor insists on seeing you immediately."

"Who is it?"

"He conceals his identity. But he gave me a token he said you would recognize."

"Show it to me."

The door slid back and Hidé entered on his knees. He bowed in the darkness, shuffled forward on his knees, and handed Genji a flat, circular metal object about the diameter of a large plum. It was an ancient sword guard depicting a flock of sparrows flitting over waves.

"I will receive him. After an appropriate interval, show him in."

Hidé hesitated. "Would it not be prudent to require him to unmask first?"

"Prudent, but unnecessary."

"Yes, lord." Hidé backed out, still on his knees, and drew the door closed behind him.

Heiko pulled her underkimono around herself and slipped out of the bed. "I will withdraw."

"Where to?"

Heiko remembered. They were in the maids' quarters, the only remaining undamaged wing of the palace. She and Genji occupied the main room. All the others each had several occupants. There was no spare room to which she could go.

"I will wait outside."

"It's far too cold. Besides, I prefer your presence."

"My lord, I am hardly in any condition to appear before anyone other than yourself." Her hair flowed unbound over her shoulders to her hips. She was practically naked. No makeup remained on her face. Genji had lately taken a fancy to seeing her without it. It would take at least an hour to become minimally presentable, and then only with Sachiko's help.

"These are extraordinary times. Normal rules do not apply. Prepare yourself as best you can."

Heiko arranged her hair in a fair semblance of the ancient Heian style, a middle parting with the long tresses loosely bound with a single ribbon. Several layers of inner kimono, deftly arranged, mimicked the loose robes of those times. Powder and rouge were so lightly applied, she appeared to wear none at all, yet they vivified the brightness of her eyes and the smile implied by the shape of her lips.

"You amaze me," Genji said when she reentered, tea tray in hand.

"How so, my lord?"

"You look as if you have just stepped from a painting of the Era of the Shining Prince." He gestured at his own hastily tied kimono. "In contrast, I appear to be exactly what I am. A man just roused from sleep."

She was saved from making modest protestations by the guest's arrival. He was a large man cloaked from head to foot. There was an awkwardness to his movements that seemed faintly familiar to her. She had seen him before. Where?

Hidé and Shimoda stayed close to him, behind and on either side. The slightest suspicious move would cost him his life. The man's clear, gradual movements showed he understood this very well. Even his bow was slow and deliberate.

"Forgive my untimely intrusion, Lord Genji."

A portion of his cloak masked his face, revealing only his eyes. Tiny as they were, they displayed obvious surprise when he saw Heiko.

"I am prepared to speak in your presence only."

Genji gestured at Hidé and Shimoda. The look of concern on both men's faces deepened. Neither made a move to leave.

"You may wait outside," Genji said.

"Yes, lord." Hidé and Shimoda bowed without taking their attention from the possible assassin. Their eyes remained on him as they backed out of the room.

After the door closed, Genji could still visualize them as clearly as if he could see through wood and paper. They were poised on the other side, hands on their swords, ready to burst through the door within a heartbeat.

The man looked at Heiko once again. "We are still not alone, my lord."

Genji said, "If you cannot trust Lady Heiko, then I cannot trust you." He motioned to her. She bowed and moved forward with the tea.

Now Mukai was faced with a genuine and unexpected dilemma. In order to drink the tea, he would have to unmask. If he refused the tea and remained cloaked, the conversation would not take place. Since Genji already knew who he was—this was their second meeting—there could be only one purpose in requiring him to identify himself to Heiko. To test their reaction to each other. Did that mean he suspected her? Or him? Or both of them? Or was it just a game he was playing with the geisha he thought her to be? There was an even greater problem, of course. If he unmasked, Heiko was sure to report the visit to Kawakami. Then Mukai would follow Gojiro into the interrogation chamber, and soon thereafter into the very same disposal pit. Unless he denounced Heiko now as a spy and assassin. No, that would not work. Genji would never believe it without proof, and Mukai had none to offer. He cursed himself for not considering the possibility of Heiko's presence. Because of the bombardment, he did not think she would be at the palace. Mentally exhausted by the myriad of uncomplementary possibilities, he gave up trying to find a way out. He uncloaked and took the offered tea.

Heiko displayed no surprise, no hint of recognition. This was because she had recognized Mukai a moment earlier by his tiny, closely set eyes and the bulbous lump of nose beneath the cloth that covered the rest of his face. She assumed he had been sent by Kawakami in some devious misdirection strategy. Mukai was an odd choice for such a move. A natural dullard, through and through.

Genji saw no reaction from Heiko, which meant nothing. He knew her self-control was remarkable. Mukai's flitting eyes answered one question, at least. Heiko and Mukai were acquainted. That meant betrayal was a near certainty. Whose betrayal and by whom was not yet established.

Mukai bowed low to Genji. "I regret to inform you your messenger, Gojiro, was captured by the Shogun's agents on his way out of Edo."

"That is indeed unfortunate," Genji said. "Did he respond to questioning?"

"No, my lord, he did not."

Genji said, "I will honor his loyalty and courage by raising all three of his sons in rank. Is there any possibility of recovering his body?"

"No, my lord. That is impossible."

Apart from his sorrow at the death of a trusted old retainer, Genji wasn't especially concerned about Gojiro's failure to leave Edo. He had volunteered knowing that capture, torture, and death were his likely fate. Saiki had sent another messenger at the same time, one that had probably already reached Akaoka.

"Thank you for your valuable report."

"There is more. Your other messenger was also captured."

"Are you sure?" Genji chose his words with care. He didn't want to give Mukai information he didn't already have. It was always possible his apparent betrayal of Kawakami was a ruse engineered by the Sticky Eye himself.

"Falconers are stationed at strategic intervals between Edo and Akaoka. Lord Kawakami is well aware of your late grandfather's enthusiasm for carrier pigeons and suspected you would employ them as well. Your army will not receive the order to mobilize."

"Then our situation is grave, indeed." Now help could not come until Saiki reached Akaoka. If he reached it.

"Might not one of your commanders at home order mobilization on his own initiative?"

"My commanders are Japanese," Genji said, "not outsiders. Initiative is a deadly foreign impulse, don't you know? They will await their orders, as they have been instructed to do."

"You must leave Edo nevertheless, my lord. Even if Lord Kawakami does not order your assassination, antiforeign elements are very likely to take action. The bombardment has inflamed emotions to dangerous heights." Mukai paused. He took a deep breath to fortify himself before speaking again. "Though my family is a hereditary vassal of the Kawakami clan, our castle lies in relative isolation in the snow country, on a high cliff above the Sea of Japan. In ancient times, it never fell to siege, not even when Oda Nobunaga himself led an army against it. No one will expect you to strike out in that direction. It may be your best alternative. In the meantime, other messengers can be sent to Akaoka. Eventually one will get through. Until then, I believe I can ensure your safety."

"Your generosity astounds me," Genji said, truly astounded. "Such an act would put you in open rebellion, not only against the Kawakamis, but the Shogun as well."

"I am prepared for the consequences, my lord."

"I will consider your offer," Genji said, intending no such thing. "I must advise you, however, the safest course of action for you would be to return to your former allegiance."

"Never," Mukai said, his voice full of uncharacteristic vigor. "As my ancestors stood with yours at Sekigahara, so will I stand with you now."

"Even if the result is the same?"

"It will not be," Mukai said. "Every portent shows you have the gods' favor."

Mukai was an extremely serious person who would not understand laughter now, so Genji did not laugh, despite the strength of the impulse to do so.

Everyone who believed in his prophetic ability saw omens everywhere. Yet he himself saw only uncertainty.

Genji returned the sword guard to Mukai. He would present it again should the need arise.

"So your family has secretly kept this for all these years?"

"Yes, my lord." Mukai bowed low and respectfully took the oval of filigreed steel with both hands. "Ever since the battle. To remind us where our true loyalties lie."

Would they ever escape Sekigahara? Even if the Tokugawas were overthrown, wouldn't they and their supporters then wait their turn to fight yet another "decisive battle"? One hundred years from now, after the outsiders have conquered Japan along with all the rest of the world, if such was the future, will we at last have forgotten Sekigahara?

After Mukai departed, Genji idly asked that very question of Heiko.

"I don't know, my lord. I do know that Sekigahara has nothing to do with that gentleman's adherence to you."

"Of course it does," Genji said. "What other motive could he have?"

"Love," Heiko said.

"Love?" Genji was surprised. He had noticed no telling look or gesture pass between Heiko and Mukai. "You mean he, too, is in love with you?"

"No, my lord." Heiko couldn't keep herself from smiling. "Not with me."

• • • • •

Twenty-five samurai walked away from the old abandoned hunter's shack in the Kanto foothills.

None was equipped for hunting. One of the two men at the head of the group turned to the other.

"The meeting settled nothing."

"Was that unexpected?"

"No, it was not. But I had hoped for better."

"The fact that the meeting took place at all could be considered a triumph." He turned and gestured at the men following along the trail back toward Edo. "Look at us. Twenty-five men wearing the crests of a dozen lords. In another time, not so long ago, it would have been unthinkable to see such mingling of those with different clan loyalties. We are transcending ancient limitations, my friend. We are of the generation that will create a new ideal. By our sincere determination, we will bring forth the virtuous rebirth of the Japanese Nation."

The first man who had spoken regarded his companion with undisguised admiration. He felt his chest filling with the righteousness of their cause. Truly, they were Men of Virtue.

Others in the group engaged in more idle conversation.

"Did you hear about the kimono Heiko wore two weeks ago?"

"I did more than hear about it. I saw it."

"No!"

"Yes. Her garments were covered with embroidered images of grotesque and gaudy foreign roses. Worse yet, they were of the kind some fools call the American Beauty Rose, as if 'American' and 'beauty' can make sense together."

"Have we degenerated so far that even in the realm of roses, we must admire alien blossoms?"

"For these outsider-worshipping traitors, our own roses are beneath notice."

"All roses are foreign," yet another man said. "The ones we have came from Korea and China in olden times."

"Once we have a science of our own, we can know which flowers are truly Japanese, and admire only those."

"Science is an outsider abomination."

"Not necessarily. A gun can shoot in any direction. So, too, science can be a tool in our hands as well as in theirs. Science can be used to strengthen Japan, so I have made it my mission to understand science. This cannot be unpatriotic."

"Indeed, it is most laudable that you are willing to make such a sacrifice, to risk pollution in order to strengthen our cause. I bow to you in gratitude."

"Surely the chrysanthemum is Japanese."

"Of course. That is beyond question."

The chrysanthemum was a sacred symbol of the Imperial Family. To doubt its lineage was in itself an unvirtuous act.

"With science, we can prove it was the original Japanese flower."

One of the leaders held up a cautioning hand. "Quickly. Into the woods."

A few moments later, a horseman appeared in the near distance, ascending the same trail the twenty-five samurai were using to descend. Behind him were five more horsemen—or more accurately, three horsemen and two traveling companions of the gentler gender.

· · · · ·

Shigeru frowned. "Is it wise to be so casual?"

"Casually is the only way we will manage this escape from Edo," Genji said. "If we show any concern at all, suspicions will arise. We have already successfully viewed winter cranes and entered the foothills unmolested. The casual strategy is sound."

Shigeru didn't see why that made it necessary to ride into the midst of two dozen unidentified and concealed samurai, as they were now doing, without any preparation for battle. He knew better than to argue with Genji, however. His young nephew's apparent softness and malleability were exactly that—apparent, not real. Genji was at least as stubborn and inflexible, in his own way, as the late Lord Kiyori had been. Shigeru moved to the rear of the party. That was the most vulnerable position. He hoped an attack, if it occurred, would begin there.

"Forgive me, my lord," Hidé said, "but I must agree with Lord Shigeru. I saw two dozen men, but there could be more behind them, perhaps many more. They could easily be assassins sent specifically to intercept you."

"They could just as easily be an innocent group of friends on an afternoon stroll. Let us proceed. And please, do not take any action without a direct order from me."

"Yes, lord." Hidé, unable to keep the worried expression from his face, spurred his horse forward into the lead position. If they were indeed assassins, perhaps they would attack him first, giving his lord a better opportunity to escape.

Emily looked questioningly at Lord Genji. He smiled and said, "There are some men on the trail ahead. There is no reason to expect any trouble." He gently urged his horse forward.

"I am sure you are right, my lord," Emily said, moving forward alongside him, "for we travel in peace, without ill intentions, and will surely attract none."

"Is that a Christian belief?" Genji asked. "Such a balance of intentions?"

" 'As ye sow, so shall ye reap.' Yes, I think so."

"Do you share that view?" Heiko asked Stark.

"Experience has taught me otherwise," Stark said. He discreetly felt for the pocket pistol concealed under his jacket.

When they reached a point where the trail widened slightly, samurai suddenly appeared on all sides of them. Though their swords were not drawn, they were clearly ready for immediate deployment.

"Outsiders are not permitted here." The one who spoke stood slightly in front of the others. "This is yet a part of Japan unruined by their infectious presence."

"Clear the way," Hidé said. "A Great Lord honors you with his passage."

"We would be honored," said a second man who now also stood apart from the rest, "if the lord in question were truly great. I see, however, that the one of whom you speak is infamous for his groveling at the feet of outsiders. I will not yield to such a one."

Hidé's hand went to the hilt of his sword. As fast as he was, Genji spoke before he could unsheath his blade.

"We need not stand on ceremony," Genji said. "The day grows late. All of us have a wish to be elsewhere, do we not? Then let us proceed. There is no need for anyone to yield. Choose one side of the path, and we will use the other."

"Spoken like the weakling you are," said the first man. "Your grandfather was a warrior worthy of

290 · Takashi Matsuoka

respect. You are but the degenerate leavings of a dying line."

"Hidé." His lord's warning voice was the only reason the man's head was still on his shoulders. Hidé relaxed his grip on his sword and took a deep breath, attempting, though not quite succeeding, in calming himself.

"If that is the case," Genji said, "then I am certainly beneath the notice of such virtuous men as yourselves. Let us leave it at that and part company now."

"Perhaps we should do as he says," the first man said to the second. "It would be cruel of us to deny him the pleasures to which he has become accustomed."

"Yes, that is so," said the second man. He turned an arrogant sneer on Genji. "We have heard that you squeal with delight nightly as barbarian ogres stretch your bleeding asshole with their stinking animal penises."

"And that you gurgle like a contented baby during the day as you suck the foul emissions from those very same diseased organs."

"You are sadly misinformed," Genji said. "The only outsider with whom I have shared intimacies is this one beside me."

Several of the samurai laughed derisively.

"She is a treasury of delights you cannot begin to imagine," Genji said.

The first man said, "You are a fool, or mad, or both. Or perhaps blind. Look at her. Your mount is more like a human woman than she. Granted, they are about the same size, with noses of the same length. The coloration of your horse, however, is vastly more beautiful than the ghostly shades of your companion."

"And her odor. Rank beyond description."

Genji smiled benignly. "You are obviously not close enough to inhale her true scent. When excited, she emits a perfume from her private regions akin to opium fumes, and then, a kind of sexual ecstasy overcomes her. Consider the fine bones of her hands. How nearly transparent her skin. Excited, she generates a force akin to lightning, and when she touches you, small shocks travel from her body to yours. That is why her color is so strange. The very matter of her being has been transformed."

While Genji distracted their adversaries, Hidé and Shigeru subtly shifted their positions. If a charge became necessary, they would be able to attack with maximum effect. With swords and hooves, they would take out half the opposing group in the first moments of combat. Those who were left would be entirely manageable. Hidé recalled an often-repeated axiom of their clan—one Okumichi cavalryman was the equal of any ten samurai on foot. That being the case, and he did not doubt that it was, the advantage was actually with them, and not with these so-called Men of Virtue. Hidé and Shigeru exchanged a quick glance, acknowledging their readiness.

"Notice her breasts?" Genji continued. "So unnaturally full, so protuberant." Under the pretext of talking about Emily, he moved forward two paces, putting more of himself and his horse between her and the belligerent samurai. He thought he would be able to cut down the closest men quickly before they could do any harm. "Her breasts ripen monthly. Indeed, they are ripe as we speak. They are filled, not with milk, but with a fiery ambrosial dew. To touch most of her is to touch ice, because all her bodily heat is in but three places—her breasts, her mouth, her vagina."

Emily wondered what Genji was saying to his new acquaintances. Whatever it was, it must be fascinating, for many of them stood openmouthed, and not a few of them stared in her direction. She smiled at them in response, trusting her friendliness was in harmony with Genji's.

Stark didn't know what Genji was saying, either, but he knew what he was doing. All three of the Okumichi samurai had maneuvered themselves into better fighting positions. A battle was imminent.

Stark counted twenty-five swordsmen on the other side. None of them had firearms, at least not in the open. Twenty-five against Genji, Hidé, and Shigeru. Not good odds, even though they were mounted and their opponents were not. Stark had only the small .32 caliber pocket pistol ready to deploy. Six bullets and no reloads handy. If he had his bowie, he could account for another one or maybe two, but he didn't. At best, they could take out half. The other half would kill them for sure. Or worse. He looked toward where Emily was, next to Genji. Heiko was beside him. He would kill Emily with his first shot and Heiko with his second, to save them the agonies these men surely had in store for them before they died. Then he'd shoot the closest four and trample as many more of the others as he could before he went down himself. He was ready. His shoulders relaxed. He had no more thoughts.

Momentarily stunned into silence by Genji's wild discourse, the first man now recovered his voice, and spat out his words. "Keep your polluted fantasies to yourself. It is trouble enough for us to deal with that stench."

The second man said, "We cannot say with certainty whether that foul odor comes from those unwashed horses, your bestial bedmate, or your own decaying and degenerate self."

"Enough!" Shigeru could take no more. He spurred his horse forward as the Men of Virtue drew their swords. "Apologize to your ancestors now, for when we are done with you, we will cast down their altars, disinter their remains, and discard them in the offal pits of the outcasts."

The leading ring of samurai moved forward to meet him, then fell back as they recognized him.

"Shigeru!"

"Impossible! He's dead!"

After momentarily freezing in place, the samurai turned and fled in every direction. All except the two who had been doing the talking. They both fell to their knees and pressed their heads against the ground.

"Please accept my apologies," the first man said, "and spare my aged parents."

The second man said, "My children are still innocent infants. Let my blood wash them clean."

The two men moved at the same time. The first one gripped the blade of his katana with both hands and, with blood pouring from his mutilated palms and fingers, thrust it deep into his throat. He pitched sideways, his life gurgling away through the wound, his mouth, his nostrils. The second man placed his blade in his mouth and slammed his head forward. The hilt hit the ground, driving half the length of the weapon through the back of his skull. Somehow, the sword balanced him. Held up by a gruesome tripod of sword and knees, he died spasm by spasm.

Emily fainted dead away. She would have fallen had not Genji caught her in his arms. He half expected her heft to knock him from his steed. Surprisingly, she wasn't as heavy as she appeared to be. Nor as large, close up this way. Her exaggerated bodily shape and her bizarre features had distorted his awareness of her actual proportions.

Shigeru began to dismount.

"Not necessary," Genji said.

"I should identify them," Shigeru said. His face burned. Only blood would cool his rage.

"Let it pass," Genji said. "These are trying times for us all. They were misguided, but their sincerity was unquestionable. Let us honor their sincerity and forget the rest."

Shigeru bowed. But when Genji moved on, he dismounted anyway. He examined the crests on their kimonos and memorized their faces. Genji was too compassionate. Certain words could never be recalled. They were beyond forgiveness.

One man had mentioned parents, the other children. Later, when the present crisis was past, he would find them and do what needed to be done.

Shigeru remounted and urged his horse forward.

* * * * *

"I don't understand," Emily said. "Everyone was just talking. Lord Genji even seemed jovial. Then, suddenly..." Her body trembled uncontrollably. She tightened her grip on Stark, hoping he would hold her more tightly, too. He did. It didn't help. She still trembled. She had never imagined she would see anything so terrible, such senseless violence, all the worse for being self-inflicted. One moment those two men were talking. The next, they had consigned their immortal souls to everlasting damnation by taking their own lives. And for what? The sight of their awful wounds, the sound of the blood in their throats, would she ever be able to forget these things? She didn't think she would, and trembled more.

"Their way of thinking is very different from ours," Stark said, which explained nothing. The hostile samurai had a seemingly insurmountable advantage in numbers. Yet a few words spoken by Shigeru and they melted fearfully away. Why? He didn't know. Two of them had killed themselves in particularly painful ways. If they were so willing to die in agony, they certainly didn't lack courage. Why hadn't they attacked instead? He didn't know.

The warlord and his uncle sat conferring a short distance away. Heiko, showing not the least sign of distress, busied herself with Hidé, building shelters from the bamboo he cut down. As delicate as she appeared to be, the recent violence had apparently not affected her at all.

Stark didn't understand what had happened any more than Emily. "I wonder if we are as much of a mystery to them."

"That cannot be," Emily said. "Our actions follow reason, as God intended."

· · · · ·

"It would be wise to continue to travel through the night," Shigeru said. "It is doubtful those who fled will return. Other pursuers, however, may be close behind us."

"It would be wise," Genji said, "but it is also

impossible. Emily cannot travel. The shock has been too much for her."

"Shock?" Shigeru glanced in the outsider woman's direction. "Why is she shocked? She should be relieved. Thus far, combat has been unnecessary."

"She is not accustomed to seeing men immolate themselves," Genji said. "At least, not with swords. Death by gunshot may not be quite so disturbing to her sensibilities."

Shigeru had no patience for such a discussion. He broached another, more important subject. "Several of our recent adversaries wore the crest of the Great Lord of Yoshino. This means he will soon know of our location and probable direction. Shortly thereafter, the Shogun will know as well, since Yoshino is an ally of the Tokugawas."

"Not necessarily," Genji said. "I doubt their meeting was sanctioned by any of their lords. They were acting on their own. Therefore, they were technically, and perhaps in fact, committing treason. They will not reveal our location if it means they must also confess to a crime that will ruin themselves and their families. We are safe."

Shigeru said, "Nevertheless, as a precaution, we should loop farther north, and turn west just south of Mushindo Monastery. It will add two days to the journey, but it will also put us on a path less prone to interception."

Hidé and Heiko rejoined them. Hidé said, "The shelters are ready, my lord."

"Thank you. I will stand the first watch, Shigeru the second, and you the third."

Hidé said, "There is no need for you to do such menial duty, my lord."

"There are only three of us. If I do not bear my

share, in short order you and Shigeru will be too tired to be of any use. I will stand the first watch."

"Yes, my lord."

Heiko smiled at Genji.

"Something amuses you?"

"An idle thought, nothing more."

"And what is the idle thought?"

"We are proceeding farther north?"

"Yes, for two more days. Why?"

"Is not the renowned impregnable fortress of the Mukai family to the north?"

Genji reached for her, but he was not fast enough. With a giggle, she slipped away.

"Come back."

"Patience, my lord."

Heiko stopped a short distance away from the outsiders and bowed. "Emily, Matthew." She gestured at one of the lean-tos she and Hidé had erected. "We are to stop here for the night. Please try to get some rest. After tonight, we may not have such leisure until we reach Lord Genji's castle."

"Thank you, Heiko," Emily said.

Emily was put to bed under several layers of blankets. Stark and Heiko sat with her until, at last, she fell asleep. When Heiko rose, Stark stopped her.

"Who were those men?"

Heiko searched her memory for the right word. "Outlaws."

"Why did they run away instead of attacking?"

"They recognized Lord Shigeru."

"There were two dozen of them, against four men on our side."

"Yes," Heiko said. "They were too few and knew it. So they ran."

Stark was sure Heiko didn't understand his

questions. The answers she gave made no sense. Nowhere in the world do two dozen men run from four. "Why did those two kill themselves?"

"They were apologizing for their harsh words."

"Apologizing. By stabbing themselves with their own swords?"

"Yes."

"What did they say that required such an action?"

"Disrespectful things," Heiko said, "which would be disrespectful for me to repeat." She bowed. "Good night, Matthew."

"Good night, Heiko."

Stark didn't fall asleep until near dawn. He heard Heiko giggling. Later, the warlord's uncle woke and disappeared into the woods. Several hours later, he returned and Hidé assumed the watch. Stark wanted to offer his services, but he didn't. He didn't want to insult someone inadvertently and have to apologize with his life. He had to live until Ethan Cruz was dead.

· · · · ·

"You don't really believe what you said about Mukai?"

"I do. The way he looked at you. The way he said 'My lord.' And so often. 'My lord.' At every opportunity, as if by saying it, he possessed you."

"Mukai's ancestors fought beside mine at Sekigahara. That is the only reason for his allegiance."

"If you believe that, you are as gullible as a pubescent farm girl."

"A sparrow sword guard has been in his family for generations."

"According to him. He could have purchased it

at any pawnshop. Sekigahara is his excuse, not his reason. Love always finds a way."

"Ridiculous. And not amusing. Stop laughing."

"You're right. I shouldn't laugh. I should be angry."

"What reason do you have for being angry?"

"Because you are considered more beautiful than I. By some, at least."

"Mukai is not in love with me."

"One day, when you are living a pampered existence in his castle high above the swirling northern sea, you will know otherwise."

"The world has not deteriorated to that extent. Nor will it in my lifetime."

"Is that prophecy, my lord?"

• • • • •

That night and the following morning, a heavy snowfall blanketed the Kanto Plain. From his office in Edo Castle, Mukai watched the world turn white. Genji was somewhere out there, a hunted fugitive. His heart ached when he thought of how the young lord must be suffering in the harsh weather.

He had tried to get the assignment to intercept Genji, but Kawakami had taken it upon himself. So he was stuck here in Edo, helpless to give aid to the one he loved more than life itself. Could any fate be crueler?

He looked at the sword guard in his hand. Sparrows flitting above the waves. It was when he had seen it in Seami's shop that he had realized the truth of his feelings for Genji. Until then, he had not understood the source of the lingering malaise that had plagued him since the previous spring. He had attributed it to the unease everyone felt at the increasing presence of outsiders in Japan. In fact, spring was when he had first seen Genji.

"There is the next Great Lord of Akaoka," Kawakami had said, pointing him out at a gathering before the Shogun. "When the old man dies, the line is finished."

Mukai saw a youth whose incredible beauty left him speechless. He knew he should express agreement with Kawakami, but his mouth would not form the words.

That would have been that. Nothing further would have occurred. But that very evening, listening to a discussion about the poisonous values of the outsiders, his life began to come into focus for the very first time.

"Happiness is the main goal of outsiders," Kawakami said.

"That is hard to believe," Lord Noda said. "No society based on such a shallow, self-centered concept can survive beyond a few generations, at best."

"I don't know how long they will survive," Kawakami said. "Nevertheless, it is a fact."

"They are strange," Lord Kubota said, "but they cannot be that strange."

"It is written into their supreme law," Kawakami said. "Happiness is declared to be a right guaranteed to everyone."

"To individuals?" Mukai said.

Kawakami shot him an irritated look. His function was to attend, listen, and appreciate, not speak. Mukai bowed apologetically. Mollified, and feeling magnanimous that night, Kawakami answered him. "Yes. To individuals."

"How perverse," Lord Noda said.

Mukai silently agreed. Perverse, without question.

The goal of society was order, and the only way to order was the correct establishment of place. Civilization required it. Everyone must know his place, accept it, and behave accordingly. Anything else would result in chaos. Happiness. What an idea. Mukai felt an excitement he thought at the time was righteous indignation, which was the appropriate response.

Then he saw the sword guard and something broke open inside of him. Before he knew it, he was weeping.

"My lord," Seami the shopkeeper said, "are you unwell?"

The sparrows in midair. Though they were but inanimate representations in filigreed steel, were they not freer than he would ever be?

Genji's beauty.

His own ugliness.

The emptiness of place.

Happiness. A pure, individual, personal, selfish happiness. To think of oneself and to forget all else. Even better, to disappear into the bliss of unbridled love. If he could be with Genji, he would vanish, and only Genji would remain, beautiful, so very beautiful.

And so he wept as Seami stood by, helplessly wringing his hands.

Mukai purchased the sword guard for the first figure Seami named, without haggling. He would gladly have paid twice as much. With it, he invented a fictitious ancestor who had fought with the Okumichis at Sekigahara. It gave him a reason to meet privately with Genji.

Now, as snow continued to fall, and his large,

blunt-fingered hand tightly clutched the sword guard, Mukai made the most fateful decision of his life.

Within the hour, he left Edo Castle, bound for his home on the Sea of Japan. He was a minor lord, with a mere two hundred armed vassals. No matter. He would summon them all and rally to the sparrow-and-arrows banner of the Okumichi clan. If the young lord was to die, then he, too, would die.

The thought of perishing in the same place and at the same moment as Genji brought an exquisite vision of nearly unendurable beauty to his imagination. It was too much to hope for. Yet it wasn't impossible. They could die in each other's arms, the blood of love beautifying them both in the eternal moment of death.

A joyous warmth flooded Mukai's bosom. Winter itself was banished.

Unashamed, he admitted the truth he felt to the core of his being.

The outsiders were right. Nothing was more important than happiness.

· · · · ·

Sohaku and Kudo guided their horses through the deep snow.

"There they are," Kudo said.

Two thousand samurai were bivouacked in the clearing ahead. At their center was a command tent. A quarter of the men were armed with muskets as well as the usual complement of swords and lances.

"No sentries are posted," Kudo said. "That is careless."

"The country is at peace," Sohaku said, "and besides, who will attack the Shogun's army so close to Edo?"

Kawakami, dressed ostentatiously in full battle armor, greeted them effusively as they entered his tent.

"Lord Kudo, Reverend Abbot Sohaku, welcome."

Sohaku said, "Thank you for seeing us in such extraordinary circumstances, Lord Kawakami."

"Nonsense. Some sake, to cut the chill?"

"Thank you."

"I trust you were able to depart from Edo without excessive difficulty."

"Yes, thanks to you." Sohaku emptied his cup, which an attendant immediately refilled. "Regrettably, we were forced to kill the men who were keeping watch on the palace. Otherwise our departure would have been too easy, and suspicions would have been aroused. We are not yet certain of the loyalty of all of our men."

"Understood," Kawakami said. "I expected nothing else. I therefore assigned my own least reliable men to the watch. Therefore, it could be said that we have already exchanged mutual favors." He bowed, and Sohaku and Kudo did the same. So far, the depths of their bows were precisely equal. "What is your strength?"

This was the second test. The first, which they had passed, was entering Kawakami's camp alone, without a contingent of bodyguards. Now they were being asked to reveal their numbers and armament.

"One hundred and twelve samurai," Sohaku said without hesitation, "all mounted, all armed with muskets of the Napoleonic type, and carrying twenty rounds of ammunition apiece."

"Are they your own hereditary vassals?"

"Mine or Kudo's, most of them. About a dozen are direct retainers of the Okumichi family."

Kawakami frowned. "Would it not be most sensible to eliminate those without delay?"

"The situation is sensitive," Sohaku said. "Our men are samurai of the most conservative and traditional type. Anything smacking of the cowardly or underhanded will undermine my own position. Murdering a dozen men loyal to their liege lord would not be helpful in that regard."

"Having them in your midst is excessively dangerous," Kawakami said.

"I agree. At midday today, I will announce my allegiance to the Shogun, giving as my reason the need for national unity in the face of a likely barbarian invasion. We must set aside old grievances and unite, as our ancestors did when the Mongols invaded Japan six centuries ago. I will say that Kudo and I have concluded, regrettably, that Lord Genji is not prophetic but insane, as is his uncle, Lord Shigeru, whose heinous crimes are well known among our men. To follow him blindly is not loyalty but cowardice. True loyalty is adherence to the ancient ideals embodied by our late lord, Kiyori. We must uphold the honor of the Okumichi house by establishing a regency. Lord Genji will be taken into protective custody, and we will henceforth act in his name."

"You are quite an orator, Reverend Abbot. Had you remained in a monastic setting, you would undoubtedly have led many listeners to *bitoku*."

"You are too kind, Lord Kawakami. As a true samurai, you could expound just as well on the nature of essential moral virtue."

"What of those whose doubts are not dispelled by the clarity of your words?"

"Their loyalty to Lord Genji, misplaced though it is, will be honored. They will be permitted to depart directly for Akaoka." Sohaku accepted another serving of sake. "Do you think any of them will successfully evade your forces?"

"I sincerely doubt it."

"So do I."

Kawakami said, "There is still Lord Shigeru to consider."

"He is the murderer of Lord Kiyori. We will deliver him to his proper fate."

Kawakami nodded. "Excellent. However, I am troubled by one aspect of your plan."

"Please share your concern."

"Lord Genji alive will continue to be a serious danger, even in custody. His reputation for prophecy, specious though it is, has a powerful hold on the popular imagination."

Sohaku smiled. "Unfortunately, though we will try to preserve his life, Lord Genji will be killed in the confusion. We will bear his honored ashes back to Cloud of Sparrows for interment."

"Shortly thereafter," Kawakami said, "the Shogun will announce the raising of your house to the lordship of Akaoka. Lord Kudo, as your most valued retainer, will have his lands and stipend adjusted appropriately."

"Thank you, Lord Kawakami." This time, when they exchanged bows, Sohaku and Kudo inclined their torsos more deeply than their host.

Kawakami said, "My forces will move down the coastal road at top speed. Lord Genji will likely try to slip through to the Inland Sea somewhere west of Kobe. I will be waiting for him."

"Only if he evades the main body of our

cavalry," Sohaku said. "I will intercept him in the mountains at Yamanaka Village. Before he left for his crane viewing, he said he would try to join us there."

Kudo said, "I will trail Lord Genji with twenty of our best marksmen. We will do our best to eliminate Lord Shigeru with sniper fire before he leaves the mountains."

Kawakami raised his cup. "May the gods favor those who truly possess virtue."

• • • • •

Seasick though they were, Taro and Shimoda pulled resolutely at their oars. If they were not plummeting down the sheer faces of oceanic cliffs, they were looking up at massive watery avalanches. Or so it seemed to them. If their tiny boat was inundated, as appeared likely at any moment, they were surely doomed. Land was nowhere in sight.

Not that they could see it even if it were. They were already nearly blind from the ceaseless ocean spray.

Taro leaned close to Shimoda. "Which way is Akaoka?"

"What?" Shimoda strained to hear him over the perpetual thunder of collapsing waves.

"Are we going in the right direction?"

"I don't know. You think he does?"

Saiki, at the helm, was the picture of confidence.

"I hope so."

"The gods of weather, oceans, and storms favor us," Saiki said. A wave crashed over the boat, soaking them all despite the oilcloths they wore over their clothing. Saiki bailed with one hand and controlled the rudder with the other. From time to time, he adjusted the angle of the sail.

Taro—wet, cold, nauseated—couldn't stop shivering. "Then the gods have a strange way of bestowing their blessings. We seem to be in grave danger."

"The opposite is true," Saiki said. "We are invisible in such heavy seas. The Shogun's patrols will never find us."

Saiki had grown up on the water. In the carefree days of his youth, when he was a low-ranking samurai without special responsibilities, he spent many happy hours in the wild waters off Cape Muroto, hunting whale with the fishermen who had been his childhood playmates. As the giant animals passed the cape, the fishermen would row their longboats alongside one, leap on its back, and drive a spear straight into its brain. If their aim was true, the whale was theirs. If not, they were the whale's. The spearman would fall into the ocean to drown while the boat, bound to the wounded whale by spear and line, was towed to sea. Usually fishermen were able to cut the line and return home. Sometimes they were never seen again.

"Row harder," Saiki said. "Maintain this angle to the waves."

With luck and a continuing east wind of bearable velocity, they would reach Akaoka in three days. Five hundred men would be ready to ride immediately. In two weeks, the entire army would be poised for war. Saiki hoped Lord Genji survived that long.

Another huge wave smashed into the boat.

Saiki turned his full attention to the sea.

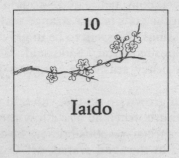

10

Iaido

The katana has been the weapon of the samurai since time immemorial. Consider the inner meaning.

Our blade is honed only on a single edge. Why? It is because with the dull edge against our flesh, the katana becomes a shield. This cannot happen with a double-edged sword. One day, in the midst of a melee, you may owe your life to the dull edge rather than the sharp one. Let this contrast remind you that attack and defense are one.

Our blade is curved, not straight. Why? It is because in a cavalry charge, a curved blade is more efficient than a straight one. Let this curvilinear aspect remind you that a samurai is first and foremost a mounted warrior. Even afoot, comport yourself as though you are astride an angry warhorse.

Make these two truths part of your being. Then your lives will be worth living, and your deaths will not fail to be honorable.

SUZUME–NO–KUMO
(1334)

The snow had been cleared from the meadow and a low platform erected there. On each side of the wooden square, a small tent had been raised under which the judges would sit. All was in readiness.

"The air is crisp, but not frigid. The wind is just strong enough to flutter our banners. The overcast sky diffuses the light. Conditions are perfect, my lord."

Hiromitsu, Great Lord of Yamakawa, nodded happily. "Well, let us begin." He took the chief judge's seat in the tent on the east. His chamberlain took the second seat on the west, his cavalry commander the seat on the north, and his infantry commander the last seat, on the south.

It was the tradition in Yamakawa Domain for the lord, his senior retainers, and his best swordsmen to leave the castle at the beginning of each New Year and encamp in the nearby woods for a day and a night and the following day, there to hold an *iaido* tournament. The presence of women and children was not permitted. This rule had been established in ancient times to spare the families of the samurai who took part unnecessary anguish. In those days, each contest involved real katana with real blades. Though the strike was supposed to stop just short of actual contact, excitement, old grudges, the value of the prize that went to the winner, and the simple wish to excel in the presence of their liege not infrequently led to bloodshed, maiming, and even death.

Of course, katana were no longer used. They had been replaced long ago by shinai, mock swords of split and bound bamboo. Two hundred and fifty years of peace had taken its toll on the fighting spirit. That was one way to look at it. The other, which was

310 · *Takashi Matsuoka*

Hiromitsu's way, was to see it as keeping what was of value and discarding what was not.

Thirty-two samurai would take part in the matches, which were arranged as single eliminations. The winner would progress to the next set of matches; the loser was out. So sixteen men would go to the second round, eight to the third, and four to the fourth, before the final two met to determine the champion, and the winner of the finest three-year-old warhorse in the domain.

Hiromitsu was about to signal the beginning of the tournament when one of his sentries came running.

"My lord," the man said, gasping for breath, "Lord Genji and his party ask permission to pass."

"Lord Genji? Isn't he in residence in Edo this year?"

"Apparently, not anymore."

"Guide him forward. He is most welcome, as always." Genji had the Shogun's permission to leave Edo, or he did not. If the latter was true, it would be better for Hiromitsu not to know, so he would not ask. There was no question of refusing to see Genji, however, or denying him the right of passage. They were allies of long standing. Not that they knew each other personally. They did not. Their ancestors had fought together at Sekigahara. Or at least, Hiromitsu's paternal ancestors had been on the losing side. His maternal relatives had stood with the winners, the most prominent of whom were the ancestors of the present Shogun. He was therefore also an ally of the Tokugawas, technically speaking. This was the perfect situation for the mild and unambitious Great Lord of Yamakawa. His clan's history required him to show the utmost respect and hospitality to both sides, and at the same time gave him a reason to refrain from actively participating on behalf of either in the event of civil war, which seemed more imminent with every passing day. Fortunately, his fief was small, produced no significant quantity of vital resources, was situated well outside the likely fields of battle, and controlled no important routes. His neutrality would therefore offend no one.

A broad smile on his face, Hiromitsu politely walked forward to greet his guests as they arrived. Many things surprised him about the travelers. There were only six of them, for one thing. An exceedingly small group to accompany a Great Lord so far from home. Second, only three of them were samurai. Two were outsiders, a man and a woman, both of the usual grotesque appearance. They were far beyond the usual limited sphere in which they were permitted free movement, and would have had most of his attention if it were not for the final member of the group. She was a woman whose beauty was so astonishing, Hiromitsu mistrusted his eyes. Surely such perfection was not possible.

"Welcome, Lord Genji." Though he did not know the Great Lord of Akaoka on sight, it was easy to know which man to address. He was the one flanked by the two samurai, one of whom was Shigeru. Hiromitsu had recently received a report, now obviously erroneous, that the famed duelist had been killed by his own clansmen under scandalous circumstances. "Welcome to you also, Lord Shigeru. You arrive at an auspicious moment. We are about to begin our annual New Year's iaido tournament."

"I regret our intrusion," Genji said. "We will make it brief by continuing immediately on our way."

"Oh, no, please. Now that you are here, stay and observe. My men are not of the level of your renowned warriors. They do their best, however, which is all anyone may be asked to do."

Genji said, "Thank you, Lord Hiromitsu. We will gratefully accept your hospitality."

Shigeru said, "That may not be prudent."

"We are far ahead," Genji said. "Some among us would benefit from a rest." He turned to the woman behind him. She bowed deeply. "This is Lady Mayonaka no Heiko."

"I am honored to meet you, Lady Heiko." During the past year, her name had been on the lips of everyone who had traveled to Edo. The descriptions he had heard fell far short of the reality. "Your fame has reached even this remote place."

"A completely undeserved fame, my lord."

Her voice suggested the resonance of the finest chimes. He stared at her speechlessly for a moment or two longer than was appropriate before he realized his mouth was actually open. Embarrassed, he turned to his chamberlain and saw that he was similarly awe-stricken.

"The outsider gentleman is Matthew Stark. The lady is Emily Gibson. They have come to help in the building of the mission house adjoining Mushindo Monastery."

Hiromitsu bowed politely to the outsiders. "Welcome. Prepare places for our guests," he said to the chamberlain.

"Yes, my lord. For the outsiders, too?"

"For all members of Lord Genji's party."

"My lord, what of our rule regarding the presence of women?"

"Suspended," Hiromitsu said, assisting Heiko from her saddle. "Lord Genji, please take my place as the judge on the east. Lord Shigeru will replace the chamberlain as the judge on the west."

"Your suggestion is very gracious, Lord Hiromitsu," Genji said. "But we would prefer to observe free of responsibility. I understand betting is also a part of this tradition."

Hiromitsu laughed heartily. "Excellent, most excellent. But you are at a disadvantage. You don't know anything about the abilities of any of my men, so would not know whom to favor." His already happy mood was elevated further by Heiko's presence. She had taken the sake from his adjutant and was now pouring for him. The elegance of her posture alone would have made water intoxicating.

"I thought to wager on one of our company," Genji said, "if you will permit his participation. I believe it would be highly entertaining."

Hiromitsu's jovial mood completely evaporated. "If Lord Shigeru is to take part, I will concede the contest before we begin. All thirty-two contestants together are not his equal."

"My uncle has no tolerance for bamboo training tools," Genji said. "I doubt he would agree to use them."

"That is correct," Shigeru said. "Only live blades cut through to the truth."

"Lord Genji, I cannot allow this," Hiromitsu said, freely permitting his horrified feelings to show on his face. "How can I begin the New Year by bringing corpses home to new widows and orphans?"

"You cannot," Genji said, "nor would I suggest any such thing. Heaven would surely exact a harsh retribution on us all if we committed such an atrocity. I had in mind, not my uncle, but the outsider, Stark."

"What? Surely you're joking?"

"Not at all."

"My men would consider that an insult of the most egregious kind, Lord Genji. They may not have the reputation of your samurai, but they are samurai nonetheless. How can I ask them to test their skill against such a person?"

"I would not suggest it unless I thought it worthy of a wager," Genji said. "I will award one hundred ryo in gold to the man who defeats Stark. Furthermore, I will wager with you whatever you wish. I believe Stark will win the tournament."

If Hiromitsu was shocked before, it was nothing compared to how he felt now. Madness surely ran through the Okumichi line. What was he to do? He could hardly take advantage of an obvious lunatic. One hundred ryo was ten times the annual stipend of the average retainer. Yet to refuse would be to offend, and he was loath to do so, not with the grim, deadly, and equally insane Shigeru so close at hand. What a dilemma!

"If Stark fails to defeat everyone he faces, Lady Heiko will entertain you for a week the next time you are in Edo. At my expense. Is that agreeable with you, my lady?"

Heiko smiled at Hiromitsu, then looked demurely downward as she bowed. "To be paid to spend time with Lord Hiromitsu is a double reward."

"Well, uh, well," Hiromitsu said. A week with Heiko. It was too much to expect that any mutual affection would blossom, a kind of affection leading to more than casual friendship. It was too much to expect. But it was possible. "Please permit me to address my men. We can proceed only with their consent."

"Of course. In the meantime, being an incurable optimist and expecting approval, I will prepare my champion. May I borrow a pair of shinai? And let me propose an additional incentive. Win or lose, every man who faces Stark will receive ten gold ryo."

His eyes dancing with visions of himself and Heiko in Edo, Hiromitsu went to convince his men. Initially, they were reluctant to engage in such a ridiculous charade, even for a small fortune in gold ryo. What convinced them was Genji's side bet with their lord.

"A week with Lady Heiko?"

"Yes," Hiromitsu said. "One week in Edo with Lady Heiko."

His loyal retainers bowed. "We cannot deny you such a prize, my lord, even at the cost of our own dignity."

"Where there is loyalty, there is always dignity," the grateful Hiromitsu said.

"My lord." The sentry assigned to watch his guests reported in. "Lord Genji, Lord Shigeru, and the outsider went into a bamboo grove. To practice."

A murmur of chuckles rose from Hiromitsu's men. The sentry did not join them.

"The outsider is very fast," the sentry said.

"He knows how to use a sword?"

"It appeared that Lord Genji was giving him his first instruction."

"Iaido takes years to master," the chamberlain said. "If Lord Genji thinks to teach an outsider the art in a few minutes, then he is surely the maddest of all the Okumichis."

Hiromitsu said, "You say he was fast."

"Not at first, my lord. But by his fifth draw, yes, he was fast. Very fast. And accurate, too."

"Have you been drinking, Ichiro?" one of the men said. "How can anyone learn how to use a sword in five draws?"

"Silence," Lord Hiromitsu said. "Were you close enough to hear their conversation?"

"Yes, my lord, but Lord Genji and the outsider spoke in English. I could only understand what he and Lord Shigeru said."

"Which was?"

• • • • •

He followed the two mad lords and the outsider into a bamboo grove, matching his steps with theirs so his would be inaudible.

"I'm sure you have a reason for making us look like fools," Shigeru said.

"Stark will win," Genji said.

"Is that prophecy?"

Genji laughed and did not answer.

The outsider said something in his slurred, barbaric tongue. Genji replied in the same language. Only one word was in Japanese. Iaido. The outsider said something that sounded like a question. He, too, used the word "iaido." Genji stopped five feet away from a single stalk of bamboo ten feet tall and four inches thick. Suddenly, his hand went to his sword, steel flashed, and the blade sliced cleanly through the bamboo. After a moment, the upper part of the stalk separated from the rooted trunk and fell to the ground.

• • • • •

"Lord Genji is surprisingly good," the sentry said.

"So poetry, sake, and women have not occupied his entire attention all these years," Hiromitsu said. "It was a ruse. His grandfather, Lord Kiyori, was a wily old man. He must have trained his grandson in secret."

* * * * *

When the bamboo fell into the snow, Genji said something in the outsider's language. The outsider asked another question. Shigeru's name came up. Genji replied.

"What did he say?" Shigeru said.

"He asked why you cannot represent us in the tournament. I told him you do not play at fighting."

Shigeru grunted. "Your strike was good. The stalk stood for a full heartbeat before falling."

"When grandfather struck," Genji said, "he cut so cleanly and so swiftly, the stalk stood for five heartbeats as if whole."

The outsider spoke. Again he used one Japanese word, "iaido." He seemed to be protesting. In answer, Genji stood before another bamboo stalk. His right hand went across his body to the left, where his sword was belted. The blade came out and slashed through the stalk. This time it stood for two heartbeats before falling. He turned to the outsider and spoke again. He made a strange movement with his right hand, as if pulling a much shorter blade.

"A gun and a sword are very different," Shigeru said.

Genji said, "Not so. They are both merely extensions of the man holding them."

* * * * *

318 · Takashi Matsuoka

Genji removed his swords and replaced them with one of the borrowed shinai. The other he gave to the outsider. He spoke a few unintelligible words, and the two men faced each other.

As soon as the outsider's hand moved, Genji whipped his shinai from his belt and struck the outsider in the right temple.

The second time, Genji moved first. Before the outsider could respond, he was hit once again, in the right shoulder.

The third time, their movements were nearly simultaneous, but the result was the same. Genji's shinai reached the outsider's forehead before the outsider's reached Genji's neck.

On the fourth draw, the outsider had his first victory, a clean blow to the temple.

By the fifth, he was able to hit Genji before the lord could draw his shinai completely out of his belt.

•   •   •   •   •

"Which proves nothing," one of the men said. "What great feat is it to defeat someone like Lord Genji?"

"Besides," said another, "he must have let the outsider win in order to puff up his confidence."

"Perhaps," the sentry said. But his tone and expression said otherwise.

•   •   •   •   •

They started back toward the tournament platform. The sentry slipped away. As he left, he heard a few more words.

Shigeru said, "Does he know why you are doing this?"

"No. But he trusts me."

. . . . .

"What arrogance," one of the men said. "He seeks to humiliate us for his own entertainment."

"I wonder," Hiromitsu said.

"What other motive could he have?" the chamberlain said.

"He may be fulfilling a prophecy."

"My lord, that is sheer foolishness," the chamberlain said. "He is no more a prophet than you or I."

"Do you know that for a fact?" Hiromitsu asked. "No, and neither do I. Let us proceed with caution. Toshio. You will face the outsider first. Be attentive."

"Yes, my lord."

. . . . .

Iaido usually began in a seated position. The contestants knelt at opposite ends of the platform, bowed, and moved deliberately toward each other on their knees. When they were at an appropriate distance, usually between five and ten paces, they would draw their swords and strike in one smooth motion. There was no parrying. There was no second chance. The winner was the man who drew his sword most swiftly and struck with accuracy.

In deference to the outsider, who was incapable of sitting properly on his knees, the rules were modified to permit standing confrontation. Also, to keep the numbers even, a samurai chosen by lot withdrew.

Despite the sentry's report, Toshio was overconfident. He was so busy glaring disdainfully at Stark, he was struck in the neck before his shinai cleared his belt. The second man, more alert, fared no better. The outsider struck him in the shoulder of his sword arm as he moved to deploy his weapon. The third was disqualified for drawing too soon and charging, rather than drawing and striking in one movement as required. The chastened samurai was pitifully apologetic.

"It was the heat of the moment," he said, pressing his forehead to the floor of the platform and weeping openly. "I lost all discipline. It was unforgivable."

"No," Hiromitsu said. "You are in shock, as we all are. Lord Genji, how long has this outsider been in Japan?"

"Three weeks."

"He mastered iaido in three weeks?"

"In five minutes," Genji said. "He never tried it before today."

"I don't mean to doubt you, but that is difficult to imagine."

"The outsiders have a similar art. Instead of swords, they use guns. Stark is an accomplished practitioner."

"Ah. We were wrong to take him lightly simply because he is an outsider."

"When we let ourselves see only what we expect to see," Genji said, "we view the contents of our own minds and miss what is truly before us."

Was Genji alluding to his ability to see the future? It certainly seemed that way to Hiromitsu. In fact, it almost seemed as though he were saying he had known the outcome of the contest before it began. If he knew something so trivial, would he not also know the result of the larger matters facing them, the largest of them being the impending civil war? Hiromitsu decided he must discuss the issue with the other Great Lords in the region at the earliest opportunity. Something remarkable was taking place here. Perhaps it extended well beyond a mere iaido tournament.

Genji said, "Since you did not know of his background, it would be unfair to hold you to the wager. I will withdraw Stark from the contest."

"Oh, no, Lord Genji, we must continue. This is most entertaining. Besides, the risk is all on your side. I wagered nothing."

"Neither did I," Genji said, "since the outcome was never in doubt."

Genji was definitely claiming foreknowledge. Here, then, was a chance to test him. Hiromitsu said, "If you will permit it, I would like to make substitutions for the final two rounds."

"Please do so."

Hiromitsu assigned his infantry commander, Akechi, to face the outsider next. If the outsider survived, then he would face his cavalry commander, Masayuki. Akechi struck the outsider cleanly in the right rib cage. But the strike came a moment after the outsider hit him in the neck.

Masayuki was the best swordsman in Yamakawa Domain, and the equal of the best anywhere, save Shigeru. If he could not defeat the outsider, then surely mystical forces were at work. Only the power of an undeflectable prophecy could accomplish such a thing.

Masayuki and the outsider drew at the same moment. Both their strikes were true. Masayuki hit the outsider in the forehead. The outsider hit Masayuki in the right temple.

"Simultaneous strikes," the chamberlain said from the judge's seat on the west.

"It appears so to me as well," Hiromitsu said.

"Do you have a differing view, Lord Genji, Lord Shigeru?"

"No," Shigeru said. "It looked simultaneous."

"Then I have lost the wager," Genji said.

"Neither of us has lost. It is a tie."

"I have lost," Genji said, "because I said Stark would win. He has not."

Masayuki bowed to the outsider. The outsider extended his hand.

"They shake hands instead of bowing," Genji said. "He is acknowledging your victory."

The outsider and the samurai shook hands.

"Well done, Masayuki," Genji said. "You have won a fine warhorse and one hundred gold ryo for yourself, and what will surely be an entertaining week for your lord."

Masayuki bowed low. "I cannot accept the prizes, Lord Genji. The outsider's blow landed before mine. He is the winner."

"Are you certain?" Hiromitsu said.

"Yes, my lord." He bowed again. His pride would not allow him to claim a victory he knew did not belong to him. "I deeply regret my failure."

Genji said, "It is no failure to do your best and honestly accept the results."

"Well," Hiromitsu said, "what a surprising outcome. For me, if not for you, Lord Genji."

Shigeru said, "My nephew is rarely surprised."

"So I have heard," Hiromitsu said.

The chamberlain said, "Where shall we deliver the prize?"

"There is no need for delivery," Genji said. "Stark will ride it."

"My lord," the chamberlain said, "this is a

warhorse, not a tame prancer. It will kill any but an expert horseman."

Genji smiled. "Would you care to wager on it?"

His guests declined Hiromitsu's offer of lodging at his castle for the night. He did not ask why they were in a hurry to continue their journey to wherever they were going. He was certain that Genji, with his foreknowledge of the future, was already as good as there.

• • • • •

Shigeru said, "You made clever use of your reputation."

"For contests and gambling?"

"For prescience and mystical powers. Hiromitsu is now convinced you somehow transformed an outsider into a master of iaido in minutes. Or that you knew, thanks to your gift of foresight, that the impossible would happen, that he would win. An excellent strategy."

"Still a gamble," Genji said. "I thought Stark's ability with a gun would transfer to a sword, at least in this limited way. It was a guess, not a certainty."

"Then, in addition to everything else, you are lucky as well. I congratulate you for that, also. If you are sufficiently lucky, your other attributes will be amplified by it."

"Luck was with us this time anyway," Genji said. "Our present pursuers will get little assistance from Hiromitsu. And later, if the Shogun tries to mobilize the north against us for war, I think every lord in Hiromitsu's circle will be extremely slow to respond." He looked around at the surrounding mountains. "Aren't we near Mushindo Monastery?"

• • • • •

Jimbo bowed in gratitude to the hot spring for providing the surrounding growth of unseasonable plants with the heat they needed to flourish in the midst of winter. He bowed to the old pine tree for giving the shiitake mushrooms the shadow that protected them from sunlight. He bowed to each mushroom before he plucked it, thanking them for giving up their existence so that he and other humans could continue theirs. There were enough of the succulent fungi here to make a feast. He took only what he needed to enliven the simple meal he planned for the village children. Shiitake was a delicacy. They would enjoy it. He moved around the hot spring collecting savory herbs and edible flowers. The simpleton, Goro, loved to eat flowers.

Thinking of children, he paused, and, pausing, felt himself flooded with intense sorrow and regret. He bowed in apology to two children no longer upon the earth, two whose lives he had cruelly ended. He thought of them many times every day, always picturing them reborn in heaven or the Pure Land, in the arms of Christ Our Lord or Kannon the Compassionate One. He pictured their innocent faces bright with eternal happiness. But he never forgot how they looked when they had breathed their last earthly breaths. He asked Christ to redeem his soul and Kannon to bathe him in her all-forgiving love.

He met Kimi, one of the little village girls, on his way back to Mushindo.

"Jimbo, someone is coming this way! Outsiders!"

Jimbo looked where Kimi pointed. On the other side of the valley, six riders guided their steeds along a precipitously narrow path on the mountainside. They were too far away to recognize. Two of them, a man and a woman, were definitely outsiders. Were they the two True Word missionaries Lord Genji had mentioned?

Kimi stepped out into a clearing and yelled out at the top of her little lungs, "Hello! Hello!" She moved her small, thin arms in the biggest rotations she could manage.

The third horseman in the line waved back. Something about the gesture made him think of Lord Genji.

"They saw us. Let's go greet them, Jimbo."

"They're not coming here, Kimi. They're just passing by."

"Oh, no. How disappointing. I wanted to see more outsiders."

"I'm sure you will," Jimbo said, "when the time is right."

"Jimbo! Jimbo! Jimbo!" Goro's powerful voice echoed through the valley.

"We're up here, Goro!" Kimi turned to go back down the path. "I'd better get him. He gets lost easily."

Jimbo watched the riders until they disappeared into the next valley.

• • • • •

The trail ahead forked in three directions.

"We will separate here," Genji said. "Heiko, you will guide Stark along the windward trails of these mountains. I will go with Emily through the valleys. Shigeru will backtrack and thin the ranks of our closest pursuers. That is likely to be Kudo and his men. He likes snipers, so be careful. Hidé will remain here. Find several locations from which you can launch ambushes. If any get this far, delay them as long as you can."

"Let the women travel together," Shigeru said. "Stark should go with you."

"I agree," Hidé said. "The prophecy says an outsider will save your life in the New Year. With our own eyes, we have seen Stark wield a shinai after a few minutes of instruction. It is clear he must be the one. He cannot fulfill his part if he is not with you."

"This wilderness is filled with bandits and deserters," Genji said. "Two women alone will not last long."

"I am not so helpless, my lord," Heiko said. "Lend me your short sword and I will get us through. I promise."

"You will get through because Stark will get you through," Genji said. "There is no use arguing. My mind is made up. The New Year is long. Who is to say when the saving will take place? And who is to say who will do the saving? Perhaps it will be Emily, not Stark. Prophecies are notoriously difficult to interpret."

"This is no time for jests," Hidé said. "Stark will be of great help if you are confronted. Emily will only burden you with her care."

"I am a samurai," Genji said, "with two swords and a bow. Are you saying I am incapable of defending myself and one companion?"

"Of course not, my lord. It is simply wisest to keep risks to a minimum."

"It is settled. We will meet again in Akaoka."

Genji explained his plan to Stark and Emily.

"May I speak privately with Emily?" Stark said.

"Please do."

Stark and Emily rode off a short distance. He

took the small .32 revolver from his jacket and offered it to her.

"You may need this."

"It will be more useful in your hands. Or perhaps you should give it to Lord Genji."

"He might not be able to protect you."

"If he cannot, how can I? I've never fired a gun in my life."

"You hold the grip like this," Stark said, "cock the hammer back, and pull the trigger. It's simple."

"Is there not a matter of aiming?"

"Press it against your target." He held the gun against his own temple. "You won't need to aim."

Emily understood. Matthew was preparing her for disaster. If necessary, he was giving her a way to escape a fate worse than death. He didn't know she had already suffered it. And she was a Christian. Not as good a one as her late fiancé, but still a Christian. She could not take her own life under even the most terrible of circumstances.

"Thank you for thinking of me, Matthew. But what of Lady Heiko? Can we rightly think of ourselves before others, especially others we are pledged to save in Christ's name? How can you protect her if I have your gun?"

Stark dismounted. He undid his saddle pack. Inside was a knitted sweater. He unrolled it and took out the .44 revolver she had seen him save from the ruins of the palace. His holster was next. He belted it on, tied the leather thong around his thigh, and slipped the big gun in. He slowly eased it in and out a few times, testing the resistance of metal against leather.

When he offered her the .32 again, she took it, not because she intended to use it, but to give him some peace of mind. They both had a long way to go. It would not help if he were worrying about her during his own perilous journey.

When Hidé saw the gun, he said, "If he has two, we should ask him to give the other to Lord Genji."

"No man, not even an outsider, can be asked to surrender his weapon to another," Shigeru said. "He will give it if he wants to. Otherwise, it is not our place to say anything at all." He bowed to Genji from his saddle. "May our ancestors watch over you and safeguard you on your journey home." He turned and spurred his horse away. Within a few moments, he could neither be seen nor heard.

"I promised to show you my castle, Lady Heiko, and soon my promise will be fulfilled."

"I look forward to it, my lord. Farewell." She and Stark continued on the trail going northward.

"No one will pass this way while I live," Hidé said.

"It is enough if you delay them without sacrificing your life. There are few men I can trust completely. You are one of them. Be sure to meet me at Cloud of Sparrows."

"Lord." Greatly moved, Hidé was unable to say more.

Genji led Emily away before he was forced to witness more tears from his lachrymose chief bodyguard.

· · · · ·

The storm lasted longer than Saiki thought it would. Five days later, they were still being lashed by wind and wave.

"We will be within sight of land in another two hours or so," Saiki said.

"You said that two hours ago," Taro said. He and Shimoda were exhausted. Their hands bled from the constant rowing necessary to keep the boat's bow turned into the waves.

Saiki strained his eyes. There was a turbulence in the water ahead of them. Whirlpools rarely occurred this far from land. Perhaps it was uncharted reef.

"There may be danger ahead," he said. "Be prepared to change course quickly."

The water under the boat itself began to move upward. Just as Saiki realized what was causing it, one of them breached twenty feet away.

"Sea monsters!" Taro said.

"Whales," Saiki said. Two more broke the surface nearby, a mother and its calf. He had never seen them near Akaoka this late in the year. Perhaps mild weather had kept this pod in the north longer than usual. He acknowledged them with a bow as they passed. Once he had hunted them. Now he would only watch as they swam by.

Then the water beneath them exploded, splintering the boat and throwing the three men into the sea. The powerful turbulence of the passing whale sucked Saiki deep underwater. He fought his way to the surface at the same instant his burning lungs forced his throat open. There was an odd taste in the water. He looked at himself, expecting to see a wound. Instead, he saw blood, gallons of it. There wasn't that much in his entire body. More bubbled up from below him. He felt the warmth of the crimson current just as a whale with a harpoon in its back surfaced not ten feet away. It stared at him with a huge, baleful eye.

Was it only a whale, or the ghostly incarnation of one he had killed long ago? Had its spirit come back seeking retribution? Karma was inescapable. Now he was paying for his crimes against fellow sentient beings. Did not Buddha say all life is the same? He would die drenched in this ghostly blood, and his lord's hopes for rescue would die with him. His own life could now be measured in minutes. He wouldn't last long in the frigid winter sea.

Then he saw the dorsal fins cutting the stormy surface of the water. Sharks. The ghosts of the whales he had slaughtered would be completely satisfied. As he had killed and eaten them, now he would be killed and eaten by the carnivores attracted by the blood in the water.

"There!" He heard a man yelling. "There's another one!"

When he turned toward the voice, he saw a longboat moving rapidly in his direction.

• • • • •

The fishing boat was from Kageshima Village, the very village where he had spent much of his youth. The wounded whale had been fleeing when it crashed into Saiki's boat. It was not a karmic specter after all.

"Shimoda is badly injured," Taro said. The fisherman had plucked them from the water first. "Several ribs are broken, and his left leg."

"He'll heal," one of the fishermen said. "My cousin had both his legs shattered, and he lived. Of course, he doesn't walk very well anymore."

"What were you doing so far from shore in such a small craft?" another asked.

"These men and I are in the service of Genji, Great Lord of Akaoka," Saiki said. "It is vital that we reach Cloud of Sparrows as quickly as possible. Can you take us there?"

"Not in such rough seas," said the man sitting at the tiller. He was the eldest among the fishermen, and the captain of the longboat. "If you are samurai, where are your swords?"

"Don't be impudent," Saiki said. "Obviously, we lost our swords in the ocean."

"Samurai are not supposed to lose their swords."

"Silence! Behave as befits your station."

The man bowed, but not very deeply. Saiki would deal with him once they were ashore.

One of the fishermen had been staring at Taro. "Aren't you one of Abbot Sohaku's men?"

"Do I know you?"

"I delivered dried fish to the monastery three months ago. You were working in the kitchen."

"Ah, I remember. What a coincidence that we should meet again in such a way."

"Are you still the abbot's vassal?" the captain asked.

"Of course. As my father was before me."

"Good," the captain said.

Saiki said, "What is a fisherman doing questioning the loyalty of samurai?"

"Seize him," the captain said.

Several of the fishermen fell on Saiki and swiftly bound him with harpoon line. They restrained Taro but didn't tie him.

The captain said, "Abbot Sohaku has declared a regency. Our lord, Fumio, follows Sohaku. You said you are still his vassal, too. Are you?"

Taro looked at Saiki. "I'm sorry, Lord Chamberlain, but I must obey my oath. Yes, I am still Abbot Sohaku's vassal." The fishermen released their grip on him.

The captain pointed at Shimoda with his chin. "Tie that other one up, too."

"That won't be necessary," Taro said. "He is already bound by his injuries."

"Tie him anyway. There is no telling with samurai. Even if he was dying, he'd be dangerous."

Night fell as they came ashore. Taro was given a bath and a change of clothing. Saiki and Shimoda were unceremoniously placed in a corner of a hut and watched over by two fishermen armed with harpoons.

"The domain is on the brink of civil war," the captain said. He was also one of the village elders. "A third of the retainers have avoided choosing sides so far. The others are split evenly between Genji and Sohaku."

"Should we not permit these two to bathe, also?" a man asked. Saiki recognized him. Twenty-five years ago, he had helped Saiki take his last whale.

"Not important," the elder said. "Soon they will be dead."

Saiki said, "How can you turn against a Great Lord who can see the future as clearly as you can see yesterday?"

"We may seem like stupid peasants to you, sir samurai, but we are not that stupid."

"I have witnessed his ability with my own eyes," Saiki said.

"Is that so? Then tell us what will happen to you."

Saiki stared disdainfully at the man. "It is my lord who is prescient, not me."

"And he never told you your future?"

"I serve him, not the other way around."

"How convenient."

"He predicted Sohaku and Kudo's treachery, and so sent me here to raise the army. In the meantime, Lord Shigeru will take care of many of the traitors."

"Lord Shigeru is dead."

"Believe what you wish. I grow tired of this foolishness." Saiki closed his eyes, seemingly oblivious to his fate.

"Sir?" The elder addressed Taro. "It's not true, is it?"

"It is," Taro said. "I rode from Mushindo Monastery to Edo with Lord Shigeru, and left him there with Lord Genji not five days ago."

The fishermen hastily conferred.

"We must ask Lord Fumio for instructions. If Lord Shigeru is alive, it will be very dangerous to fight his nephew."

"Who will go?"

"One of the elders."

"I will go," Taro said. "It would be disrespectful for a peasant to convey such a message to your lord when a samurai is available to do so. In the meantime, see that these two are secured and that no harm comes to them."

"Thank you, sir. We will do nothing until you return with instructions from our lord."

Six hours later, the village was asleep. Even the two guards watching over their prisoners dozed. Taro slipped silently into the hut. He broke the first guard's neck, took his harpoon, and drove it straight into the other's heart. Both men died without making a sound.

"I swore an oath to Sohaku," Taro said, freeing Saiki and Shimoda. "I also swore one to Hidé that I would help him guard Lord Genji with my life. That oath takes precedence."

"I cannot travel," Shimoda said. He held a harpoon in his hands. "Don't worry. I will give a good accounting of myself before I die."

Saiki took a long last look at the village before he and Taro entered the forest. He would never see it this way again. When the rebels were put down, he would return with troops and personally lead the extermination of Kageshima. Much of the happiness of his own youth would die along with it. He did not try to restrain his tears.

Truly, the whales will be fully avenged then.

* * * * *

Shortly after they parted from Lord Genji, Heiko excused herself to change. She didn't ask Stark about the gun he wore, or how he had managed to defeat five experienced samurai with a weapon he'd never even seen before today. He wasn't sure he knew himself. Genji had known he'd win. He'd seen Stark use a gun once, and from that, he knew Stark could quick-draw a sword. Or, if he didn't know, he was willing to gamble on it.

The horse under him pawed at the snow-covered ground and pulled against the reins. Stark patted his neck and murmured soothingly, and the horse calmed down.

When Heiko returned, she looked completely different. The colorful kimono was gone, and so was the elaborate coiffure. She wore a simple jacket, and the same loose pants the samurai wore, and riding boots, and a wide round hat over her loosely braided hair, and a short sword in her sash. She hadn't asked him about the gun or the iaido, so he didn't ask her about her clothes and her sword.

"The trail we will take is little used," Heiko said.

"We are unlikely to encounter bandits. They prefer places with more traffic. The danger will come from Sohaku. He knows these mountains, too. He may have sent men ahead of us."

"I'm ready."

She smiled. "I know you are, Matthew. So I am very confident we will reach our destination safely."

They traveled for two days without incident. On the third day, Heiko halted her horse and raised her hand to her lips for silence. She dismounted, handed Stark the reins, and disappeared into the trees ahead. She returned an hour later. Still motioning for silence, she gestured for him to leave the horses and follow her.

From the crest of the next hill, they could see thirty samurai armed with muskets congregated at a bend in the trail, which was now blocked with a barricade of logs five feet high. When she was sure Stark had seen what there was to see, she led him back to their horses.

"Sohaku," she said.

"I didn't see him."

"He wants us to think he's taken the rest of the men elsewhere."

"He hasn't?"

"Not very far. If you wanted to pass the barrier without a fight, what would you do?"

"I saw a narrow path along the hillside. It begins out of sight of the barricade. I'd go that way at night." He thought for a moment. "We'd have to leave the horses. It's strictly a footpath."

"That is what he wants us to do," Heiko said. "He has men hidden in the trees along that path. Even if we get past them, we will be on foot. He will catch us long before we are safe."

Stark recalled what he'd seen. He hadn't noticed any sign of anyone hiding, but of course, he wouldn't, not if they were any good at it. "What will we do?"

"I have watched you ride. You are a good horseman."

"Thank you. So are you."

Heiko acknowledged his praise with a bow. She indicated his gun. "How good are you with that?"

"Good." This was no time for false modesty. She wouldn't bc asking if she didn't need to know.

"Are you accurate while riding?"

"Not as accurate as I am standing still." Stark couldn't keep the grin off his face. This delicate little woman planned to charge the barricade.

· · · · ·

"No sleeping," the barricade commander said. "If they try to pass, they'll try at night."

"Nobody's going to come this way," one of the samurai said. "They'll see the barrier and take the other trail, as Sohaku said they would."

"If they see you sleeping, they might change their minds. Now get up and pay attention." The commander glared at the next man. "Did you hear me? Wake up." He slapped the man's head. The man toppled over, lifeless. The commander looked at his hand. It was wet with blood.

"Eeeee!" Another man in front of the barrier fell, clutching at the razor-edged throwing star lodged in his throat.

"We're under attack!" the commander yelled. He looked in every direction. They were under attack, but from where and by whom?

Something came rolling down the hill. The commander raised his musket to fire. The body landed at his feet. It was another of his men, with his throat neatly cut from ear to ear.

"Ninjas!" someone screamed.

Fool! That would only spread panic. When this was done, he would punish whoever had called out. He couldn't immediately place the voice. Which one of the men sounded so girlish?

He turned to give orders and saw someone small standing right in front of him, face cloaked. Only the eyes were visible. They were very beautiful eyes. The commander felt a wetness spreading across his chest. He opened his mouth to speak, but he no longer had a voice. As he fell, he heard gunfire. It didn't sound like muskets. His head against the ground, he heard the hooves of galloping horses. A moment later, two horses leaped over the barrier in front of him. The rider of the first horse was firing a large handgun. There was no one in the saddle of the second horse. Good. At least they had gotten one of them.

Before he could speculate as to which one, blood stopped flowing to his brain.

· · · · ·

Stark waited by the stream. It was exactly where Heiko said it would be. When Stark rode at the barrier with Heiko's horse in tow, he expected to run into heavy musket fire. Sohaku's men were firing, but not in his direction. When he jumped the barrier he saw several bodies already down. He hadn't shot them.

Heiko came silently out of trees. How had she gotten there so fast?

"Are you well?" she asked.

"Yes, fine. You?"

"A musket ball grazed my arm." She knelt by the stream, washed the wound, and deftly tied a bandage over it. "It is not serious."

Heiko's horse neighed. There was a gurgle in it that didn't sound right. It neighed again, more weakly this time, and fell over on its side.

Stark and Heiko knelt beside the fallen animal. It was still breathing. Soon it wouldn't be. A bullet had torn through its neck. The snow was dark with blood.

"Your prize horse is strong," Heiko said. "It will carry us both until we can find another."

She climbed on behind him. She was so light, he was sure his horse wouldn't even notice her.

Who killed more men back there, Heiko or him?

Stark wondered if every geisha was so multitalented.

· · · · · ·

Sohaku rushed back to the barrier with his main force as soon as he heard the first gunshot. He found eighteen of the thirty men he'd left there dead or seriously wounded.

"We were attacked by ninjas," one of the survivors said. "They came at us from every direction."

"How many were there?"

"We never saw them clearly. That's how it always is with ninjas."

"Was Lord Genji with them?"

"I didn't see him. But he may have been among the horsemen who jumped the barrier. They passed very quickly, firing their guns as they rode through us."

"Guns?" Hidé and Shigeru had each taken a musket when they rode out of Edo with Genji. The presence of guns probably meant that Genji had been with them. If they had split into two or three groups, which was what Sohaku would have advised had he been with them, the guns would have gone with the lord. "Did you count them?"

"Yes, Reverend Abbot. There were at least five, perhaps ten."

Sohaku frowned. Five or ten guns. Plus an undetermined number of ninjas. That meant Genji had been reinforced somehow. By whom? And from where? Was it possible that his allies were already rising up to support him?

"Send a messenger to Kudo. Tell him to rejoin us."

"Yes, Reverend Abbot. Should the messenger go immediately?"

The hesitancy he heard angered Sohaku. Were his men so weak a single encounter had broken their spirits?

"If not now, when?"

"Forgive me for making a suggestion unasked, sir, but might it not be prudent to wait until morning?"

Sohaku looked down the trail. The dim light of the new moon was just bright enough to make a man imagine shadows within shadows. Such imaginings created vulnerabilities ninjas would not fail to exploit. Some of them were with Genji. Wouldn't some also lurk behind precisely to prevent what Sohaku now intended?

His anger faded. "Do so in the morning, then."

"Yes, Reverend Abbot."

But when dawn came, a messenger arrived before his departed.

• • • • •

Kawakami waited for Genji to come down from the mountains to the Inland Sea. He wondered idly whether Kudo had managed to shoot Shigeru. It was of no real importance. If he still lived, he wouldn't for much longer. Among Kawakami's two thousand men was a battalion of five hundred musketeers. No swordsman could stand against five hundred guns, not even Shigeru.

Genji's fate would be worse. Whatever protections he enjoyed as a Great Lord he had forfeited by leaving Edo without the Shogun's express permission. Such a flagrant violation of the Alternate Residency Law automatically raised the assumption that he was in rebellion. The Shogun did not suffer traitors lightly. Arrest, trial, and condemnation lay ahead. Many questions would be asked. Many secrets would be revealed. Everyone would see then who knew and who didn't. Before Genji was ordered to commit ritual suicide, he would be humiliated and disgraced, destroyed in a trap Kawakami had been crafting for nearly two decades. He hadn't known then Genji would be his victim. The grandfather, Kiyori, had been Great Lord of Akaoka at the time, and Genji's wastrel sire, Yorimasa, was next in line. He was the one Kawakami had been thinking of when his brilliant plan came to him as if in a vision. Such was the depth of his own foresight that the one was as appropriate as the other. He couldn't help feeling deep satisfaction at his own wisdom, and why shouldn't he?

"Lord, a courier from the Shogun has arrived."

"Show him in. Wait. Have we had any word from Mukai?"

"No, my lord. He seems to have left Edo. No one knows where he has gone, or why."

This was the most disturbing news Kawakami had heard in a long time. Mukai was not particularly important. But he was always so dully predictable, so stolid, so very much just there. That was his chief, perhaps his only real, virtue. For him to act so out of character was unsettling, especially in this time of crisis. Kawakami would make his displeasure abundantly clear when he next saw his assistant.

"Lord Kawakami." The courier went to one knee and bowed in the manner appropriate to a samurai in the field. "Lord Yoshinobu sends his greetings."

Yoshinobu was the head of the Shogun's Council. Kawakami took the letter from the courier and opened it hurriedly. Perhaps the situation in the capital was so critical that the Council had decided to take more drastic action against Genji. This could be an order abolishing the Okumichi clan without delay. If so, the Shogun's forces would immediately besiege Akaoka Domain's famous fortress, Cloud of Sparrows Castle. Since Kawakami's troops were already halfway there, he would be the one executing the order.

But it was not to be.

Kawakami's disappointment was so great, his chest actually hurt. The Council had retroactively approved the withdrawal of the lords and their families from Edo. In addition, the Alternate Residency Law was temporarily suspended until further notice. Genji was no longer a traitor. He was a loyal lord obeying the Shogun's commands.

"Is the Shogun also withdrawing from Edo?"

"No, my lord." The courier handed Kawakami another letter.

The Shogun's Council ordered all Allied Lords

to ready their armies for deployment in the Kanto and Kansai plains should it become necessary to resist an outsider invasion directed toward the Imperial Capital of Kyoto or the Shogun's Capital of Edo. The Shogun would lead the forces in the Kanto from Edo Castle. According to Yoshinobu, one hundred thousand samurai would soon be ready to fight the invaders to the death.

Kawakami was tempted to laugh out loud. A hundred thousand samurai with swords, a few outdated muskets, and even fewer and more outdated cannons would soon be a hundred thousand corpses in the event of an outsider invasion.

"A squadron of warships bombarded Edo with great effect," Kawakami said, "and at no loss to themselves. What if the outsiders just keep doing more of the same?"

"They cannot conquer Japan with warships alone," the courier said. "Eventually, they will have to come ashore. When they do, we will behead them as our ancestors beheaded Kublai Khan's Mongols."

The courier was one of many such samurai, obsessed with the sword and living in the past. The outsiders had siege mortars that could fling explosive shells the size of men five miles. They had horse-drawn cannons that could be moved swiftly from placc to place, cutting down thousands here, then thousands many miles elsewhere, in the space of a few hours, and the outsiders had many of those cannons. They had rifles and handguns that used self-contained cartridges instead of separate powder and ball. And most important of all, they had been killing each other with the predecessors of these deadly weapons during the two and a half centuries Japan's samurai had slumbered in the Tokugawa peace.

Kawakami said, "We will meet their war machines with our swords and our fighting spirit, and we will show them what we are made of." Flesh. Bone. Blood.

"Yes, Lord Kawakami," the courier said, his chest swelling with pride, "we will."

· · · · ·

Hidé prepared his ambush well. He found a dozen places suitable for his purposes in the hills surrounding the crossroads. He had both his and Shigeru's muskets. He would fire them from one position, then run to the next and shoot arrows. When he reached the next, he would reload and fire the muskets again. This wouldn't fool Sohaku or Kudo, but they couldn't be sure, and that uncertainty would slow them down.

So far, no one had come. Three nights ago, he thought he heard an outburst of shooting from the windward direction. Lady Heiko and Stark had gone that way. He had a feeling they'd successfully escaped from whoever had been shooting at them. His confidence in Stark was very high ever since the iaido tournament. Lady Heiko was in good hands.

He was less sure about Lord Genji. His foreknowledge of future events should keep him safe. Yet, as the lord himself said, prophecies were not always easy to understand. He would have been much more at ease if Stark had accompanied the lord.

Hidé stopped thinking about prophecies and focused his attention completely on what he could see and hear. Someone was approaching from behind him. Was he so dull that the enemy had managed to circle around without alerting him? He raised his musket and prepared to fire. It was a lone man. He was leading rather than riding his horse, which pulled a makeshift sled behind it. There were two bundles on the sled. They appeared to be bodies wrapped in blankets.

Hidé lowered the musket. It was Shigeru.

Fear chilled him more than the winter day.

Whose bodies were on the sled?

11

Yuki to Chi

From the strategic point of view, I must of course regret our loss in that battle. Defeat is never to be lightly accepted. However, I cannot help but feel that from the aesthetic point of view, there could not have been a more exquisitely beautiful result.

The white of the lightly falling snow. The red of the spilling blood. Was there ever a white more white, or a red more red, colder snow, or warmer blood?

SUZUME–NO–KUMO
(1515)

Kudo began to worry when the second scout did not return. When the third one also failed to report, he ordered a retreat. In retrospect, he knew that was an error. Samurai going backward were not as confident as samurai going forward.

One of the men he had assigned to the rear guard came galloping toward him.

"Lord, the others have disappeared!"

"What do you mean, disappeared?"

"One moment they were there, the next, they were gone." He looked fearfully over his shoulder. "Someone is hunting us."

"Shigeru," someone else said.

"Return to the rear," Kudo said. "You, you, and you. Go with him. People don't disappear. Find them."

The men he had assigned sat on their horses and looked at each other. No one made a move to obey.

Kudo was about to chastise them harshly when the rider at the front of the column screamed. His hands clutched at the shaft of the arrow jutting from his right eye socket.

• • • • •

Shigeru would have preferred to let Kudo and his men continue their plodding pursuit awhile longer. Then he would have killed half of them as they advanced, and the other half as they retreated. There was a certain pleasing symmetry in that. Unfortunately, it was necessary for him to abandon such aesthetic considerations.

He looked at the huge stone structure looming through the trees. Massive smokestacks spewed foul-smelling fumes into the sky. Dark ashes fell like the shadows of dead snowflakes, turning the landscape black. Humbled, spiritless men in loose gray uniforms, heads nearly shorn of all hair, moved self-propelled carriages out of the building and into neat rows outside. The ground beneath him vibrated. Was it caused by the laughter of demons?

His visions were still evanescent and transparent, and therefore bearable. But they were rapidly growing more vivid, more grotesque, more frequent, and, worst of all, more convincing. So far, he could tell the difference between future vision and present reality. That wouldn't last much longer. He had been separated from Genji for only two days. At his present rate of deterioration, in two more days, he would once again become the blithering lunatic he had been at Mushindo Monastery. In such circumstances, patience was not a virtue. Haste was.

The hooves of his horse made little noise as it stepped into the snowy meadow. Yesterday, Shigeru would have trusted the animal's instincts and ridden through the image of the fiery prison and the broken men inhabiting it. Today, the will to do so was already gone. He went around it.

Kudo was down to sixteen men. They were probably the best marksmen he could muster. Their aim might be good, if they waited to sight a target before firing. But their discipline was poor, their courage weak. Only four of them had been killed, yet those remaining were already defeated, fleeing in panic from a single unseen attacker. He was pleased none of them were samurai he had trained.

Shigeru let an arrow fly toward an outrider's throat. He didn't wait to see whether he hit his target or not. A strangled scream and answering gunfire told him he had. Musketballs snapped branches and whirred through the leaves. Not one came close to where he was or even to where he had been. Pathetic. Perhaps the outsiders would conquer Japan in less time than he had thought. They certainly would if this was the level of resistance they could expect.

He watched Kudo struggle to bring his men into a defensive circle within a stand of tall pines. As the traitor's marksmen continued to fire at nothing, Shigeru moved up the trail.

• • • • •

Kudo fumed. The situation was utterly ridiculous. Fifteen men armed with muskets surrounded by what was almost certainly a single opponent. That the opponent was Shigeru mattered not a whit. If it were a matter of swords, it would be entirely different, of course. But they were modern musketeers against one archaic lunatic. They could shoot him down before he was anywhere close enough to cut anyone. Shigeru was a master of the bow, true enough. Five corpses testified to that. Yet if his men maintained their discipline, they would know where he was by the trajectories of the arrows that came their way.

Kudo held his position for almost an hour though there was no longer an immediate threat. He knew Shigeru was long gone, probably to set another ambush. He stayed where he was to give his men time to calm down. The greatest danger was that they would continue to dissipate their advantage in numbers and weaponry through mindless fear.

"Shall we surrender?" he said mildly. "I think we should. After all, we outnumber him only fifteen to one, we have only muskets to oppose his bow, and we are surrounded. Or at least I think we are. How is it that one man can surround fifteen? Please clear up this mystery for me."

The men exchanged chastened glances.

"Forgive us, Lord Kudo. We let ourselves fall prey to Shigeru's reputation. You are right, of course. There is no reason for us to huddle like frightened children."

"I take it you are once again ready to be samurai?"

"Lord." The men bowed.

Kudo divided his force into three groups of five. They would move together, separated but well in sight of each other. They would be far enough apart that Shigeru would be able to shoot at only one group at a time, revealing his position, and allowing all fifteen guns to come to bear.

Kudo said, "Even if we fail to hit him the first time, we will have located him. Our three groups will drive him like game, trap him, and shoot him down."

"Yes, lord."

"Whoever fires the fatal shot will have the honor of removing his head and presenting it to Abbot Sohaku."

"Thank you, lord."

Kudo led the most exposed men, the ones on the downward slope of the hills to the left. He hoped Shigeru would attack them first. He would dearly love to be the one to put a bullet between the madman's eyes. Since Shigeru always did the unexpected, he was more likely to hit the center, where he would be exposed to the most concentrated fire. That meant he would have to attack them from behind. Kudo's eyes looked forward. All his attention was in his back. He would sense rather than see. Shigeru was not the only true samurai in the clan.

A riderless horse bolted from the trees on the right.

None of the men fired.

Had the horse slipped free or had Shigeru intentionally released it to distract them? It didn't matter. The tactic, if that's what it was, hadn't worked. No one panicked. And now Shigeru was on foot. Without his horse, his speed and mobility were greatly reduced. Kudo's confidence began to rise.

The low winter sun moved in its shallow arc

toward nightfall, and still there was no attack. Shigeru was waiting for darkness to minimize Kudo's numerical advantage. Out in the open, in three groups, they would be easy prey. But only if they continued their present tactic, which Kudo had no intention of doing.

He scanned the landscape. It was a trusted axiom of war that he who chose the field of battle secured a key to victory. The valley widened here. In the middle of the small plain was a low hill, an island of seven pines rising from the snow. If they encamped there for the night, they would enjoy the advantage of clear sight lines in every direction. Even in the slight light of the new moon, a man would stand out against the freshly fallen snow. Stealth, the main advantage Shigeru enjoyed, would be lost. It was perfect.

Which was precisely why his suspicions were aroused. Everything he had seen, Shigeru surely had seen as well. It had to be a trap.

"Approach with caution. Look carefully into the branches of the trees. He may think to come at us from above."

They moved forward, muskets at the ready. When they reached the base of the hill, Kudo sent seven men forward, one to examine each tree.

"No one here, lord."

Something was amiss. Every warrior instinct he possessed told him so. He walked slowly around the hill. There was no place for a man to hide, even one as adept at hiding as Shigeru. Still, he felt deep unease.

"Lord?"

Perhaps, seeing how obvious the possibilities were for both ambush and defense, Shigeru had continued down the valley. There was a narrow gorge below that would be an ideal place for one man to confront many. Perhaps he waited there. Perhaps.

Finally, finding no reason to delay further, Kudo said, "We will camp here. Each group will take its turn maintaining the watch."

"Yes, lord."

At the base of the hill, the scent of the pines grew strong. Kudo stopped.

"Fall back!"

"Do you see him, lord?"

Kudo did not. But he had made a mistake and realized it just in time. He had looked up. He had not looked down. Pine trees dropped their needles in profusion. Three small hollows were full of them.

He drew his sword.

"Cover me."

He advanced to the closest hollow and stabbed vigorously into the blanket of pine needles. Nothing. The second and the third hollows produced the same result.

Shigeru was not above. He was not below. There was nowhere else he could be. He had not laid a trap here. He was mad, but he was also brilliant. And patient. Stealth and patience were inseparable qualities.

"Secure the horses there. You. Climb that tall pine. Keep watch."

Shigeru awaited them elsewhere. They were probably safe for the night. So his reasoning told him.

Kudo was unable to sleep. He went back to the three hollows filled with pine needles and probed them with his sword once again.

The sentry in the tree said, "Lord, a horse approaches. I see no rider."

It was Shigeru's warhorse. It approached for a

distance, neighed, and shied back, as if it wanted to come closer, but was afraid to do so.

"It wants to join our horses," the sentry said.

Its hesitancy was understandable. Warhorses tended to mistrust people in the absence of their masters.

The reason for its desire to come forward was less obvious. Did it really seek equine company? Is that what was moving it toward them?

Kudo's persistent uneasiness sharpened. There was trickery of some sort here. He leaned up against the tree to get a better view.

"Are you sure no one is with the horse?"

"No one is in the saddle, lord, and no one hides behind it."

"Under it, perhaps?"

The sentry peered harder into the distance. "I don't think so, lord. The horse's girth seems normal in profile."

"Would you stake your life on it?"

The sentry's answer came without delay. "No, lord."

"Shoot the horse."

"Yes, lord."

Kudo's hand came away from the pine tree sticky with resin. An unusual amount seeped from a long line in the bark where the trunk had partially splintered. The venerable pine had been weakened by age, disease, and storm, then suffered this injury. When the sentry above shifted his position, the tree creaked alarmingly. That sound evoked a strong sense of kinship in Kudo. Trees and men were not so unalike.

"You'd better come down and climb another," Kudo said. The recoil from the musket might be too much for the wounded tree.

"Yes, lord."

Kudo examined the line of damage more carefully. It formed an unusual pattern, almost like a—door!

The tree trunk exploded outward.

Kudo recognized the wild, resin-covered face at the same moment the blade penetrated his chest and cleaved his heart and spine. Not enough of his life remained for him to enjoy the satisfaction of knowing his intuition had been right all along.

• • • • •

Drenched in the traitor's blood, Shigeru slashed at men and demons with both swords. Shouts and gunfire came dimly to his ears. He could barely hear anything other than the heavy fluttering of the huge metal dragonflies hovering overhead.

Their eyes were blinding beams of light.

Their circular wings rotated impossibly above them.

Their spawn, hideously elongated segmented worms of steel, shot past him at high speed, as if on tracks. Through their gaping pores, he could see the bodies of thousands of the doomed crushed against each other.

The gleaming blades of swords flashed in arcs and circles.

Gouts of blood fountained into the air.

Bodies and body parts littered the snow.

Men screamed and died until only one man remained screaming.

Shigeru screamed until his lungs were empty and his consciousness left him.

Only then did the dragonflies depart.

• • • • •

He woke to a vision of teeming millions. Humans swarmed like insects as far as he could see. Windowed pillars of stone, glass, and steel rose toward the clouds. Inside, yet more people jammed together like flightless drones in hives. More nests were below, for dull-eyed hordes shuffled into gateways and disappeared underground.

He stumbled back and fell over the corpse of a horse. Slaughtered men and animals covered the hill. His own horse stood a short distance away, regarding him suspiciously.

When he looked up, the vision was gone. For how long?

He went searching among the dead. Kudo lay faceup by the splintered trunk of a fallen pine. He lifted the body by the topknot and severed the traitor's head. When he returned to Cloud of Sparrows, he would mount it on a spear and leave it to rot outside the castle.

"You won't be lonely," Shigeru said to the head. "Your wife and your children will be there with you."

It took two hours of coaxing before his horse permitted him to remount. Shigeru rode north as fast as he could. He prayed it was fast enough.

• • • • •

All around him was fire. He was in Edo, and Edo burned. Instead of clouds, winged cylinders filled the sky. From them fell canisters that broke apart into glowing embers, which in turn exploded into flames as they hit the city.

Winds whipped by the firestorm sucked the air from his lungs.

Half-charred people copulated in the ruins as they died.

Shigeru gripped the reins of his horse and trusted it to lead him on.

If one more night passed before he rejoined his nephew, it would be too late.

• • • • •

When they saw the horseman in the distance, the seven shoddily dressed men scurried into the nearest thicket to hide. They carried a random assortment of weapons—three pikes, four spears, an old-fashioned double-edged longsword, and two flintlock pistols without flint, powder, or bullets. Though they were more boys than men, fear and privation had marked their haggard faces with the signs of terminal old age. Fourteen eyes sank back into the dark hollow pits of their sockets; jawbones and teeth jutted against nearly fleshless skin. Their skulls were all too apparent behind the thin veils of their faces.

"If we killed him, we could eat his horse," one of them said wistfully.

His nearest companion snorted derisively. "Like we ate the other two horses?"

"How was I to know they had a gun?"

"And such a gun," another said. "It fired many times without being reloaded once."

"I'm sure Ichiro and Sanshiro are impressed, too, whether they are in the Pure Land or some demonic realm."

A short sob escaped the first man. "We were from the same village. We grew up together. How can I face their parents? Or Shinichi's?"

"Shinichi's been dead a long time. Why think about him?"

"He should have jumped into the woods with

us. He was a fool, running away down the road like that."

"His arm was chopped off."

"His skull was split in two."

Though weeks had passed, the incident was fresh in everyone's mind. It had begun their current streak of deadly bad luck. Taken from their villages, they had been marching to join Lord Gaiho's main army on the Inland Sea when they came across a handful of samurai from another domain. Those samurai were as ferocious as they were few. In a brief battle, ten of their number were killed and the troop shattered. With all of their own officers dead, they didn't know what to do. So they ran away. They had barely survived by foraging like deer and rabbits. They were farmers, not hunters. Every effort to bring down wild game failed miserably. Then two days ago, desperate with hunger, they had attacked a gentle-looking samurai and his outsider companion for their horses, and Ichiro and Sanshiro had been shot dead.

The first man fingered the ring of wooden prayer beads around his neck. "I thought I'd return these to his mother, and apologize for living while he died."

"It's not his mother you want to see. It's his sister. A real beauty, she is."

"None of us will see anybody's mother or sister, including our own. We're deserters, fool. They'll be executed for our crime, along with the rest of our families, or sold into bondage, if they haven't been already."

"Thank you. That's truly comforting."

"Maybe this one doesn't have a gun."

"He's a samurai with two swords. That's bad enough."

"Maybe not. Look. He's wounded."

His clothes were dark with bloodstains. Clotted gore covered his face and hair. As they watched, he harshly pulled the reins and brought his horse to a sudden halt.

"No, no," the samurai said. "Not that way. There are too many of them."

"What does he see?"

"Something that's not there. He's lost a lot of blood. I think he's dying."

"Then our luck has changed at last. Let's get him."

"Wait. He's coming this way. We can take him by surprise."

"Behind those towers," the samurai said. "We'll sneak past them." He pulled his horse away from the clear trail ahead. Looking fearfully over his shoulder, he rode toward the rock-strewn slope where the seven men hid.

"I can taste it already," one of the men said, salivating.

"Quiet. Steady. All together. Now!"

· · · · · ·

A belt across his lap kept him from escaping the seat into which he was strapped. An unknown force pressed him backward. His ears were filled with a faint and persistent whine, like the sound of a high wind, only dead, not alive. The walls curved toward a low ceiling barely higher than a man's head. The room was narrow and very long. Seats like his were in front, behind, and to the right. Each one he could see held a prisoner like himself. To the left was a small window with rounded corners. He didn't want to look through it, but a will stronger than his forced his head to turn.

He saw a huge city ablaze with light. It was rapidly falling away. Either it was sinking into the pit of hell, or the compartment containing him was rising from the earth. Neither was possible.

He was not yet a slave. But soon he would be. His mind was in the tightening grasp of demons.

    •   •   •   •   •

He saw the world through mists of blood. A sword in each hand, he no longer bothered to hold the reins. Let the horse go where it will. He would kill demons as long as he could, then he would die.

He no longer knew where he was. Stone and steel were everywhere. Here and there a few trees, a few hedges, sprouted through like unwanted weeds. In the distance, foul gases billowed into the air from giant smokestacks. Joyless swarms filled the streets of the endless city, the broken slaves of unseen masters. An extensive and elaborate system of smooth stone roadways ran in every direction. But this did not make travel easier. Vast multitudes of metal carriages jammed into every space. They moved with excruciating slowness while emitting noxious fumes from small pipes at the rear of each vehicle. Surely the people within were dying a slow death. Sunlight barely seeped through the gray haze. Not even a heap of burning corpses would create a fouler stench. '

No one else seemed to notice. People sat in their vehicles and walked the streets, inhaling poison with every breath. They stood in good order upon platforms, packed tightly against each other body to body, in neat rows, waiting their turn to be devoured by metal worms.

    •   •   •   •   •

Shigeru stopped. He stood waist-deep in snow. A beast snorted behind him. He twirled quickly, his swords ready to strike, expecting another demonic assault. Instead, he saw only his horse a short distance away, following the trail Shigeru had plowed with his own body. He looked around. He was halfway up a ravine. He saw snowdrifts, trees, nothing else. Were the visions gone? It was too much to hope for. Yet so it seemed.

Wait.

Something dangled from his shoulders.

A human head. No, not one. Eight of them.

"Ahhh!"

He slashed wildly at the extra heads sprouting from his body. Demonic possession was transforming him into a hideous mockery of human life. The only escape was death. He dropped his katana and turned the shorter wakizashi's blade toward his chest, the point aimed at his heart.

The last head rolled against a small pile of fallen branches mostly covered by snow. The dead face stared at him. It was Kudo. Shigeru lowered the blade. After decapitating Kudo, he had tied the head to his saddle. He didn't remember slinging it over his shoulder. He looked down at his torso. There were a few superficial wounds where he had slashed himself. Nothing else. He wasn't undergoing any kind of metamorphosis. He picked up one of the other heads by its hair. No topknot. Not a samurai. An emaciated face he didn't recognize. Not anyone he remembered killing. The other six heads told him as little.

Shigeru looked up at the sky. It was a blue of the purest kind, seen only in the winter, in the countryside far from human habitation. He saw no monstrous dragonflies. He heard no demons wailing. The visions were definitely gone. This was the first time he had experienced a spontaneous remission from so virulent an episode. Perhaps Genji had not been responsible the last time either. Perhaps it was some kind of mysterious internal mechanism that periodically relieved the torture, if he survived each barrage of insanity long enough. This slew of visions had been brief compared to the ones that had led him to confinement at Mushindo Monastery. Perhaps they would soon cease altogether on their own.

Shigeru walked down the slope to where Kudo's head had rolled.

There was something odd about that mound of snow. Branches stuck out of it too evenly. Someone had placed them there.

Shigeru put the head down. He drew his sword and approached the suspicious shape. It was roughly triangular. A sniper might build a blind in such a way. But why here? He stood away from the likeliest lines of fire and scraped at the snow with the tip of his sword. A chunk fell inward and a hole appeared.

The mound was hollow.

Two bodies were inside.

12

Suzume-no-kumo

Can you be like the blind before a painting, the deaf in the midst of music, the dead at a banquet?

If you cannot, then throw away your katana and your wakizashi, your six-foot bow, your hawk-feathered arrows, your warhorse, your armor, and your name. You lack the discipline to be a samurai. Become a farmer, priest, or merchant.

Also, avoid beautiful women. They are too dangerous for you.

SUZUME–NO–KUMO
(1777)

Emily had her lies neatly arranged. She was ready to tell Lord Genji that she and Matthew were now betrothed. It was a custom among American ecclesiastics of their faith, she would say, for one to take the place of another when death intervened. Her marriage to Zephaniah would have been one of faith, not love, and so would her marriage to Matthew.

Though it seemed entirely too far-fetched, she

relied on the vast differences in their cultures to make her words believable. So many Japanese customs were incomprehensible to her, she thought it safe to assume the reverse was also true, and the unreasonable would therefore not undergo the usual level of scrutiny. Matthew had agreed to support her claims. That would help. She would eventually have to create another reason for staying, since he had no intention of marrying her, nor did she have any wish for him to do so. When the time came, she knew she would think of something simply because she had to. She would never return to America. Never.

To her great relief, for she was not good at lying, she had not had to say anything at all to justify her continuing presence in Japan. When Lord Genji announced that they would leave Edo for Akaoka, his domain on the southern island of Shikoku, he simply assumed she and Matthew would go with him.

Now she alone traveled with the soft-spoken young lord. Matthew went on another path with Lady Heiko. The uncle, Shigeru, had gone back the way they had come. Hidé stayed behind at the junction of the parting ways. Though nothing was said, it was apparent that their hosts were concerned about possible pursuit. Following the naval bombardment, had one of the imperial perpetrators—Britain or France, or perhaps Russia—invaded Japan in an attempt to expand its colonial empire? She knew the United States would not be involved in such an immoral act. America, once a colony itself, abhorred the subjugation of independent peoples. It favored the Open Door Policy, which allowed all nations to interact freely as they chose, with no recognition of any empire's claim of proprietary spheres of influence. She remembered

Zephaniah teaching that lesson. Of course, he had been Mr. Cromwell then, not Zephaniah. May he rest in peace.

It was not as cold in the valley as it had been higher up in the mountains. Earlier in the day, they had turned toward the southwest. She could tell by the direction of the sun's movement across the sky. They followed a path beside a shallow stream that moved just enough not to freeze over completely. Their horses' hooves made soft crunching sounds as they stepped through the thin crust of ice that had formed on the surface of the snow.

Emily said, "What is your word for snow?"

"*Yuki.*"

"Yuki. A beautiful word."

"You will not think so if we must remain in it much longer," Lord Genji said. "There is a small hermitage not far from here. It is rough and rustic, but a better place than a camp in the woods."

"I grew up on a farm. I am used to rough and rustic."

He smiled in amusement. "Yes, I can almost picture it. Surely you did not grow rice?"

"We grew apples." She was silent for a while, remembering the happiest times of her childhood, her handsome father, her beautiful mother, her sweet young brothers. She refused to let the more recent past destroy all the joy she had known before. "Orchards and paddies are quite different. Yet it seems to me that the nature of farmwork is the same whatever the place, whatever the crop. We are tied to the seasons and the vagaries of weather, and that is the essence."

"Vagaries?"

" 'Vagaries' are unpredictable changes. The singular is 'vagary.' " She spelled the words out.

"Ah. Vagary. Thank you." He would remember the word. So far, he had done so with every new one that had come up. Emily was impressed.

"You are a quick learner, Lord Genji. Your pronunciation and your vocabulary have improved markedly in just three weeks."

"The credit is yours, Emily. You have been a most patient teacher."

"A good student always makes the teacher look good," Emily said. "And certainly if any credit is due to teachers, then Matthew deserves it, too."

"For Heiko's progress, yes. For mine, you are solely responsible. I find Matthew's way of speaking more difficult to understand than yours. Am I mistaken in thinking your accents are quite different?"

"You are not mistaken."

"Your words are clipped, which is somewhat like Japanese. He talks more like this, with a kind of odd melody."

He imitated Matthew's leisurely slur and twang with such exactitude, Emily burst out laughing.

"Excuse me, my lord. You sounded so much like him."

"There is nothing to excuse. Your laughter does raise a concern, however."

"It does?"

"Yes. In Japan, men and women speak quite differently from each other. If a man were to speak like a woman, he would be the object of much ridicule. I hope I am not committing that kind of error with your language."

"Oh, no, Lord Genji. I assure you, you sound very much like a man." She blushed. That wasn't quite what she had meant to say. "The differences in speech between Matthew and me are solely a matter of region, not gender. He is from Texas, in the south of our country. I am from New York, which is in the northeast. The regional differences are quite strong."

"That is a great relief to know. Ridicule is a particularly powerful weapon in Japan. Many have died, many have been killed, because of it."

They hold life in low regard, Zephaniah had said. They will kill and die for the most ridiculous of reasons. If two samurai passing in the street should accidentally bump their sheathed swords, a duel is immediate and terminal. Someone must die.

Surely that is an exaggeration.

Do you know me to exaggerate?

No, sir.

Not sir. Zephaniah. I am your betrothed now, remember.

Yes, Zephaniah.

Their prickly sense of honor is utterly outrageous. If a samurai is spoken to with insufficient politeness, he will take it as a deadly insult, an attempt by the speaker to ridicule him. If he is spoken to with excessive politeness, the result is the same. Pride goeth before destruction, and a haughty spirit before the fall.

Amen, Emily said.

By our own example, we will teach them humility, and lead them to redemption thereby.

Yes, Zephaniah.

Lord Genji said, "Then when English comes into more extensive use in Japan, I can be confident that I am speaking it properly?"

"Yes, without any doubt whatsoever."

"Thank you, Emily."

"You are welcome, Lord Genji. May I make a correction in your usage?"

"Please."

"You said, 'when' English comes into use in Japan. 'When' applied in such a way suggests inevitability. A better choice in this case would be 'if.' "

"I meant to suggest inevitability," he said. "My grandfather predicted it."

"He did? Forgive me for saying so, my lord, but that seems highly unlikely. Why would significant numbers of your people learn our language?"

"He didn't say why. He might not have foreseen the cause, only the result."

Emily was sure he wasn't using the right word. "To foresee is to know in advance."

"Yes."

"Surely he didn't know of events before they took place?"

"Yes, he did."

His answer chilled her. He was claiming a power for his grandfather that was given only to those chosen of God. That was blasphemy. She tried to lead him away from that terrible sin.

"Lord Genji, only Jesus Christ and the Prophets of the Old Testament knew of things to come. Our duty is to seek an understanding of their words. New prophecies cannot occur. Christians cannot believe such a thing."

"This is not a matter of belief. If it were, I would choose not to believe. Life would be less difficult."

"Sometimes people guess, and coincidence makes the guess seem prophetic. But it is an appearance only. By the grace of God, the Prophets alone foretold the future."

"I wouldn't call it grace. It has been more like a family curse. We have borne it because we have had no choice. That is all."

Emily said no more. What could she say? He spoke as if he believed himself to have the gift as well. If he persisted in such thinking, not only was he damned for blasphemy, he was in danger of madness as well. His delusions would make him see portents and signs where none existed, and his actions would be shaped by those misleading figments of his imagination. She must be patient. And diligent. The delusions of centuries would not fall away in a day or a week or a month.

A warm radiance of righteousness filled her bosom. There was a reason Christ had placed her in this place and time. That reason was clear to her now. She made a silent vow to Him. She would save Lord Genji's soul though it cost her life. May God show His divine grace and infinite mercy to them both.

They proceeded for a time in silence.

When the shadows of the mountains completely covered the valley, Lord Genji said, "We won't reach the hermitage before nightfall by the usual route. Let us go this way. We will have to lead our horses rather than ride them. Do you think you can manage? The distance is much less."

"Yes, I can manage."

They veered away from the stream and went straight up the steep hillside. Near the top, they came to a small open meadow. The scene sparked her memory. It looked so much like a similar meadow in Apple Valley. Even the snow blanketed it the same way. Was it coincidence that she had come upon a scene so reminiscent of long-ago days? Or had her longing recast the alien landscape into shapes and shadows more familiar to her?

"It's perfect for snow angels." She hadn't meant to speak. The words just slipped out.

"What are snow angels?"

"Have you never made them?"

"I never have."

"May I show you? It will only take a minute."

"Please."

Emily sat down on the snow in as ladylike a manner as she could manage. She reclined, and stretched out her arms and legs as far as they would go, being careful to keep the hem of her skirt from rising above the ankles of her boots. Then she vigorously brushed the snow with her outstretched limbs. She giggled, realizing how silly she must look. When she was finished, she got up without disturbing the shape she had made.

"Do you see it?"

"Perhaps the angel's image must be in mind before one can see it."

Emily couldn't hide her disappointment. It was really a very fine snow angel. "Perhaps."

"Emily?"

"Yes?"

"May I ask your age?"

"I will be seventeen next month."

"Ah," he said, as if that explained something.

He said it in the way adults often did when dismissing a child. She let her irritation get the best of her. "And what is your age?" Normally, she would never be so rude.

Lord Genji didn't have a chance to answer.

Several men leaped out from behind the trees. Shouting loud war cries, they rushed forward and stabbed at him with spears and pikes. He managed to turn the first attacker away with his hastily drawn sword, but the two behind him drove their blades into his back. The circle around him tightened.

Emily was too stunned to move.

Triumphant shouts rose from their attackers as Genji went down. Blood splattered the snow around him.

"Genji!" Emily cried.

The mention of his name stopped them. The men—there were nine of them—pulled away, fear in their faces. She heard Genji's name repeated. She also heard another name she knew.

• • • • •

"Oh, no. He's Shigeru's nephew."

"This is terrible. We manage to surprise a samurai, and it turns out to be Lord Genji."

"A lord's horses are as tasty as anyone else's."

"Shigeru will come after us. And he won't kill us quickly. I hear he loves to torture first."

"We need those horses. There's many a meal on those haunches. I'm not going hungry any longer."

"I'd rather be hungry than dead."

"I agree. Let's apologize and go."

"Look."

The lord lay where he had fallen. The ugly outsider woman tended to him, murmuring in her harsh, ungraceful tongue. The snow beneath him was crimson.

"We can't stop now. It's too late."

"Let's use the woman before we kill her."

"What are you saying? We're not criminals."

"Yes we are. We might as well go all the way. They can chop our heads off only once."

"Aren't you curious to see what she looks like? I've heard their bodies are covered with coarse hair, like a wild boar."

"I heard it was more like the fur of a mink, down there, in her nether regions."

The men looked at her.

"Wait. Make sure the lord is dead first. Samurai are strange creatures. As long as he breathes, he can kill, even if he has to rise from his deathbed to do it."

"He's dead. See? She speaks to him and he doesn't answer."

"Take no chances. Slit his throat."

• • • • •

Emily didn't know what to do. She felt Genji's blood go from warm to cold to ice within moments after it seeped through his clothing and into hers. He was wounded in his chest and his back. She had to staunch the bleeding soon, or he would die. With his clothing on, she couldn't determine the exact location or nature of the wounds. She had to undress him first. But if she did that, would he not die from exposure before he died from loss of blood? It was a terrible dilemma. If she did nothing, he would die anyway.

When she had called out Genji's name, the bandits had instantly ceased their attack and withdrawn a short distance.

They stood together arguing. Occasionally, they looked in Genji's direction. Shigeru's name came up several times. Once, four of them made as if to leave, but their leader pointed at Genji and said a few words. He must have been convincing, for the men stayed.

"Perhaps they repent of their actions," she said, "and will assist us to make amends."

Genji breathed but did not speak.

"We are in Christ's hands, all of us."

Their discussion over, the men approached. She thought they were coming to help. The ceasing of the attack and the mention of Shigeru's name gave her that hope. Then she saw their knives.

Emily hugged Genji close, shielding his body with her own. The bandits shouted loudly, whether at each other or at her she didn't know. One of them grabbed her arms. The others wrenched Genji from her grasp. Her assailant pushed her down on her back and began pulling her skirt up. The leader shouted something at him, and he turned, shouting back.

She remembered Matthew's gun.

While the man holding her was distracted, she took the revolver from her coat pocket, cocked the hammer as Matthew had shown her, held it under the man's chin, and pulled the trigger.

Blood, bone, and flesh exploded into the air and showered the men holding Genji.

She cocked the hammer, placed the end of the barrel against the next closest man's chest, and pulled the trigger again. By the time he fell backward, his companions were already running away downhill as fast as they could go. She fired twice more at their retreating backs but missed each time.

What should she do now?

She had a badly wounded man in her arms, a gun with two bullets, and two horses. There were bandits nearby who might return to resume their murderous assault. She didn't know where she was or in which direction the hermitage lay. She couldn't find her way back to the crossroads where Hidé waited, or forward to Akaoka. Even if she could, Genji couldn't travel. If she did nothing, they would both freeze to death during the night.

She pulled Genji beneath the trees. There were too few of them to provide the protection she had hoped for against the rising wind or from the snow that once again had begun to fall. They needed a better place.

She found a suitable hollow in the nearby ravine. It took all her strength to drag Genji there. She couldn't move him a second time. The shelter would have to be built around him.

Their first night out of Edo, Hidé and Heiko had used branches to make them. Now she would have to do the same.

One Christmas, when she had complained about the cold, her mother had told her about the Eskimos who lived in the far north, in the land of endless winter. Their houses were made of ice, yet were warm inside. Those cold walls kept the colder air outside and retained within the air warmed by human life. So her mother had told her, and drew a picture of a round ice house on a plain of ice, with happy, round-faced Eskimo children building snowmen outside. Was it true or a fairy tale? Soon she would know.

She leaned the branches at an angle as she had seen Hidé do. He easily cut what he needed. She tried, and failed. There was an art to wielding the sword that she didn't possess. She took the best branches from among those already on the ground. With her shawl spread over them like an awning, and a layer of snow upon that, she built a roof. She filled in the gaps at the base of the lean-to with more snow. It wasn't round like the one her mother had drawn. It was more of a rough wedge. But it was a serviceable ice house.

She went inside and closed the entrance with yet more snow, leaving just a small opening so they wouldn't suffocate. Was it warmer? She thought it was. If it wasn't exactly cozy, at least it shielded them from the wind.

· · · · ·

Emily knew nothing about wounds. Genji's certainly looked grievous. The one in his chest exposed the bones of his rib cage. The two in his back went deep. Blood pulsated from them with every beat of his heart. She took off her petticoat, tore it into strips, and wrapped his damaged torso as quickly as she could. When she picked up his clothing to re-dress him, the cloth crackled with frozen blood. There were blankets in the packs the horses carried. She covered Genji with her coat and went outside to get them.

The horses were nowhere in sight. She saw marks in the snow that might have been their hoofprints. It was hard to tell for sure. Falling snow obscured the tracks. Saying a silent prayer, she followed them anyway. Yes. There was one. She was relieved to see it was the mild-tempered mare she had ridden, and not Genji's unruly stallion.

"Here, Cinnamon." Cinnamon was the name of her horse in Apple Valley. It had a reddish hue, like this one. She clicked her tongue and held out her hand, palm up. Horses liked that.

The horse snorted and shied away. Did it smell the blood on her clothing?

"Don't be afraid. Everything is fine and dandy." She spoke in her most soothing tones and walked toward the horse as it continued to back away. She talked and walked and the distance between them slowly shrank. "That's a good girl, Cinnamon. Good, good girl."

She was a hand span away from her mare's bridle when she heard a strange growl behind her. She reached for the gun that wasn't there. It was in her coat, and her coat was on Genji. She turned, expecting to see a wolf. It was Genji's stallion, head lowered, pawing the snow with his forefeet. Her mare pranced away out of reach.

Emily stepped slowly backward. She didn't want to do anything that would make the stallion charge. She didn't try to talk to it. She doubted it would respond to sweet words. She was only ten yards away when it leaped suddenly into a gallop, but not in her direction. Her mare sauntered over the hill. Genji's stallion pursued it.

Emily's relief didn't last long. She hadn't paid enough attention to where she was going as she followed the mare. Though she looked in every direction, she couldn't see the shelter. She couldn't even see the ravine. She was lost.

The snowfall steadily grew thicker, as if the snow clouds themselves were dropping to earth in a single body.

Melting snow was beginning to soak through her clothes. Her hands and feet were already numb. She and Genji would soon die. Tears froze on her cheeks. She was not afraid of death for herself. It was Genji's fate that tore at her heart. He would perish alone in this wilderness so far from his home, with no one to hold him, no one to say words of comfort as his soul went down to Purgatory, the inevitable doom of all who died unbaptized. She had promised God she would save his soul, and she had failed.

She sank down in the snow and wept.

No, no, this wouldn't do.

She choked back her sobs. She had promised God. As long as the life He had given her was in her body, she would do her best to fulfill her vow. What she felt was not genuine sorrow; it was self-pity, the darkest aspect of the sin of pride.

Think.

The snow obscured everything more than a few feet away in every direction. Since she recognized no landmark anyway, that was of small importance. Her feet showed her the incline of the mountain. If she could remember whether she had gone downhill or uphill after the mare, she might be able to find her way back.

Downhill.

She thought the mare had gone downhill. That meant the shelter was somewhere above her present position. It couldn't be too far away. She had walked very slowly. She took a careful step into the deepening snow, then another, and another. She followed her feet up the mountainside. With her fourth step, her foot went into the snow and found no ground beneath it. She toppled over the hidden precipice headfirst. Her momentum threw her downhill, head over heels. She didn't stop until she slammed into something hard.

It was the lean-to.

She had been going in the wrong direction. If she hadn't fallen into the ravine, she would have wandered in the storm until the cold sent her to her eternal rest. New snow covering the shelter rounded its edges. Now it looked more like the Eskimo ice house her mother had drawn. She scraped away the snow and went inside.

Genji was alive, barely. His breath was shallow and infrequent. His skin was cold and nearly blue. Without more heat, he would be dead in minutes. She had no blankets with which to cover him. She didn't know how to make a fire. Her mother had told her Indians did it by rubbing two sticks together. She was sure it wasn't quite that simple. No, the only heat she had to offer was the warmth of her own body.

Which was the greater sin? To lie with a man not her husband, or to sit idly by while he died? The first commandment was not to kill. Surely that had precedence. And she wouldn't be lying with him in the strictest biblical sense. This was an attempt at rescue, not an act of fornication, lust, carnality, or adultery.

Emily lay down next to Genji on his left side, away from the wound in his rib cage. Her coat covered him, and she herself was fully clothed. She wasn't "lying" with him at all. Nor was she doing much good. The heat of her body was being dissipated by the clothing between them.

She closed her eyes in prayer. She asked God to look into her heart and see the purity of her motives. She asked Him to forgive her if her judgment was wrong. If He could save only one life, she asked Him to save Genji's, for she was baptized and he was not.

She quickly stripped off her clothing, everything but her pantaloons. She removed his also, with the exception of his loincloth. She was careful not to notice anything she should not. She used his bloodstained robe as a sheet over the pine needles, and her coat as a mattress over that, then placed Genji upon it. She covered his body with hers as fully as she could without putting too much weight on him. The bleeding had stopped, but pressure could tear the wounds open. She used their remaining clothing to make a snug cocoon around them.

There was no warmth, no softness in Genji's skin. He wasn't even shivering anymore. Hugging him was like hugging a block of ice. Rather than her thawing him, it seemed he would freeze her instead. But the heat from the core of her body, pressed so tightly against his, was stronger than the cold.

A single bead of sweat appeared on his upper lip.

His breathing deepened.

She fell asleep with a smile on her lips.

· · · · ·

Genji woke blind, feverish, pain tearing his body. He was bound in such a way that he could barely move. Someone pressed down on him, holding him against the ground.

"Eeeyyy!"

He bucked and twisted and reversed positions on his assailant. Now he was on top.

"Where are we?" He was a prisoner. That much he knew. But whose?

The reply came in a strange voice speaking garbled words that made no sense. It was a woman's voice. He had heard it before. It had been in a dream. Or a vision.

"Lady Shizuka?" Was she here, a prisoner, too?

She spoke again. Again he understood nothing. She tried to free herself from his grasp. He tightened his hold on her wrists and she stopped struggling immediately. Her voice had a soothing tone. She was explaining something to him.

"I don't understand what you're saying," Genji said.

Lady Shizuka, if it was her, continued murmuring in her secret language.

Why was he blind? Had his eyes been put out? Or was he in a dungeon, sealed away below the ground, far from sunlight? Was this woman a tool of his torturers? Kawakami. The Shogun's Sticky Eye. It was something he would do. Use a woman. He thought of Heiko. The woman beneath him wasn't Heiko. Was she? No. He would understand Heiko. Wouldn't he?

"Heiko?"

The familiar voice spoke again, more excited this time, and just as incomprehensible. Except for two words. "Genji" and "Heiko." Whoever she was, she knew him. The voice was familiar, but the body wasn't. It was larger than Heiko's. Or so it seemed. He wasn't sure of anything.

He faded in and out of consciousness. Each time he awoke, he could see a little better. The walls glowed, emanating light. Instead of hair, gold filaments sprouted from the woman's head. Her eyes were a blue void, like the sky. Something sparkled at her neck. It was something he had seen before in another vision.

•   •   •   •   •

The young man drives his sword deep in Genji's torso....

He feels blood pulsating from his chest....

An extraordinarily beautiful woman says, "You will always be my Shining Prince."

Her beauty is not entirely Japanese. He doesn't recognize her, but her face brings a longing to his heart. He knows her. Or will. She is Lady Shizuka.

Smiling through her tears, she says, "I finished the translation this morning. I wonder whether we should use the Japanese name, or translate the title into English as well. What do you think?"

"English," Genji says, meaning to ask what she has translated.

Lady Shizuka misunderstands him. "English it is, then. . . . She would be so proud of us."

Who would be so proud? He has no voice to ask. Something sparkles at her long, smooth throat.

· · · · ·

It was what he saw now at this woman's throat. A small silver locket no larger than his thumb, marked with a cross upon which was emblazoned a stylized flower, perhaps a lily.

· · · · ·

"Lord Genji?"

He had fallen unconscious again.

She gently brought his arms back under the cover and closed the cocoon. He would be as warm above her as below. Blood dripped onto her breast from his chest wound. The binding on his back was wet as well. His exertions had torn open the wounds. If she tried to move him, he might awake and resume his struggle against the phantoms of delirium, and so do himself harm.

Their new position was somewhat awkward and

disconcerting, however. As long as he slept, it was not a problem. When he was awake, even in his feverish state, she found herself experiencing embarrassment. There was no rational reason for it. Neither he nor she was doing anything wrong, and no sinful intentions whatsoever were manifest. Yet the fact that he was now atop her was necessarily disturbing. It created an appearance of wrongdoing, though of course there was no one to observe it, and so no one to draw an erroneous conclusion.

Moving him entailed too great a risk. Better the appearance of wrong than the actual doing of it, for it was surely wrong to cause him to injure himself.

She grew drowsy as dawn brightened the packed snow around them. Soon, she, too, was asleep.

Snow continued to fall well into the day.

· · · · ·

"In another hour, they would have been dead," Shigeru said. "She made a vent in the shelter, but snow covered it. They were slowly suffocating."

Hidé looked toward the fire, where Lord Genji and Emily slept. He had dressed the lord's wounds and fed them both. They would survive.

Shigeru showed Hidé the .32 revolver. "It holds four expended bullets and two fresh ones. I think she fought off whoever attacked Genji. Who knows? There may have been bodies nearby under the snow." He said nothing about how he had found them, Genji and the woman nearly naked, wrapped together as one in a single sheath of their clothing. He didn't know if the woman had fired the gun and saved Genji that way. He knew she had saved him with her body. With the wounds he had suffered, and the loss of blood, he would have frozen to death without her.

"Lord Shigeru," Hidé said, eyes wide with astonishment. "Do you realize what has happened?"

"Yes. The prophecy has come true. An outsider met in the New Year has saved Lord Genji's life."

IV

THE BRIDGE OF LIFE AND DEATH

13

Apple Valley

The sages say happiness and sorrow are one. Is this because in finding the first, we also find the second?

SUZUME-NO-KUMO
(1861)

I am not much of a samurai after all," Genji said. He was in the Great Lord's main bedroom in Cloud of Sparrows Castle. It did not feel like his room. His grandfather's presence was still very strong here.

"How can you say such a thing, my lord?" Saiki said. "You survived under the most perilous of circumstances. That is exactly what a samurai is expected to do."

Saiki and Hidé knelt at the bedside. Genji lay on his left side as Dr. Ozawa tended to his wounds.

"You sailed through ocean storms, were attacked by whales, and held captive by traitors," Genji said. "Those are what I would call perilous circumstances."

Genji flinched as some dried blood came away with an old dressing. Both samurai inhaled audibly and leaned forward as if to lend assistance.

"I'm sorry, my lord," Dr. Ozawa said. "That was clumsy of me."

Genji waved off the apology. "I was taken completely off guard by a ragged gang of starving deserters, defended by Emily, and rescued by my uncle. Not exactly a tale we will want to recite at my next birthday festival."

"You suffered grievous injuries that would have killed a lesser man," Saiki said. "Your fighting spirit kept you alive. What is more important in a samurai than fighting spirit?"

"A modicum of ordinary alertness, perhaps."

Hidé could restrain himself no longer. He pressed his forehead to the floor and kept it there, not deeming himself worthy to look up at his injured lord. He allowed himself to make no sound. His shuddering shoulders alone indicated the depth of his grief.

"What is it, Hidé?" Genji said. "Get up, please."

"It is all my fault," Hidé said. "You were almost killed because of my negligence."

"You weren't even there. How can you accuse yourself of negligence?"

"Because I should have been. I am your chief bodyguard. To permit you to face peril without me was unforgivable."

"You made your point very forcefully at the time," Genji said. "I ordered you to stay behind, over your protests, and Shigeru's. You could do nothing else."

"I could have followed you without your knowledge."

"Hidé, get up and stop this nonsense. There is no

one to blame but me. I have grown so used to having good and faithful men around me, I have lost the ability to protect myself. If anyone should be weeping in shame, it is I, not you."

"I agree with Hidé," Saiki said. "Your injuries are indeed due to his failure. He should have disregarded your order and continued to watch over you without your knowledge. For such disobedience, he would later be obliged to commit suicide, of course, but in the meantime, he would have guarded you, as his duty demanded."

"And what if Kudo and his men had come to those crossroads? No one would have been there to stop them."

"Lord Shigeru killed them all," Saiki said. "There was no need for Hidé to keep watch."

"We didn't know that then," Genji said. "And who is to say what would have happened if Hidé had done as you say he should have. Perhaps the prophecy would have been thwarted, and you would be viewing my corpse instead of teaching me the wisdom of disobedience."

Hidé looked up.

Saiki sat speechless.

Genji smiled. When all else failed, he could always fall back on prophecy. What a handy device.

Dr. Ozawa said, "Your wounds are clean, my lord. There is no sign of infection. Remarkably, you have not suffered from any serious frostbite, either. I am at a loss to explain how that is possible. Lord Shigeru said he found you buried in a mound of snow."

"I was not alone," Genji said. "My companion had knowledge of Eskimo lore. She was able to put that knowledge to good use."

"What is 'Eskimo'?" Dr. Ozawa asked. "An outsider medical technique?"

"A technique, certainly," Genji said.

"With your permission, I would like to discuss Eskimo with her. Perhaps Lady Heiko would serve as translator?"

"I am sure you will find such a discussion enlightening," Genji said. He wished he could be there. It would be very entertaining. Emily would tell the truth. She always did. Lying, she said, was a sin against Christ. How flustered and embarrassed she would be, how she would struggle to explain what she had done without revealing too much. He imagined the scene and laughed.

"My lord?"

"I'm just happy to be recovering so quickly. Thank you for your help, Dr. Ozawa."

"Don't overexert yourself too soon. A relapse would be dangerous."

Genji rose from the bed. Normally, he would just stand there while attendants put his clothing on for him. Upset at himself for his incompetence in the woods, he insisted on dressing himself.

"I may not be much with a sword," he said, "but I am a marvel with a sash."

"It was your first real battle," Saiki said. "You will do better the next time."

"Could I do worse?"

"You are too hard on yourself, my lord," Saiki said. "During the uprisings in the western part of the domain—this was before you were born—I saw blood spilled for the first time. I regret to say, I threw up and soiled my loincloth. Simultaneously."

"No!" Genji said. "Not you?"

"Unfortunately, yes," Saiki said.

Genji laughed and Hidé joined him. Saiki laughed, too. He neglected to mention that he had been thirteen years old at the time, and the blood he had seen was that of the two heavily armed farmers he had just killed with his first full-sized katana. He was glad his story had lifted Genji's spirits. A small sacrifice in dignity was inconsequential.

"Oh, excuse me. Am I interrupting a conference?" Emily stood at the doorway. Her dress was similar to the one she had worn before, but fashioned of silk instead of cotton. Her petticoats, her pantaloons, and her stockings, too, were silk. Her old clothes had been ruined in the wilderness. Seamstresses in the castle had used them as a pattern to make replacements. She would have preferred cotton, which was more properly humble. But to refuse these gifts of well-meant charity would be unkind. So for the first time in her life, she was dressed in silk from head to toe. Even the padded coat, as frumpy and oversized as the old one, was of the same fine material.

"We were just concluding," Genji said. "Another minute or two. Please come in."

"Lady Emily," Saiki said. He and Hidé bowed deeply as she entered. "I am happy to see you well and about."

Genji noticed the elevated level of politeness Saiki employed. She was now "Lady Emily" instead of "the outsider woman." The fulfillment of the prophecy had worked a significant change in her status. Genji was glad. Almost entirely alone in a foreign land, widowed before she was even married, her life was hard enough. A little kindness would reduce her pain.

Genji said, "He expresses happiness at seeing you in good health."

"Please thank Mr. Saiki for me. I am happy to see him safe as well."

"She thanks you for your good wishes, Saiki, and is happy to see you safe. Do we have anything further to discuss?"

"No, my lord," Saiki said. "The rebellion against you has been crushed. All that remains is to mete out punishment. Lord Shigeru has already carried out the most difficult actions. I will take one hundred men to Kageshima Village tomorrow morning. That will be that."

"I think it will be sufficient if you execute the village elders," Genji said. "Accompany it with a stern admonition to the others regarding the importance of loyalty, not merely to their immediate lord, but to the Great Lord of the domain."

"That is not the usual procedure, my lord."

"I know."

"I wonder how wise it is to be kind at the present time. It may create the impression that you lack the will to do what is necessary."

"I have precisely the will to do what is necessary, and that is what is necessary. There will be more than enough killing in the days ahead. If we must kill, then let us concentrate on our enemies and not our own peasants."

"Yes, my lord."

Saiki and Hidé withdrew. At the doorway, Hidé said, "I will wait with the horses."

Genji was about to tell him his presence would not be required. They were not going far. Hidé's determined facial expression stopped him. It was obvious he would not be riding anywhere alone for some time.

"Very good, Hidé."

Emily said, "Are you sure you are well enough to ride, my lord?"

"We will saunter," Genji said. "We will do no galloping. I'll be fine."

"Perhaps we should just take a walk instead. I have yet to see much of the castle. What I have seen is very beautiful."

"And you will see it. But today, we must ride. There is something I want to show you."

"What is it?"

"Come with me and find out."

Emily laughed. "A surprise? I used to love surprises, when I was a child. Oh. Do you think Matthew would like to come with us?"

Genji said, "He's busy practicing. Listen."

The muffled sound of gunfire came from the distance.

"Anyway, this is something I want to show you, not him."

"It grows ever more mysterious," Emily said.

"But not for long," Genji said.

•　•　•　•　•

The final head was that of an infant not yet one year of age. Shigeru stuck it on a spear at the end of the row of heads outside the front gate of the castle. Winters in Akaoka Domain were warmer than they were in the mountains of the main island of Honshu. Kudo's face was already rotten beyond recognition. The others were fresh, their recent agonies still alive in their expressions. Kudo's wife, two concubines, five children, widowed mother, brother, brothers-in-law, sisters-in-law, uncles, aunts, cousins, nephews, and nieces. Fifty-nine heads in all.

Kudo's family was now extinct.

Heiko bowed and approached him. "A most gruesome task, Lord Shigeru."

"And a necessary one."

"I don't doubt it," Heiko said. "The river of karma flows inexorably."

"May I be of some assistance to you, Lady Heiko?"

"That is my hope," Heiko said. "Shortly, Lord Genji will be going for a brief excursion. Lady Emily will accompany him. They will, of course, pass this way."

"Of course. The lord always uses the front gate of the castle, no matter where he goes."

"This display will horrify Lady Emily beyond measure."

"It will?" Shigeru looked at the neat row lining the south side of the road. "Why? It appears that everything is in proper order."

"She is of a particularly tender nature," Heiko said, choosing her words with great care. "Also, being an outsider, she doesn't understand the workings of karma. The presence of children, especially, will cause her much sorrow. I am afraid she will be unable to continue the outing with our lord."

"And you suggest I do what?"

"Remove the heads."

"I don't see how I can do that. It has been a tradition since time immemorial to show the fate of traitors at the main gate of the castle, and to keep them there until the flesh rots from the skulls and the carrion eaters have picked them clean."

"A tradition worthy of perpetuation," Heiko

said. "Might you not consider modifying it slightly, just for now? Could the display not be moved temporarily to Lord Kudo's residence?"

"The traitor is no lord, and no longer has a name."

"Excuse me," Heiko said, bowing. "I meant to say, the traitor's former residence."

"I was on my way there to burn it to the ground."

Heiko blanched. "Not with the servants inside?"

Shigeru smiled grimly. "That was my intention. Our lord, being the supremely compassionate and excessively forgiving master that he is, ordered that they be sold into bondage instead."

Heiko took a relieved breath. "Then may I make a suggestion?"

"I was under the impression that you have been doing so all along."

"With your permission only, Lord Shigeru. May I suggest that you burn the residence as you have planned, and then place these reminders upon the ruins. Would that not be an effective alternative?"

Shigeru imagined how it would look. Fifty-nine heads on the ends of spears protruding from the smoking wreckage of treason. "Very well, Lady Heiko. It will be done."

"Thank you, Lord Shigeru."

She did not stay to watch him accomplish the task.

· · · · ·

On their way from the castle, Genji, Emily, and Hidé met Stark and Taro on their way back.

"Do you never run out of bullets, Matthew?" Emily sat astride the horse instead of sidesaddle.

Genji had talked her into wearing pants like his, flowing wide-legged trousers called "hakama." It was, he said, entirely appropriate for ladies. She remembered Zephaniah's advice to follow the customs of Japan so far as they did not violate the dictates of Christian morality. Hakama seemed benign enough. They were so loose, they seemed more like a skirt than pants in the Western sense.

"I've made a mold to cast new bullets," Stark said, "and our hosts have powder aplenty." He held out spent cartridges in his hand. "These I can reuse several times."

"You will be a most Christian soldier, I hope," Emily said, "and fight only for righteousness' sake."

"My mission is righteous," Stark said. "That's a certainty."

Taro said to Hidé, "Where are you going?"

"Not far. If you are free, come with us."

"I'll do that. Mr. Stark is meeting Lady Heiko. She's a better guide for him anyway, since she can speak his language."

Hidé and Taro rode some distance behind the lord and lady. In their own domain, this close to the castle, attack was highly unlikely. Nevertheless, Hidé observed their surroundings with unceasing attention.

"How is his shooting?"

"Amazing," Taro said. "I never imagined such a thing was possible. He draws and fires his gun faster than any iaido master can draw a sword. Faster even than Shigeru, I think."

"So I told you."

"Yes, you did. I thought you were joking. Now I know you were not. He's accurate, too. At twenty paces, he hits his target with the first shot nine times out of ten, and always with the second. I wonder why he practices so hard. There is no one in Japan against whom he can test his skill."

"He is a warrior like us," Hidé said, "and war is coming. That is reason enough."

Emily watched Genji closely. If he showed any signs of strain whatsoever, she would insist on their return. So far, he seemed fine. Being home was no doubt a great help. The climate in his domain was much milder than that of Edo. There it was winter, with all its harshness. Here it was more like early spring.

"Are winters here always so mild?"

"It is rarely colder," Genji said, "so we have little need for Eskimo skills."

"My lord, please."

"Perhaps our population would be greater if it snowed."

Emily looked away, her face hot with embarrassment. She was sure she was as red as an apple ready for plucking.

Genji laughed. "I'm sorry, Emily. I couldn't resist."

"You promised you would never mention it."

"I promised I would never mention it to others. I said nothing about reminiscing with you."

"Lord Genji, that is very ungentlemanly of you."

"Ungentlemanly?"

" 'Un' is a prefix meaning 'not.' A gentleman is a person of good character and high principle. 'Ly' is a suffix meaning 'having the character of.' " She turned as stern a gaze on him as she could manage. "Your present behavior does not demonstrate good character and high principle."

"An unforgivable lapse. Please accept my most profound apologies."

"I would, were you not smiling in such obvious amusement."

"You are smiling, too."

"It is a grimace, not a smile."

"Grimace?"

She refused to explain.

They rode inland in silence. Every time she cast a surreptitious glance his way, that little smile was still on his lips. She wanted to be upset with him, but she couldn't manage it. At the same time, to act as if nothing had been said would be wrong. His jests were inappropriate, given their relationship. She was a missionary and he was the lord sponsoring her mission. Nothing had happened to change that.

She paused and looked back at Cloud of Sparrows. When she had first seen it, her dismay had been painfully keen. This was a castle? Then where were the great walls and towers of stone, the parapets, the ramparts, the crenellations and embrasures, the drawbridge, the moat? The only stone was in the base, loose-packed and unmortared, atop which stood elaborate pagodas of wood, stucco, and tile. Castles were the abodes of knights, like Wilfred of Ivanhoe. Never could she imagine him, resplendent in his armor plate and chain mail, shield and lance in hand, atop his mighty charger, coming forth from such a place. Like beauty, castles were different in Japan. As much as one difference had proved a genuine blessing, so had the other been a great disappointment.

How much her views had changed in two short weeks. Cloud of Sparrows appeared so light to the eye, its seven stories seemed to float above the rocky sea cliff. Its stone base swept upward in an elegant concave parabola to support walls of stucco as white as summer clouds. Atop the walls were the arches and curves of roofs covered with gray terra-cotta tiles. From where she sat atop her mare, some two miles distant from the castle, she could, with little effort, see the tiles as flocks of sparrows taking flight. There was an ethereal elegance here that made the heavy stone structures of her former imaginings seem pitifully earthbound in contrast.

Genji said, "Are you very angry, Emily?"

She smiled and shook her head. "No. I only think it proper not to joke about certain things."

"You are right. I will not joke about it again."

They came to a moderate rise in the terrain. Before they crested it, she thought she caught a familiar scent. She quickly dismissed it as a trick of her suppressed homesickness. A moment later she looked into a small valley and grew dizzy in her saddle. The air she breathed suddenly seemed thin, as if she had climbed to a great height.

"An apple orchard." Her voice was a whisper.

It was not large, perhaps a hundred trees. When they rode down among them, and they surrounded her, they might as well have been ten thousand. She stood in her stirrups, reached up, and plucked a bright red fruit.

"Why, these are very much like the apples we grew on our farm," Emily said.

"Perhaps they are the same," Genji said, "Are apples native to America?"

"No, European settlers brought them. A man named Johnny Appleseed spent his life planting them all across the country. Or so I was told. It might be a fairy tale, not history."

"There is often little difference between the two," Genji said. He reached up to take hold of a branch, gasped, and lowered his arms. His injuries frustrated his effort. "I used to climb into these branches and have imaginary conversations. My companions were always very wise."

"I used to climb, too," Emily said, "and play games with my two brothers."

"Imaginary brothers?"

"Real. Tom and Walt."

"Are they missionaries, too?

"No. They died in childhood."

"And your parents?"

"They also have passed away."

"We are both orphans, then." He looked up into the branches above. "I suppose you are no longer able to climb."

"I beg your pardon?"

"Trees. Can you still climb them? If my injuries permitted, I would go to the very top with ease."

"I could do the same," Emily said.

"Of course."

"You seem doubtful, Lord Genji."

"Well, you don't look like much of a tree climber."

"That sounds like a dare." She and Tom and Walt exchanged dares all the time. The last time she was in a tree, she'd leaped from one branch to another on a dare. The branch she landed on broke. She clung to it as it swung toward the ground and barely avoided serious injury.

I'm sorry about breaking the branch, Father.

Better the branch than you. But you must not do that again.

Yes, Father.

You are very beautiful, Emily. You will be much less beautiful with a crooked leg, or a crooked back.

Yes, Father.

He always told her how beautiful she was. When he had said it, it had made her feel wonderful. How different that word was now.

Emily took off her coat and laid it across her pommel. She reached up, firmly grasped the branch above her, and left the saddle. She swung back and forth, gaining momentum, and finally threw first one leg then the other over the branch. She twisted herself around and sat, her legs swinging gaily under her, a triumphant smile on her face.

Genji bowed deeply from his saddle. "Forgive me for doubting you. You are an excellent climber indeed. When I am healed, we must have a contest."

"And what will we stake?"

"Stake?"

"The prize the loser gives the winner."

Genji said, "If you win, I will give you this orchard."

"Oh, no, that is far too much. That makes it gambling, not a game."

"Very well," Genji said, "win or lose, I will give you this orchard. You can give me something in exchange. Then we are not gambling, are we?"

"I cannot accept a gift so grand," Emily said. "And even if I did, I have no means to care for it properly."

"I will give you means as well. The three villages in this valley and the next."

"No, I cannot accept. My purpose is to spread the word of God, not to take for myself."

Genji gestured at the rise they had come over to

enter the valley. "You can build a church there. Is that not what you have come to do?"

"I thought the land for our mission was in another province."

"You can build here, too. I promise, your church will always be full."

Emily laughed despite her concern. He would keep his promise by issuing a command. Messengers would ride into the villages. The peasants would drop to their knees, press their heads to the ground, and hear the words of their lord. On Sundays thereafter, they would fill the pews as they had been ordered to do. They would listen to a translated sermon that meant nothing to them. When baptism was offered, every man, woman, and child would come forward to accept it.

"You cannot force people to believe, my lord. They must look into their hearts and come to the truth on their own."

"I promise, I will come to your church, and look into my heart."

"Lord Genji." She didn't know what else to say.

"You saved my life. You must let me thank you with a gift."

"I could just as well say you saved mine. Neither of us would have survived without the other."

"Then you owe me a gift as well. I will give you Apple Valley. What will you give me?"

Emily had to lean against the trunk to keep from falling. "Apple Valley?"

"That's what my mother called it. Ringo-no-tani. Apple Valley, in English." His smile remained. The expression in his eyes changed. "She was from the north. Her father's domain was renowned for its apples. She was very young when she married, not many years beyond childhood. She missed her mother and her sisters. She missed her playmates. She missed the trees she climbed as a child, and the fruit she picked and ate in their boughs. She missed the childish garlands of blossoms she wore on her head. My father planted this orchard for her in the hopes it would ease her sorrow and, perhaps one day, even bring her joy."

"And did it?"

"She was happy when the seedlings were planted. She put a few into the ground herself. She never saw the trees, or the blossoms, or the fruit. She died that winter, in childbirth. Her newborn, my sister, died, too."

"I'm so sorry."

"The sages say happiness and sorrow are one. Whenever I am here, I understand their meaning."

Leaves and branches obscured the surrounding landscape of steep Japanese mountains. The nearness of the Pacific Ocean was masked by the scent of apples. Perched above the ground, her feet dangling in the air, Emily felt her concentration dissolve. She looked down and saw Genji on his warhorse, and it was he who was out of place, not herself. The incongruity of a samurai in her orchard made her laugh.

Her own laughter brought her back.

Coming back, she began to weep.

"My home was in Apple Valley," Emily said. "Another Apple Valley."

After a time, Genji said, "This place was yours before you ever saw it."

•　•　•　•　•

"Lady Emily is quite nimble for such a large person," Taro said. They watched her swing herself up into the tree.

"She is not really that large," Hidé said. "When those two fools killed themselves, she fainted in our lord's arms. He held her easily. Her proportions are not what we are used to, and so we misjudge her size."

"Now that I regard her with that knowledge, I see you are entirely correct." Taro made the maximum possible effort to gain the right perspective. Lady Emily had brought Lord Kiyori's prophecy to fruition. It would not do to see her as large, or ungainly, or ugly. Loyalty compelled them to cast her in the best possible light. "In fact, there is a kind of ladylike daintiness to her. In an outsider sort of way."

"True," Hidé said. "I feel great contrition now for my former mistaken views. Surely, in her own land, where standards are based on other ideals, she is considered quite the beauty, much as Lady Heiko is in ours."

Much as he wanted to, Taro could not bring himself to agree with his friend. With some effort, he could conceive of her as attractive to outsiders, some of them at least. But a beauty on the order of Heiko? What could he say? His skills were with sword and bow, not words.

"That might be, if the basis for such a comparison existed," Taro said. "Lady Heiko is a geisha of the first rank, and Lady Emily . . ." He battled mightily to cut through to safety. "Do geishas exist in Lady Emily's country?"

"It is my understanding they do not," Hidé said. He was apparently having difficulty with his own words as well. His brow was deeply furrowed with the unaccustomed effort of sustained thought.

"That is also my understanding," Taro said.

"Then, is it appropriate to speak of Lady Emily and Lady Heiko in the same terms?"

"Not appropriate at all," Hidé said, brightening with relief. "Clearly, I misspoke. My admiration for her caused me to go a bit too far. We do her no favor by exaggerating her merits."

"No, we do not," Taro said. Enthusiasm returned to his voice. "They are profoundly apparent. They do not require false amplification."

"In any case, how important is something as superficial as outer beauty?" Hidé moved the conversation to safer ground. "What really matters is the beauty within. There, Lady Emily is second to none."

"You have clearly expressed the key point," Taro said, much relieved by the shift in focus. "True beauty lies within."

The two samurai smiled happily as they sat on their horses and kept watch over their lord and Lady Emily. Between them, they had resolved an important issue. Now they knew how to think about an important person who did not quite fit into the usual order.

· · · · ·

Heiko said, "You did not mention the details of our journey to Lord Genji."

Stark said, "He didn't ask."

They sat in chairs in a room overlooking one of the castle's inner gardens. It was one of several furnished to meet Emily and Stark's needs. This particular room was crowded with six chairs, four tables, a large couch, a writing desk, and two dressers. Outsiders were unlike Japanese. What they thought was good, Japanese thought was bad, and vice versa. Genji's servants took this as their guiding principle.

404 · *Takashi Matsuoka*

In their zeal to make the honored guests feel at home, they did for them the opposite of what they did for their lord. Where he had much space and few furnishings, the guests had many furnishings and little space. The servants exerted themselves to the utmost to create an environment completely unlike one in which they themselves would be comfortable. In this they had succeeded admirably.

"I intend to tell him myself," Heiko said, "today."

"Your secret's still your secret," Stark said. "I'm not saying anything."

"Thank you for your restraint. I appreciate it very much. Secrets are impossible to keep. You will not speak of it, I know. But word of the fight at the barricade will eventually reach Lord Genji. He will realize the truth."

"Will that cause problems?"

"Yes, I believe it will."

"He doesn't know about your other skills."

"No."

"Why did you use them?" Stark said. "We might have sneaked through okay, and if we didn't, I would have shot our way through. Swords are no match for a six-gun."

"I could not put your life at risk any more than I had to. Before he died, Lord Genji's grandfather made a prophecy. He said an outsider Lord Genji meets in the New Year will save his life. I was certain you were the one."

"If I was, then nothing would have happened. I had to live to do what the prophecy said I would do. If I died, then I wasn't who you were waiting for. Nothing lost."

"Prophecies cannot be trusted to fulfill themselves," Heiko said. "Without our most sincere efforts, the outcome may be much different from what we hope for. If you were the outsider intended to save him, but were killed before you could do it, then another would have come forward. But not the right outsider. Lord Genji would live, because the prophecy said he would. But he might be maimed or crippled or put into a coma."

"Is that how it works?" Stark said. He didn't believe any of this. But she wanted to talk, so he listened. "How did Lord Genji's grandfather get into the prophecy business?"

"He was born with the gift of foresight. He had many visions throughout his life."

"Was he always right?"

"He was."

"Why didn't he tell everyone it was Emily?"

"Visions are always incomplete. Though life is preordained, its precise unfolding depends on what we do. Past karma determines the first. Present karma the second."

"Karma?"

"Perhaps your word is fate, but a living, constantly changing fate."

"Fate is fate," Stark said. "It's there. It doesn't change. We just don't see it until we walk into it. Or it walks into us."

· · · · · ·

Sometimes, when Stark was in the vicinity of El Paso, he'd stop by Manual Cruz's establishment, which had the best dozen whores in Texas, according to its proprietor. Stark never actually counted more than eight at any one time. As far as he could tell, none was better than whores anywhere else in town, much less the state.

"Poetic license," Cruz said. "Picks a man up. Puts him in an optimistic frame of mind. Good for him. Good for business."

"What's poetic license?"

"You come here for a lesson in the intricacies of language, boy, or to get screwed, glued, and tattooed?"

"I came to fuck a whore," Stark said, "not to get anything affixed."

"Literal-minded cuss, aren't you?" Ethan said. Ethan was Cruz's adopted son. He wore his gun low on his hip the way Stark did, and kept his shoulders relaxed the same way. One day, Ethan would figure out he was Matthew Stark, the gunfighter with the big reputation, and call him out. Or he would figure out that he and Stark were in the same line of work and suggest a partnership. One or the other, one of these days.

Cruz laughed. "Go ahead. Take a good look and make your best selection."

Stark didn't patronize Cruz's establishment because of the superior quality of its merchandise. He went there because it was the one closest to the edge of town. Towns made his chest and throat tight. He didn't go into them any more than he had to.

If location was what recommended the place, it was also what kept him away most of the time. He couldn't stand the rank odor of the pigsty next door. In that regard, he appeared to be in the minority. Cruz always had more business when the prevailing wind came toward the bar than when it blew away from it. Which was fine as far as Stark was concerned. The only thing he disliked more in a whorehouse than the stench of pigs was a crowd of fornicating drunks. He always checked the wind when he rode into El Paso, and so never had to deal with either.

He wasn't sentimental. He didn't have a favorite whore. He was twenty years old, and he'd killed three more men in gunfights since he'd killed Jimmy So Fast, and he didn't know if he'd live to be twenty-one. No one had come after him in over a year, but he wasn't fool enough to think that meant no one would. He gave four bits to Cruz and took the closest of the best dozen upstairs.

That time, which was the second to the last time he ever went to Cruz's, it happened to be Mary Anne.

She was nothing special, except she was older than the others, older than any he'd been with. She was kinder, too, and when he spilled himself all over her thigh before he could get inside her, she shushed him, and held him close, and told him to rest awhile, it was okay, he could give it another go without giving Cruz another four bits. He told her it was always hard to hold it in the first time off the trail, he was with a woman so infrequently was the reason. She said shush and just held him until he was ready.

When he was finished he must have fallen asleep because what he did next was wake up. A dim lamp burned on the table. Mary Anne was asleep next to him. The wind being the way it was, blowing from the wrong direction, business was slow. She was in no hurry to go back downstairs and sit in a hard chair in an empty bar.

He had to piss. He turned to get out of bed and saw two little girls staring at him. They stood right up next to the bed. The littler one, she couldn't have been more than four or five, had her thumb in her mouth. The other one, older by a couple of years, had a protective arm around her sister's shoulder. He could tell they were sisters by the family resemblance. He knew whose daughters they were the same way. The sheet hanging from a pole on the other side of the room had been spread out when he'd gone to bed with Mary Anne. Now it was pulled back and he could see the little bed on the other side.

"Hi, there," Stark said. How was he going to talk them into turning away so he could get his pants on?

"We didn't know anyone was here," the older girl said. "It was quiet."

"I'll be going as soon as I can get dressed," Stark said.

The younger girl picked his pants up from the chair and brought them to him.

"Thank you."

"You're welcome," the older one said for her.

He looked back at Mary Anne, thinking the sound of voices would wake her. No such luck. She was a very sound sleeper.

"We were sleeping," the older girl said, "but Louise woke up thirsty, so I was going with her to get a drink of water."

"You're a good girl," Stark said, "to be looking after your little sister that way."

"Even when we're not sleeping," the older girl said, "nobody knows we're there. We're quiet as church mice, so our mommy can do her job."

"You're always behind the sheet?"

"No, silly. We go to Mrs. Crenshaw's house during the day, excepting Saturdays and Sundays. On Sundays we go to Sunday school at the church." She looked at her alcove and looked back at Stark and giggled. "How could we stay in that itty bitty space all the time?"

"Why aren't you at Mrs. Crenshaw's now?"

"Because it's nighttime, and it's Saturday." This time, both girls giggled. "Don't you even know what day it is?"

"Becky, Louise, what are you doing up?" Mary Anne lifted her sleepy head from the pillow.

"Louise is thirsty, Mommy."

"Then give her some water and go back to bed."

"Yes, Mommy. 'Bye, mister."

" 'Bye." Stark got up and put on his pants as soon as they were out the door. "They're not going down to the bar, are they?"

"Sure. That's where the water is."

"You could keep a pitcher in your room. Right there by their bed."

"They don't want that." Mary Anne rolled over on her back with the sheet pulled up demurely around her neck and watched him dress. "They think the smell of pigs gets in the water and makes it dirty."

Stark didn't want to say it, it was none of his business. But he said, "This is no place for kids."

"This is no place for me, either," Mary Anne said, "but here they are, and here I am. There are worse. Cruz lets them stay with me, and nobody bothers them. That's something to be grateful for. He says he doesn't abide pederasts, and he means it."

"What's a pederast?"

"One who takes pleasure in molesting a child."

Stark remembered the orphanage and the surprised look in the night supervisor's dead eyes after Stark cracked his skull open with a hammer. "I don't abide pederasts either."

"You don't have to leave. They'll drink their water and go back to sleep."

"I hear voices," Stark said, listening to the laughter in the bar. "Customers."

"More than enough girls to handle whoever's there." Mary Anne took a deep breath. "I get lazy when the east wind blows. The air's so nice, and there aren't many visitors."

Stark took another four bits out of his pocket and put it on the table next to the lamp.

"I told you, you don't have to pay for the second time. It was really the first time, if you think about it." She smiled at him. It wasn't the kind of smile a whore smiled when she was making fun of you or when she was trying to trick you out of more money. It was a nice smile.

"I'm going down to Mexico to work a mine," Stark said. He was actually on his way to Missouri to rob more banks. He thought it might make a better impression if he didn't say so right out, before he really knew her. "I'll be back in the spring."

"I'll be here," Mary Anne said.

It was the first time Stark had ever lied to a whore. There wasn't any reason to before. Why did he want to make a good impression on Mary Anne? Because she was the mother of two children? That was a damned foolish reason, if that's what it was. Nothing holy about motherhood. His own mother, her identity forever unknown to him, had left his infant self on the steps of a church in Columbus, Ohio, wrapped in a blanket and with nothing else, not even a name. He got Matthew because that was the Apostle next on the name list. He didn't know how he got Stark. He had no soft spot for mothers. Maybe it was because Mary Anne was kind and had a nice smile. Maybe it was because Becky and Louise were cute little girls who didn't belong in a whorehouse. Those were damned foolish reasons, too. Stark had no fondness for children, not even memories of himself as one.

It was the first time he'd lied to a whore, and it was also the first time he'd told a whore he'd come back to see her. He thought that was his second lie, after the one about going to Mexico to work in a mine.

But it turned out he was telling the truth when he told what he thought was his second lie. Mary Anne and Becky and Louise were on his mind all the time he was in Missouri. He was thinking about them at the wrong time in the bank in Joplin and almost got his head blown off by a farmer with a shotgun, except the shotgun shell misfired and Stark shot the farmer in the leg. He didn't get any money, and he also didn't get killed. The posse from Joplin was still on his trail when he reached the Texas panhandle. Those were some stubborn men in Missouri. He didn't have any of their money, and they were still chasing him two states away. He made a decision during that long ride. He decided to go see Mary Anne and try to figure out why he was still thinking about her and Becky and Louise.

"See what I mean?" Cruz said when Stark walked in the door. "Poetic license puts a man in an optimistic frame of mind. The wind's blowing the wrong way for you, yet your spirit's picked up. I mean a deep thing when I say these are the best dozen whores in Texas."

"Where's Mary Anne?" Stark said.

"Well, that's a first. You actually want to see someone specific, do you?"

"Where is she?"

"You said spring." Mary Anne stood at the top

of the stairs. "It's still winter, and you're here already. Was the mine played out?" She smiled that gentle smile of hers and he knew why he was back. He was in love.

"What mine?" Stark said.

"The one in Mexico."

That was the trouble with lies. You had to remember which ones you told to whom. It was easier to tell the truth. He'd tell the truth to Mary Anne as soon as he was alone with her.

"Are you busy?"

"Just putting the kids to bed. They'll be asleep in a few minutes. Come on up."

"Not an all-nighter," Cruz said. He exaggerated his inhalation and exhalation with sound and gesture. "Nothing like the smell of pigs to fill a whorehouse. The best dozen's going to be doing a lot of bouncing tonight."

"I'll pay up front for the night," Stark said. "How much?"

Cruz narrowed his eyes, his brain calculating there in his ax-dented skull. "It's not just the companionship. It's the profit from the bar I lose when it's just you up there instead of a line going up and down."

"How goddamned much?"

"Ten American dollars."

Stark took silver dollars out of his saddlebag and dropped them on the card table in front of Cruz. They were part of his savings from his previous, more successful forays into Missouri.

"Jesus, boy," Cruz said, checking the coins and finding them genuine and satisfactory in every respect. "You haven't been robbing banks, have you?"

"Seen any reward posters with my face on them?"

"Not yet."

Stark went up the stairs to Mary Anne. The girls were in bed but still awake. The sound of fucking came through every thin wall. They didn't seem to notice.

"Hi, mister," Becky said. As usual, Louise didn't say anything.

"Hi, Becky. Hi, Louise."

"Hey, you remember our names."

"Sure I do."

"What's yours?"

"Steve."

"Hi, Steve."

"Now, Becky," Mary Anne said, "you know it isn't polite to call an adult by his given name. You call him Mr. . . . What's your last name?"

"Matthews."

"You call him Mr. Matthews."

"Hi, Mr. Matthews."

"Hi."

"Good night, Mr. Matthews."

"Good night."

Mary Anne went to pull the sheet shut.

"You don't need to do that," Stark said.

She gave him a funny look.

"We're just going to talk, that's all."

"You paid ten dollars to talk all night?"

"That's right. Is it okay with you?"

"It is if you don't have anything funny in mind."

"Funny like what?"

"Like talking dirty and having the kids hear you. Like making them watch while you do things."

"What the hell kind of man do you think I am?"

"I don't know," Mary Anne said. "You're in a whorehouse. I'm a whore. You pay ten dollars and say all you want is talk, I have to wonder why."

"I love you," Stark said. The words came out before he intended. He was hoping to work his way around to it. Now maybe he wouldn't have to.

"Oh, is that it?"

He thought Mary Anne would be happy to hear it, or at least surprised. Instead, she looked disappointed and very tired.

His feelings hurt, he said, "I guess you hear that all the time from your many admirers."

"More often than you'd know," she said. "I wouldn't call them admirers. Just men temporarily in a strange soft place in their lives, lost in some kind of dream. It's not me they want, or Becky and Louise. It's themselves, only seen in another way. It doesn't last. Then they get scared mean. Blame me for things not being the way they want them to be. I've been through it. You'll get over it."

She went to her bed and lifted up a corner of the mattress. From the small roll of bills she found there, she peeled half away and put the rest back. She took his hand and put ten dollars in it. Then she closed the curtain between them and the girls and guided Stark to her bed.

"They'll fall asleep in a few minutes. Then we'll have some fun and you can go back to Mexico." The tears in her eyes didn't keep her from smiling. "It's sweet of you, Steve, it truly is. Your feelings aren't real. You're so young you don't know it yet, but you will."

"Don't tell me about my feelings," Stark said. "I'll tell you." And he did.

He told her about the orphanage, the hammer,

and Elias Egan; about the card game, the jammed Volcanic Pistol, and Jimmy So Fast; about the three gunfighters he'd shot dead. He told her about the banks in Missouri; about the trading posts in Kansas before the banks in Missouri; about the horses and cattle in Mexico before the trading posts in Kansas. He told her about the money he'd been saving without knowing why he was saving money.

"I almost got shot in Joplin because I was standing there with my gun in my hand, thinking about what I was going to do with the money, and I knew what I was going to do, and I was so surprised I knew, I didn't notice the farmer until he started trying to unjam his shotgun."

"You were thinking of all the pretty things you could buy if only you had a woman to buy them for." Mary Anne still looked weary, like someone listening to a story she'd already heard.

"No," Stark said, "I was thinking I'd like to have a ranch in the Texas hill country. Raise cattle. If you know how to rustle them, how hard can they be to raise, is what I was thinking. Build a cabin that's not too cold in the winter and not too hot in the summer. Spend enough time out in the open and that becomes important to you."

"I expect it would," Mary Anne said.

"I was thinking about a place I rode through two summers ago, north of Ashville, and I knew where to build the cabin. I was thinking about the cabin and I saw you inside, cooking a stew with beef from a steer we'd raised ourselves, and outside I saw Becky taking care of Louise, in the shade of an ironwood grove, and when they're thirsty, they get clear water from their own well." Stark reached out and took Mary Anne's hand in his. Still smiling and looking sad, she started to pull her hand away. He said, "We don't see nor hear nor smell not one damned pig."

She stopped trying to free her hand. After that, she looked in his eyes for a long time before she came softly into his arms.

The next morning, she said, "Ethan is fast with that gun of his. When he's back, he'll come after us, even if Cruz lets me go, which he won't."

"Cruz will let you go," Stark said, "and Ethan won't know where to look."

"There's a two-man–sized savage from the Pacific Ocean rides with him, tracks like an Indian."

"If they find us," Stark said, "they'll soon enough wish they hadn't."

"Oh? And why is that? You have a lot of friends in Texas, do you?"

"Have you heard of Matthew Stark?"

"Who hasn't?" She looked at him, thinking. "Now I remember. People say he's the one who outdrew Jimmy So Fast, not you. No wonder your story sounded so familiar."

"I'm Matthew Stark."

Mary Anne knew Matthew Stark was the fastest gun in west Texas, a mean, scar-faced giant of a man who beat whores to death while fucking them. She started laughing because this sweet, handsome boy was either lying or crazy. Then she started crying because she and her daughters weren't going anywhere, not with a liar or a lunatic, take your pick. It took Stark nearly another hour to convince her that he and his reputation had gone their different ways some time ago. He thought telling her who he was would make her feel safer and stop her worrying about Ethan. Instead, it almost lost her for him.

He waited until Mary Anne and Becky and

Louise were finished packing their meager belongings in a decrepit trunk held together with a length of rope. Then he checked both his pistols and went downstairs.

"Well, you sure as hell don't look too rested," Cruz said, "for a man who's spent all night in bed."

"We need to talk a little business." Stark sat down at the card table across from Cruz. The whoremaster was exactly where he had been last night, except he was eating a pork chop instead of dealing poker, and sitting alone instead of with a trio of suckers.

"Wind's still blowing from the same direction. Price's still ten dollars the night."

"There are no more nights for her," Stark said. "She's leaving."

"Sure she is," Cruz said, "if you have five hundred dollars. That's what she owes. Pay it, you can do what you want with her. She'll be back, you know, once you get your head out of your ass and wake up."

Stark had more than five hundred dollars. But he needed all his money to buy the ranch in the hill country. "I'll give you a hundred."

He saw Cruz's eyes shift and, following them, saw the bartender coming around the bar with a double-barreled shotgun. He dove to the left toward Cruz while the blast turned the table to kindling. His first bullet went through the bartender's right shoulder, his second through the man's right thigh. The bartender dropped the shotgun and fell to the floor clutching at his spurting wounds with the one hand that still worked. When he looked back at Cruz, he saw a derringer aimed his way. Stark shot him in the face. The big .44 bullet undid the ax dent on its way out of Cruz's skull.

Some people didn't know when to quit. Stark did. He never robbed another bank or visited another whorehouse. He thought he'd never kill another man, either, and maybe he'd have been right about that, too, if it had been up to him.

• • • • •

All the while she was making her confession, Heiko kept her hands on the mat before her and her head bowed. She didn't have the courage to look at Genji's face. What must he be thinking of her, this fiendishly duplicitous woman who claimed to love him even as she awaited the command to kill him? The silence following her final words of contrition was almost unbearable. Only her pride kept her from weeping. That would be too shameless an appeal to his manly compassion. She didn't let a single tear fall. He would kill her or, gentle soul that he was, he would only cast her out. No matter which act he chose, this was her last day on earth. She would not live without him. If she was sent from the castle alive, she knew precisely what she would do.

She would go to Cape Muroto.

Six hundred years ago, the first Great Lord of Akaoka, Genji's ancestor Hironobu, had won the battle in the woods there, establishing his sovereignty. Today, there was a small Buddhist temple belonging to an obscure Zen sect at the top of the sheer cliffs crowding against the sea. Nine hundred and ninety-nine steps went up from the rocky shore to the temple. She would stop on each one and affirm her eternal love for Genji. She would beg Amaterasu-o-mikami, the Sun Goddess, to bathe him in her divine light for all his long and fruitful life. She would beg Kannon, the Compassionate One, to see the sincerity in her heart and reunite her with him in Sukhavati, the Pure Land beyond all suffering.

When she reached the top, she would thank the gods and Buddhas for granting her nineteen years of life, her long-departed parents for bringing her into the world, Kuma for protecting and nurturing her, and Genji for the love she had not deserved. Then she would step from the edge into the Great Void, without fear, without regret, without tears.

"How would you have done it?" Genji said.

"My lord?" Heiko still didn't look up.

"My assassination. What technique would you have used?"

"My lord, I beseech you, please believe me. I could never have done anything to harm you in even the least way."

"Hidé," Genji said.

The door slid open instantly.

"Yes, lord."

Nothing in Hidé's face showed whether he had heard any part of the conversation. His hand, however, rested on the hilt of his sword.

"Ask Hanako to bring sake."

"Yes, lord."

Heiko knew he would not go himself. He would send Taro, who was behind the door on the other side of the room. Hidé would remain where he was, ready to burst in if needed. He would not leave his lord undefended in a room with a treacherous female ninja.

Genji was about to offer her a purifying ritual libation before he passed sentence. His graciousness

tore at her heart. She barely managed to continue restraining her tears.

"I suppose you would have done it at night,
when I was asleep. That is the kindest way."

Heiko could not reply. If she spoke another
word, her emotions would betray her. Trembling,
silent, she kept her eyes on the mat.

"My lord." Hanako's voice came from the other
side of the door.

"Enter."

Hanako's eyes were red and swollen. She bowed
and came in with a tray in her hands. Upon the tray
was a flask of sake and a single cup. Genji, of course,
would not drink with Heiko. She would drink alone,
repentant, and prepare to accept her fate.

Hanako bowed low to Genji. Then she turned
and bowed with equal depth to Heiko. As she did so,
a sob left her throat, and a shudder ran through her
shoulders. She wept piteously.

"Lady Heiko," she said, and sobbed again.

"Thank you for your friendship," Heiko said.
"Orphans that we both are, we were kindly made sisters by fate, for a little while."

Unable to control herself any longer, Hanako got
to her feet and ran crying from the room.

"Do outsiders weep as much as we Japanese?"
Genji said. "I doubt it. If they did, instead of science,
they would have kabuki, like us." He looked down
at the tray. "She brought only one cup. What was she
thinking? Oh, well."

To Heiko's amazement, he picked up the cup and
held it out to be filled. Stunned, she could only stare
at him.

Genji said, "I prefer it hot to cold, don't you?"

Not knowing what else to do, Heiko took the

flask from the tray and poured for him. He drank and offered the cup to her.

"My lord," she said. She made no move to take the cup from his hand.

"Yes?"

"I cannot drink from the same cup as you."

"Why not?"

"The condemned cannot touch that which has touched the lips of the lord."

"The condemned? What are you talking about?" He took her hand in his and put the cup into it.

"My lord," Heiko said. "I cannot. My crimes would only be made more heinous."

"What crimes?" Genji said. "Am I dead? Am I crippled? Are my innermost secrets betrayed to my enemies?"

"I did not reveal my true nature to you, my lord."

Genji sighed. "Do you think me such a fool?"

"My lord?"

"The most beautiful geisha in Edo chooses as her lover one of the least of the Great Lords. She does so because I am so handsome, charming, and witty. Of course. What other reason can there be? Fool that I am, it never occurs to me that subterfuge is in play, does it?"

Genji lifted the flask. Heiko had to put her cup out to keep him from spilling sake all over the mat.

"I knew you were working for the Sticky Eye," Genji said. "There was no other possibility. The man carries a grudge beyond all reason. I knew, and I assumed all along you knew I knew, and knew that I knew you knew. We are not children or outsiders, after all. Such superficial deceit is the norm. It is like saying hello. We could hardly have begun without it, could we?"

He gestured for her to drink. She was too shocked to disobey. He retrieved the cup and she poured for him.

"You cannot ignore my treachery," Heiko said, "or let it go unpunished. Your vassals will lose all respect for you."

"Do I deserve punishment?"

"You, my lord? No, of course not. You have done nothing wrong."

"Then why should I punish myself?"

"You should not. I am the one who should be punished."

"Really? Fine. Make a suggestion."

"It is not for me to say."

"I command you to make a suggestion."

Heiko bowed. "Execution or banishment are the only choices, my lord."

"On the one hand, you are a geisha and my lover. On the other, you are a ninja and an agent of the Shogun's secret police. How is it possible to avoid compromise of one kind or another? We live in a world of myriad conflicting loyalties. It is not purity, but the nature of the balance we achieve that displays our true character. I see no fault in either of us. We are both hereby pardoned."

"My lord, you must not forgive me so lightly."

Genji took both her hands in his. She tried to pull away, but he would not release her. "Heiko, look at me." She would not. "The punishments you suggest would cause me unendurable anguish. Is that just?" She didn't speak. He released her.

"So the love you claim you have for me is so weak, you prefer death," Genji said.

"Kuma and I were the only surviving ninjas of our clan," Heiko said. "How can I ignore my vow and live? I would dishonor him as well as myself."

"If you die, I will have no life, just a joyless semblance of it. Must I pass such a sentence on myself?"

"There is nothing else we can do. It is our karma."

"Is it? Who else in the castle knows of this besides Stark?"

"Everyone, by now. Bad tidings travel swiftly."

"I mean officially."

"Only you, my lord."

"There lies the solution," Genji said. He sat thoughtfully for several moments. "You only pretended to work for the Sticky Eye. All along, you have been reporting to me. Even now we are hatching plans whereby you can continue to convey useful misinformation to Kawakami, lulling him into a false sense of security. When we are ready, we will spring the trap and catch him in a fatal error."

"That is utterly ridiculous. No one will believe it."

"It is not necessary that anyone believe. Only that they pretend to do so, as we will pretend. Hidé, Taro."

Doors on both sides of the room slid open.

"Lord."

Genji said, "The time has come to reveal my most secret strategy to you. Enter and close the doors."

"Lord."

When Genji finished his revelation, both Hidé and Taro bowed deeply to Heiko.

Taro said, "Our thanks to you, Lady Heiko, for risking your life in such a dangerous endeavor. Our ultimate triumph will owe much to your courage."

Hidé said, "I pray to the gods and Buddhas that I can attain even a fraction of your merit."

The voices of both men were steady. Tears flowed freely from their eyes, however, tears they pretended were not there.

"Would there be samurai or geisha without kabuki?" Genji said. "We are so fond of melodrama, are we not?"

When she looked at him, she saw tears in his eyes, too, and the sight broke her resolve.

"Genji," she said, and said no more, silenced and blinded by her own tears.

14

Sekigahara

When attacking, await the right moment.

When waiting, be poised like a boulder on the edge of a ten-thousand-foot precipice.

When the right moment manifests itself, vanish into the attack like a boulder plummeting into the void.

SUZUME–NO–KUMO
(1344)

Kudo's failure to return from the mountains did not surprise Sohaku. He had hoped his ally would eliminate Shigeru. He had hoped, but he had not expected it. What had surprised him was the presence of ninjas on Genji's side. With Kudo and Saiki, he had been one of the three main commanders of the domain's army. No ninjas followed the sparrow-and-arrows banner. At least, not to his knowledge. Could such a thing have been done so secretly that he had not learned of it? It seemed impossible. Kudo would have known and told him. Saiki would have known, and it would have shown on his face. Not even someone as wily as Lord Kiyori could have fooled all three of them. Could he? Even if he had, the arrangement would have collapsed immediately upon his death. Pacts with ninjas were sealed with personal oaths.

There was no possibility Genji employed them on his own. He didn't even know where to find them. Sake and geishas were his realm, not spies and assassins. And what ninja would trust the word of such a frivolous weakling? Unless they, too, were swayed by fools' tales of his prophetic powers. No, ninjas were deeply immersed in the fundamental realities of life. They were not so easily misled.

That left only one other highly distressing candidate. Kawakami. Ninjas were known to be among the operatives of the Shogun's secret police. Had the Sticky Eye planned all along to eliminate Sohaku and Kudo to weaken Genji? Perhaps he never intended to accept their switch in loyalties. Kudo could have died in a trap set by Kawakami there in the mountains. Yet that also seemed improbable. It wasn't a smart move. The smart move, if Kawakami intended to betray them, was to let Kudo kill Shigeru, have Sohaku help trap Genji, then kill all three at the same time.

None of the alternatives made sense. Sohaku had to attain clarity, and soon, or his actions would not yield good results, and he had to act, also soon. He had less than eighty men with him. His vassals in Akaoka were either dead or his vassals no longer. Until he knew what Kawakami's intentions were, he couldn't risk returning to Edo. Instead of protection, he might find arrest and interrogation.

At least his family was safe. When he had become abbot, they had moved to his father-in-law's domain on Kyushu, the southernmost of the four main islands of Japan. They were therefore safely out of reach of Shigeru's vengeance.

Abandoning all hope and fear, he needed to find the calm at the very core of his being. Then a governing solution would present itself on its own.

There was only one place he could go.

Mushindo Monastery.

• • • • •

Kawakami grimly looked through his telescope at the fleet of British and French warships anchored in Edo Bay. Arrogance of such magnitude was inconceivable. Only recently, they had bombarded the city. Now they sat there as if nothing had happened. No, it was far worse than that. They acted as though they were the wronged party.

Some southern lords had fired on outsider merchant ships in the Kuroshima Strait. In retaliation, the British and the French had blasted the forts to rubble, then had proceeded to Edo to destroy the palaces of the offending lords. Their aim being as crude as their understanding, the outsiders had bombarded the Tsukiji district rather indiscriminately. Instead of repenting, they demanded payment of an indemnity to compensate them for the damage suffered by their merchant ships, formal apologies from the responsible lords, and a promise from the Shogun that such an act would never be repeated.

Disturbing as these events were, none was as mortifying as the reports he had received from the battlefront. When British marines had come ashore, the courage of the samurai in the Kuroshima forts had evaporated. Faced with disciplined troops, massed rifles, and supporting artillery, they had fled in abject terror. Six hundred years ago, their ancestors had fearlessly met and defeated the Mongol hordes of Kublai Khan. Now they ran away without even putting up a fight. What a shameful day in the long history of their warrior nation.

The Shogun had been unable to decide on an appropriate response. Some hotheads advocated a declaration of war against the outsiders, all of them. Others, more frightened but not necessarily more reasonable, urged immediate acceptance of the outsiders' demands. Consensus was needed to keep the government from splintering. To achieve it, the Shogun had taken an unprecedented step. Instead of making a decision and issuing proclamations, he had invited all the Great Lords, even those not allied with him, to come to Edo, meet in Council, and work with him to forge a united answer. He was, in effect, offering to share power with his traditional enemies, the excluded clans who had been waiting since Sekigahara to wreak vengeance on the Tokugawas. The stage was set for an historic reconciliation.

The possibility that it would actually occur sickened Kawakami. It would mean the end of his patiently devised plans to destroy the pretentious Okumichi clan. Worse, in such uncertain times, their reputation for prophetic vision might enable them to rise even higher than the undeserved heights to which they had already been elevated by popular opinion. Kawakami could almost picture it.

Genji would attend the conference. He would make some offhand comment that the Shogun would regard as serious advice. Action would be taken. In one of those coincidences that often seemed to materialize around the lords of Akaoka, the result would be better than anyone could have imagined. The

Shogun, in his weakened state and clutching at every phantom hope, would then be moved to appoint Genji to his inner council of advisors. Kawakami didn't need to be a prophet to know his own future once that happened. The vengeful Genji would manufacture a pretext forcing the Shogun to order Kawakami's ritual suicide. He had served the Shogun faithfully for his entire life. Yet if his master had to choose, of course he would choose Genji. If he believed what the Shogun believed, Kawakami would do the same in his place. Secret police chiefs were easy to come by. Prophets were another matter.

What an atrocious turn of events.

But wait. None of this had yet occurred. And it would not if Genji never reached Edo. Kawakami had one last chance. It would have to be unofficial this time, since Genji was no longer an outlaw, had never been one, thanks to the retroactive suspension of the Alternate Residency Law. The country was in turmoil, however, and unexpected things happened at such times.

Sohaku had sent word that he was temporarily retiring to Mushindo Monastery. This had irritated Kawakami. Now he saw it was actually a fortunate development. On his way to Edo, Genji would pass between Mushindo and Yamanaka Village. Kawakami intended to be in the village at the appropriate time, along with his personal vassals, some six hundred in number. All armed with Napoleonic muskets, and all well versed in their use. Yes, everything considered, the situation was not necessarily evolving in an entirely unsatisfactory direction.

The only other worry, and it was a minor one, was his assistant Mukai's continuing mysterious absence. Kawakami had sent three messengers to the dullard's tiny northern domain. None had returned. This was very strange, very strange indeed. Had some domestic emergency drawn him away and embroiled him so completely he was unable to reply? Kawakami remembered Mukai's wife, whom he had met on a number of unavoidable social occasions. She was nearly as characterless and homely as her husband. The same could be said of his two concubines. They seemed to exist only to fulfill the expectation that a lord of his rank would have at least two of them. No overwhelming passion was even remotely imaginable.

Sooner or later, Mukai would show up with an entirely rational, entirely boring reason for his return home. Perhaps he had stupidly interpreted the Shogun's permission to leave Edo as an order to do so. That was precisely the sort of decision he would make without Kawakami to instruct him.

He dismissed his concern. More pressing matters demanded his attention. His spies were keeping watch on Akaoka. Heiko still shared Genji's bed. His opportunity would come soon enough.

· · · · ·

"One, I strongly advise against this journey," Saiki said. "Two, if the journey is made, I strongly advise proceeding in force. No less than a thousand men. Two thousand would be better. Three, I strongly advise traveling in company with at least one other lord, preferably one considered reliably neutral by both sides. This will reduce the likelihood of ambush along the way."

"Thank you for your sincere concern," Genji said. "Under other circumstances, the danger would surely be as great as you fear. But I go to Edo at the Shogun's invitation. That alone ensures safe passage."

"Ten years ago, that would have been true," Shigeru said. "Now the Shogun is no longer in firm control of the realm. Outsider warships blast his capital city with impunity. More and more often, his own Allied Lords as well as Excluded Lords disregard his authority as they will. In many domains, the regimes of the Great Lords themselves are shaky. Saiki is right. You should not go."

Genji turned to Hidé. "What do you think?"

"Whether you go or not is a decision beyond my competence, lord. If you do go, then I agree with Lord Saiki. You should go in force. A thousand men will be sufficient, if you take the best."

Genji shook his head. "If I march on Edo with a thousand men, the Shogun will see it as an act of aggression, and rightly so."

"Inform him ahead of time," Saiki said. "Say you will station them well outside the city, but within reach of the Kanto Plain, should the Shogun desire that they join with his forces against the outsiders. We can use Mushindo Monastery for the purpose."

"In any event, we will stop there on the way," Genji said. "Emily wants to check on the status of the mission building. Do you know if construction was ever begun?"

"No, my lord." Saiki fought back the irritation he felt. He was very grateful to Lady Emily for saving Genji's life. Yet he found it intolerable that concern for her irrelevant missionary work should intrude into a discussion of such seriousness. "Is it your intention to permit Lady Emily to accompany you to Edo?"

"It is."

"Then I must add a fourth suggestion," Saiki said. "Four, I strongly advise against her doing so."

"Quiet Crane Palace is being rebuilt," Genji said. "Emily must oversee some aspects of the construction. She cannot if she isn't there."

Saiki gritted his teeth. "Is architecture one of her talents?"

"No. But our architects need her advice about the design of the chapel."

"Chapel?"

"I have ordered a small Christian church incorporated into the design."

"What?" Saiki was aghast.

Shigeru laughed, which surprised everyone. He so rarely did. "Why be concerned, Saiki? A thousand years ago, Buddhism was an outsider religion brought here by Chinese and Korean missionaries. Now it is as Japanese as we are. A thousand years hence, the same will be said of the Christianity these new outsiders bring."

Saiki said, "I did not realize you were of such an optimistic bent, my lord."

"I am learning from my nephew as we go along."

"You believe it is prudent to allow a woman to go on this potentially perilous expedition?"

"Not a woman," Shigeru said. "Several women. Lady Heiko and Hanako will come along, too."

Saiki refrained from exhibiting any further consternation. He only said, "My fifth suggestion is that we approach this journey with the seriousness that it deserves."

"Heiko misses Edo," Genji said, "and Hidé should not be deprived of every opportunity to ensure himself of an heir."

"The greatest danger is not passed," Saiki said,

not permitting himself to react to the frivolous nature of such reasoning. "It still lies ahead."

"And when it comes, we will meet it," Genji said. "Until then, let us not indulge ourselves in needless worry."

Saiki bowed. How ironic if they had survived their recent perils only to die on a mundane trip to Edo. Such was the nature of karma, and it was to karma that he now bowed as much as to his lord. "I hear and obey, my lord."

"Thank you, Saiki."

"How many men shall I prepare?"

"Oh, twenty or thirty should be enough. We won't be in Edo long."

"Our scouts report that Sohaku is at Mushindo," Hidé said. "If he is still coordinating his actions with Kawakami, the thousand men Lord Saiki suggests are far from excessive."

"Mushindo will be clear well before Genji gets there," Shigeru said. "The nameless traitor will soon be doing all his coordinating with none other than hungry ghosts."

· · · · · ·

"I can hardly believe my eyes," Emily said. "First an apple orchard. Now this."

She and Stark were in the midst of winter roses. They were the whitest white and the reddest red, and every shade of pink between them, from pale to deep.

Stark said, "This garden deserves its fame."

Emily gave him a questioning look.

"Heiko told me another name for the castle is Rose Garden Keep."

"Rose Garden Keep," Emily said. "Cloud of

Sparrows. Such poetry to describe a fortress sadly dedicated to war."

"War is poetry to the samurai," Stark said.

"Why, Matthew, you seem to have acquired much understanding of them during your recent travels with Heiko."

"We had some opportunity to talk," he said. Then he clenched his jaws shut. It was better not to say any more. Heiko said she'd tell Genji all about it. Maybe she would, maybe she wouldn't. It was her business, not his.

They had been led to the rose garden by Hanako after Emily managed to convey her desire to be outdoors rather than in. The overabundance of chairs, tables, desks, and lamps in her room made her somewhat claustrophobic, and the parlor she shared with Stark was no better. Servants had brought out the incongruously plush sofa chairs upon which they sat. Emily reminded herself to tell Lord Genji about lawn furniture. He seemed eager to learn as much as he could about American civilization, as well as the American language.

"She seems such a delicate creature," Emily said. "The privations of the wilderness must have caused her considerable discomfort."

"She did okay." Stark tried to shift the conversation elsewhere. "You and Lord Genji had more of an adventure than we did. If the rumors are true, you're an angel who performed miracles to save his life."

Emily turned away and stared intently at a distant rosebush. She hoped he had not seen the color that had risen into her face.

"Oh, rumors. You know how those are. Someone who knows nothing says something, and the nothing grows and grows."

"Heiko doesn't seem the type to gossip. She said Lord Shigeru told her he found you and Genji in a snow house you'd built. Did you really build a snow house?"

"It was just a shelter of branches upon which snow happened to fall."

"She said Lord Genji told her you kept him and yourself warm with knowledge you learned from Eskimos."

"I have never met an Eskimo in my life," Emily said, as adamantly as she could.

"I didn't think you had," Stark said. "She must have misunderstood him. Or I misunderstood her. So how did you do it?"

"Do what?"

"Stay alive. You were lost for almost two days in a raging snowstorm. You did something to keep from freezing, didn't you?"

"The shelter shielded us from the wind," Emily said. She could not lie. Nor, God help her, could she tell the whole truth. That would be more embarrassing than she could bear. "Though the walls around us were of snow, they were nonetheless walls. They separated us sufficiently from the elements such that it was noticeably warmer within than without."

"That's good to know," Stark said, "if we're ever in a similar situation."

"I am sure we will not be," Emily said. She reached out to a brilliant red blossom. "I wonder what variety this is?"

Genji said, "American Beauty."

Emily turned and saw him standing a short distance away. His obvious amusement told her he had been there long enough to hear at least some of her excruciating conversation with Stark. Seeing the distress in her face, he immediately effected a more serious mien. He stepped up to the flower she had caressed, drew his short sword, and barely grazed the stem with its edge. The blossom separated from the bush and fell into his hand. Thorns dropped away as he touched them lightly with his weapon.

He bowed and offered the tamed rose to Emily.

"Thank you, my lord."

"That's a strange name for a Japanese flower," Stark said.

"It is the name here only," Genji said. "One of my ancestors had a—" He was about to say, vision. Remembering how much his use of the term had disturbed Emily, he said instead, "—dream. The following morning, he issued a proclamation declaring the most splendid roses blossoming within the castle would henceforth be known as American Beauty roses."

Emily thought Genji's explanation sounded suspiciously like another visionary claim. But her curiosity was aroused.

"Of what did he dream?"

"He never revealed its exact nature. That very day, he joined his army to that of the Takeda clan. He was with them when they attacked the palisades at Nagashino, perhaps the most famous cavalry charge in our nation's history. He died in a firestorm loosed from the massed muzzles of enemy muskets, along with thousands of other mounted warriors. No one has made such a charge since."

"His dream led him to that folly?"

"Yes. Before the attack, he told his vassals to have no fear. The arrival of American Beauty within the walls of Cloud of Sparrows signaled the ultimate triumph of our clan. His dream, he said, guaranteed it."

Before she could stop herself, Emily said, "Why, that was quite mad." She wished she could bite her tongue off. "I'm sorry, my lord, I misspoke."

Genji laughed. "He tried to force reality to fit what he dreamed. Madmen often do. Unfortunately, this is not an uncommon failing in my family. Neither is a tendency to fatally misinterpret dreams. His successor let the proclamation stand as a cautionary reminder."

"That was wise of him," Emily said, trying to make up for her clumsy gaffe with compensatory praise.

"And it would have been even wiser if he had remembered it himself," Genji said. "His own dreams convinced him to side against the Tokugawas at Sekigahara. He was killed, our clan nearly destroyed, and here we are today, on the permanent list of the Shogun's most untrustworthy adversaries."

Emily felt both sympathy and disapproval. The clash between them put an unfamiliar scowl on her face. She said, "These are surely signs that such dreams should be seen for what they are. Dreams only. It is written in the Holy Bible, 'Prophesying serveth not for them that believe not, but for them which believe.' "

"Perhaps. It doesn't trouble me very much, one way or the other. I dream much less frequently than my predecessors."

While his tongue, lips, lungs, and larynx formed these words, the world around him vanished, and Genji found himself elsewhere.

· · · · · ·

A gentle wind cools his somewhat feverish skin.

White blossoms fill the branches above and imbue the air with their sweetness.

Apple Valley is in bloom.

It must be spring.

The enveloping beauty tightens his chest and brings tears to his eyes. He is happy, and yet—

What conflicting emotions are these he feels? He isn't sure. The future Genji may know. The visionary one does not. Just as it was in his first experience, he inhabits the person he is yet to be. The hands holding the reins, resting on the pommel, are not so different from the hands that gave the rose to Emily. If this day is distant from the present one, it is not so distant that he has entered old age.

Genji lets his horse go where it will. He has no destination. He waits. For what? Impatience drives him from his saddle. He paces back and forth. Looking up, he sees the branch upon which Emily sat when he gave her this valley. Heiko made her confession to him on the same day. He thinks of the two women and smiles.

The beautiful geisha who knows more than she should.

The naive outsider who knows only what she wants to know.

He thinks of them and is reminded once more of the cruel limitations of prophetic vision.

He senses the vibration in the ground before he hears the hooves of the galloping horse. When he looks toward the rise at the mouth of the valley, he sees a steep-roofed building with a bell tower. Atop the tower is a white Christian cross. Hidé rides past Emily's church at top speed. Without waiting for him to arrive and deliver the message, Genji leaps back onto his horse and spurs it toward Cloud of Sparrows.

Servants are gathered in the courtyard. They bow as he arrives. He rushes into the castle. From the far end of the corridor, he hears the cries of a newborn infant coming to him from his own bedroom. His urgent steps quickly take him there.

A maid holds the baby for him to see. It is the mother he is concerned about, not the child. He gives it only a cursory glance. Before he can enter the inner room, Dr. Ozawa steps out and closes the door behind him.

"How is she?"

"The birth was a very difficult one," Dr. Ozawa says. His face is grim.

"Is she out of danger?" Genji says.

Dr. Ozawa shakes his head. His bow is deep. "I am sorry, my lord."

A single unalloyed emotion surges through him at the doctor's words. Grief. He drops to his knees.

Dr. Ozawa kneels with him. "You are a father, Lord Genji."

Genji is too broken by his sorrow to resist as the baby is placed in his arms. Something sparkles at its throat. Though tears obscure his vision, he recognizes it immediately. He has seen it twice before.

Once in another vision.

Once in a mound of snow.

A small silver locket marked with a cross upon which is emblazoned a single stylized flower, perhaps a lily.

• • • • • •

Dr. Ozawa said sternly, "I warned you against overexertion, my lord."

Genji rested on a bed in a room overlooking the rose garden. He didn't remember coming here. He did remember falling unconscious.

"I was only talking."

"Then you were talking too much. Please talk less."

Genji sat up. "I'm fine."

"People who are fine do not collapse without reason."

"Vision," Genji said.

"Ah." Dr. Ozawa faced the door. "Hanako."

The door slid open and Hanako looked in. "Yes, Doctor." She smiled at Genji through her worried expression and bowed to him.

"Bring tea," Dr. Ozawa said.

"Sake would be better," Genji said.

"Tea," Dr. Ozawa said again.

"Yes, Doctor," Hanako said, and withdrew.

"Shall I tell you?"

"If you wish," Dr. Ozawa said. He had been the clan doctor for nearly forty years. Kiyori and Shigeru were his patients before Genji. He knew all about the visions. "I doubt I can provide any useful insights. I never have so far."

"There is always a first time."

"Not necessarily. Sometimes, there is not even a first time."

Genji described what he had seen in as much detail as he could. He waited for Dr. Ozawa to speak, but he only sat quietly and drank his tea.

"This one is like the first," Genji said. "It confuses more than enlightens. Who is the child's mother? It must be the Lady Shizuka of my first vision. The child wears the mother's locket. But in the first, Lady Shizuka is alive, and I am dying, and in this one the reverse seems true. An irresolvable contradiction."

"So it seems."

"Do you believe I have seen what must be, or what could?"

"Everything your grandfather shared with me has come to pass." Dr. Ozawa sipped his tea. "However, I know he did not share everything. Nothing your uncle has said has materialized. So far. Yours is yet another, entirely different situation. You have had two visions and will only have one more. And that will be the end of it for you. That is a more fortunate circumstance, I think, than either Kiyori's or Shigeru's. You have neither too much clarity nor too little. Rather, just enough to increase your alertness."

"You didn't answer my question."

"How can I?" Dr. Ozawa said. "What do I know of the future? I am a mere physician, not a prophet."

"Such philosophical neutrality is not helpful," Genji said. "I need counsel."

"I hesitate to offer what could only be opinion and not considered advice," Dr. Ozawa said.

"I would welcome it nonetheless."

"Then you should speak to a woman."

"Yes," Genji said, "but which one?"

"That should be obvious."

"Oh? Please tell me."

Dr. Ozawa bowed. "I meant it should be obvious to you, my lord. You are the one with the vision."

• • • • •

Heiko listened without interrupting. When he was finished, she remained silent. Genji understood. It must not be easy for her to learn that he would father a child with another woman. But with whom could he share his experience? He trusted no one else as much.

"One thing alone is clear to me," he said. "Before any of this can come to pass, Shizuka must meet Emily, because the locket she wears, the one she gives to our child, is the one that is presently Emily's. Beyond that, I am at a complete loss."

She said, "Did you not once tell me of an outsider master and his blade? I cannot recall his name."

"Are you thinking of the story of Damocles and the suspended sword?"

"That is not it." Heiko thought. "His name was not entirely unlike that of Zen Master Hakuin Zenji. Hakuo. Hokuo. Okuo. Okkao. Okkao's Blade. Something like that."

"Occam's Razor?"

"Yes, that's it."

"What of it?"

"When you say one thing is clear to you, you are not using Occam's Razor."

"Oh? You have mastered outsider thinking?"

"There is little to master here. As I recall, Occam's Razor says, when faced with multiple possibilities, the one requiring the simplest explanation is most likely to be correct. You have not chosen the simplest explanation."

"I have limited myself to only that part of the vision that can be explained. How have I not applied Occam's Razor?"

"You are assuming Shizuka, whom you have yet to meet, will be the mother. That the identifying locket somehow comes to her from Emily, and then goes to the child. There is a simpler explanation."

"I fail to see it."

Heiko said, "The child gets the locket directly from Emily."

"Why would Emily give her locket to my child?"

"Because it is her child, too," Heiko said.

Genji was shocked. "That is utterly preposterous. Also, insulting. And neither is it in conformity with the rule of simplicity. For her to be the mother of my child, we must first sleep together. I do not see a simple, direct path to that, do you?"

"Love tends to simplify the most complex and difficult of situations," Heiko said.

"I am not in love with Emily, and she certainly is not in love with me."

"Perhaps not yet, my lord."

"Not ever," Genji said.

"And how do you feel about her?"

"I have no feelings for her, not the kind of which you speak."

"I have seen you laughing with her," Heiko said, "and she smiles often in your company."

"We nearly died together," Genji said. "Because of that, we have a bond we did not have before, yes. A bond of friendship, not a bond of love."

"Do you still find her repulsive and ungainly?"

"Not repulsive. But only because I have grown accustomed to her appearance. 'Ungainly' is also a rather harsh term." Genji recalled the way she lay in the snow, waving her arms and legs to create her snow angel. He pictured her clambering into the apple tree without the least self-consciousness. "I suppose, in her own outsider way, she has a certain innocent grace."

"You speak of her as though she is someone for whom you have affection."

"I will admit to liking her. It is a long way from liking to loving."

"A month ago, it took all your discipline for you to even glance in her direction. Now you like her. Love does not seem so inconceivable."

"There is a critical difference between the two. Sexual attraction."

"Which she does not generate?"

"Please."

"Of course, there is an even simpler explanation," Heiko said.

"I hope it is more pleasant as well," Genji said.

"That is for you to say, my lord, not I." Heiko looked down at her hands clenched in her lap. "New conditions would not have to arise leading you and Emily to bed if you have already been there."

"Heiko, I have not bedded Emily."

"Are you certain?"

"I would not lie to you."

"I know you would not."

"Then what are you saying?"

"You were delirious when Shigeru found you."

"Unconscious. I had been delirious earlier."

"You and Emily were inside a snow-covered lean-to for a day and a night before you were discovered." She looked up and her eyes locked with his. "My lord, do you remember precisely how you stayed warm?"

· · · · · · ·

"I am so happy to see you well," Emily said. "We were all very worried. Please, sit down."

"Thank you." Genji's inner self was in turmoil. It was only fitting that his outer self be in equal agony, a condition immediately provided by the misshapen outsider chair. His spine shifted out of alignment as soon as he sat, and his organs pressed unnaturally against each other, restricting the flow of *ki* and causing the accumulation of dangerous toxins. Excellent. Now he was thoroughly ill at ease.

"Lady Heiko said you wished to speak with me."

"Did she tell you why?"

"Only that it was a matter of some delicacy." Emily looked at him. "It might have been better for me to come to your rooms instead of you to mine. Perhaps you haven't completely recovered from the recent episode."

"There is nothing to worry about," Genji said. "It was only fatigue catching up with me. I am more rested now."

"I was about to have tea." Emily went to a table with an outsider tea service on it. "Would you care to join me? Heiko was kind enough to acquire some of the English variety."

"Thank you."

Any delay was welcome. How was he to raise the question? He couldn't imagine a less manly, more humiliating act than asking a woman—a woman with whom he was not on the closest terms, and an outsider on top of it—whether he had bedded her because he couldn't remember if he had or not!

Emily lifted a small decanter and poured a portion of thick white fluid into their cups. Then she added black tea. Its perfumed scent failed to conceal the fermented nature of the leaves used for brewing. Finally, she added sugar and stirred.

Her first sip brought a bright smile to her face. "It has been so long, I had forgotten how delicious it is."

Genji tried the strange mixture. As soon as it

touched his taste buds, he gagged. Politeness prevented him from doing what instinct demanded, which was to instantly spit out the foul concoction. The cloying sweetness, the strong bergamot odor, and the wholly unexpected presence of greasy animal fat combined to create an intolerable assault on his senses. Too late, he realized what the white fluid was—thickened milk from the grotesque udders of cows.

"Is something wrong, my lord?"

The potent liquid in his mouth prevented him from responding. He steeled himself and swallowed. "Ah, I am surprised, merely, at the taste. Our tea is not so strongly flavored."

"Yes, the difference is significant. It's a wonder they are made from the same leaf."

They spoke of differences and similarities long enough to allow Genji to set aside his cup without drawing attention to the fact that he did not drink from it a second time.

Still unable to directly approach the actual subject of his visit, Genji sought to reach it in a roundabout manner.

He said, "When we were together in the snow, I noticed something."

Emily's cheeks immediately became inflamed. She lowered her gaze to her teacup. "Lord Genji, I will be in your debt to a very great extent if you will never mention the matter again."

"I understand your discomfort, Emily, truly I do."

"Forgive me for expressing doubt, sir." She briefly raised her dizzyingly bizarre blue eyes to cast a hurt and disapproving look his way. "You seem to have found a particular amusement in frequent and public allusions to it."

"For which I sincerely apologize." Genji bowed. Now that he found himself in an analogous position of profound embarrassment, he knew her feelings could not be very different from his. "I did not previously treat your concern with the appropriate regard."

"If your apology is heartfelt and true, then you will drop this matter now and forever."

"I promise to do so afterward. Regrettably, we must speak of it one last time."

"Then you will understand if I do not take your apology seriously."

Genji knew of only one way to demonstrate his sincerity. It was something he did daily at the shrine of his ancestors. He never performed the act before living persons outside the Shogun's palace, and he had never imagined he would for an outsider. He went to his knees and bowed all the way to the floor. "I ask only because I must."

Emily knew pride was everything to samurai. The sight of the lord of the domain humbling himself to her brought tears of shame to her eyes. Who was the conceited one here? Whose was the arrogance? The vanity? It was written in the Book of Job—Wilt thou condemn me, that thou mayest be righteous? She, too, fell to her knees and took his hands in hers.

"Forgive my self-serving vanity. Please ask what you must."

Genji was too shocked to speak right away. He was utterly unaccustomed to having his person seized in such a way. Indeed, had any of his bodyguards been present in the room, Emily's head would now be rolling on the floor. To touch a Great Lord without his permission was a capital offense.

"The wrong is mine," Genji said. "Do not blame yourself."

"I do, I must," Emily said. "What a dangerous and insidious thing is pride."

It was several minutes before they were back in their chairs and she was sufficiently restored to allow the discussion to continue.

"It might have been nothing, only delirious imagining," Genji said. "In the snow, I saw a piece of jewelry at your throat."

Emily reached into the neck of her blouse. A thin silver chain came up with her hand, and on the chain was the silver locket with the cross and the stylized flower.

"Was it this?"

"Yes," Genji said. "What is on the cross?"

"A lily in a form known as the fleur-de-lis. The Kings of France took it as their royal symbol. My mother's family was originally of French extraction. The fleur-de-lis was a reminder of this."

She clicked it open and leaned forward to show him what was within, a miniature portrait of a young woman who closely resembled Emily. "This was my mother's mother, at seventeen years of age."

"An age you will soon attain."

"That's right. How do you know?"

"I asked you, when you made the snow angel."

"Of course." Remembering, she smiled. "You did not think much of my angel."

"A failure of my perception rather than your art."

Emily sat back and sighed in relief. "Well, that was not so bad. I was expecting—I don't know what I was expecting, but I thought the line of questioning would be far worse."

There was no way to avoid asking the more difficult question.

"I'm not finished," Genji said.

"Go on, then. I am ready."

She looked as ready as he felt, which was not ready at all. But there was nothing else to do, so he went on.

"After I was injured, my memory is fragmented and hazy. I remember lying with you. Naked. Were we?"

"Yes, we were."

"Did we do more than lie together?"

"What do you mean?"

"Did we make love?"

Emily turned away, shocked that he could even mention such a thing. Though it seemed impossible, more color rose into her cheeks.

"It is very important that I know," Genji said.

She could neither face him nor say a single word. Finally, after her silence extended from moments into minutes, Genji stood.

"I will forget this conversation and the events leading to it." He slid the door open and stepped into the corridor. He was closing the door when she spoke.

"We shared our warmth," Emily said, "to save our lives. Nothing more. We did not—" To speak so explicitly was agonizing. "We did not make love."

Genji bowed deeply. "I am very grateful for your candor."

He walked away without the relief he had hoped to receive. Emily was not already pregnant. Also, Lady Shizuka remained to be met. These were good things. But his hopes were rapidly diminishing. The other possibility Heiko had mentioned—that he would fall in love with Emily—was no longer as unimaginable as it had seemed. During his visit, as he had spoken of their time in the snow, and recalled what he had seen and sensed, and had watched the innocent emotions so guilelessly displayed on her face, something truly unexpected occurred.

He had found himself growing excited.

* * * * *

"I continue to believe Lord Genji and Lord Shigeru will lead our clan to its destruction," Sohaku said. "Therefore, I do not regret my decision."

He had led seventy-nine samurai out of the mountains and back to Mushindo Monastery. The sixty who remained sat assembled before him in the meditation hall. The others had disappeared before the meeting. Sohaku did not doubt more would soon follow them. Events had conspired against him.

He had failed to kill the two remaining Okumichi heirs.

By now, Kudo's head was rotting on the end of a spear outside Cloud of Sparrows. And the Shogun's proclamation suspending the Alternate Residency Law had made Sohaku, and not Genji, the outlaw.

Kawakami insisted their plans could still succeed. He could afford to say so. He was the head of the secret police and the Great Lord of Hino. He had place and knew it. Sohaku had none. Nothing was left for him but a final bold stroke. It didn't matter that it would change nothing whether the result was triumph or defeat. The only important consideration was how he would die, how he would be remembered by his family and foes. He had once commanded the finest cavalry in all the domains of

Japan. He preferred attack to a more passive ritual suicide.

According to his scouts, Genji had left Akaoka for Edo accompanied by less than thirty samurai. Sohaku had twice as many men now. He would not have them for long. He doubted he would have ten when he rode from the temple.

Sohaku said, "Tomorrow morning, I will meet Lord Genji in battle. You are released from your oaths of loyalty to me. I urge you to either seek a reconciliation with him or service with another lord."

"Hollow words," an angry man in the fourth rank said. "Released from our oaths or not, we are still bound by our actions. Reconciliation is impossible. And what lord will accept traitors like us?"

"Be silent," another man said to him. "You knew the risks. Accept your fate like a man."

"Accept yours," the angry man said. His sword flashed suddenly. Blood spurted from the severed arteries of the man who had admonished him. The attacker fought his way through the three ranks separating him from Sohaku.

Sohaku neither stood nor drew his sword.

The man was almost upon him when another samurai cut him down from the back.

"Forgive him, Reverend Abbot. His family did not succeed in escaping from Akaoka in time."

"There is nothing to forgive," Sohaku said. "Every man must make his own decision. I will leave my swords here and go to the meditation hut for one hour. Then I will return. If any among you wish to accompany me into battle, wait here."

No one took him up on his invitation to come and kill him. When he returned to the main hall an hour later, he found the two corpses gone. Everyone else remained in their places. He would have fifty-eight men against Genji's thirty.

Sohaku bowed deeply to his loyal retainers.

"I have no words to express my gratitude to you," he said.

The brave and the doomed returned his bow.

"It is we who are grateful," a man in the first rank said. "We could not follow a finer lord."

•   •   •   •   •

"The Reverend Abbot declines to coordinate his attack with yours," the messenger said. "He will sally forth from the monastery at dawn."

Kawakami understood. Sohaku knew death was his fate no matter what happened to Genji, so he chose to die sword in hand. He was no longer concerned about the success or failure of the campaign itself. That had become irrelevant.

"Extend my thanks to the Reverend Abbot for informing me of his actions. Tell him I will pray to the gods for his success."

"Lord."

Kawakami was with his six hundred men at Yamanaka Village. Of these, only one hundred were primarily swordsmen. They were there to protect the others, a regiment of musketeers, against close-quarters assault. He did not expect it to come to that. Even though Sohaku outnumbered Genji two to one—that is, if he retained all his men, which Kawakami doubted—he would fail in his attack. He would fail because his sole concern was to display his courage, not to win. Die-hard cavalryman that he was, he would probably intercept Genji at the Mié Pass. The slopes there were ideal for a downhill charge from both sides. If he did that against a force such as Kawakami's, he and all his men would be cut down long before they could draw a single drop of blood with their swords. But the Okumichi clansmen were not musketeers. Like Sohaku, they were living relics of another era. They would meet the charge with one of their own, and the two sides would clash with katana and wakizashi, with yumi, yari, naginata, and tanto, with the weapons and wild courage of their ancient ancestors.

They were doomed, all of them. Sohaku would die in the Mié Pass. Genji and Shigeru would die at Mushindo, where they would go after defeating Sohaku. Kawakami, of course, would be waiting for them there. He would take the heads of the last Okumichi lords to the shrine of his ancestors in Hino Domain.

After two hundred sixty years, the Battle of Sekigahara was about to end.

· · · · ·

In several lengthy sessions, Genji listened to Shigeru speak of his visions. His uncle described occurrences so strange they could occur only in a distant future, if at all. Devices that allowed communication over great distances. Flying craft. Unbreathable air. Undrinkable water. The now-fecund Inland Sea full of dying fish, its coasts inhabited by deformed wretches. Populations so dense people crushed up against each other within carriages miles long and thought nothing of it. Large numbers of outsiders everywhere, not just in the restricted zones around Edo and Nagasaki. Wars so brutal and so vast whole cities disappeared in flames in a single night.

Genji decided to have Shigeru's words recorded in the family annals and left for posterity. They did no good now. His hope that his own visions would be clarified by them was completely frustrated. Except in a single unwelcome respect.

In Genji's vision of his death, he saw something Shigeru saw in every one of his own: There were no men with topknots, swords, or kimonos. Samurai were extinct. Inconceivable though it seemed, this at least would occur in Genji's lifetime.

He looked at the men riding with him. Was it really possible? In a few short years, would they all be swept away in the outsiders' total conquest of Japan, as Shigeru believed?

Hidé and Taro rode up alongside. Hidé said, "My lord, we are approaching the Mié Pass."

"Do you really think we are in danger here?"

Taro said, "Yes, lord. Abbot Sohaku was my commander for five years. This is precisely the kind of terrain he favors. He can attack at high speed from both sides of the valley."

"Very well," Genji said. "Tell Heiko and Hanako to drop back with Emily and Matthew."

"Yes, lord," Hidé said. "How many men shall I assign to guard them?"

"None. If Sohaku awaits, he will not bother them. My uncle and I are his only interest."

"Lord."

Genji turned to Saiki. "You didn't add your views."

"Your instructions were quite appropriate, my lord, and complete. There was nothing to add." Saiki was at peace. Whatever would happen, would happen. He did not know whether he would live or die. He knew he would act as a loyal retainer should. This was enough to know.

Heiko was not happy with the instructions she

received. She obeyed them, nevertheless. She had already promised to do so as a condition of her pardon.

Until I say otherwise, you are a geisha only. You will not use your other skills against either Sohaku or Kawakami. Agreed?

I can agree about Sohaku, but not about the Sticky Eye. He must be eliminated at the earliest possible moment.

I did not ask for your opinion. Do you agree, or do you not? His expression was without the slightest sign of humor.

Yes, my lord, I agree.

So here she was, dressed in a fancy, cumbersome traveling kimono of great beauty and little combat utility, in the saddle of a mare as tame as the one bearing Emily, and without weapons of any kind, apart from her bare hands.

"Lady Heiko," Hanako said.

"Yes?"

"If you should need them, there are throwing daggers in my right saddlebag, and a short sword in my left."

"Lord Genji has forbidden me to have them."

"You do not have them, my lady, I do."

Heiko bowed in gratitude. "Let us hope they are not needed."

Emily said to Stark, "What if the man you seek is not at the monastery?"

"Then I'll keep looking."

"And if he died in the epidemic?"

"He didn't."

Through Heiko, he had spoken with Taro about the outsider monk at Mushindo. The Japanese called him Jimbo, which was a shortened form of the man's name, Jim Bohannan. Since the Japanese word for monk was *bozu*, it was also a pun. Whatever he called himself, his description fit Ethan Cruz exactly.

What's a pun? Stark asked.

A play on words, Heiko said, a certain sound conveying more than one meaning.

Oh.

Heiko and Stark looked at each other. They both laughed.

Stark said, I guess you'll have to teach me English before you teach me Japanese.

"I don't know in what way he offended you," Emily said, "but vengeance is a bitter fruit. Better by far to forgive. 'If ye forgive men their trespasses, your heavenly Father will also forgive you.' "

"Amen," Stark said.

• • • • •

"Shigeru is not among them," the scout said.

"Of course not," Sohaku said. "He is circling to ambush us when we set the ambush he expects us to set."

He laughed, and his lieutenants laughed with him. Like all dead men, they were slightly giddy at finding themselves still upon the earth, and were completely without fear. One of them took his musket from its sheath, looked at it as if he had never seen it before, and dropped it on the ground. Other muskets fell until they had all been discarded.

Sohaku turned to the five ranks of cavalrymen behind him. "Are you ready?"

A samurai stood in his stirrups, raised his lance, and yelled at the top of his voice, "Ten thousand years!" Soon the cry was taken up by all. Men who had been laughing a moment earlier were now weeping and screaming out the same words in a single united voice.

"Ten thousand years!"

"Ten thousand years!"

"Ten thousand years!"

Sohaku drew his sword and spurred his horse into a charge.

· · · · ·

Emily heard the loud exclamations from the road ahead.

"Banzai! Banzai! Banzai!"

"Has someone come to greet Lord Genji?" she asked.

"Yes," Heiko said.

"What does 'banzai' mean?"

"It is an ancient way of saying 'ten thousand years.' The true meaning is more difficult to explain. I suppose you could say it is an expression of deepest sincerity, deepest commitment. The speaker is expressing his willingness to trade eternity for this single moment."

"Ah, then these are Lord Genji's allies," Emily said.

"No," Heiko said. "They are his deadly foes."

Stark drew both his guns and kicked his horse toward Genji.

· · · · ·

When they entered the pass, Sohaku's men were not met by a countercharge, as they expected, but by a volley of musket fire from the trees on their left flank. A quarter of their number fell, many because their horses had been struck. Following their commander, the rest wheeled and attacked uphill toward the tree line. Two more devastating volleys shattered their ranks. Only then did Genji's men become cavalrymen again, mounting their own charge out of the trees.

Sohaku aimed himself straight at Genji. He cut through the first two men he met. The next, Masahiro, was a samurai he had trained, and trained well. Masahiro deflected the blade directed at him and rammed Sohaku's horse with his own. Sohaku felt his knee snap. With only one leg to use for leverage in the stirrups, he was hard-pressed to keep Masahiro from striking a lethal blow. This delay saved his life.

Stark rode up next to Genji with a revolver in either hand and shot at the closest attackers. He fired eleven times, and nine of Sohaku's men fell dead from their saddles. Masahiro's vigorous efforts kept Sohaku at a distance. That was the only reason the twelfth bullet missed his heart. He saw Stark point the big revolver at him, and he saw the puff of smoke. Strangely, he heard nothing. An invisible blow of great weight struck the left side of his chest. Then a feeling of weightlessness threatened to lift him skyward. He pushed himself forward onto his horse's neck, trying not to lose consciousness and fighting desperately to stay in the saddle.

"Reverend Abbot!" Someone took hold of the reins, he wasn't awake enough to know who. "Hold on!" The horse galloped beneath him. How shameful it was to die of a gunshot wound without once having crossed swords with an Okumichi lord.

• • • • •

When he heard the shouts of Sohaku's men, Shigeru knew he had made a mistake. There was no one waiting in ambush. He rode to the crest of the hill just in time to see the charge. By the time he arrived, it was over.

Saiki said, "We lost but six men. Sohaku rode straight into our guns."

"It was a reenactment of Nagashino," Genji said. "He used tactics that failed three hundred years ago."

"It suited his purpose," Shigeru said. He dismounted and began looking among the enemy dead.

"He is not among the fallen," Saiki said. "After Mr. Stark shot him, one of his men led him away."

"And you permitted it?"

"I was not standing idly about," Saiki said. "More pressing matters demanded my attention."

Shigeru didn't bother to reply. He leaped back onto his horse and spurred it toward Mushindo Monastery.

"This way of fighting was very effective, my lord," Saiki said.

"You do not exhibit the happiness your words suggest," Genji said.

"I am an old man," Saiki said. "My way is the old way. To be in a battle decided by guns brings me no joy."

"Even when you are on the winning side?"

At last, Saiki smiled. "It is better to be on the winning side. That, at least, I can happily accept."

It did not take long to dispose of the wounded among the enemy. In deference to Emily, Genji forbade decapitations and, further, ordered the bodies covered as well as they could be while she rode past.

He thought Shigeru would find Sohaku quickly and be waiting when he reached Mushindo Monastery. His former cavalry commander appeared to have suffered a fatal wound from Stark's bullet. He could not have ridden far. But as Genji approached the walls of the monastery, his uncle was nowhere to be seen. Apparently, Sohaku had stayed alive long enough to require a more extended pursuit.

Saiki said, "My lord, please wait here until we are certain no trickery lies ahead." He rode ahead with Masahiro.

"Your marksmanship is most impressive," Genji said to Stark. "There must be few in America who are your equal."

A huge explosion prevented Stark from answering.

The meditation hall disintegrated, throwing debris in every direction. Several in their party were struck in this way and instantly killed. A section of heavy beam broke the forelegs of Genji's horse and threw both animal and rider to the ground. At almost the very same moment, the surrounding woods erupted in massed musket fire.

Heiko pulled Emily from the saddle and covered her with her own body. If she was to be the mother of Genji's heir, no injury must come to her. All around them, men and horses died. Their corpses absorbed the bullets that continued to rip through the air. Heiko could not raise her head to see what had happened to Genji and Stark. She silently pleaded with Amida Buddha to shield them with her radiant benevolence.

As if in answer to her plea, voices in the woods called out, "Cease fire! Cease fire!"

The shooting stopped. Another voice said, "Lord Genji! Lord Kawakami invites you to approach and discuss the terms of your surrender!"

Heiko saw Taro and Hidé pulling Genji out from under his dead horse. He said something to Hidé.

The chief bodyguard laughed and bowed to his lord. Then he said, "Lord Genji invites Lord Kawakami to approach and discuss the terms of *his* surrender!"

Anticipating a resumption of the attack, every survivor in Genji's party pressed themselves even harder against the ground. But after a few moments of silence, there was a reply from the woods.

"Lord Genji! You are surrounded by six hundred men! There are women and outsiders with you! Lord Kawakami will guarantee their safety if you will meet with him!"

Hidé said, "An obvious trick."

Genji said, "Perhaps not. He has no need for tricks. We cannot escape. All he need do is tighten the ring of guns around us and we will all be dead soon enough."

"My lord," Hidé said, "surely you are not accepting his invitation?"

"I am. Obviously, he wants to tell me something badly enough that he is willing to delay the pleasure of killing me."

"Lord," Taro said, "once he has you he will never release you."

"Oh? Do you foresee that?" That silenced all protest, as Genji knew it would. Any reference to prophecy always did.

· · · · ·

The satisfaction Kawakami felt demanded the utmost possible prolongation. He gestured at the variety of food and drink his adjutant had placed before Genji.

"Will you not partake of some refreshment, Lord Genji?"

"Thank you for your hospitality, Lord Kawakami, but I will not."

Kawakami bowed, signaling that he did not take offense at his guest's refusal.

Genji said, "I confess, I fail to see the reason for this meeting. Our positions must appear definitive. My lieutenants are of the opinion that you intend to seize me."

"I have given my word to the contrary," Kawakami said, "and I intend to keep it. I wished to see you before your death, which we both know is imminent and inevitable, so all will be clear between us in the end."

"You speak as though we were outsiders. Clarity and finality are what they seek and, therefore, what they find. We are infinitely more subtle." Genji smiled. "Never-ending ambiguity is the essence of our understanding. Therefore, nothing will be clear between us, and there will never be an end, no matter who lives and dies here today."

"From your words, one would think there is a question as to who that will be."

Genji bowed. "I am being polite. There is no doubt whatsoever."

Kawakami didn't permit Genji's outrageous implication to anger him, or his persistent smile to irritate him the way it usually did. Instead, he returned the smile with one of his own, and continued in a friendly conversational manner. "Of course, I do not conceive of permanence. I am neither child, idiot, nor outsider, that I would believe such foolishness. I mean only to clarify what is amenable to clarification, and end only that which can be ended. My principal motive, I am not averse to admitting, is that in doing so, I will experience the pleasure of definitively exposing the falsity of your prophetic abilities."

"Those abilities themselves being of an ambiguous nature, I regret, for your sake, that aspect of your presumed triumph will also not materialize."

"Please save your sympathy for those who will benefit from it, while you are still able to give it." Kawakami gestured with a look. His adjutant came forward with a pine box wrapped in white silk, bowed, and placed it between Genji and Kawakami. "Permit me to honor you with this gift."

"Since I have none to give you in return, I must decline your gracious offer."

"Your acceptance of itself will be a gift of more than equal value," Kawakami said.

Genji knew what was in the box, not by virtue of any vision, but by the expression on Kawakami's face. With a bow, he took the box, untied the silk, and opened it.

· · · · · ·

Shigeru rode at an unhurried pace toward Mushindo Monastery, his posture relaxed, his face expressing no concern. His senses, however, were fully alert. He knew he would find Sohaku, and he knew he would kill him without great difficulty. Kawakami was a more serious problem. Sohaku's attack—a bold single-front cavalry charge unsupported by infantry—clearly had not been part of any strategy Kawakami had devised. That meant another, more devious, much deadlier trap lay somewhere ahead. The Sticky Eye would never mount an open attack, no matter how great his numerical advantage in men and arms. Some form of ambush. Snipers, most likely, firing from a long, safe distance away.

He entered the valley below the monastery, rode into a copse of trees—and disappeared.

· · · · · ·

"Where is he?" the first sniper asked.

"Keep your voice down," hissed the second. "Shigeru has ears like a witch."

"But where did he go?"

"Stay calm," said the third sniper. "Remember the reward we'll get for bringing back his head."

"There. I saw something move among those trees."

"Where?"

"There."

"Ah, yes, I see him." The first sniper exhaled in relief.

"Wait. It's just his horse."

"What?"

All three snipers leaned forward.

"I don't see any horse."

"There. No, it's just a shadow."

"I'm getting out of here," the first sniper said. "Gold doesn't do a dead man any good."

"Stop, you fool. Wherever he is, he's too far away to do us any harm. He must cross that clearing. It'll be easy shooting."

The second sniper got up and ran after the first. "If it's so easy, you do it."

"Fools!" But the third sniper got up and ran after the second.

· · · · · ·

"Something's happening. Look." One of the trio of snipers in the second position pointed at the three men abandoning their post on the next hilltop.

"Shut up," hissed the leader, "and get back down."

The man did as he was told. But he began to look nervously in every direction instead of down toward the valley.

· · · · ·

Three sniper posts. Two, now that one was abandoned. Shigeru continued to wait. Within minutes, the remaining snipers also fled.

Shigeru frowned. Such lack of discipline was sickening to behold, even when it occurred among foes.

He urged his horse forward once again.

· · · · ·

"Father."

It was a child's voice. His son's.

"Nobuyoshi?"

There was no answer.

He looked to every side and saw nothing. For once, he would welcome a vision if it brought Nobuyoshi back to him, even for the briefest moment, even as a ghoul drenched in blood, holding his own head in his arms, pronouncing curses on Shigeru.

"Nobuyoshi?"

He willed himself to see what was not there. So many times before, against his will, he had seen. Surely, once, just once, he could see as he wished?

But he saw only trees and the winter sky. No visions, no delusions, no meeting with the dead. Had he heard the voice at all?

"Lord Shigeru. You do me honor." Sohaku was astride the trail ahead accompanied by one samurai.

Distracted by thoughts of his son, Shigeru had almost ridden into him. Sohaku did not display any sign of the gunshot he was reported to have suffered. His armor was unblemished, his posture was erect, and his voice, when he spoke, was strong.

"Imagine no such thing. I come to take your head. Nothing more."

Sohaku laughed. "You will be disappointed. They are overvalued. Mine, certainly, has not done me much good. Has yours, Yoshi?"

"No, Reverend Abbot, I regret it has not."

Shigeru spurred his horse into a charge. A heartbeat later, Sohaku and Yoshi responded. At the instant before they met, Sohaku leaned forward against his horse's neck and cut upward toward both Shigeru and his mount. Yoshi struck downward. Shigeru, anticipating both moves, deflected Sohaku's blow and avoided Yoshi's, slicing halfway through the latter's thigh and severing his femoral artery. Yoshi fell as Shigeru wheeled his horse around. Sohaku, slowed by his broken knee, could not match Shigeru. By the time he turned, Shigeru was already charging from his left side. Sohaku twisted in his saddle and blocked Shigeru's downward katana cut, but with the shorter wakizashi now in his left hand, Shigeru sliced cleanly through Sohaku's right shoulder joint.

• • • • •

Sohaku experienced each moment that followed with such completeness that there was no sense of sequence.

Blood spewed from the ruined stump of his shoulder. Had he ever seen a brighter red?

His hand still clenched his sword, only now, sword, hand, and arm were at an unaccustomed distance from him, on the ground at the hooves of his horse.

He floated weightlessly in the air, the earth above, the sky below.

Shigeru's face appeared before him, bloodsplattered, full of anguish. Sohaku felt a depth of sympathy he could not express in words.

Sunlight flashed from the blade arcing through the air. He recognized the elegant form, the metallurgical pattern at its edge, and the nearly white hue of its steel. There were only two swords like it in all the realm. The katana and wakizashi together called the Sparrow's Talons.

A headless body fell away beneath him. It was missing a right arm. It wore his armor. It was not important.

Sohaku disappeared into the infinitely bright light of Amida Buddha's compassion.

* * * * *

Shigeru held Sohaku's head up and looked at him face-to-face. If he had any thoughts about the recent frequency with which he had been killing friends and relatives, he did not have them long.

"Fire!"

Thirteen of the forty musket balls that flew through the air toward him found their target. Though they knocked him down, none of them created an immediately fatal wound. Shigeru got to his feet. As he stood, his katana fell out of his paralyzed right hand. Bullets had shattered his forearm and elbow on that side. He ran toward the trees opposite those from which the volley had come. He had nearly reached them when twenty musketeers stepped out of concealment in front of him and fired their weapons at point-blank range.

He fell a second time. When he tried to rise, not even a finger moved. He was not surprised to see Kawakami looking down at him.

"Cut off his head," Kawakami said.

"He's still alive, my lord."

"Then wait. Bring them here. Show him." The adjutant held the Sparrow's Talons so Shigeru could see them. "Please watch, Lord Shigeru." Two men held him up. A third man with a heavy ax struck at both katana and wakizashi until they broke in half.

"Good," Kawakami said. "Now cut off his head."

Kawakami made sure his own triumphant face filled Shigeru's eyes. How satisfying that this was the last thing the great warrior would see in his wretched lifetime.

But Shigeru's vision had already gone elsewhere.

"Father!" Nobuyoshi called out as he ran toward Shigeru. There was no blood, no decapitation, no cursing. The boy laughed and pulled a small, colorful butterfly kite aloft behind him. "Look what Cousin Genji made for me!"

"Nobuyoshi," Shigeru said, and smiled.

· · · · ·

Kawakami had prepared Shigeru's head with fastidiously correct etiquette. The eyes were closed, the face was clean with no expression of pain or suffering, the hair was immaculately neat, and sandalwood incense almost completely masked the smell of blood and incipient decay.

"Thank you, Lord Kawakami," Genji said. "Your

generosity surprises me. I thought you would intend to present this to your ancestors."

"Oh, I will do so, Lord Genji. Please do not concern yourself on that account. When you are dead, I will recover both this head and yours."

"May I inquire as to the location of the body? When I return to Cloud of Sparrows, a more complete cremation would be desirable."

Kawakami laughed, though he did not feel like laughing. His guest had not reacted with the horror and fear Kawakami expected. If Genji had any hope of rescue, it must lie with his uncle. The sight of Shigeru's head should have broken him. He signaled to his adjutant, who closed the box and wrapped it once more in silk.

"Unfortunately, the body, as well as that of Abbot Sohaku, was in the meditation hall. You may think of the cremation as already having taken place."

"Thank you once again for your hospitality." Genji bowed and prepared to depart.

"Please don't rush off. There is yet another item on our agenda."

Genji sat back. The small, constant, aggravating smile was still on his lips. But not for long. Kawakami willed his anger to subside. He wanted no negative emotions to interfere with his perceptions of what would happen next. These were memories he would treasure and recall for years to come.

Kawakami said, "I understand you have been most fortunate in securing the affections of an incomparable beauty, Lady Mayonaka no Heiko."

"So it seems."

"Yes, so it seems," Kawakami said. "How different seeming and the real so often are. What seems like love may be hate or, worse, an act designed to confuse and distract. What seems like beauty may be ugliness of such depth that it cannot be imagined." He paused, expecting a witty retort, but Genji said nothing. "Sometimes, what seems and what is are not the same, and yet both are real. Heiko, for example, seems to be a beautiful geisha, and she is. She is also a ninja." Again he paused. Again Genji said nothing. "Do you doubt me?"

"No, Lord Kawakami, I have no doubt you are telling the truth."

"You don't seem surprised."

"As you have pointed out, we are well advised not to place too much emphasis on what seems to be."

"Lord Genji, please do me the courtesy of pretending you believe me to possess a modicum of intelligence. Obviously, you know of her dual character."

"For the sake of argument, let us assume so." Now Genji paused and looked at him with what Kawakami believed was heightened anxiety. "There is more, of course."

"Of course. Since you know she is a ninja, then you must also know she is in my employ."

"I would come to that conclusion, yes."

"And I knew, of course, that you would uncover all of these facts before very long." Kawakami permitted the satisfaction he felt to show on his face. "Like all clever people—and you are very clever, Lord Genji, no one would deny you that—you tend to disregard the cleverness of others. Did you really think me such a fool that I would expect Heiko's secret to remain secret?"

"I must admit, I formerly had such thoughts," Genji said. "I see they were mistaken."

"More mistaken than you realize. You thought I sent Heiko into your bed so she could betray you, possibly even kill you, at a moment I deemed propitious. Not unreasonable, since this is the assignment Heiko also thought she had. Perhaps the two of you have discussed this in some detail by now?"

Kawakami gave Genji an opportunity to respond, but he did not.

"How could I have such a plan? For Heiko to do such things, she would need to be treacherous and deceitful to a grotesque extent. No external semblance of beauty could conceal such ugliness from a man of your subtle understanding. On the contrary, my true purpose demanded an entirely different sort of woman. One possessed of great sensitivity, passion, sincerity, depth. Exactly Heiko, in other words. Like a doting father, I had only one wish for her. That she find true love."

Kawakami paused again, savoring the pendant moment. The growing dismay on Genji's face intoxicated him.

"May I permit myself to hope that she has?"

* * * * *

Before Kawakami ascended to the title of Great Lord of Hino, which was then held by his uncle, he fancied himself slighted by Yorimasa, the son and heir of Kiyori, Great Lord of Akaoka. The occasion was unimportant. The injury, real or imagined, merely added heat to the already existing hatred established by Sekigahara. It further offended him to see such a drunken, opium-addicted wastrel esteemed for the visionary abilities that supposedly ran in his blood. Kawakami knew true vision was based on having information that others did not want known. Acquiring this required diligence, skill, and a natural ability carefully nurtured. Inherited magic had nothing to do with it.

He contemplated for some time the retributive actions open to him. A duel was out of the question. Even intoxicated, Yorimasa was deadlier with a sword than Kawakami on his ten best days combined. And if, against all probability, he somehow managed to prevail, he would then have to deal with Yorimasa's younger brother, Shigeru, whose reputation was already beginning to rival the legendary Musashi's. Defeating him left the realm of the improbable and entered that of the clearly impossible.

Assassination was more reasonable. The Kawakami clan had, through an historical accident whose origins had grown vague over time, the allegiance of a small clan of ninjas. When Kawakami imagined Yorimasa's death in such a covert manner, he felt not the slightest joy. It wasn't important that everyone knew who was responsible. But Yorimasa had to know before he died, or where was the satisfaction?

The answer came to him one day when he was accompanying Ryogi, the procurer, on a tour of villages in the outlying parts of Hino Domain. Kawakami's interest in geishas had led him to secretly invest in several of the leading houses. His interest was not in sex, however, but information. Geishas knew things no one else did.

"Some who fancy themselves connoisseurs say manner is everything," Ryogi said. "This is the accepted view of the old Kyoto school, of course." Ryogi laughed. "It is the view of blind men. Appearance, my lord, is far more important. Behavior can be compelled. Appearance is either there or it is not. A woman cannot be forced to be beautiful."

Kawakami nodded assent, though he did not agree, because that is what required the least effort. He did not spend time with Ryogi to exchange words with him. The old procurer was crude, harsh, stupid, given to foul habits of every kind, and profoundly repulsive in almost every way imaginable, including personal hygiene. He had only one positive attribute, the astounding ability to see rare beauty in a woman when she was still a very young child. Because he was held in such low regard, Ryogi's discoveries never found their way to the best geisha houses and were therefore never properly nurtured. The beauty that eventually blossomed was invariably wasted in some low-level brothel in the worst parts of the Floating World. That was how Ryogi had come to his attention. Kawakami had, on several occasions, noticed the most extraordinarily beautiful faces staring out from behind the wooden bars of some of the very worst brothels in Edo. Upon inquiry, he discovered two things. First, the women, prematurely ruined by years of ill use no matter how young, were invariably unsuitable for his purposes. Second, each and every one had been sold to the proprietors by one particular man.

Kawakami was accompanying Ryogi on this procurement mission because he hoped to learn the skill himself. In this he had been unsuccessful. The three little girls selected in the villages they had visited were pretty enough, but he could discern no common feature or quality hinting at the beauty Ryogi assured him was there.

"Thank you for the lesson," Kawakami said. He gestured to his assistant to give Ryogi his payment.

Ryogi took the gold coins with an obsequious bow. "Isn't there another village in the last valley? I see smoke. And I think I smell something, too."

"*Eta*," Kawakami said. Eta were the hereditary outcasts who did the foulest necessary work. They were disdained by even the most lowly peasants.

"Butchers?" Ryogi said, sniffing the air like a mongrel.

"Leather workers," Kawakami said. He turned his horse in the other direction, back toward the castle and away from the disgusting odor the shifting wind now strongly blew his way.

"I'll take a look," Ryogi said. "You never know where beauty may be found, eh?"

Kawakami was about to bid him good day when he thought better of it. To know what others did not sometimes required going where others declined to go.

"Then I will accompany you awhile longer."

"My lord," his senior bodyguard said. "Do not risk pollution by entering an outcast village. There is no reason. How can there be beauty among those who skin and work the hides of slaughtered beasts?"

"And if there is," another bodyguard said, "what man can overcome his disgust enough to bother with it?"

"Nevertheless, we will continue with our guide."

As soon as he saw the child, about three years of age, Kawakami knew. He didn't need Ryogi to tell him, though Ryogi did.

"She will devastate many men," Ryogi said, "before she is worn down by them. Who are her parents, her siblings?"

The gathered outcasts continued to press their heads to the ground. No one spoke. They were all too stunned and frightened by Kawakami's presence. Never before had a samurai, much less the heir himself, set foot in their village.

Kawakami said, "Answer."

"Lord." A man and a woman shuffled forward on their hands and knees without lifting their eyes from the ground. Two boys and a girl, between five and eight years old, followed their lead.

"You, woman, look up."

She did so with great hesitancy, lifting her head, but not her eyes. Her face was remarkably pretty, though she was past the first blush of youth, and her form not entirely inelegant. If Kawakami had not known, he would not have guessed her cursed lineage.

"Not bad," Ryogi said. "But the mother is nothing compared to what the daughter will be."

At Kawakami's signal, one of the bodyguards dropped some coins on the ground. The little girl was put on one of the three broken nags Ryogi had strung along behind his horse. The party departed.

At Hino Castle, Kawakami paid Ryogi a bonus for his excellent instruction. The procurer left for Edo the next morning, along with his four new pieces of human merchandise. That night, he stopped at a way station. When he did not come to breakfast, the innkeeper went to check. He found Ryogi's neck slit from ear to ear. Three of the little girls had exited this life in the same way. The fourth was missing.

As he had been instructed, Kuma the Bear took the eta child to his own village, the home of the small clan of ninjas to which he belonged.

"What's your name?"

"Mitsuko."

"I'm your uncle Kuma."

"You're not. I don't have an uncle Kuma."

"Yes, you do. You just didn't know until now."

"Where's my mommy?"

"I'm so sorry, Mitsuko. There's been a terrible accident. Your mommy, daddy, brothers, and sister have all gone on to the Pure Land."

"No!"

· · · · · ·

"Kuma you have already met," Kawakami said, "though the introduction was not formal. Your outsider friend, Stark, shot him right after the bombardment of Edo. Perhaps you remember?"

"I do."

"Needless to say, Mitsuko—you know her by her professional name, of course—is not an orphan." He signaled to his adjutant, who poured sake for him. This was an occasion that called for something more festive than tea, even if he had to drink it alone. "Both her parents are still alive, as are her two brothers and older sister. There is a remarkable family resemblance among them all. Particularly between Mitsuko and her mother and sister. It is quite pronounced, now that she is an adult. Naturally, the inescapable hardships of eta life have taken their toll. But not on Mitsuko. Are you sure you will not partake of some sake, Lord Genji? It is genuinely of the best quality." He was sure Genji did not miss his emphasis on the word "genuinely."

"No, thank you."

"Have you no words of wit or wisdom to offer, my lord?"

"I do not."

"A pity you failed to foresee this."

"Not really," Genji said. "No harm has been done. My feelings are unaffected by your slander."

"Your feelings?" Kawakami laughed. "They should be the least of your concerns. A Great Lord sharing his bed with an eta, the polluted offspring of stinking, offal-eating, hide-stretching degenerates. I am sorry you will not survive to experience the furor this news will excite when it becomes public. It will put an unfortunate and indelible stain on the reputation of your clan, even as it is extinguished. The only thing better—or worse, depending on your viewpoint—is if you and Heiko had children, or even married. Regrettably, the pressure exerted by outsiders has forced a compression of events. Things do tend to speed up when they are around, don't they?"

"No one will believe such a ridiculous allegation," Genji said.

"Do you think not?" Kawakami said. "Picture mother and sister standing by her side. Will anyone have the slightest doubt then?"

"That will not happen," Genji said.

"Oh? Do you foresee that?"

Genji smiled. It was a slight smile, and lacked the assurance of his former smile, but it still irritated Kawakami. "I have foreseen what is necessary. And heard the same. With your permission, I will impose upon you no longer."

Kawakami's adjutant and bodyguards looked at him, waiting for the signal to cut Genji down. He did not give it. Let him return to Heiko. Let him look at her now and feel what he must inevitably feel. Such agony that Kawakami could imagine was worth more than Genji's immediate death.

Patience had its own pleasures.

. . . . . .

Never more than now did Genji feel the painful limitations of prophecy. As hopeless as his situation seemed, he knew he would not die here. He had to live to be assassinated in another place, at another time, and to meet Lady Shizuka, who will weep for him, and to have his third and final vision. Yet what good did that knowledge do him? He had blindly entered a trap of the worst kind.

Eta.

He could attempt a pretense with Kawakami but not with himself. The revelation of Heiko's origins devastated him.

Eta.

In Genji's entire life, not one had even been permitted in his sight. Butchers, leather workers, waste handlers, grave diggers, corpse carriers.

Heiko was one of them.

Eta.

He fought down a wave of nausea.

"My lord, are you unwell?" Since Genji's return, Hidé had waited patiently for his lord to break his silence. Only concern that he might have been poisoned by the treacherous Kawakami made Hidé speak first.

"I have bad news," Genji said. In his absence, his remaining men had built a wall of dead horses around their tiny redoubt. Their thick bodies rendered the position essentially bulletproof. Genji would have been more able to appreciate this ingenuity had the animal corpses not reminded him so forcefully of what he had just learned. He did not look at the faces gathered around him. If he did, he would have to look at Heiko or she would notice his failure to do so, and he could not look at her just yet. Instead, he kept his eyes on the silk-wrapped box he had brought back with him.

"Lord Shigeru is dead."

The shocked gasps Genji heard told him the men had hoped what he had hoped. That Shigeru would arrive at the last minute and somehow miraculously scatter the hundreds of enemies who surrounded them. Shigeru could do it if anyone could, and only Shigeru.

"Is it certain, my lord?" Hidé said. "Kawakami is full of tricks. Might this not be one?"

Genji bowed to the box and unwrapped it. As he did so, he noticed Heiko speaking softly to Emily, who immediately dropped her gaze to the ground in front of her. He felt gratitude for Heiko's kindness, and shame at his own persisting inability to perceive her in other than the most distressing light.

There was another gasp when he opened the box. Several of the men began to sob. Soon all were weeping. The eleven samurai who had survived Sohaku's charge and Kawakami's ambush, some of them badly wounded, were all men Shigeru had trained. Harsh, exacting, relentless, and merciless, he had been the last of the old-style masters of the arts of war. No member of the clan had been more feared, hated, and revered. His loss tore at the warrior essence he had helped to forge deep within each man's heart.

Emily, unable to contain her emotions, said to Heiko in a choked voice, "Must war be waged so cruelly? Is not death terrible enough?"

"Death is not terrible at all," Heiko said. "Only dishonor is terrible. For Lord Kawakami to present Lord Shigeru's head to his own clan is an insult of the worst kind. That is what these men mourn. Their failure to defend Lord Shigeru from such shame. It is their own dishonor they feel most keenly."

Stark had pulled his saddlebags during the lull. He had two loaded six-shooters, forty bullets for the .44, and eighteen for the .32. When nightfall came, he would break for the walls of the monastery. With luck, he'd survive to reach it, and inside he'd find Ethan Cruz and kill him. He hoped the explosion hadn't already done it.

"Hidé, tell Lady Heiko and Lady Emily that they must leave us now," Genji said. "Lord Kawakami has guaranteed their safety. Mr. Stark is also free to go if he chooses."

"Yes, lord." Hidé went to tell Heiko.

Heiko had heard Genji's words quite clearly, since their makeshift fortress was not large and she was no more than ten paces from him. She wondered why he didn't speak directly to her. Since his return, he had not looked her way once. Had Kawakami said something to shake his trust in her? Surely, no matter what it was, Genji would not believe him. If there was any certainty in an uncertain world, he must know her love for him was true.

Before Hidé could speak, Heiko said, "I will not go."

"My lady, there is no choice in the matter," Hidé said. "Lord Genji has commanded it."

Heiko swiftly drew her dagger and held the edge against her throat. One swift stroke would open her jugular vein. She said again, "I will not go."

Emily, aghast, said, "Heiko," but Heiko ignored her.

Stark, who was directly behind her, thought of seizing her arm. As soon as he thought it, her head shifted in a way that made him give up the idea. She was ready for it and he wouldn't be in time.

Hidé looked at Genji. "My lord."

Genji knew Kawakami would not kill Heiko if he could help it. She would be displayed along with her relatives as final proof of his greatest triumph. Her humiliation would be more grievous than Genji's death. He could spare her that agony simply by insisting that she leave. He had no doubt she would slit her throat without a heartbeat's hesitation. But he couldn't do it. Whatever else he felt about her, he also loved her. He could not be the instrument of her death. There was still hope. His vision promised life. Perhaps in securing it, Heiko could be protected.

Genji finally looked at her. He bowed deeply to her. "I hope I prove worthy of such loyal attachment."

Heiko lowered the dagger. She returned his bow and said, "The attachment does not depend on worth or loyalty, my lord."

Despite himself, Genji laughed. "So unconditional? Then my debt to you is great indeed."

"Yes," Heiko said, in a very geisha-like way, "how will you ever repay it?"

Now the men laughed, too. Lord and lady behaved in an utterly unworried manner. How could they themselves act otherwise? Tears were wiped away.

Emily said, "Heiko, what were you doing?"

"Making a demonstration," Heiko said. "Sometimes, words are not effective with samurai."

Genji said, "Emily, Matthew, you are free to go. My adversary will not harm you."

"Free to go where?" Stark said.

"No doubt, he will conduct you safely to the

American consul's residence in Edo. You will be able to board the next ship for America."

"America's not my destination," Stark said. He gestured toward Mushindo Monastery with his .44. "That is."

Emily said, "I believe I have already told you, Lord Genji, my mission is here in Japan."

"We are surrounded by several hundred men," Genji said, "who will try their best to kill us with guns and swords in a very few minutes. Do you really want to be here then?"

"I will be where God chooses," Emily said.

Stark smiled and cocked the hammers of both revolvers.

Genji bowed and turned his attention to his men. "Lord Kawakami intends to retrieve my uncle's head when he comes for mine. I do not plan to oblige him in either case."

"We will take his instead," Hidé said. "We will leave it to rot outside the walls of his own burning castle."

"Yes!" many voices exclaimed together.

"Why wait? Let us take it now!"

"Stop," Genji said, just in time to prevent half of his handful of men from making an immediate suicide charge into Kawakami's guns. "Sometime past, I received a vision which clarifies the present. This is not the end." He did not add that his vision did not necessarily indicate the survival of anyone other than himself. His statement had the desired effect. He could see confidence returning in the men's eyes and posture. "Of course, anyone eager to commit suicide anyway has my permission to attack."

Whether a coincidence of timing or brought on by Kawakami's anger at hearing such good cheer among the doomed, the surrounding guns opened fire. Volley followed volley without pause. Musket balls tore into their animal-flesh walls in such profusion, the worst-hit parts began to disintegrate. Waves of bullets whistled through the air over them.

Were what he had seen truly visions? Genji began to doubt it. It seemed far more likely now that his head and his uncle's would soon be hanging from the pommel of Kawakami's saddle—or perhaps, since the Sticky Eye seemed to be rather excessively fastidious, from his adjutant's. But he recalled a rule his grandfather had once told him.

The foreseen can be depended upon to occur in an unforeseen manner.

Hidé saw the smile on Genji's face and felt his confidence soar even as the situation appeared to deteriorate at an accelerated pace. Most of the horses, ripped by musket balls, began to fall apart and liquefy. A foreleg bounced off Hidé's shoulder and splashed into the bloody mud. Within the circle of shredded animal flesh, everyone was soaked in horse blood. A hell realm was materializing around them. Yet Genji smiled. Hidé tightened his grip on his sword. More than ever, he was certain of their victory. How it would occur, however, was still a great mystery.

· · · · ·

"If possible," Kawakami told his adjutant, "take Genji and Heiko alive. In any case, do not damage the lady's face."

"Yes, lord. But they may both be dead already, and their faces destroyed as well. We have fired many hundreds of bullets at them."

"All we have done is kill the same horses over

and over again," Kawakami said. "They're waiting for us to go and get them. Then they'll fight. Put down the guns and go in with swords."

"Yes, lord."

"Wait. Have your ten best shots retain their guns. Assign them to shoot the outsider with the guns as soon as he shows himself."

"Yes, lord."

Kawakami watched from a safe distance, as always. His men stacked muskets and drew swords. Once they would have been eager to do it. No longer. Now they believed in the superiority of guns. So did Kawakami. Not because his six hundred guns had prevailed against the ten or twenty swords on Genji's side. That proved nothing. But because guns had killed the invincible Shigeru with ease. A single farm boy with a musket could have done it. With two weeks of training, a peasant with a gun could defeat a samurai who had spent years honing his skill with a sword. There was no argument against it except historical inertia.

New tactics still remained to be developed. Or learned from the outsiders. It took no great insight to use guns in defense of a position or in ambush. Attack was still problematic, especially against an opponent similarly armed. The need to stop and reload seemed an insurmountable obstacle to a sustained offense. How did the outsiders do it? Kawakami was determined to learn. When he was finished with Genji, he would turn his full attention to gunnery and its strategies. Perhaps there was a master among the outsiders akin to Sun Tzu. If so, Kawakami would study his version of *The Art of War*. The Tokugawa grip on the Shogunate was weakening. It would be wrested from them soon, but not in the ancient manner, by samurai with swords. The new Shogun would take power with guns. He could be the one. Why not? If the old rules no longer applied to war, they would not long apply to hierarchical precedents. Lineage would matter far less than firepower.

Guns. He needed more guns. Better guns. Bigger ones. Cannons. Warships.

Wait. It wouldn't do to get ahead of himself. First, Genji.

Kawakami moved forward, but with caution. Genji's men, few as they were, also had muskets. How tragic if he were shot dead at the moment of his greatest triumph. He was careful to keep a protective screen of trees between himself and the enemy.

· · · · · ·

"Why have they stopped shooting?" Hidé asked.

"My head," Genji said. "To take it, they must use swords."

Taro cautiously peered past the protective carcass in front of him. "Here they come."

Genji looked at his men. Every one of them held a sword. Discarded muskets lay in the bloody mud. It would be more efficient to meet the attack with a volley of gunfire before engaging with swords. But efficiency was not on their minds. They were samurai. At the decisive moment of life and death, only a sword would do.

Genji drew his own sword. Perhaps he was the last Okumichi, and as the last, he was the one with completely false visions. There was no assassination awaiting him in the future. There was no Lady Shizuka, no heir waiting to be born, no third vision. Everything had been delusion. He looked at Heiko and saw her looking at him. Their smiles were simultaneous. No, not everything had been delusion.

"Prepare yourselves," Genji said to his men. "We will attack." That was the way for samurai to die. In the attack. Like a boulder plummeting from an infinite height into the endless void. "Ready..."

A volley of musket fire from the walls of Mushindo Monastery drowned out the rest of his command. Half the front rank of Kawakami's samurai went down. The advance immediately became a disorderly retreat, with panicked men running in every direction away from Mushindo. A second volley followed, and more of Kawakami's men fell.

Genji saw the barrels of about forty muskets on the wall. Who were they? He didn't have time to speculate. A new disturbance broke out in the rear of Kawakami's position. The ground beneath him reverberated with the impact of horses' hooves.

"Cavalry!" Hidé said. "Someone is attacking Kawakami!"

"Reinforcements!" Taro said.

"How?" Hidé said. "Our domain is three days away for a man on a swift horse."

"Look out," Taro said, "they're coming back."

Kawakami's battalion, now desperately trying to escape the cavalry charge, ran back toward Mushindo. Devastating musket fire greeted them again. But as the musketeers reloaded, the deluge of frightened men resumed. Genji and his few samurai had to fight desperately to keep from being overrun. Blades flashed in every direction. The blood of dying men and dead horses mingled in the mud. Genji heard Stark's guns fire twelve times, then no more.

There was no time to reload. Stark picked up a sword, held it with both hands, and swung it like an ax, gouging bodies, shattering skulls, and chopping off limbs.

Heiko and Hanako stood at the center with Emily between them, slashing and stabbing at whoever came close.

One of Kawakami's men got behind Hidé, who was already engaged with several others, and cut at him.

"Hidé!" Shouting his name in warning, Hanako threw herself in the way. The falling blade severed her left arm above the elbow.

Horsemen burst from the woods. Makeshift sparrow-and-arrows pennants flew from their banner staffs. They hacked and trampled their way through the retreating mass toward Genji, shouting his name as a war cry.

"Genji!"

"Genji!"

"Genji!"

Heiko said in an astonished voice, "Do you see who it is, my lord?"

"Yes, I see," Genji said. "But can I trust my eyes?"

＊ ＊ ＊ ＊ ＊

"I ordered an end to the shooting," Kawakami said angrily.

"Those were not our guns, my lord. The shots came from within the monastery."

"Impossible. Anyone there would have been killed in the explosion."

"Perhaps more of Lord Genji's men have since arrived." The adjutant looked fearfully over his shoulder. "From the start, it seemed unlikely he would travel with so light an escort. Could this have been a trap, my lord?"

"That is also impossible," Kawakami said. "If it were so, Genji would never have met with me. He would not risk himself unless he had no choice."

Kawakami could see his men retreating from the monastery toward him, and in rapidly worsening disorder. "Our forces appear to be moving in the wrong direction."

"The unexpected gunfire has caused some confusion," the adjutant said.

"Then go forward and restore order."

"Yes, lord." But the adjutant did nothing to urge his horse forward.

Kawakami was about to unleash a torrent of invective when he was interrupted by shouts behind him.

"Genji!"

"Genji!"

"Genji!"

Shouting the Okumichi war cry, mounted samurai crashed through the undefended rear of Kawakami's position. Caught on foot without their own horses, with their muskets stacked and unreachable, trapped between volleys of gunfire and charging cavalry, Kawakami's battalion dissolved in total panic. Many threw down their swords and ran for the only exit from the trap, the road back to Edo. Bullets, swords, and horses' hooves decimated them as they fled.

Kawakami and his adjutant were surrounded before they could go very far. Their resistance being feeble, both were captured with little drama.

"Hold," Kawakami said. "I am more valuable to you alive than dead. I am Lord Kawakami." Despite being a captive, his sense of importance was undiminished. This was merely a setback, not a permanent defeat. "Despite the banners you fly, you are not Okumichi samurai, are you? Who is your lord? Take me to him."

· · · · ·

For fifteen years, Mukai had been a loyal, subservient assistant chief of the Shogun's secret police. He did what his lord, Kawakami, told him to do, without much concern about the frequent anguish and very occasional satisfaction his work produced. The purpose of life was not to seek particular joys, after all, but to venerate and obey those above, and to command and discipline those below.

Almost too late, he had learned that such an existence was not life, but no more than living death.

This was life.

The raw animal power of the charging warhorse beneath him was nothing compared to the vital energy surging through his own being.

"Genji!"

"Genji!"

"Genji!"

Electrified by an almost painful ecstasy, Mukai felt himself to be the living embodiment of the Lightning God as he led the charge to Genji's rescue. His love had showed him possibilities he had never before dared to imagine. Acting on his love had liberated him forever. The happiness he felt was selfish, personal, utterly pure. He had no thought of duty, family, place, history, tradition, obligation, face, or shame. There was nothing in him but his love, and there was no world except the unity of himself and Genji.

One hundred eighty loyal retainers had followed him in the desperate ride from his tiny northern domain. They had been convinced to do so by Lord Genji's prophecy of certain victory. Genji had not, to Mukai's knowledge, made such a prophecy. Mukai had simply lied, and lied extremely well. Love had mysteriously given him the eloquence he needed. His retainers, so used to a clumsy, self-effacing, tongue-tied lord, were amazed into belief and obedience.

Now, the sparrow-and-arrows banner flying over him as in his dreams, Mukai was beyond fear and hope, life and death, past and future. He struck at the men obstructing his path with joyous abandon.

"Genji!"

He shouted the name of his love, a declaration, a battle cry, a sacred mantra.

Mad with fear of flying bullets and crashing horses' hooves, many of Kawakami's men tried to find sanctuary within Genji's circle. The press of so many panicky swordsmen threatened to do what Kawakami's planned assault had not. Genji and his companions were on the verge of being overwhelmed.

Had he come this far only to arrive moments too late? Mukai cursed the poor grasp of strategy that failed to tell him where Kawakami would set the ambush; had he been blessed with a better military mind, he would have known where to go and would have arrived days ago. He cursed the wretched sense of direction that had led him down one wrong path after another on his way through the mountains; with a better knowledge of the stars, of wind patterns, of the seasonal movement of birds, he would not have lost precious hours going east instead of west; he cursed the fifteen years he had spent in windowless interrogation chambers; an active out-doorsman would have known the geography of the region, and this would have remedied any failure of strategic wisdom or directional acuity.

No! They could not die apart. Not after love and fate had brought them so close. He broke away from his bodyguards and charged headlong into the swirling mass of men and swords.

"Genji!"

Slashing wildly left and right at every head he saw, he forced his way toward Genji's position. The sheer multitude of enemy weapons soon brought down his horse. He barely felt the spear thrusts and sword cuts that tore at his body. Genji. He had to reach Genji. He continued to fight his way forward on foot.

"Lord Mukai! Wait!" His retainers struggled to catch up.

"Genji!"

"Mukai!"

He leaped over the wall of horses to Genji's side. "My lord." He bowed. "I have come as I promised."

"Watch out!" Genji used his sword to deflect a blow aimed at Mukai's back. "We should dispense with the courtesies for now. Let me just say, I am very surprised, and very happy to see you, Mukai."

"My lord," Mukai said.

As love had given him eloquence, now it took it away.

"My lord."

It was all he could say.

Genji was drenched in blood from head to toe. Whether it was his own, that of his enemies, or from the shattered remnants of horses, Mukai could not say. Did it matter? In this doomed and precious moment, together with Genji, fighting at his side against the most impossible of odds, all sense of self and other disappeared. There was neither subject nor object, nor absence of subject and object. There was neither the passage of time, nor the absence of its passage. What was within him and what was without? Not only was he unable to find an answer, the question itself was nonsense.

"My lord."

For several desperate moments, it seemed the end had come. There were too many of Kawakami's men, and too few of Genji's. For every one they cut down, three more took their place. Then, just as the ring of swords began to close around them for the final time, another volley of musket fire came from the walls and all resistance collapsed. All at once, as if a silent command had passed among them, Kawakami's men discarded their weapons and threw themselves on the ground.

It was over.

Mukai said, "You have triumphed, my lord."

"No," Genji said, "you have triumphed, Mukai. This victory is yours alone."

Mukai smiled a smile so radiant he felt certain his whole body glowed.

"Mukai!" Genji caught him in his arms as he collapsed.

"Lord!" Mukai's retainers came forward. He waved them off without taking his eyes away from Genji's face for a single moment.

"Where are you hurt?" Genji said.

Mukai didn't care about his wounds. He wanted to tell Genji dreams came true not only for visionaries but for ordinary men like himself, too, if they were completely sincere. He wanted to say he had dreamed of this very moment with perfect clarity—the blood, the embrace, the death, the fearlessness, and, most especially, the eternal, transcendent, ecstatic oneness beyond all limitations of perception, definition, and understanding.

Then he no longer wanted even that, and there was only the smile.

"Lord!" Mukai's men watched in shock as Genji lowered their lord's body to the ground. He had told them Genji had prophesied victory. He had said nothing about his own death.

"Lord Mukai is dead," Genji said.

"Lord Genji, what are we to do? Without Lord Mukai, we are masterless. He has no blood heir. The Shogun may well confiscate his fief."

"You are the loyal retainers of a most loyal and self-sacrificing friend," Genji said. "All who wish may enter my service."

"Then we are henceforth your vassals, Lord Genji." Mukai's former lieutenants bowed deeply to their new lord. "What do you command?"

"Well, well," Kawakami said, "how touching, and how dramatic. Perhaps one day this will appear as a scene in a kabuki play about your life, Lord Genji." He looked down at them from his saddle, his expression as confident as always. Intimidated by his status, Mukai's men accompanied him as they would a guest rather than a captive. In vivid contrast to everyone else, he and his adjutant wore immaculate clothing unblemished by combat.

"Dismount," Genji said.

Kawakami frowned. "Permit me to caution you against getting carried away. The only change is an improvement in your chances of survival." He was no swordsman. His art was otherwise. It was, ironically enough, knowledge, that very quality the Okumichis supposedly possessed beyond all other men. It was knowledge that would give him the ultimate victory. "If you negotiate intelligently, you may actually enjoy significant benefit. May I suggest—"

Genji reached up, grabbed Kawakami's arm, and threw him to the ground.

Kawakami, choking and gagging, lifted his face out of the muddy gore. "You—"

Genji's sword arced above Kawakami and sliced through most of his neck in a downward cut from right to left. The dead man's head flopped between his shoulders, held there by spinal gristle. Blood fountained into the air for an instant, then subsided as quickly as blood pressure dropped to nothing. The corpse fell forward into the mud, the head still between the shoulders, the stupefied face staring at the sky.

Genji looked at the adjutant. He had been in the tent when Kawakami had spoken of Heiko's origins.

"Lord Genji," the adjutant said.

"Kill him," Genji said.

The two men on either side of the adjutant struck immediately. The corpse struck the ground in three pieces—head, right shoulder, and the rest.

Genji looked at the cowering prisoners, perhaps three hundred in number. They were rank-and-file samurai, unlikely to have been privy to any important information. Kawakami had always been fascinated by knowing what others did not. He could not enjoy that advantage by sharing with many. The adjutant knew. Probably, Mukai had also known. Who else? His wife? His concubines? Other geisha? Even if he went on a countrywide killing spree, he couldn't be sure of eliminating every possibility. With Kawakami gone, it might not be necessary. Few would dare bring forth such outrageous allegations without supporting evidence. That, of course, was the key. The supporting evidence.

Genji said, "Check the monastery for more explosives. Once it is clear, prepare the bath."

"What of the prisoners, lord?"

"Release them. Without their weapons."

"Yes, lord."

He would deal with the evidence as soon as he could. First, he had a meeting with the Shogun to attend.

• • • • • •

Miraculously, Saiki had not been killed by the massive explosion inside the monastery. He was unconscious when Mukai's musketeers found him, covered with the remains of Masahiro and his horse. He was groggy as he lay on the litter bearing him toward Edo. His ears were still ringing and he couldn't hear anything else. But what bothered him most was that he had missed Kawakami's decapitation. That he would have liked to see. When his hearing was restored, he would ask Hidé for a detailed report.

• • • • • •

Ethan Cruz wasn't in the monastery. But he was somewhere, and he was alive. He had to be. Stark looked back. This was the second time he'd passed this way. He remembered the trail. He'd find his way here from Edo.

And he'd find Ethan Cruz.

• • • • • •

Emily didn't feel the saddle under her. She hardly felt her own body. Though her eyes were open, nothing she saw made any impression upon her mind.

She was in shock.

So much blood.

So much death.

She tried to recall a comforting line of biblical verse. Nothing came to her.

•   •   •   •   •

In that moment when it had seemed they would all die, Genji's eyes had met hers, and he had smiled at her in his familiar way. Since then, he had once again begun avoiding her. He was careful not to let it appear so. But Heiko could tell. Nuance and subtlety were among her special talents.

What had Kawakami said to Genji at their meeting?

•   •   •   •   •

Hanako looked up at Hidé from the litter where she lay. She was very proud of him. With every crisis, he matured further, grew braver, became more focused. Even his posture astride his horse was changed. He was well on the way to becoming the fine samurai she had always known he could be. All he lacked was a wife appropriate to his station in life.

She said, "I release you from our marriage," and turned her head away. No tears flowed from her eyes, and she controlled her breathing so as not to give the appearance of distress.

Hidé said to Taro, who rode alongside him, "She is delirious."

Hanako said, "I am no longer fit to be your wife."

Taro said to Hidé, "Yes, delirium without a doubt. Even the mightiest of warriors, suffering grievous injury, sometimes babble nonsense in the aftermath. Blood loss and shock, I believe, are the causes."

Hanako said, "You need a life companion who is unmaimed, who can walk behind you without bringing you shame and derision."

Hidé and Taro continued to ignore her. Hidé said, "Did you see her fling herself beneath the sword?"

"Magnificent," Taro said. "I have seen such actions in kabuki plays, never in real life."

"Whenever I see her empty sleeve," Hidé said, "I will remember with deep gratitude what it cost her to save my life."

"I cannot hold a tray," Hanako said, "nor properly hold a teapot or sake flask. Who can stand to be served by a cripple with only one arm?"

"Fortunately, she still has her sword arm," Taro said. "Who knows when you will once again need her at your side?"

"True," Hidé said. "And one arm is more than sufficient to hold an infant to her breast, or the hand of a child as it learns how to walk."

Hanako could restrain herself no longer. She trembled with emotion. Hot tears of love and gratitude spilled from her eyes in great profusion. She wanted to thank Hidé for his steadfastness, but words could not find their way past her sobs.

Taro excused himself with a bow and rode to the rear. There among Mukai's former vassals, he, too, gave way to uncontrolled tears.

For once, Hidé remained dry-eyed. With the steely self-control he had learned in combat, he allowed no tears to fall, no cries to rack his body. His sorrow for Hanako's injury was profound, but it was nothing compared to the respect he had for her samurai-like courage and the ever-growing love he felt.

The rigor of war and the joy of love. Truly they were one, not two.

Hidé sat erect in the saddle and rode toward Edo.

15

El Paso

Words can damage. Silence can heal. Knowing when to speak and when not to speak is the wisdom of sages.

Knowledge can hinder. Ignorance can liberate. Knowing when to know and when not to know is the wisdom of prophets.

Unimpeded by words, silence, knowledge, or ignorance, a fluent blade cuts cleanly. This is the wisdom of warriors.

SUZUME–NO–KUMO
(1434)

Jimbo looked among the hardy winter plants for sustenance. The act of looking, done with gratitude and respect, was nourishing in itself. Old Abbot Zengen had told him of adepts who had gone so far on the way, they no longer needed to eat. They lived on the air they breathed, the sights they saw, and the pure meditations they accomplished. He had not believed at the time. Now it didn't seem so far-fetched.

From time to time, Jimbo paused and thought of Stark. He knew his former adversary would eventually arrive. He didn't know when. He didn't think it would be very long. Had he been among the small party of samurai and foreigners that had passed Mushindo Monastery three weeks ago? Perhaps. There was no point in speculation.

There were two certainties. Stark would come, and Stark would try to kill him. He wasn't concerned about his own life. That had stopped mattering to him a long time ago. Or maybe not so long. It only seemed that way. Stark's life was what interested him. If he killed Jimbo, his anguish would not decrease. A hunger for revenge drove him from past murders to his next. Jimbo's death at his hands would only increase his suffering and his burden of evil karma. What was to be done? If he showed Stark the new man that he himself had become, a man of true inner peace, liberated from the pain and suffering of hatred, would he, too, see the way? Jimbo would present himself without fear and ask forgiveness. If it was not given, he was ready to die.

He would not fight.

He would not kill.

Never again would he raise his hand in violence.

A small movement on the mustard leaf caught his eye. He carefully removed the tiny beetle and released it on the ground. It scurried rapidly away on six busy legs, its two antennae flicking in every direction. The beetle didn't see him. Its life, as vivid and as fragile as his own, was on a different scale. He bowed respectfully to his fellow sentient creature and continued collecting his supper.

The brush behind him rustled. He recognized the

small, quick movements. It was Kimi, the smart little girl from the village.

"Oh, Jimbo," Kimi said. "You're so quiet I didn't know you were there. I almost stepped on you."

"Thank you for not doing so."

Kimi giggled. "You're so funny. Have you seen Goro? He went looking for you an hour ago. I'm afraid he got lost again."

Jimbo and Kimi both were still. They listened.

"I don't hear him calling your name," Kimi said. "Maybe he wandered into the next valley."

"Please find him. When he gets lost, he gets excited. When he gets excited, he gets careless."

"And then he gets hurt," Kimi said. "If I find him before it's time for your evening meditation, I'll bring him to see you."

"That will be fine."

" 'Bye, Jimbo." She bowed with her hands together in *gassho,* the Buddhist gesture of peace and respect. She had been the first of the village children to imitate Jimbo in this way, and now all the rest did, too, following Kimi's lead as they usually did.

" 'Bye, Kimi." Jimbo returned her bow and her gassho.

Jimbo arrived back at the gates of Mushindo just as two galloping horses approached from the west. He recognized the former monk Yoshi as the rider in the lead. The second man, slumped forward and barely keeping his saddle, was the Reverend Abbot Sohaku.

· · · · ·

Both men were badly wounded, Sohaku more seriously than Yoshi.

"Help me bind him," Yoshi said. "Quickly, lest he bleed to death."

"I will do it," Jimbo said. "Look to yourself. You've been stabbed and cut as well as shot."

"These?" Yoshi gestured at his wounds and laughed. "Superficial."

A large-caliber bullet had entered Sohaku's chest on the left side, penetrated the lung, and blown open a fist-sized hole in his back. It was a wonder he was still alive, but alive he was.

"So, Jimbo," Sohaku said, "what words of wisdom do you have for the dying?"

"Nothing special. We are all dying, are we not?"

Sohaku laughed, briefly. A dribble of blood from his mouth put a stop to that. He said, "You sound more and more like old Zengen every day."

"Reverend Abbot, you must lie down."

"No time. Bind me." He turned to Yoshi. "Go to the armory. Get me another set of armor."

"Yes, Reverend Abbot."

Jimbo said, "You will not need armor where you are going."

"You are mistaken. I am going to battle. I will need the armor to hold me together, or I will never get there."

"Abbot Sohaku, you will fight no more battles."

Sohaku smiled. "I refuse to be killed by a bullet."

Jimbo sealed the wound as best he could with a poultice of medicinal herbs, then wrapped a length of silk tightly around Sohaku's torso. The external bleeding had stopped. Nothing would end the bleeding within except death.

Yoshi helped Sohaku into the new armor and tied the laces securely. His torso, loins, and thighs were now covered by plates of iron, lacquered wood, and leather. He took the helmet but declined the steel collar that would protect his throat and neck, and the lacquer mask for his face.

"Reverend Abbot," Yoshi said, "you risk decapitation."

"Who do you think is coming after us?"

"Lord Shigeru, without a doubt," Yoshi said.

"At my best, with the wind and light in my favor, and every god smiling on me, could I defeat him?"

"Under those conditions, perhaps."

"And wounded as I am, what are my chances?"

"None, Reverend Abbot."

"Exactly. So I prefer to give him the opportunity for a clean strike."

Jimbo said, "Go or stay, death is the result. So stay and die in peace."

"At the end, all my debts have come down to a single one. What I owe Lord Genji, what I owe my ancestors, what I owe myself are the same. Death in battle."

Sohaku bent his leg into the angle it would take when he sat in the saddle. Yoshi tied it in that shape with leather straps. He helped Sohaku to his horse and boosted him into the saddle.

"How is it that you are fighting against Lord Genji?" Jimbo said.

"His supposed prophecies are leading the clan to ruin. I thought to save it by overthrowing him. I failed. Now I must apologize."

Jimbo said nothing.

Sohaku smiled. "You are thinking ritual suicide is the usual form. That is correct. This particular case calls for combat. It is always far more satisfying to slay a rebel than to find him already self-slain. The sincerity of my apology requires that I do what best suits those to whom I am apologizing."

"I understand," Jimbo said, "though I do not agree. If you must die, then it is far better to do so without again raising your own hand in violence. Your karma would be less burdensome."

"You are mistaken, Jimbo. It is my karma that requires combat." Sohaku bowed. The effort made him grimace in pain. "Remember me to your God or Buddha when you go to him. If he's there."

• • • • • •

"Why are you going to the mountains to meditate?" Kimi asked. "I thought that was why you have a meditation hall."

"Jimbo," Goro said, smiling happily.

"For a time, I must be away from everyone and everything," Jimbo said.

"Will you be gone long?"

"Jimbo, Jimbo, Jimbo."

"No, not long."

"We'll wait for you here."

"Your parents will miss you."

Kimi laughed. "My parents have eleven children, silly."

"Then I will see you when I return," Jimbo said. He bowed, his hands in gassho. Kimi did the same.

"Jimbo, Jimbo, Jimbo," Goro said.

• • • • • •

The mountain hut Jimbo used for solitary meditation was less a structure than the suggestion of one. It was made of old branches loosely tied together.

There was more of sky above him than roof, the walls barely obscured his view of the surrounding trees, and neither seriously impeded wind or weather. Old Abbot Zengen had built the hut. It was very much like his single–brush-stroke renderings of mountains, animals, and people. What was not there more vividly described the subject than what was.

Sohaku's words weighed heavily on Jimbo.

It is my karma that requires combat, he had said.

Was this also Jimbo's karma?

He was not the man he had been. Of this he was certain. Less clear was whether he had completely liberated himself from the past. Had he abandoned all sense of self as he believed, and was he thus acting solely to guide Stark toward his own liberation from anguish? Or were the deceptions of a most subtle and insidious pride binding him yet more tightly in delusion?

Jimbo's breathing deepened, and deepened yet more. Inhalations and exhalations grew imperceptible. The contents of his mind and the contents of the world were not to be distinguished. He entered the vast emptiness at the same moment it entered him.

• • • • •

Mary Anne came out of the cabin with a bright smile on her face, expecting to see Stark. When she saw Cruz, she turned and ran back inside.

Cruz grabbed her before she could turn the shotgun on him and hit her in the temple with the barrel of his pistol. The two little girls screamed and held each other.

By the time Tom, Peck, and Haylow came in, Cruz had already stripped Mary Anne naked.

"What about the little bitches?" Tom said.

"Better take them outside," Haylow said. "They don't need to see this."

"Strip them, too," Cruz said. Mary Anne wasn't quite conscious. He stood her up against the wall, raised her hands together above her head, and drove his knife through both palms, pinning her there. She woke up screaming.

"Jesus, Mary, Joseph," Peck said, "all the blessed saints, Mother of God, and the Holy Trinity."

"Ethan," Tom said.

Haylow shielded the little girls and held them against his big body.

"I said strip them," Cruz said.

"Not them," Tom said. "They ain't done nothing."

"They were born," Cruz said. "Are you doing what I said or not?"

Tom and Peck looked at each other. They looked at Cruz. His shoulders were loose and his hand was close to his pistol.

Peck said, "We always do what you say, Ethan, you know that."

"I don't see you doing it."

Haylow's face was wet with tears. He didn't say anything. He didn't make a sound. He punched the older girl hard in the jaw, then he punched the younger one. Both girls were lifted off the floor by the force of the huge man's blows, and landed hard. They might have been alive. They were as still as the dead. He undressed the younger one very gently, while Tom and Peck, following his example, did the same for the older one.

"No, no, no!" Mary Anne screamed hopelessly.

Cruz picked the older one up by her hair and held her face an inch away from Mary Anne's.

"What's her name?"

Mary Anne screamed and wept.

Cruz said to Peck, "Give me your knife." Peck gave it to him. Cruz held it against the girl's throat. "I said, what's her name?"

"Becky," Mary Anne said, "Becky. Please, please—"

Cruz drove the knife into the girl's belly and slit her open to her heart. He dropped the small corpse at the screaming woman's feet and went for the younger girl.

Tom ran out of the cabin.

Peck fell to the floor and backed away on the seat of his pants. When he hit the wall and couldn't back away anymore, he turned and vomited, and kept vomiting even after his stomach was empty.

Haylow just stood there, crying.

"What's her name?" Cruz said.

"Oh, God, oh, God," Mary Anne said.

Cruz put the child on the table and got the ax from beside the stove.

"Louise!" Mary Anne screamed, as if the name would save the life. "Louise!"

Cruz struck so hard, he cleaved the table under the girl in two. The severed head bounced on the floor and rolled to the foot of the bed. He stared at Mary Anne and said very quietly, "Now it's your turn."

She couldn't have heard his voice over the sound of her own screams.

· · · · ·

Jimbo didn't know how long he'd stayed in meditation. When he opened his eyes, the light was the same as when he'd closed them. A moment had passed, or days. When he moved, the moisture frozen in his clothing crackled. His knees, tight from being bent, ached as he took his legs out of the lotus posture. More than a moment. Two or three days, at least.

He left the hut and went to the pile of rocks near the streambed. During the floods that came every ten years or so, these rocks were streambed, too. Now they were dry. Jimbo removed several of them until he saw the oilcloth. He reached in and pulled out the package. Where should he unwrap it? Here in the open? Back at Mushindo? No, he knew the perfect place. He went back into the hut.

In a structure that was more not-hut than hut, the man who was more not–Ethan Cruz than Ethan Cruz took on the appearance of what he had once been.

Here was his hat, crumpled and crushed out of shape. He made a hat block out of twigs and wet the hat with snow melted in his hands. By tomorrow morning, it would look right. Right enough, anyway.

Here were his shirt, trousers, jacket, and boots. They smelled of old sweat and mold. He put them on.

Here were the barrels and stock of his double-barreled double-ought shotgun. He reassembled it. In a separate oilcloth were six shells. He loaded the shotgun and discarded the spares. He wouldn't need to reload.

Here was his holster, and in it, the .36 Colt Manual Cruz had given him a lifetime ago.

You told me you've been herding cattle, boy.

Yes, sir. That's what I said, and that's what I've been at.

Uh-huh. That's what you've been at is what I've heard, and more. Might you have neglected a small detail about your herding?

I'm not sure what you mean, sir.

You can cut the sir shit, Ethan. The detail I mean, and you know it, is you've been herding cattle attained by hangable means.

They can only hang me once. Highway robbery's hangable, and if they want me for that, they'll come soon enough anyway. And there're those two fools I had to shoot in here. That's hangable, too.

Why, you've grown up to be a rustler, a highway robber, and a fast gun, boy.

Ethan waited, expecting a lecture.

Cruz said, You've done me proud. Make me feel like my life's had some kind of reason after all. Sure don't get any reason mongering whores, let me tell you.

Cruz offered his hand to shake.

I'm the father of Ethan Cruz. Well, stepfather. Close enough. Goddamn. Sometimes things turn out all right after all.

That night, Cruz gave Ethan the .36 Colt off his own hip.

Many favor the .44 Army model. Heavier bullet, surer kill, they reason. But there is a singular virtue to the .36 for a man who has the wherewithal to perfect his aim. It's half a pound lighter than the .44. You can draw it that much faster. One day, when it's the other man down and dying, you'll remember me with a special fondness.

Ethan felt his chest tighten. He wanted to tell

Cruz he'd remember him with a special fondness, .36 Colt or no .36 Colt, but he didn't. Ethan wasn't a man of many words. So all he said was, What if you need it? It won't do you any good on my hip.

Ethan could see by the smile on Cruz's face and the wetness that sprang up in his eyes that he took his meaning without it being said. Cruz was the man of many words that Ethan wasn't, but on this occasion, he didn't discourse on it as he might have. In fact, he didn't say anything at all for a while. He just sat there smiling.

Then he said, Need it for what? I'm not getting into any gunfights. Cruz showed him his derringer. This is more than enough for this old gambling whoremonger. Any shooting be done, be done at a range so close it be no range at all.

· · · · ·

When Jimbo returned to the monastery, most of it was gone. Charred ruins lined a huge pit where the meditation hall had been. The ashes of funeral pyres were everywhere. All that remained intact were the outer walls, the bathhouse, the abbot's solitary meditation room, and the temporary prison hut Sohaku's men had constructed for Shigeru.

Most of the village children seemed to be here, playing in the wreckage and speculating on the bits and pieces they found.

"Look. Here's someone's forearm bone."

"No it's not. It's just a piece of wood."

"Arm. See? The knob at the end."

"Horrible. Throw it away."

"Be careful. Here comes an outsider."

"That's the one who was with Lord Genji. The one with two guns."

"It isn't him. It's another."

"Run! He's going to kill us!"

"Jimbo," Goro said, smiling and shuffling forward. "Jimbo, Jimbo."

"No, Goro, don't. It's not Jimbo. Come away, quickly."

Kimi said, "It *is* Jimbo." She went running up to him, her eyes wide with surprise. "Why are you dressed like that?"

"I have to do something I can't do in the other clothes." He looked at the pit. It looked like all the powder in the adjacent armory had exploded at once. "What happened?"

"There was a great battle while you were gone—"

"Hundreds of samurai died—"

"Lord Genji was trapped—"

"Jimbo, Jimbo, Jimbo—"

"—Shigeru's head in a box—"

"—muskets on the walls—"

"—mounted samurai charged—"

"—covered in blood from head to toe—"

Not all the jumble of information was clear. He heard enough to know the outsider with Lord Genji was named Su-ta-ku and had survived the battle. As soon as the fighting ended, he had searched the ruins of Mushindo for Jimbo. A woman of unbelievable beauty, certainly a famous geisha, had asked Kimi if she knew where Jimbo was, and Kimi had told the lady he had gone into the mountains to meditate. The lady had then spoken to Su-ta-ku in his own language. Kimi didn't know what she had said.

In answer to the children's demands, he told them about his timeless meditation, the moisture turning to ice in his clothing, the visitation of three angels sent by Maitreya, the Buddha of Future Times, proclaiming the eternal happiness of the village children, for they were all to be reborn in Sukhavati, the Pure Land of Amida, the Buddha of Compassionate Light.

That night, after the children were gone, he walked through the altered grounds of the monastery. Stark had been here. He would be back. Was Jimbo a better gunfighter than Stark? Once, maybe. Not now. He hadn't been practicing, and Stark certainly had. Stark would drop him before he had his gun clear of his holster.

That would be too easy. Jimbo would take him from ambush. Stark was too angry and too grieved to be as careful as he should. An ambush would work.

•   •   •   •   •

It was some days back in Edo before Emily was sufficiently recovered for Stark to leave. The process was speeded by Genji's encouraging her to take an active part in the design of the chapel for the rebuilt Quiet Crane Palace. There were still dark circles under her eyes, and her lightness of spirit had yet to return. That would take more time. The horrendous carnage she had seen at such close quarters wasn't easily forgotten. Still, she was smiling once again.

"Must you really go back to the monastery so soon?"

"Yes, Emily, I must."

She looked at the .44 on his hip and the .32

tucked into his belt and didn't ask any other questions. "You'll come back?"

"I intend to."

Emily suddenly put her arms around him and hugged him tightly. He could feel her tears on his neck. "Be careful, Matthew. Promise me you'll be careful."

"I promise."

Genji sent Taro and a contingent of five samurai to escort Stark. They understood that they were to allow Stark to proceed to Mushindo alone once they reached the village. He spoke no Japanese and they spoke no English. They rode in silence.

Stark thought the silence would suit him, but it did not. Memories came. He couldn't keep them away. His hatred of Cruz was not as strong as his love for Mary Anne.

Mary Anne said, This is the happiest day of my life, Matthew, I swear it is.

Mine, too, he said.

He stood with Mary Anne, Becky, and Louise in the shade of ironwoods on land he lawfully owned. I thought I'd build our cabin here. Over there, a garden. Flowers and vegetables. Range the herd there.

Becky said, Where's the pigs going to be?

No pigs, Stark said.

Becky blinked in disbelief.

No pigs, she said to Louise.

No pigs, Louise said.

Mary Anne looked at Stark.

Why, those are the very first words she's ever spoken.

No pigs? Stark said.

Mary Anne nodded. No pigs, she said.

No pigs, Louise said.

No pigs, Becky said, laughing.

Soon they were all laughing. They laughed so much, they couldn't keep standing. Later, they all sat under the ironwoods and just smiled and smiled.

Louise never became exactly what you'd call a talker. That was Becky's specialty. But she did say a word or two from time to time after that. Sometimes the shape of a cloud would make her speak, or the presence of the wind, or its absence. Sometimes she'd have a short conversation with an ironwood or a passing deer. And when she was happy, which was often, Stark would hear her mumbling to herself, No pigs.

If he kept thinking about them, his thoughts would slow his hand down and tighten his shoulders and Cruz would shoot him dead without half trying. He knew it, but he couldn't stop himself. He could just about see them before his eyes, smiling, laughing, talking.

· · · · ·

Stark tied his horse to a tree and walked toward the monastery with the .32 in his left hand and the .44 in his right. He wasn't going to a quick-draw contest. This wasn't iaido with guns. He would find Ethan Cruz and kill him. That's all. He had to be careful. Cruz could be anywhere. Stark wished he had a shotgun.

· · · · ·

The little troop of children followed Kimi over the back wall of Mushindo.

"Be quiet," she whispered. "We'll be punished if we're caught."

One of the other little girls put her hand over Goro's mouth. "Quiet."

Goro nodded. When the girl removed her hand, he put his own hand over his mouth.

They hid behind the fallen timbers of the meditation hall and watched the abbot's hut. The new outsider was coming from the village. Jimbo was probably in the hut meditating. When the stranger came, Jimbo would come out to meet him. They were dressed very much alike. What did they plan to do? Whatever it was, they would surely do it together.

· · · · ·

Jimbo stood completely motionless in the shadow of a tree and watched Stark approach the monastery. He was twenty yards away with his back toward Jimbo, a gun in each hand. When Stark went through the gate, Jimbo quietly put down the shotgun he held. He'd already removed the shells and put them in his pocket. Now he followed Stark.

· · · · ·

Just inside the gate, Stark moved to the side, keeping his back against the wall. He thought he heard something move in the wreckage. Cruz could be there. Or he could be inside the hut, the bathhouse, the cell. Or he could be behind them. Or under them. Or obscured in any shadow. He checked his guns again. They were both cocked. He stepped away from the wall and walked slowly toward the wreckage. Someone was definitely there. It had to be Cruz. Stark hoped Cruz, if he really was there, had only pistols like he did. If he had a carbine or, worse, a shotgun, he would cut Stark down before Stark was close enough to do him harm.

Stark moved forward. He had no choice.

"Not another move, Stark."

Stark felt the cold metal touch of a gun barrel against the back of his neck.

"Drop the guns or die."

* * * * *

Jimbo knew Stark wouldn't disarm. Not now. Not after hunting him so long and coming so far and finally finding him. Not even if finding him meant it was Cruz's gun—because it was Cruz he thought he'd found—against his head instead of the other way around. Not even if it meant he would die instead of Cruz. He had come looking for death. If it couldn't be Cruz's, his own would do.

"Any other than you drop the guns," Jimbo said, saying what Cruz would say, "I blow your head off."

Stark did exactly what Jimbo expected him to do. He dove to one side and spun around as he fell, firing both guns even before he had a clear shot. Jimbo had him in his sights all the way. His heart was calm, his hand was steady, his aim undistorted by emotions. He pointed the barrel of his .36 slightly to the right of Stark and fired less than half a heartbeat before Stark's heavy .44 bullet tore through his chest.

"Jimbo!"

This time it wasn't Goro, but Kimi. Horrified, she leaped to her feet and started running toward Jimbo. The other children were close behind, Goro with his hand still over his mouth. But when Stark stood, they stopped and dropped to their knees, bowing respectfully. In the village, Lord Genji's samurai had told everyone Stark was the equal of a lord, and must be so honored. They pressed their foreheads to the earth even as they held each other and cried.

Jimbo saw nothing but sky and felt nothing bodily at all. At first, he thought he was adrift from his physical being, that this was the very moment before his consciousness dissolved back into the void. Then he saw Stark.

Stark stood over Cruz. It seemed as though he'd spent his whole life looking for him. Now he'd found him. He'd shot him. The eyes looking up at Stark were clear. There was no pain showing in the face.

Jimbo wanted to tell Stark his family hadn't suffered, he'd shot them clean when he'd found them and they'd died right away. This is what he wanted to say, but the bullet had torn his heart and his right lung and he didn't have a voice left. It was just as well. Telling the lie was more a mercy to himself than to Stark. Stark didn't want words from him, he wanted revenge, and he'd gotten it. Now it was up to Stark to find what he really needed. Jimbo wished God's grace for Matthew Stark, and Buddha's compassion, and the protection and guidance of the ten thousand gods. He would have smiled, but he knew it would be misunderstood, so he kept the smile in his heart.

Stark pointed his .44 at Cruz's left eye and the .32 at Cruz's right, and fired three times with the .44 and four times with the .32. He would have fired more if there had been more bullets left in his guns. But after three and after four, the hammers he kept cocking fell on spent cartridges. When he finally stopped pulling the triggers of his empty guns, he was looking at a dead body with blood, shattered bone, and gore where a face should have been. He holstered the .44, tucked the .32 back in his belt, and walked away.

The children kept their heads bowed to the ground until Stark was gone. Then they ran toward Jimbo, only to stop short when they saw what was left of him.

Only Goro kept going. He dropped to his knees beside Jimbo and screamed and moaned. He waved his arms helplessly over the body as if trying to embrace what was no longer there.

Kimi knelt beside Goro and put one of her arms across his shoulder. With stubborn determination, she overlaid her memories of Jimbo over the ruined face, and saw him as she would remember him.

"Don't cry, Goro," she said, though she was crying herself. "This isn't Jimbo anymore. He's gone ahead to Sukhavati, the Pure Land, so when we get there, he'll greet us, and we won't be afraid. Everything will be wonderful in Sukhavati."

She was sure it would be because Jimbo had said it would, and he had always told them the truth. She believed it, but she was not in the Pure Land, she was still on this sad and terrible earth, and here everything was not wonderful.

Jimbo was dead.

She and Goro held each other and wept.

· · · · ·

Stark got on his horse. He could hear the cries of weeping children inside the monastery walls. He heard them, and he felt nothing.

Not better.

Not worse.

The same as before, which was nothing at all.

He put his boot heels to his horse's ribs and the horse moved.

And the earth was without form, and void; and darkness was upon the face of the deep.

V

NEW YEAR'S DAY

*The First
New Moon after the
Winter Solstice,
In the 16th Year
of the Emperor
Komei*

16

Quiet Crane

On his deathbed, Lord Yakuo received a visit from Father Vierra. Father Vierra asked him what he regretted most in his life.

Lord Yakuo smiled.

Persistent, as the Christian priests tend to be in these matters, Father Vierra asked if it was something he had done or something he had not done.

Lord Yakuo said regret was an elixir for poets. He had lived the life of a rough, unlettered warrior, and would die as one.

Father Vierra, seeing the smile on Lord Yakuo's lips, asked if he regretted being a warrior instead of a poet.

Lord Yakuo continued to smile, but did not answer.

While Father Vierra asked questions, Lord Yakuo entered the Pure Land.

SUZUME-NO-KUMO
(1615)

A whole year has passed," Emily said. "I can hardly believe it."

"More than a year," Genji said. "You arrived on your own New Year's Day, six weeks before ours."

"Why, yes, that's true, isn't it?" Emily smiled, bemused at her own forgetfulness. "Somehow it went by without my notice."

"The children's Christmas pageant had so much of your attention," Heiko said, "it's no wonder."

"Zephaniah would have been happy to see it," Stark said. "So many promising young Christians."

They sat in the large room overlooking the innermost courtyard of Quiet Crane. The reconstruction of the palace had been so meticulously exact, every tree, bush, and pebble in the garden seemed the same as before. The view was only slightly altered, in the northeast corner, by a steeple topped with a small white cross. Genji's architects had performed brilliantly. Emily's wishes for a chapel were fulfilled while the requirement of not flaunting its existence to the rest of Edo was also met. The cross could be seen from almost every inner vantage point within the palace and from nowhere outside of it. A strategic placement of walls and tall trees with especially dense foliage was employed for the purpose.

The chapel was not used for sermons or services of the usual kind. Emily was not a preacher. She was far too shy, and not nearly as certain as a preacher must be of the exclusive truth of her faith. In a year, she had seen enough of charity, compassion, selflessness, devotion, and every Christian virtue displayed by nonbelievers to doubt exclusivity was part of God's plan. Great is the mystery of godliness, she said to herself, and added a silent amen.

Instead of preaching, she taught Sunday school to curious children. Their parents, often followers of both Buddha and the Way of the Gods, apparently had no objection to lessons from yet another faith. How one person could even think of believing in three religions at the same time was yet another of the many unimaginable mysteries Emily had encountered in Japan.

The stories and parables she told, translated by Heiko, found great favor among her young listeners, who steadily grew in number. Lately, some of the mothers had been staying to listen, too. So far, none of the men had come. Genji had offered, but she could not permit it. If he came, his vassals would follow out of duty, and their wives and concubines and children, all out of duty to Genji, and not from the hunger for God within their own breasts.

The samurai all practiced the disciplines of the Zen sect, a religion without preaching, indeed without any doctrine she could perceive, all serious and grim and silent. Was it a religion at all? She once asked Genji to explain it to her, and he just laughed.

There is little to explain. I only play at it. I am too lazy to truly do it.

What is done?

He sat in the contortionist position called the lotus, with each foot on the opposite thigh, and closed his eyes.

And what is it you are doing? It seems to me you are doing nothing at all.

I am letting go, Genji said.

Letting go? Letting go of what?

First, bodily tension. Second, thoughts. Third, everything else.

To what end?

You are so much a person of the West, Genji said, always thinking of ends. The means are the end. You sit. You let go.

And once you have let go, then what?

Then you let go of letting go.

I don't understand.

Genji smiled, uncrossed his legs, and said, Old Zengen would say that's a good beginning. I'm not a good example. I never get beyond letting go of bodily tension, and often I don't even get that far. When the Reverend Abbot Tokuken comes down from the mountains, he will explain better. He was old Zengen's best disciple. But we shouldn't count on it. He may have attained such clarity, he can no longer speak at all.

You say such silly things sometimes, she said. The greater the clarity, the more precise the explanation, the more perfect the transmitted understanding. That is why God gave us the gift of speech.

Zengen once told me, the greatest clarity is profound silence. In fact, those are the words that sent Tokuken into the mountains. He heard them, and the next day he departed.

When was that?

Five or six years ago. Maybe seven.

Emily smiled to herself. She thought she could be in Japan for the rest of her life and still not understand. She looked up and saw Genji smiling at her. Perhaps it wasn't so important to understand after all. Perhaps what was most important was to care.

"Good morning, lord." Hidé bowed at the entrance to the room. Hanako, bowing behind him, cradled their newborn.

"Have you named him yet?" Genji said.

"Yes, lord. We thought to call him Iwao."

"A good name," Genji said. " 'Steady as stone.' May he be so, like his father."

Hidé bowed, embarrassed at the compliment. "The father is thick as stone, anyway. I hope the son will be brighter."

"May I hold him?" Heiko said.

"Please," Hanako said.

She moved with such ease and grace the absence of her left arm did not call attention to itself. Rather, one sensed only an unusual degree of gentleness in her every movement. She had, Heiko thought, gained in womanliness rather than lost.

Heiko said, "What a handsome boy. He will surely break many hearts in the years to come."

"Oh, no," Hanako said, "I will not permit it. He will fall in love once, and he will be true from beginning to end. He will break not a single one."

"Hidé, call in our clan historian," Genji said. "Your son is apparently destined to be the first and last of his kind."

"You may laugh at me," Hanako said, also laughing, "but I see nothing lacking in a simple, straightforward heart."

"That is because you have been fortunate," Heiko said, "to win the affection of just such a one."

"I am nothing of the sort," Hidé said. "My tendencies and habits are toward laziness, insincerity, and dissipation. If my behavior is better than that, it is only because I no longer have the freedom to be worse."

"Easily cured," Genji said. "Say the word and I will instantly dissolve this most inconvenient marriage."

Hidé and Hanako looked at each other warmly.

Hidé said, "I fear it is too late. I have grown too used to my captivity."

Stark said to Emily, "May I wish you a happy birthday now, Emily, since I won't be here on that day?"

"Thank you, Matthew." Emily was surprised he remembered. "Thank you very much. Time passes so quickly, it will be no time before I'm an old maid." She said it sweetly, not to elicit a compliment or a denial, but as something she truly looked forward to. The more beautiful a woman, the more she had to lose with the change of every season. Here in Japan, she had at last no beauty at all, and so nothing whose presence or loss called for the least lamentation.

Heiko said, "You're not even close to being an old maid. Eighteen is considered only the beginning of womanhood, the time of the first true blooming."

Genji said, "We have a saying. 'Even cheap tea tastes good on the first brewing. Even a witch's daughter is beautiful at eighteen.' "

Emily laughed. "Why, Lord Genji, I don't know if I should take comfort in that."

"Really, my lord," Heiko said, "is that your best compliment?"

"I suppose it doesn't exactly illustrate the point, does it?"

Heiko saw by the way Emily looked at Genji, her very eyes smiling, her skin aglow, that she had taken no offense.

"Shall I?" Hanako asked.

"Certainly," Heiko said, giving her back her son.

"How far will you go?" Hanako said.

"Nothing has been decided," Heiko said. "I think, perhaps, San Francisco, for the time being. At least, until the civil war in America is at an end."

"How exciting. And how frightening. I cannot imagine living outside of Japan."

"I cannot imagine it, either," Heiko said. "Fortunately, experiencing it, I will not have to imagine."

"What an honor," Hanako said, "that Lord Genji has chosen you to be his eyes and ears across the sea."

"Yes," Heiko said. "A high honor indeed."

America? Why must I go to America?

Because I trust no one else so completely.

Forgive me for saying so, my lord, but if exile is the reward, it would be more comforting to be trusted less.

You are not being exiled.

I am being forced from my homeland, across the sea, to a barbarous land whose ways are completely unknown to me. If this is not exile, what is it?

Preparation for the future. I have had a vision. In a very short time, everything will change. Anarchy and upheaval will destroy the ways we have followed for two thousand years. We must have a place of refuge. That is your task. To find such a place.

Genji, if you no longer love me, just say so. Such an elaborate ruse is unnecessary.

I love you. I will always love you.

Your words and your actions are not in harmony. A man does not send the woman he loves half a world away.

He does if he intends to join her.

You will leave Japan? Impossible. You are a Great Lord. You may well become Shogun in time. You cannot leave.

How much of the impossible has already happened, Genji said, foreseen in vision after vision by one Okumichi after another. It seems impossible, yes, but can we doubt it? You will go to America, and one day, I will follow.

When will that day come?

I'm not certain. Perhaps another vision will instruct me.

I don't believe you.

After all that we have been through, how can you doubt me? Why would I ask you to go, if it were not true? Why would I commission Stark to guide and protect you? Why would I send a fortune in gold with you? Heiko, as strange as it seems, the only explanation is the one I have given you. This is proof of my love, not proof of its absence.

She consented. What else could she do? She believed he loved her still. She could see it in his eyes, and feel it in his touch. But he was lying to her. About what, and why?

Ever since he had gone to talk with Kawakami before the fight at Mushindo Monastery, something had changed. What had Kawakami said? Genji claimed he had said nothing special, had only invited him to a meeting so he could taunt him. That couldn't be true. Kawakami had said something. What?

Emily said, "Are you not from Texas, Matthew?"

"I am."

"Then will you fight in the war when you return home?"

"He cannot fight," Genji said, "at least, not right away. He is to establish a trading company and hold it as our proxy."

"I will not fight in any case," Stark said. "I was a child in Ohio. I became a man in Texas. How could I bear arms against either?"

"I am glad of it," Emily said, "in that you will not fight for slavery."

"Lord." A samurai knelt at the doorway. "A messenger from the harbor has arrived. The morning tide has begun to flow. The ship must soon depart."

"Still bound to the tide," Genji said.

"Not for much longer," Stark said. "Captain McCain told me the *Star* will be outfitted with a steam engine when it ports in San Francisco."

"Steam may liberate ships," Genji said, "but not our hearts. Like the sun and the moon, we are tied forever to the gravity of the sea."

"Isn't it the other way around?" Emily said. "Doesn't the sea respond to the movements of the sun and moon?"

"For us it is the opposite," Genji said, "and always will be."

Heiko, Hanako, and Emily poured sake for the men. Then Genji, Hidé, and Stark poured sake for the women. They raised their cups together for the last time.

"May a bold tide bear you forth," Genji said, looking straight into Heiko's eyes, "and the tide of remembrance bring you home."

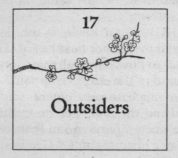

17

Outsiders

*Gods and Buddhas, ancestors and ghosts, demons
and angels, none of them can live your life or die
your death. Neither foreknowledge nor seeing into
the minds of others will show you the way that is
truly yours.*

    This much I have learned.
    The rest is for you to discover.

SUZUME–NO–KUMO
(1860)

Emily stood with Genji at the window overlooking Edo Bay. The *Star of Bethlehem* was still visible, just barely, on the brink of the horizon.

"You will miss her very much," Emily said.

"I know she will find happiness where she goes,"
Genji said, "so I am happy for her."

   •   •   •   •   •

Genji's thirty men were dressed in black, anony-
mous as ninjas. He recognized Hidé and Taro, because

he knew them so well, and several of the others by their horses. Behind the scarf that masked his own identity, he grimaced. What did it say about a leader that he knew a horse better than he knew a man? Perhaps, if that leader was a cavalryman, it said a good thing, and not a bad. Perhaps.

"There is one easy way out of the village," he said. "Do not obstruct it. Let them come to you. Watch for anyone trying to go over the surrounding hills. Forty-one men and boys, and sixty-eight women and girls. Every one must be accounted for. Am I understood?"

"Yes, lord." The men bowed. No one asked why they were in disguise. No one wondered aloud why their lord had such an interest in a miserable eta village in Hino Domain. No one questioned his need to lead the attack himself. They understood all they were required to understand, that they would enter the village and kill every living person, so they said, Yes, lord, and bowed.

"Then let us proceed."

Swords drawn, Hidé and fifteen men charged through the village. The horses thundering among them roused everyone not already wakened by the dawn sun. Some were already outside engaged in the earliest tasks of the day. They were cut down at once, many others the moment they stepped from their dwellings. When they reached the other end of the village, Hidé's men dismounted and came back toward the center, killing everyone they encountered. The remaining samurai entered from the near side on foot or circled the outskirts to catch those who tried to flee.

Genji did not hesitate. He killed along with his men. He killed men who tried to fight with farm tools, and he killed men who ran. He entered hut after hut and killed children in their beds, and mothers who shielded their infants, and the infants. He looked at the faces of the dead and saw no one he sought.

Perhaps Kawakami had lied. That so many people should die because of it pained Genji, but he knew the pain would be greater if Kawakami had told the truth. Hope for the lesser pain was on the rise when he entered the last hut near the center of the village.

Hidé was already inside. He was staring at a woman huddling in fear with her daughter. Between them was an infant, gurgling in innocent contentment. A young man stood protectively in front of them, a threshing tool in his hands. An older man, the father of the household, lay dead at their feet.

"Lord," Hidé said, his horrified eyes going from the women to Genji and back again.

Genji couldn't bring himself to look at her right away. Hidé's eyes told him what he would see. He examined the fallen man. Was there a hint of Heiko's determination in the set of the older man's mouth? He thought there was.

He heard someone enter behind him and stop suddenly.

Taro said, "Lord." There was the same tone of shocked distress in his voice that had been in Hidé's.

Genji could avoid it no longer. He forced himself to look up and saw his own damnation.

In the older woman, a blurred and undeniable reflection of Heiko's face peered fearfully at him through the years and toil of outcast life. The young woman clinging to her was clearly her daughter. Her rough prettiness, her bloom of youth, were reminders of the greater, subtler beauty with which Genji was so familiar. The brave young man with the threshing tool must be her husband, the infant their child. Heiko's mother, sister, niece, and brother-in-law. On the ground, her father. Somewhere, in another part of the carnage, he knew he would find her two brothers.

"Lord," Taro said again.

Genji said, "Let no one else enter this hut."

"Yes, lord," Taro said. Genji heard him step out.

"You may join him," Genji said.

"I will not leave you alone," Hidé said.

"Go," Genji said. He wanted no one to witness his crime. Let it be his eternal shame alone.

"I will not, my lord," Hidé said, and moving suddenly, he cut down the youth in the next instant. Before Genji could react, the next quick strokes of Hidé's blade felled the two women, then, with but the slightest hesitation, sliced open the baby's throat.

"Taro," Hidé said.

Taro stepped in. "Yes?"

"Take Lord Genji to his horse and ride with him to our gathering place. I will complete the task with the rest of the men."

Taro bowed. "I will do so."

Genji stumbled out into the morning light. He hardly knew what he was doing, or where he was going.

"My lord?" Taro tried to lead him to his horse.

"No." Genji stood and watched as Hidé searched among the corpses, taking great care to examine their faces. He pointed out the bodies of two men. Genji knew they must be Heiko's brothers. These were dragged into the hut Genji had just left, and the hut was set on fire. Only when all the bodies were counted and they and the entire village were ablaze, only then did they mount their horses and ride away.

Was Genji's guilt less because Hidé had prevented him from doing the actual killing? No. It was Hidé's sword, but it was Genji's intention. And what had he accomplished? The living evidence was gone. It didn't guarantee that Heiko's secret would remain one. Others may know, in other villages. Some surviving intimates of Kawakami could have heard a hint or two while sharing sake with him and viewing the moon. Killing the family had been a necessary measure, but he couldn't kill enough people to securely seal away the truth even if he killed half the nation. The only place Heiko was sure to be safe was outside Japan. The truth would not follow her that far, and if it did, it would have no meaning.

In America, few even knew Japan existed, much less eta.

•   •   •   •   •

Genji didn't deny missing Heiko. Had Emily wished he would? She couldn't read his expression. There was a smile on his lips, of course, the small smile that was always there. Was there a hint of sorrow in his eyes? There had to be.

She felt a tiny pang in her heart she hoped was not jealousy. What did she truly feel? Heiko had been her very best friend in Japan, and a true friend indeed. Emily would miss her sorely, though her continued presence would certainly have further complicated her already tangled emotions. Love was hard enough when it was plain and simple, as it was for Hidé and Hanako. How much harder it was when two women were in love with the same man, and those two women were close friends. Not that there was any kind of competition, or even a hint of awareness about her feelings on either Genji's or Heiko's part. Emily was not a consideration. She was an outsider, grotesque, misshapen, and very difficult to look upon. She would not be loved. But she was free to give away her heart, even if no one else ever knew. That was enough. Wasn't it? Or did she wish to be thought beautiful once again, as she had been in America? Sometimes she thought she did, despite the pain it would inevitably bring to her, if only Genji thought she was beautiful, too.

"How can you be so sure?" Emily said. "Happiness is not necessarily every person's lot."

"Just a feeling."

"A feeling. You're not claiming to have dreamed of her happiness, I hope."

"No. I'll have no more dreams, not of the kind you mean."

"Do you really accept that?" Emily's question was earnest. If he would surrender all pretensions to prophecy, he would be that much closer to salvation.

"Well," Genji said, "just one more. Will you allow it?"

Emily frowned and looked away. "It's not a matter of my allowing or not allowing anything, Lord Genji, as you well know. And please stop smiling at me that way. I am not amused in the least by blasphemy."

Genji didn't stop smiling. He did stop speaking, however, and after a minute of silence, Emily regretted the harsh tone she had used with him. His attitude toward religion was painfully unserious. If every future patron of Christianity in Japan were like him, it would not be long before the True Word was just another sect of Buddhism or the Way of the Gods, not by design, but by a benign and neglectful absorption. This disturbed her, but not as much it once did, not as much as it still should. When she thought of Genji, religion was no longer the first thing on her mind.

"Can you still see it?" Genji said.

"Yes, I think so," Emily said. "There." A flash of white at the edge of the world. A sail on a mast of the *Star of Bethlehem*. Or windblown spray from the crest of a distant wave.

When had she fallen in love with him, and why? How could she do something so foolish, so hopeless, so certain to end in misery?

"My lord." Taro bowed at the entrance of the room.

"Yes?"

"I regret to inform you there was an incident in Yokohama earlier today."

"What sort of incident?"

"Some of Lord Gaiho's men made remarks. Ours felt compelled to respond."

"With remarks of their own?"

"No, lord. With swords. Five of our men were hurt, none seriously."

"That many? Have our skills eroded so badly in so short a time?"

"No, lord." For the first time since he began his report, Taro looked pleased. "Seven of Lord Gaiho's vassals have returned to the source, and an equal number are likely to follow in short order, thanks to their injuries."

"Who investigated?"

"I did, lord. Immediately after the confrontation."

"So you were in Yokohama," Genji said, "but arrived too late to prevent violence."

"No, my lord." Taro bowed deeply. "I was there when the violence began. I personally struck the first blow."

Genji frowned. "That is disappointing. You are aware that the Shogun's equanimity is lessened by signs of disorder in front of outsiders."

"Yes, lord."

"You are aware that Yokohama has a high population of outsiders, both resident and visitor."

"Yes, lord."

"Well?"

"Intolerable insults were given." Taro's eyes went briefly to Emily. "I believe I responded appropriately."

"I see," Genji said. "Yes, I think perhaps you did. You may give me a fuller report later. In the meantime, inform Lord Saiki. We are sure to receive an admonishment from the Shogun. He should prepare a formal written response."

"Yes, lord."

"Remember to speak loudly and clearly. Lord Saiki's hearing is not what it was before the explosion at Mushindo Monastery."

"Yes, lord." Taro smiled. "At Hidé's suggestion, we have begun the practice of augmenting our oral reports with written ones."

"Very good. My commendations to Hidé. And, Taro, thank you for defending the lady's honor."

"No thanks are necessary, lord." Taro bowed in Emily's direction. "She is the outsider of the prophecy."

When he was gone, Emily said, "Why did he bow to me?"

"Did he?"

"Yes. So it appeared."

"He was happy to see you, I suppose."

"I don't think so," Emily said. Her intuition told her she was one of the subjects of the conversation. She hadn't heard her name—Eh-meh-ri—but Taro had looked at her as he spoke and Genji had pointedly not done so. "I've caused trouble again, haven't I?"

"How can you?" Genji smiled disarmingly. "You haven't done anything, have you?"

"My presence alone is trouble."

"Don't be silly, Emily. That's not true, and you should know it."

"Please. I'm not quite the child you seem to think I am."

"I don't think you're a child."

"I know antiforeign sentiment is running very high. I'm afraid I'm becoming a terrible burden to you. Please tell me. What happened?"

Genji looked at her open face and the earnest, guileless expression upon it and sighed. He found it extremely difficult to lie to her, even for her own good. "Some ignorant vassals of a hostile lord made remarks. There was a minor altercation. Some of my men were injured, none seriously, according to Taro."

"And the other lord's vassals?"

"Are fewer this afternoon than they were this morning."

"Oh, no." Emily dropped her face into her hands. "I might as well have murdered them myself."

Genji sat on the chair beside hers. He sat upright on the edge as he had learned to do, instead of collapsing into it as he had in the past. His inner organs felt much better when they remained where they belonged, instead of being unnaturally crushed together. He put his hands lightly on her shoulders. "You take too much upon yourself, Emily."

As soon as she felt his touch, she began to weep. "Do I? If I were not here, nothing would be said about me, and none of your men would be compelled to do anything. How can I believe I am not responsible?"

"If you were not here, we would find other reasons to kill each other. We always have."

"No. I won't be comforted by such easy lies." With great difficulty, she stopped her tears, though she could not completely stop trembling. She faced him and said what she knew to be true, and what she wished never to say. "I should not remain so close to you."

Genji looked at her thoughtfully for a moment. Finally, he nodded and said, "You're right. I wonder why I've been so blind for so long. The solution is so obvious, so clear. To save us all from further violence, you must leave at once. Not only the palace, not only Edo, but Japan itself. If I had only seen the truth sooner, you could have boarded the *Star* this morning with Heiko and Matthew. No matter. I will make immediate arrangements for you to take the very next steamer. You'll be in Honolulu before them, and join them there for the rest of the journey to San Francisco. As soon as you are gone, we will have peace at last." He rose and walked briskly to the doorway. Once there, he stopped and turned to her. She was staring at him in astonishment. Genji laughed.

"Do you see the foolishness of your reasoning? We were killing each other for a thousand years before you arrived. Because one man stepped into another's shadow. Because a geisha served one before the other the night before. Because an ancestor of one betrayed the ancestor of another ten generations in the past. If we did not have the color of your eyes to kill for, believe me, we would have no shortage of reasons."

The effect on Emily was not what Genji had expected. She blinked in silence several times, then dissolved into sobbing so piteous, it rendered her former misery negligible.

"Emily." Genji sat beside her again. He put his hand under her chin and tried to coax her into lifting her face. She turned away and continued to sob. "If I've said the wrong thing, forgive me. I only meant to show you, by exaggeration, that your absence is no solution."

Between sobs she said, "I have been very happy here."

"You do not appear so."

"Lord." Hanako knelt at the doorway.

"Ah, Hanako, please come in. I'm at a loss."

As soon as she heard Hanako's name, Emily looked up. She ran to her and clung to her as she cried. Genji moved to join them, but Hanako shook her head.

"I will take care of her," Hanako said, and led the weeping woman away.

Genji stood where he was, alone and amazed. This was not difficult to understand. It was impossible. He dropped down into the chair, stood immediately, went to the window, noticed nothing he saw, and sat down on a cushion on the floor. Perhaps in the void of meditation, some clarity would come to him. But he was unable to release the tumult of thoughts that bound him. He was unable even to release the tension from his muscles. Where the simplest bodily control was lacking, how could he hope for mental control? He could not, so he stood, and again didn't know what to do next.

When Heiko had first suggested the possibility— so ridiculous at the time—that Emily would be the mother of his child, the seemingly insurmountable obstacle was his own feelings, or lack of them. A man did not need to love a woman in order to have a child with her. Sexual attraction, however, was required, and there was none.

And then, suddenly, inexplicably, there was.

His perception of her physical being had not changed. How could it? She was too much herself to deny, with breasts far too large for correct aesthetic balance, a waist that choked the center of her body into a tiny circle that could not help but restrict the healthy flow of ki, a torso unnaturally short and legs unnaturally long, hips too wide, buttocks excessively round and protrusive. He could not imagine such a grotesquely exaggerated shape contained within a kimono. And even if it could somehow be bound and restrained, what colors, what patterns would distract even an iota of attention from her outrageous golden hair? Elegance would be impossible.

There was also the matter of her height, if more defects needed enumeration. She was not shorter than him by a head, which was the ideal that Heiko met so perfectly. Emily was, instead, exactly as tall as Genji. When she looked at him, she did not look up. She looked straight at him with those dizzyingly blue eyes of hers.

Yet, with every passing day, he found himself desiring her more, not because of her physical attributes—he had not gone mad, after all—but despite them. Her heart was so open, so ready to see good, so blind to bad, so innocent and defenseless, so without guile and manipulation, it opened his heart as well. With her, he could let down his guard in every way, he could be himself as she was herself, plain, with first thoughts the ones that made their way into words. He desired her because he loved who she was despite how she looked. He loved her because of who he was when he was with her.

He loved her.

This realization was the great shock of his life. How had it happened? With prophecy to warn him, he should have seen it coming, but he had not. Even now, looking back, he couldn't find the time or place or event.

After he admitted the impossible had happened to him, he still had hope that Heiko's interpretation of the prophecy was wrong. Whether he desired her or not, surely she did not desire him. She was a Christian missionary almost wholly intent on spreading the gospel of her religion. One barrier was gone, but the other, even more formidable than his own resistance, remained.

Then that, too, disappeared. Emily's feelings, which she uncharacteristically attempted to conceal, were not long hidden. Any three-year-old in the palace was better at pretense than she was. Genji's last hope was Stark. Upon the demise of Emily's former fiancé, Reverend Cromwell, Stark had stepped forward as her future husband. But this hope was also disappointed. Stark was not to marry Emily. Once he helped construct the mission house he had come to build, he would return to America. Jimbo—whom he had known as Ethan Cruz—was dead. There was nothing more to keep him in Japan. In fact, Stark tarried for some months thereafter. There was nothing to keep him in Japan, but there was apparently nothing to take him quickly to America, either. Still, he was to leave, and finally this morning he did.

Emily and Genji were now separated only by her ignorance of his feelings, and his self-control. He could continue to rely on her to do her part. She was far too modest to suspect how he felt. He had no doubt about himself, either, but it was a different kind of certainty. He knew his resistance would eventually cease, and when it did, hers would, too. He knew because he finally understood the first prophecy.

Until he had, he could continue to hope that nothing would happen between Emily and himself. Otherwise the second prophecy must be a foretelling of her death in childbirth, and as their love for each other grew, it only made the end more imminent. Surely life could not be so cruel.

But now he knew it could indeed be that cruel. He had discovered Lady Shizuka's identity, not in a vision, but in an illumination of understanding, where all he already knew came together with sudden clarity. That told him tragic fulfillment was inevitable.

"My lord." Hanako knelt at the doorway.

"How is she?"

"Much recovered."

"Will she rejoin me here?"

"I think it will be better, my lord, if you go to her."

"Very well."

Hanako accompanied Genji through the corridors to Emily's room. She wished to speak, but was waiting for him to give her opportunity and permission. This Genji did.

He said, "What is your advice?"

"I would not presume to advise you, my lord."

"Of course not. Women have never presumed to advise me."

Hanako returned Genji's smile and bowed. "She is very sensitive about the project. I hope you will be able to praise her efforts, even if they fall short of perfection."

"I am sure her efforts are praiseworthy."

"Translation is a very difficult art," Hanako said. "I did not appreciate how difficult until I began assisting Heiko in Lady Emily's Sunday school. Our language and hers are so different. It is not just the words but the thoughts themselves."

"All true communication, even between two people speaking the same language, requires translation," Genji said. "In the end, our hearts must hear what cannot be spoken."

· · · · · ·

"I'm changing the dates to the Western calendar," Emily said. Her eyes were swollen and red, but the smile was back on her face, and her normal enthusiasm was in her voice. " 'The Seventh Year of the Emperor Go-toba' gives the reader of English no sense of chronology. If, instead, we say 1291, then our reader will know the event here took place at the time the last Crusader Kingdom in the Holy Land fell to the Saracens. Do you think that would be all right?"

"Yes, I think it will be fine."

"There is so much material," Emily said. "I hope I'm not taking up too much of your time, asking you to make the initial translation from the Japanese."

"I'm more than happy to do it." Genji sat next to her. When she finally looked at him, he smiled. She returned it shyly with a small smile of her own, and turned immediately back to the pages on the desk in front of her. He wanted very much to embrace her, but he did not.

"The one thing I'm very unsure of is the title."

"Emily."

"Yes?"

"I'm very sorry I upset you."

"Oh, no." She put her hand reassuringly on his. "My own oversensitivity is at fault. Really, what did you say? Only the truth."

"I sometimes joke when I shouldn't. Not everything should be laughed at."

"No," Emily said, looking down, "not everything." She began to withdraw her hand from his, but he held on.

"We are friends," Genji said. "We will have misunderstandings, as everyone does. We will never let them stand between us. Agreed?"

She looked at their hands together before she looked into his eyes. "Agreed."

"So now, let me see what you've done."

She placed the sheets of paper in front of him. "I've left the title in Japanese for now. Later, if we decide, we can substitute the English."

"Yes," Genji said, knowing that when the translation was finally finished, many years hence, the title would indeed be in English, because "English" is the last word he will ever speak in his life.

· · · · ·

The sword goes deep into Genji's chest, and everything goes white. When he opens his eyes, he sees worried faces peering down at him.

Lady Shizuka appears and, heedless of the blood,

takes him in her arms and holds him close against her breast. Tears flow down her cheeks and drop onto his face. For several moments, their heartbeats are synchronous.

"You will always be my Shining Prince," she says. She smiles at him through her tears. "I finished the translation this morning. I wonder whether we should use the Japanese name, or translate the title into English as well. What do you think?"

Genji sees that her beauty is not entirely Japanese. Her eyes are hazel, not black, and her hair is light brown. Her features are rather sharper and more dramatic than is usual, more outsider than Japanese. But not entirely so. Though there is perhaps more of her mother in her appearance than her father, her father is there, too, especially in the small smile that always seems to be upon her lips.

"English," Genji says.

"English it is, then," Lady Shizuka says. "It will be another scandal. 'Genji again,' people will say, 'and that terrible Shizuka of his.' But we don't care, do we?" Her lips tremble, her eyelids flutter, but her smile holds. "She would be so proud of us."

Yes, Genji wants to say, she would have been as proud of you as I am. But he has no voice left.

Something sparkles at her throat. Emily's silver locket, with its cross and fleur-de-lis.

He looks from the locket to Shizuka, and his daughter's beautiful face is the last thing he sees on earth.

· · · · ·

"You have made a wonderful translation," Genji says.

"Do you think so?" Emily glowed with happiness.

"But if it is, we have done it, not I. You must have your name on it, too."

"You may say I have consulted with you. No more. You are the translator."

"But, Genji—"

"I insist."

Emily sighed. There was no use arguing with him when he was being stubborn. Perhaps later she would be able to talk him into it.

"I'll get right to work on the next part."

"Enough for now," Genji said. "You will not get through the recorded wisdom and insanity of six hundred years all at once. The day is beautiful. Let us go out and view the winter cranes."

Emily laughed her delightful childish laugh.

Genji heard it and cherished it for the fragile evanescent treasure that it was.

"Yes," Emily said, standing with him and taking his arm in hers, "that's a very fine idea."

"Perhaps it will snow," Genji said.

"Genji!" Emily said, admonishment in her voice. But she smiled when she said his name.

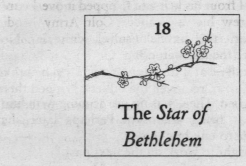

18

The *Star of Bethlehem*

Here is your katana.

To make it, steel was thrust into fire, folded, and beaten, again and again, until twenty thousand layers of purified metal became one. Of every ingot entering the flames, only one part in six survived to become blade and tang.

Consider this carefully. Clearly comprehend the difference between definition and metaphor, and the limitations of each. Only then will you be fit to unsheathe this weapon in matters of life and death.

SUZUME–NO–KUMO
(1434)

Edo fell below the horizon, then the mountaintops, and Japan was gone, and the *Star of Bethlehem* sailed on, eastbound, toward the distant shores of America.

Stark stood at the starboard railing near the aft of the ship. He took the .32 caliber Smith & Wesson pocket pistol from his belt and dropped it overboard. Next, he drew his .44 caliber Colt Army Model Revolver with the six-inch barrel, drew it more slowly than he had ever done. He held it in both hands and looked at it for a long time. Then he broke open the cylinder, removed the bullets, gripped them tightly once, and opened his hand. The six bullets fell into the sea. They were so small, they made no noticeable splash. The cylinder followed, then the frame and grip. He unbelted his holster and dropped it after the rest.

He continued to stand at the railing, very still, very quiet.

Without meaning to, he said, "Mary Anne."

Without knowing it, he began to weep.

· · · · · ·

Heiko stood at the bow of the ship and looked at the vast expanse of open ocean ahead. How would she survive in that barbarian land on the other shore? She had great wealth, thanks to the gold bullion with which Genji had entrusted her. She had the protection of Matthew Stark, whom she trusted completely as a friend and fellow warrior. But she did not have Genji. She knew she would never have him again.

His parting words to her were lies. He said he had seen in his visions that he would be the last Great Lord of Akaoka. None would follow him. Within a few brief years, there would be no samurai, no Shogun, no Great Lords, no separate domains. A civilization two thousand years old would disappear virtually overnight. So Genji said. Perhaps these were lies, too. They certainly sounded like lies. But they did not concern her. Only one lie really mattered. He had lied when he said he would join her.

She knew he would not because of what he had seen in his two visions.

In one, he meets a mysterious Lady Shizuka. Whoever she was, she could never appear in America. So Genji must meet her in Japan. In the second, his wife, concubine, or lover—he does not see her, so she could be Emily, Shizuka, or yet someone else—dies in childbirth, just after presenting him with an heir. Great Lord or not, Genji would never permit a child of his to grow to maturity anywhere but in his homeland.

He had lied, and she still didn't know why.

He had lied, and so she was bound for a land where Emily was considered beautiful. In such a place, there was one certainty, if anything was certain. Heiko would be seen as hideous and repulsive. Her fabled beauty would serve her not at all. People would turn away from her in disgust. She would be disdained, ridiculed, treated with cruelty and contempt.

She had not had to wait for time to destroy her beauty. At twenty, she had left it behind in a land already invisible beneath the horizon.

But she would not cry.

She would not fear, or despair, or weaken.

She was a ninja, after all, in the exalted lineage of Kuma the Bear, her uncle, the greatest ninja in the last hundred years. If ever she had reason to doubt herself, she had only to feel the blood running in her veins to know certainty once again. No, she was most definitely not some weeping geisha abandoned by her lover. She was on a mission from her master, Okumichi no kami Genji, Great Lord of Akaoka, a beautiful liar who would surely be Shogun of all Japan one day.

She would not dwell on her misfortunes.

She went looking for Stark. They had many things to discuss. First, they must ensure the safety of the gold. While it was unlikely to be stolen while they were aboard a missionary trade ship, they could not afford to be lax.

Stark stood at the aft railing of the ship. He was very still. As Heiko approached, his shoulders began to shake, and he fell to the deck on his knees, wailing the mindless wail of an animal impaled and not dying fast enough.

Heiko knelt next to him. Would he strike at her if she reached out? And if he did, what would she do? No, she would not anticipate. She was going to an unknown land, and her only path was unknowing itself. She would begin upon it this very moment.

Heiko withdrew from her bosom, beneath both outer and inner kimonos, a plain white scarf of the finest silk, unscented but for the scent of her own flesh, and reached out to absorb Stark's tears.

Stark did not strike out. As the silk touched his face and drank his tears, he sobbed one last time, touched Heiko's hand so gently she barely felt it, and said, "Thank you."

Heiko bowed and began to give a polite response. No words came. Instead, as she looked at his naked, sincere outsider's face, soft tears welled in her own eyes even as her lips formed a reassuring smile.

Now Stark reached toward her. Into his hand fell the first drop that left her cheek.

It glistened in his palm like a small diamond.

· · · · · ·

And the *Star of Bethlehem* sails on, and Stark says, Thank you, and Heiko's silk scarf in her silken hand absorbs his tears as her own fall across her smile and into time, and the *Star of Bethlehem* sails on.

VI

CLOUD OF
SPARROWS

Suzume-no-kumo

Scroll One, Fascicle One

*Translated from the Japanese
by EMILY GIBSON
In consultation with GENJI OKUMICHI,
Daimyo of Akaoka
In the Year of Our Lord 1861*

Late in the summer of 1291, my grandfather, father, and elder brothers were killed in battle at Cape Muroto, along with most of our valiant warriors. Thus, I, Hironobu, became Lord of Akaoka at the age of six years and eleven days.

As the victorious army of the Hojo usurpers approached, my mother, Lady Kiyomi, helped me prepare for ritual suicide. It was to take place on the bank of a stream that seasonally ran beside our castle. I dressed all in white. The sky was clear and blue.

My bodyguard, Go, stood beside me, sword raised. He would decapitate me as soon as I plunged the knife into my belly. Just as I was about to do so, sparrows began rising out of the dry streambed, hundreds and hundreds of sparrows. They flew over me in such profusion, they cast a shadow like a cloud.

The ten-year-old stableboy Shinichi, my frequent playmate, cried out, "Stop! It is an unprecedented omen! Lord Hironobu must not die!"

Go, weeping and falling to his knees before me, said, "My lord, you must lead us into battle! The gods demand it!"

How he interpreted the omen this way, he did not explain. But my retainers, joining him in tears, agreed.

"Let us die attacking defiantly as befits true warriors!"

"There are no better horsemen than the Okumichi cavalry. We will shatter their ranks in an all-out charge!"

So it was that on that very evening, I led our clan's remaining samurai, numbering one hundred twenty-one, against the Hojo army five thousand strong.

My mother, smiling through her tears, bade me farewell, saying, "When you return, I will wash the blood of our arrogant enemies from your sword."

Ryusuke was my senior surviving retainer. He intended us to charge directly into the battle array of the enemy at sunrise the next morning. We would cross an open beach filled with flying arrows, collide against horsemen more than ten times our number, then meet the pikes and spears of three thousand foot soldiers. Only after we breached their ranks would we have a chance to attack and kill the cowardly Hojo commanders.

I said, "Tonight, the enemy will encamp in the Muroto Woods. It is a ghostly place that has always frightened me. Perhaps it will frighten them, too."

Go looked at me, astonished. "The young lord has given us the key to victory," he said.

We hid in the shadows. The confident Hojo, prematurely triumphant, drank and feasted through the night. In the darkest hour before dawn, while our foes lay in drunken slumber, we infiltrated their camp, entered the tents of their leaders, and swiftly beheaded them.

Then we fired blazing arrows into the midst of the sleeping horde while screaming and moaning with the voices of ghouls from the Land of the Dead.

The enemy rushed to get their orders and found the gruesome heads of their slain lords stuck on the bloody hilts of their own swords, whose broken blades were thrust into the earth.

The Hojo army panicked and dissolved into a fleeing mob. On the beach, our archers shot them down by the hundreds. In the woods, which we knew so well, our swords took a thousand heads from their shoulders. By a stroke of fortune, dawn brought a thick and murky fog from the ocean, which confused and frightened them even more. When we departed from the Muroto Woods the next evening, we left three thousand one hundred and sixteen Hojo heads on the ends of spears, hanging like rotten fruit from the trees, scattered on the beach, and tied to the tails and manes of their blood-crazed horses. To this day, the bones of the dead roll in like flotsam when the storm waves break against the shore.

The following spring, Lord Bandan and Lord Hikari of the two closest neighboring domains agreed to join with us in a campaign against our mutual enemies. Our combined army of three thousand samurai and seven thousand foot soldiers marched first against the Hojo. Our banner was a single sparrow dodging arrows from the four directions.

When our army passed the Muroto Woods, a

second cloud of sparrows arose from the place of slaughter. Lord Bandan and Lord Hikari both leaped from their saddles and fell to their knees beside my horse. That second omen caused them to pledge their allegiance to me as their overlord. In this manner, I, Okumichi no kami Hironobu, was elevated to the status of Great Lord. I was then not yet seven years of age.

This was the beginning of the rise of our clan, the Okumichi, and the beginning of the prominence of our domain, Akaoka.

Those who come after me, pay careful attention to the words in these secret scrolls of our clan, scrolls of wisdom, history, and prophecy written in the blood of your ancestors. What I have begun, do not neglect to continue.

May all the gods and Buddhas of the ten thousand heavens smile on you who strengthen our domain.

May all the ghosts and demons of ten thousand hells hound forever those who fail to uphold our honor.

About the Author

Takashi Matsuoka grew up in Hawaii. Before becoming a full-time writer, he was employed at a Zen Buddhist temple in Honolulu. *Cloud of Sparrows* is his first novel, and his second, *Autumn Bridge,* is coming soon.

If you loved *Cloud of Sparrows,* read on for a glimpse of the stunning sequel.

Autumn Bridge

coming from Delacorte in fall 2003!

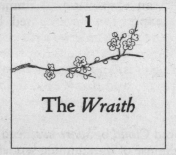

1

The *Wraith*

The Great Lord wields a sharp sword, rides a fierce
warhorse, commands unruly vassals. He has taken the
heads of ten thousand foes. His martial prowess is the
marvel of the realm. But did he not enter this world
bawling from a woman's womb? Did he not suckle
helplessly at a woman's breast? And when the cold
stars sparkle like ice in the winter sky, and the depth
of eternity chills his heart, for what does he yearn
more than a woman's embrace?

AKI-NO-HASHI
(1311)

Lady Shizuka had not changed in the slightest in
all the years Lord Kiyori had known her. Her
complexion was as smooth as the finest Ming porcelain, with the perfect pallor of a courtly woman of
the inner chamber, unlined by the passage of time,
unblemished by exposure to sunlight or hardship,
without any telltale signs of inappropriate deeds,
thoughts, or feelings. Her eyes, when they were not

regarding him—shyly or knowingly or beguilingly, as the case may be—looked off into an imaginary distance with an expression of imminent pleased surprise, an expression accentuated by her high, plucked eyebrows. Her hair was not arranged into a coiffure of the modern type with its complexity of folds, stacks, waves, and accessory devices but simply middle-parted and tied with a light blue ribbon into a loose ponytail at her shoulders, from where it continued to flow down her back in an elegance of lustrous ebony all the way to the floor. Her gowns, too, in polished and crepe silks of contrasting textures, were of the classical types, loosely fitted and layered in complementary shades of blue ranging from the brightness of a high mountain pool to the near black of the evening sky. She was the very picture of a princess of the Era of the Shining Prince. An era, he reminded himself, many centuries past.

Outside this room, the great military might of outsider nations crowded in against Japan. The gigantic steam-powered warships of America, Britain, France, and Russia now freely entered Japanese ports. Aboard those ships were cannons that could hurl explosive shells as big as men vast distances—far past the shore, even beyond inland mountains and forests—and shatter armies concealed from sight before they were close enough to know who was killing them. The ocean that separated the islands of Japan from the rest of the world was no longer a defense. The navies of the outsiders had hundreds of such smoke-belching, cannon-bearing ships, and those ships could bring more than bombardment from afar. From distant shores, they could carry tens of thousands of outsider troops armed with more cannons, and with handheld firearms as well, and land them on the shores of Japan within a few months if they so chose. Yet here in this room in the highest tower of Cloud of Sparrows Castle, the Japan of old lived. He could pretend, at least for a time, that this was the totality of the world.

She saw him looking at her and smiled. Her expression was simultaneously innocent and conspiratorial. How did she manage it? Even the most brilliant of geishas could rarely blend the two into a single look. Demurely, she lowered her gaze and covered her girlish smile with the wide sleeve of her antique Heian kimono.

"You are embarrassing me, my lord. Is something amiss in my appearance?"

"How can there be?" Lord Kiyori said. "You are and will always be the most perfectly beautiful being in all the realm."

A hurt expression came into her eyes.

"So you say again and again. Yet, when was the last time you permitted me into your bed?"

"I asked you never to speak of that again. That it happened at all is wrong, very wrong."

"Because of the difference in our ages?"

Anyone seeing her would take her to be no more than twenty, by tradition the age at which womanhood began, a highborn lady without a doubt, possibly even a virgin. Anyone looking at him would see a man of advanced years, posture unbent by age or defeat, standing in relaxed readiness, his white-streaked hair arranged in the elaborate coiffure of a samurai lord. The difference in their ages. Yes, there was that, too, wasn't there? It wasn't something he ever thought about anymore. He said, "It will never happen again."

"Is that prophecy?" Her tone was mocking but not harsh, as if she were inviting him to share in a joke rather than having one at his expense.

"You know very well it is not."

"Are you not Okumichi-no-kami Kiyori, Great Lord of Akaoka? Then surely you are a prophet, as is the leader of your clan in every generation."

"So people say."

"People say so because your actions are often not explicable except through foreknowledge. If you are not a prophet, then how can you know the future?"

"How indeed." He had always felt the burden of the curse of prophecy, but lately, for the first time in his life, he had also begun to feel the weight of time as well. Seventy-nine years. According to the records of the ancients, men of old—heroes, sages, the blessed of the sacred gods—often lived to be a hundred and more. He couldn't imagine it for himself. Indeed, it was a marvel he had lived as long as he had, all things considered. Especially present company. He had married at eighteen, lost his wife at twenty-one, and then, following eight years of almost monklike discipline, had begun to keep company with Lady Shizuka. How long had it been? This was the fourteenth year of the Emperor Komei. They had met in the thirty-first year of the Emperor Kōkaku, whose reign had lasted thirty-eight years. After him, the Emperor Ninkō's twenty-nine years intervened before the ascension of the present sovereign. Was that fifty years ago? Out of habit, he double-checked himself using the outsiders' calendar. The thirty-first year of the Emperor Kōkaku was A.D. 1810. This was A.D. 1860. Yes, fifty years.

She had said she was nineteen when they met. She looked nineteen still. Would she always? The possibility chilled him far more than the mild winter morning.

"How should I know?" Shizuka said. "You are the one with the visions, are you not?"

"Am I?"

"Surely you are not suggesting it is *I* who sees?"

"You claim to have done so in the past," Kiyori said, "so why should you not have the ability now?"

Concentration brought the slightest of furrows to Shizuka's brow. She looked boldly into Kiyori's eyes. "Are you finally conceding that possibility?"

Kiyori was prevented from answering immediately by a voice outside the door.

"The tea is ready, my lord."

"Enter."

The young housemaid, Hanako, silently slid the door open, bowed, quickly surveyed the room, and paused. How thoughtless of him. By standing distractedly by the window, he gave her no point of reference. She would not know where to serve the tea. But before Kiyori could seat himself across from Lady Shizuka, Hanako went precisely where he would have guided her, at midpoint between where he stood and where a guest would naturally seat herself in relationship to him. Hanako never ceased to impress him. From the first, when she had entered his service as a nine-year-old orphan, she had exhibited a quick intelligence and a strong intuition that was superior to that of most of his samurai.

"Thank you, Hanako. You may go."

"Yes, lord." Hanako bowed, and walking in reverse so as not to turn her back on the lord, began to withdraw from the room.

"Aren't you forgetting something?" Shizuka said, her voice so faint a whisper it could have been imaginary.

"Hanako. One moment." What had he forgotten? Oh, yes. "When the courier returns to Edo tomorrow, you will accompany him. There you will join Lord Genji's household staff at Quiet Crane Palace."

"Yes, lord." Although the command had come without warning, Hanako showed no sign of surprise. She merely assented without question, which was exactly the correct response.

"You have served me very well, Hanako. Your parents would be proud of you." Kiyori, of course, neither made apologies nor gave explanations for sending her away with so little warning.

"Thank you, lord. You have been very kind to put up with my failings for so long."

He ignored the formal expression of humility. "I will be very grateful if you serve my grandson as well."

"Yes, lord. I will do my best."

When she had gone, Kiyori said, "Why am I sending her to Quiet Crane?"

"Are you asking me, my lord?"

"I am only thinking out loud," Kiyori said. "A bad habit that has given me a reputation for more eccentricity than I deserve."

"I see," Shizuka said. "It is good that you have thoughts on the matter, my lord, since the decision is yours." She paused before adding, "Is it not?"

Kiyori smiled sourly. He was in the same fix he always got himself into whenever he had conversations with Shizuka. His reasoning in these matters, no matter how logical, was almost always wrong. Such was the difference between logic and prophetic guidance. "I am sending Hanako to my grandson because, now that he has assumed most of the formal duties of the Great Lord of our domain, he is in greater need of reliable servants than I am. This is particularly so because three more Christian missionaries are scheduled to arrive in Edo any day now, and they will live in Japan under our protection. Their presence will trigger a crisis that will determine the future of our clan. Beyond this immediate matter, I am hoping for a mutual blossoming of affection between Hanako and Genji. She is precisely the kind of woman he needs beside him in this perilous age."

"How consistent you are, my lord. Such clarity of thought, always."

"I take it I am mistaken, as usual." Kiyori poured tea for them both, a polite formality since Shizuka, as usual, did not take hers.

"The great difference in their social status is not an impediment?"

"Because the future will bring chaos, character is far more important than status."

"How wise," Shizuka said, "how liberated from the artificial strictures of social convention, how in keeping with the times."

"You disagree?"

"Not at all. My views are quite antiquated, and I know so little of the outside world, yet it is clear even to one with such constricted understanding that inherent merit is now far more valuable than inherited rank."

"You agree, yet you seem amused by my words. I take it Hanako and Genji are not destined for each other."

"There is always more to know," Shizuka said. "Whether it should be known is another matter. Do you wish to know more?"

"I wish to know no more than what I must know to insure the well-being of our clan."

"Then you know enough," Shizuka said.

Kiyori sipped his tea. His expression was placid, hiding the immense irritation he felt at her failure to tell him what he so obviously wanted to know. Would Hanako and Genji fall in love? He could not ask her, not because the question was inappropriate—it concerned the succession of the prophetic power to the generation after Genji, a singularly important matter, and not one of mere romantic speculation—but because the asking itself raised an implication he had managed to avoid for fifty years. If she was going to tell him, she would have to do so without any request from him.

When it became obvious that he would not continue the conversation, a look of sadness came into Shizuka's eyes and she became very still. This happened not infrequently during their times together. During such moments of melancholy repose, her beauty was particularly ethereal. He could not remain with her any longer and still maintain his self-control.

As he rose to leave, Shizuka surprised him. She said, "I have never asked you for a favor, my lord, nor will I ever ask another. Will you grant this one?"

"What is it?"

"If you will consent, you must do so without knowing."

To hesitate would be unmanly. "Then I consent."

Shizuka bowed deeply, her head to the floor before her. "Thank you, my lord."

Kiyori waited for her to continue. She kept her head down for a long time without speaking. When she looked up, her eyes were wet. He could not remember ever having seen her cry before.

Tears streaming, she said, "Take your evening meal here, then stay the night with me."

"This is a most unfair request," Kiyori said, genuinely aggrieved. "You know that I have sworn never to sleep with you again. Yet you have tricked me into agreeing to do what I have pledged my life and honor not to do."

"I ask only that you share my chamber, not my

bed. My blood is as purely samurai as your own. I would never deceive you into violating a pledge."

Kiyori was still upset. He may not start the night in her bed, but being in the same room with her for an entire night, how he could avoid ending there? His resolve was strong, but he was human, after all, and a man. But there was no choice. He had already agreed. "Very well, just this one night."

"Thank you, my lord," Shizuka said. She looked up and smiled at him through her tears.

Kiyori did not return her smile. It would be a very long night.

· · · · ·

While Hanako packed her belongings for the trip to Edo, she could hear two of the younger maids chattering in the next room.

"Lord Kiyori has ordered that dinner tonight be served to him in the east tower."

"No! How many settings?"

"Two! And he specifically said there was to be no saké."

"Dinner in the east tower. And no saké. How strange. He would have dinner there only if he intended to see an important guest in private. But for such a guest he would order saké, wouldn't he?"

"Perhaps he doesn't expect a guest of the usual kind."

"You don't mean—?"

"Yes!"

"His wife, do you think, or the other?"

This had gone too far. Hanako put down her folded clothing, went to the door dividing the two rooms, and slid it open. The two maids jumped, saw who it was, and sighed in relief.

"Oh, it's you, Hanako."

"Yes, it's me, fortunately. What if it wasn't? What if it had been Lord Kiyori?"

"Oh, he never comes into the maids' quarters."

"Nevertheless, stop gossiping," Hanako said. "Or if you must, then do so more discreetly."

"Yes, you're right," one of the maids said. "Thank you for reminding us." They both bowed to her.

Hanako began to close the door between the rooms again, when one of them spoke up quickly in a loud semblance of a whisper.

"Who do you think it is, Hanako? His wife? Or the other?"

"I don't speculate about it. Nor should you." She closed the door on the wide-eyed girls. After a few moments of silence, she heard them whispering to each other again.

In truth, Hanako had an opinion, of course, though she would never speak it. It would have been less distressing if Lord Kiyori were meeting his wife, Lady Sadako. But Hanako doubted that he was. During the fourteen years she had been in the service of the Okumichi clan, she had overheard bits and pieces of Lord Kiyori's private conversations many times. Though she had never heard a name, she had heard enough to know a man did not talk to his wife in that peculiarly conspiratorial manner. He was not meeting Lady Sadako. He was meeting the other.

A chill ran through her body. It stopped under her skin just short of a shudder, and bumps rose on the skin of her arms, back, and neck, as if tiny needles were poking her from within.

She wondered if Lord Genji would also meet with the other. Then she wondered whether he already had.

·   ·   ·   ·   ·   ·

Shizuka sat in meditative silence for several minutes after Lord Kiyori left the room. Then she rose and went to the window where he had stood and looked outside. Had he seen what she now saw? The evergreen hills of Shikoku Island, the heavy gray sky, the white fringes of waves whipped to life by distant ocean storms and winter winds? She should have asked him. Perhaps tonight she would. They would stand together by this window in the highest tower of their castle, and they would look out over their domain of Akaoka. It would be their last night together. They would never see each other again.

"My lady."

"Enter."

The door slid open. Her chief lady-in-waiting, Ayamé, and four other attendants bowed at the doorway. None of them bowed in the normal lady-like manner with both hands placed on the floor and the forehead lowered gracefully nearly all the way to them. Instead, they knelt on one knee only and bowed at a slight incline from the waist, the bow of warriors on the battlefield. They were dressed in trouserlike *hakama* instead of the elaborate, flowing kimonos of women of the inner chamber, and the sleeves of their abbreviated jackets were tied back out of the way so their arms could more freely wield the long-bladed *naginata* lances they carried. In addition to the naginata, each of the attendants had a short *wakizashi* sword tucked into her sash. Ayamé alone had two swords at her waist, a long-bladed *katana* in addition to the wakizashi. Except that she was a young woman of seventeen, she was the picture of a heroic samurai. Even her hair had been cut, no longer flowing to the floor and behind her, but truncated into a ponytail that stuck out barely ten inches from her head. Man or woman, how easy it would be to fall in love with someone so handsome. The others were similarly attired.

Ayamé said, "It is as you said it would be, my lady. Lord Hironobu has not returned from the hunt. No messenger has come from him. And here at the castle, none of the samurai known to be loyal to the lord and to you can be found."

"My lady," said one of the attendants behind Ayamé, "it is not too late to flee. Take a horse now and ride to Lord Hikari's castle. He will surely protect you."

"Lord Hikari is dead," Shizuka said. She went on as shocked gasps came from her ladies. "So is Lord Bandan. And their heirs and all their families. Treachery has reached almost everywhere. Tonight their castles will go up in flames. Tomorrow night the traitors will be here."

Ayamé bowed, again the short military bow of the battlefield, her eyes locked with Shizuka's. "We will take many of them with us, my lady."

"Yes, we will," Shizuka said. "And though we will die, they will not triumph. Lord Hironobu's line will continue long after theirs have been extinguished." She felt the child kick and placed a palm on her swollen belly. Patience, child, patience. You will enter the tragic world soon enough.

Her attendants bowed their heads and wept. Ayamé, the bravest of them, fought back her tears. They welled in her eyes but did not fall.

It was as dramatic as a scene in one of those kabuki plays that Lord Kiyori sometimes mentioned. But, of course, there was no such thing now. Kabuki would not be invented for another three hundred years.

. . . . . .

Shigeru alternated between great stillness and sudden movement, sliding from shadow to shadow through the corridors of his own clan castle as stealthily as an assassin. Though the ordinary eye could apprehend him if it alighted upon him, he moved in such a way that neither servants nor samurai noticed him. If they did, they would acknowledge his presence, greet him respectfully, and bow. He in turn, seeing what was not there, would draw his swords and cut them down. This was his fear and the reason for his stealth. His control was slipping and he didn't know how much he had left. His ears resonated with a riot of demonic cacophony, and his eyes had to see through an overlay of images of torture and slaughter. Though he could still distinguish the world he walked through from the world that emanated from his mind, he doubted that he could continue to do so for much longer. He had not been able to sleep for days, and the visions that kept him awake consequently grew stronger and pushed him ever more strongly toward insanity. He was widely considered to be the greatest warrior of the present era, the only samurai in two hundred years worthy to be mentioned in the same breath as the legendary Musashi. With neither excessive pride nor false modesty, he believed his reputation to be valid. But all his martial skills were useless against this enemy within.

He needed help. For weeks, as his malady worsened, he had resisted turning to the only person who could possibly help him. His father. As Lord Kiyori's only surviving son, Shigeru had been too ashamed to confess to such weakness. In every generation of the Okumichi clan, one was born with the gift of prophecy. In the generation before, it had been his father. In the generation after his own, it was his nephew, Genji. In his, the burden had been placed on Shigeru himself. For fifty years Kiyori had used prescience to guide and protect the clan. How could Shigeru go crying to him the moment his own visions began?

Now, almost too late, he had realized that he had no choice. Visions did not come in the same way to everyone, nor could everyone who had them handle them on their own. He was being inundated with a deluge of sights and sounds that made no sense at all. Gigantic freakish machines resembling monsters of fable and legend writhed over the landscape, consuming passive lines of people dressed in bizarre uniform clothing. Air in colorful, putrid layers smothered the castle and the town below. At night the sky itself growled like the belly of a huge invisible beast and gave birth to a rain of fire that washed over screaming victims below.

What did this mean? If there were visions of the future, in what direction were they pointing him? Only someone with a similar experience could understand.

The conversations of maids told him where Lord Kiyori was. In the high tower. Because he was compelled to avoid being seen, it took Shigeru the better part of an hour to travel a distance that would normally have taken only a few minutes. But he congratulated himself on getting there undetected. No one had greeted him, and so he had not found it necessary to kill anyone. Also, during the prolonged journey, his visions had abated. They would surely return soon enough, but the respite was welcome. He was just about to announce himself to his father, when he heard him speak.

"I am sending Hanako to my grandson," Kiyori said, "because now that he has assumed most of the formal duties of the Great Lord of our domain, he is in greater need of reliable servants than I am."

Kiyori spoke for a time, then paused as if listening to a response, then spoke again. He continued in this way for some time as Shigeru listened outside the door. Shigeru focused his entire attention as carefully as he could but did not succeed a single time in hearing the voice of whoever was with his father.

"Because the future will bring chaos," Kiyori said as if answering a question, "character is far more important than status." Then, after a short pause, "You disagree?" And after another pause, "You agree, yet you seem amused by my words. I take it Hanako and Genji are not destined for each other."

Hanako and Genji? Shigeru was shocked. Hanako was a maid in the castle. How could she be destined for a lord? Surely his father was not plotting some kind of devious mischief against his own grandson? Shigeru had to see his father's companion. Whenever his father spoke, Shigeru could tell the direction in which he faced by the waning and waxing of his voice, and waited for the appropriate moment to create a sliver of an opening with the sliding door. He moved slowly across the opening to scan the room within as the conversation continued.

"I wish to know no more than what I must know to insure the well-being of our clan."

Shigeru saw him sitting in the center of the room, sipping tea. The setting was for two. Another cup, filled, sat untouched across from Kiyori. Shigeru completed his survey of the room. There was no one there but Kiyori. Had the person left through a secret passage unknown even to Shigeru? That seemed highly unlikely, but what other possibility was there? Whoever it was had certainly not gone out the window. The only other way down was past Shigeru, and no one had passed him.

"What is it?" Kiyori said.

Thinking he had been seen, Shigeru went to his knees and bowed. He hesitated for a moment, not knowing what to say, and during his hesitation Kiyori spoke again.

"Then I consent."

Shigeru rose quickly. So someone was still there. Again, he looked into the room. Kiyori looked straight ahead and spoke again as if addressing someone directly in front of him.

"This is a most unfair request," Kiyori said. "You know that I have sworn never to sleep with you again. Yet you have tricked me into agreeing to do what I have pledged my life and honor not to do."

Shigeru shrank back, suddenly cold.

"Very well," he heard his father say, "just this one night."

Shigeru retreated, moving with care at first, then he fled from the castle as swiftly as he could. His father could not help him, for he, too, was insane. Or worse. Kiyori had been speaking to a woman. It might have been Lady Sadoko, Kiyori's wife and Shigeru's mother. That was bad enough. Lady Sadoko had died shortly after Shigeru's birth. But he didn't think the lady in question had been his late mother. Kiyori had said he had pledged never to sleep with her again. He would not say that to his own wife, not even the ghost of his wife.

The east tower of Cloud of Sparrows Castle, where Kiyori always spent so much time alone, had long had the reputation among gullible children and superstitious adults of being haunted. Such stories always rose around places of ancient tragedy, and what castle in Japan had not been the site of ancient tragedies? In this case, the tragedy had been treason, assassination, and gruesome murders that had nearly extinguished the Okumichi clan in its earliest days. That had been in the fall of the tenth year of the Emperor Go-Nijō. The witch and princess Lady Shizuka had spent her last hours in that very room of the tower.

His father was consorting with a ghoul dead for more than five hundred years.